Praise for Beneath a Turquoise Sky

"Beautifully written, *Beneath a Turquoise Sky* is as colorfully woven as a Navajo blanket with well-drawn characters, a fresh setting, and heartrending history. Kiersti Giron tells a tender, soul-stirring story unlike any other in this moving journey of change, forgiveness, new beginnings, and ultimately, love."

—**Laura Frantz**, Christy Award-winning author of
Courting Morrow Little

"History is full of injustice, but healing can be found when hearts submit to God's leading. Kiersti Giron has woven such moments into the story of Caroline and Tse, two people from vastly different cultures searching for their path in life, set against the early 20th century boarding school experience of Navajo children and those who held them in their care. In turns delightful and heart wrenching, the vividly rendered world of the Diné invites readers to walk those bridges between cultures and faith in a narrative rich with longing, grief, and distrust—but ultimately hope, forgiveness, and vision. Readers won't forget these memorable characters, especially the children, met in *Beneath a Turquoise Sky*."

—**Lori Benton**, Christy Award-winning
author of *Burning Sky*

"This novel takes the reader beyond romance to a heart-soaring love story."

—**Lauraine Snelling**, best-selling author of the
Red River of the North series

"A well-written book in which two hearts of two different cultures are brought together. One from Eastern USA and the other from the Red Rock cathedrals with blue sky ceilings of the territory of New Mexico. History presents itself in reference to the flood and the Long Walk inflicted on the Navajo people for reasons of assimilation. The church presents itself on the Navajo reservation to which Caroline was called to serve and Tse Tsosie to work as a hired hand. Everything is put together in a meaningful way that lends to the truthfulness of Jeremiah 29:11-12: 'For I know the plans I have for you. Plans to prosper you and not to harm you. Plans to give you a hope and a future.'"

—**Ted Charles**, "Navajo," born into the
Tó'adheedlíinii (Water Flows Together) clan and
for the *Tódích'íi'nii* (Bitter Water) clan.

Beneath a Turquoise Sky

Kiersti Giron

DEDICATION

To Ted and Evie Charles,
my "real life" Tse and Caroline.
And to all the survivors of U.S. residential schools for
Native children.
I hope this story honors your pain.

GLOSSARY OF NAVAJO WORDS

Ahe'hee' – thank you

Bilagáana – white person

Bóhólníihii – Lord

Ch'iidiis – spirits

Chaha'oh – open summer shelter shaded by leafy branches

Diné – "the people"—what the Navajo call themselves

Dinétah – ancestral land of the *Diné* between the Four Sacred Mountains, much of it now the Navajo Nation

Dólii – girl's name meaning bluebird, shortened from Dóliibaa hózhǫ, "beautiful bluebird"

Doodatsaahii – the One who has conquered death

Hágo – come

Hataałii – traditional healer or medicine man

Hogan – traditional six-sided log home

Hózhǫ nahasdlii – prayerful invocation of beauty and harmony

Kináalda – coming of age ceremony for a girl after her first menstruation

Sháńdíín – girl's name meaning sunshine

Shashyáázh – boy's name meaning "Little Bear"

Shideezhi – my little sister

ShiDiyin God – my Holy God

Shimá – my mother

Shiye' – my son

Shizhé'é – my father

Thl'izii – goat

Tse – abbreviated male name, meaning "rock"

Tsiiyééł – traditional Navajo hairstyle, a coiled bun tied with wool yarn or buckskin on the back of the head (for women) or nape of the neck (for men)

Ya'at'eeh – "it is good," common Navajo greeting

Ya'at'eeh abini – morning greeting

Yázhí – "little one"

Yeibichai – Nightway ceremony, a traditional winter ceremony for healing

CHAPTER ONE

Pennsylvania, October 1910

At the toot of an automobile horn, Caroline Haynes tensed.

She turned from adjusting the pitcher of goldenrod on the dining table for the sixth time, stepped to the window, and lifted the lace curtain.

Father's new motorcar, carrying two figures wearing linen dusters, sputtered to a stop at the front gate.

They had arrived.

Caroline hurried to the mirror in the entryway, smoothing her hair into place. Behind her, her younger brothers thundered down the stairs and tumbled into the hallway, Toby admonishing Benji to be careful.

Nothing would be the same after today. But then, nothing had been the same since five years ago. And she would make Lillian welcome. She had promised Father, after all.

"It's Father and Mother Lillian!" Five-year-old Benji threw his arms around her knees.

Would that second name always stab so?

"I know. I heard them." Caroline disentangled herself from his clinging arms. "Don't knock me over." She hadn't meant to snap.

Toby darted past, and Caroline snagged him by the arm to give his collar a tweak and his hair a smooth. He submitted for a half second, then charged out the front door. At eleven, he seldom slowed except to eat and sleep.

Benji waited, shifting from one foot to the other as Caroline fiddled with her locket.

She looked down into his eyes upturned to hers. Benji had Mama's eyes—deep blue, the shade of blueberries—the way Caroline had her honey brown hair. And Caroline had quenched the joy in them. Wouldn't this transition be hard enough on him without a crotchety sister?

"Ready, Benji-man?" She held out her hand.

With a whoop, he dragged her through the front door and down the brick pathway to the newlyweds.

Beneath a pair of goggles emerged Father's smiling, bearded face, while Lillian's brown eyes danced under the gray veil tied over her hat, her dark curls tossed by the autumn wind. She exclaimed over Toby's height and clasped Benji in a motherly squeeze.

But she wasn't Mama. She would never be Mama.

"Welcome, Lillian." Caroline stepped forward, twisting her fingers behind her back.

Still holding Benji with one arm, Lillian drew Caroline close and kissed her cheek.

Then Caroline laid her head on Father's linen-clad chest a moment as his arms wrapped her tight, only to pull away before that familiar refuge rendered her a little girl sobbing on her father's shoulder.

"Did you have a pleasant honeymoon?" Stepping back with a smile, she laid her hands on Benji's jiggling shoulders, but he wrested away. Caroline bit her lip. He wasn't much of a credit to her today. Surely Lillian would make allowances, given the circumstances.

"Indeed." Father drew his bride's arm through his.

His bride...

Shaking off memories of their wedding a month earlier, Caroline focused on her father's words.

"She thought she'd never seen anything to match those Maine seaports." He pressed Lillian's plump hand on his arm, and she flushed a deeper rose. "We had a splendid wedding tour, Daughter, thanks to you."

"I'm glad." Surely not as wonderful as the one he had shared with Mama? She searched his face and looked away from the light in his eyes, gray like her own. "Won't you come inside? I have a ham in the oven."

"Can smell it out here. What a welcome home, eh, Wife?"

Lillian darted a glance at Caroline, then smiled up at Father and squeezed his arm. Father led her up the steps of the white clapboard house where he had brought his first bride twenty-five years ago. Benji clung to Lillian's hand, but Toby lagged behind. Hands in his knickers pockets, he snuck an uncertain look back over his shoulder at Caroline.

Maybe she wasn't the only one struggling today.

Caroline's throat ached, but she gave her brother a smile that sent him up the steps and into the house. She mustn't cry, not here, not now. She had dinner to serve, a guest to set at ease. Only Lillian wasn't a guest, not anymore. Caroline turned to close the gate in the picket fence, and her gaze landed on the round-topped brass box. The mail. She had forgotten to collect it in the flurry of the day.

She pushed through the gate and leaned back against it. Drinking a deep breath of autumn leaves and woodsmoke, she let the tension drain from her limbs. Maples arched over the lane, branches lit with crimson and ochre. A chill breeze raised gooseflesh under her sleeves.

Caroline withdrew the pile of letters and circulars and snapped the mailbox door shut. She traced the initials embossed on the shiny metal—Father's strong *J*, Mama's graceful *M*, joined by the curving *H*. Jethro and Mary Haynes.

3

Mama. What would she think to see their family today? Caroline squinted into the blue October sky. "Do you give her a little window from heaven, Lord?"

She didn't know if she hoped so or not.

Caroline trudged up the porch steps, glancing through the mail. Business correspondence for her father's livery company, a letter from her friend Jenny who had moved to Atlanta last year, a new issue of *The Home Mission Monthly.* As she turned the latch of the screen door, Lillian's laugh mingled with Benji's chortle inside. Caroline loosened her grip and leaned her forehead against the doorframe.

"Caroline?"

With a start, she looked up through the screen into Father's face.

"Coming in, Daughter?" He held the inner door for her.

Caroline followed him past the carefully laid dining table into the kitchen. The scent of ham and simmering beans tickled her nose.

"Just thought I'd slice the cornbread for you." Lillian turned from the counter to smile over her shoulder, her petite form encased in one of Mama's aprons. The strings barely reached to tie a perky bow in the back.

Caroline ran her hand along the back of a chair. "Thank you."

Lillian layered the golden slices on a silver bread plate. Mama's silver bread plate. The one they only used on Thanksgiving, Christmas, Easter, and Mama's birthday. How had she found it?

Caroline stepped to Lillian's side. "We don't—"

She caught Father's eye, the tiny shake of his head.

Caroline swallowed. Did it really matter so much, just once? She turned from Lillian's questioning face and took the salad from the icebox.

"Everything looks just wonderful, Caroline. What else would you like me to do?"

4

"You're most kind, but I didn't mean for you to do anything."

"I'm glad to free you up a bit now." Lillian clasped her hands in front of the apron, sincerity in her eyes. "Goodness, you've cared for your father and brothers so faithfully all these years."

Only five years. And that was what family did. Lillian needn't act like Caroline deserved a medal. And free her up for what? Suitors weren't exactly lining up at the door for a near-spinster going on twenty-three. The knot in Caroline's stomach tightened as she creaked open the oven door to check the ham. Sweet, meaty-fragranced steam moistened her face. "Wouldn't you like to rest a bit in the sitting room before supper? I can manage."

Father chuckled from the doorway. "You forget she's no longer Widow Smythe from next door. Lillian, come upstairs and freshen up."

"Well, if you're sure . . . " Lillian reached to untie the apron strings.

"Of course." Caroline took the apron from her with a smile.

Alone in the kitchen, Caroline ran the apron strings between her fingers. Ham nearly done, cornbread sliced, beans simmering, scalloped potatoes in a covered dish. A cake sat in the pantry—the "welcome home" cake, Benji called it. All almost ready.

All except her.

With the ham and all its trimmings either eaten or tucked into the icebox for later in the week, Caroline passed out slices of cake to the rejoicing of her brothers and Lillian's protest that she couldn't hold anymore. Still, only the clinking of forks sounded for a few minutes.

Father patted his beard with his napkin and looked across at Caroline. "By the way, Daughter, Lillian has an idea for Thanksgiving."

"Oh?" Caroline paused, a bite halfway to her mouth.

"So many times in my widowed years, different families in the church invited me for Thanksgiving." Lillian glanced at Father, then back at Caroline. "I thought it might be lovely to return the favor, have some to dinner who are alone, who don't have family nearby."

Caroline laid her fork down and squeezed her hands in her lap. Thanksgiving had always been an intimate family time for them.

"What do you say?" Father speared another plummy bite of cake.

"I don't know. We've never done anything like that before." Caroline looked to Toby for help but found him absorbed in his empty plate.

"Well, we will talk it over." Lillian's eyes met hers, their brown sparkle outshining the lines at the corners. So different from the gentle blue of Mama's eyes. "Thanksgiving is such a good time to reach out to those less blessed than we."

"Of course." But surely there were other means than destroying their traditions. They had been a family before Lillian came, after all. "Whom would you wish to invite?"

"We thought of young Widow Taft and her children—they're in your class at church, aren't they, Caroline? It's been such a difficult year for them, poor dears."

"Yes, let's." Benji bounced on his chair. "I want to play with Thomas."

Lillian reached over and smoothed the stubborn curl that always stuck up on Benji's forehead. "Sit still at the table, Benji-man."

Caroline's eyes burned. That was her name for Benji, her baby she had raised since Mama left him in her care. No one else ever used that name for him. And who gave Lillian the right to correct her brother, anyway? Caroline pushed back from the table and slipped from the room.

Alone in the dimly gas-lit kitchen, she leaned against the edge of the table, trying to swallow the ache in her throat.

Laughter rang from the dining room.

Did they even notice she wasn't there? That Mama wasn't there?

She shouldn't let this bother her. She should be grateful Father had found happiness again. She should go back.

The lump in her throat tightened till she could hardly swallow. She slid into a chair and rested her head on her hand. *I can't do this, Lord.* She slipped her other hand to the locket at her neck and clung to it.

Later, with the boys tucked in and the newlyweds disappeared upstairs, Caroline rinsed and wiped the last china plate, turned down the kitchen lights, and crept up to her room. She didn't want to think about Father and Lillian just down the hall in the room where Father and Mama had slept, where Benji was born, where Mama died.

She climbed on her bed and snuggled under her quilt to lose herself in the comfort of Jenny's letter. Settling back against the pillows, Caroline slid her finger under the envelope flap and withdrew the thin sheets of paper.

Dearest Carrie-friend . . .

Caroline smiled and rubbed her thumb over the greeting. Dear Jenny. She missed the closeness of their friendship, the sister-ness they'd shared before Mama passed and Jenny was beckoned away to the mysterious sweetness of wife and motherhood.

She scanned the lines, the news of Jenny's husband's growing parish and her baby boy's "shortening" to knee-length gowns now that he was crawling, of the expectations placed on a minister's wife and the missionary teas she had to host. Finally Caroline's gaze fell to the postscript.

*I received a letter from my brother Jeremiah, with news that his
wife is expecting their first little one. He asked me to pass his greetings
on to you.*

The quick, upright script blurred. Caroline dropped her head
onto her knees and squeezed her eyes shut. *Jeremiah.* How many
tender spots from the past could this day poke?

His sun-kissed red hair and merry, freckled face swam through
a host of memories. Walking home together from school, little Jenny tagging along behind. Passing notes in the classroom. The first
time he walked her home *without* Jenny. Talking past dusk by the
front garden gate, not wanting to say goodnight. She could smell
the sweetness of the honeysuckle growing over the fence as Jeremiah perched on it, looking into her eyes with his hazel ones and
speaking with such passion of the lost millions in China's interior,
untouched by knowledge of Christ. She leaned on the rail and knew
she would travel to the ends of the earth, if he were by her side.

That baby might have been hers, if only things had been different. If Mama hadn't died … if Jeremiah hadn't left so soon to serve
with the China Inland Mission … if a young missionary woman
overseas hadn't caught his eye.

She swiped at her cheeks. All the hurt and confusion she'd
tucked away since Father announced his suit of Lillian six months
ago seemed suddenly undammed, and she didn't know how to stop
it again. *What am I supposed to do, Lord? Teach Sunday school the
rest of my life? Help Lillian?* But Lillian wanted to "free her up." She
didn't need Caroline. No one did, really.

Caroline sniffed hard and tucked the letter back in the envelope. Enough of that. She reached for the *Home Mission Monthly.*
Articles and reports and requests for aid would be a good antidote
to foolish self-pity.

She flipped through the first few pages. Her sniffs subsided as
she skimmed a report from a missionary to the Pueblo tribe. So

easy to forget there were people in need and spiritual darkness, even within America's borders.

She turned another leaf and stared into the solemn eyes of a group of children in military-style uniforms. They stood before a low stone building, dry cliffs rising behind them. "Hebron Navajo Mission School, Class of 1909," read a line below. Her eyes shifted to the article title: "Among the Navajo: Bringing the Light of Education and the Gospel to Children of the Hogans."

The report from a Rev. Abernathy carried Caroline to a land of dust storms and icy winds, of mysterious dances and medicine men, of sheepherding families in isolated six-sided log homes—*hogans.* Of children in need of schooling, of the light of Jesus. After she finished the article, her gaze rested on a notice at the bottom of the page.

Needed: Due to the failing health of founder Miss Mariah Spencer, Hebron is currently seeking a new schoolteacher for their younger pupils. Experience teaching young children is preferred. Necessary training will be given by experienced missionaries...

A tingle ran down Caroline's arms. She shook it off. No, silly, impossible to think like that. She didn't have the credentials, the experience—well, except for years of teaching Sunday school. And her family—how could she go so far from them, even now?

And yet...

Girlhood dreams, long packed away like her china-headed dolls and ruffled pinafores, resurfaced dusty and beckoning. She had dreamed of being a missionary, even before Jeremiah, following in the footsteps of Lottie Moon or the Judsons. Caroline ran a finger over the shadowy photograph, the faces of the children. So little, those in the front row, as young as Benji, as the smallest ones in her Sunday school class. So...sad, somehow.

Needed. The word beginning the advertisement seemed stamped in darker ink. Was she—after all?

Write Willis Abernathy, Hebron Navajo Mission, Shiprock, Territory of New Mexico.

Caroline lifted her head, her heart stirring with a new and unfamiliar rhythm.

CHAPTER TWO

Hebron Navajo Mission, Territory of New Mexico, October 1910

Tse Tsosie lifted his fist and rapped on the front door of the main mission building.

He stared at the doorknob as he waited, hunching his shoulders against the early morning chill, resisting the memories crowding him from all sides. The barn, the schoolrooms, the woodshed—all called to him, asking him to remember.

Tse shifted his moccasins on the rough boards of the porch. He couldn't believe he was doing this. *But I need this chance, Lord.*

The doorknob turned. Willis Abernathy stared at him, then yanked wire-rimmed spectacles off his nose. "Peter?"

Tse held back a wince at the old name. "Willis." So his boyhood friend wore spectacles now. Too many books at that fancy Bible school?

The missionary seemed about to speak, then glanced over his shoulder at the rows of wide-eyed children seated before bowls of porridge.

Breakfast time. Tse cleared his throat. "Sorry. I should have come later."

"Students, finish eating." Holding Tse's gaze, Willis tipped his head toward the barnyard. They would talk outside.

Tse sent a half smile to his young cousin, Shándíín, whose eyes had brightened at the sight of family.

An answering smile flitted across her face before the door shut between them.

Tse strode across the yard. The barn drew him as surely as in boyhood days. Willis fell into step beside him, the companionship familiar … so long ago.

A goat ambled over to the barnyard fence, and Tse scratched its head. "I heard about your aunt."

Willis glanced at him, then back at the mission.

"How is she?"

"Better, thank God." Willis sighed and rubbed a hand over his shock of sandy hair. "But her left side remains weak. Doctor says full recovery from a stroke is up to Providence."

"How are you managing?" Tse fondled the goat's ears.

"Barely." Willis blew out a breath. "I've advertised for another teacher."

Tse jerked his head up. He hadn't expected that.

"No response yet, but it's only been a few weeks." Willis crossed his arms. "So. What brings you here?"

It had to come up sooner or later. But instead of answering, Tse swung himself over the fence.

"What on … "

Ignoring him, Tse squatted and ran his hand down the goat's leg, then lifted her foot. The sides of the doe's hoof curled raggedly inward. "No time for hoof trimming anymore?"

"I've been very pressed lately. I'll have one of the boys get to it later." Willis's voice stretched tight. He always did hate having a weakness pointed out.

"Have him clean up a bit too." Tse stood and kicked at the scattered droppings mingled with old hay. "And that doe has a sore on her udder."

Willis grasped the fence. "You come here to tell me that? I've got classes to teach."

Always the sacred schedule. Tse stepped close to the fence and forced himself to meet Willis's eyes, contrary to Navajo custom.

"I need a job."

Willis blinked. "Your family kick you out?"

"No." Of course not. "My mother—she has pain in her hands, her knees, her wrists. She cannot weave." And without weaving, there were no rugs. Rugs whose sale formed the lifeline of the Tsosie family, as for so many Navajo families. He didn't have to tell Willis that. "The railroad is looking for strong workers, but I heard about your trouble, thought I would come here first."

Willis drummed his fingers on the top board of the fence. "You think you can just waltz in here and ask for a job? After . . . " He shot a glance at Tse.

Tse's jaw tightened under Willis's scrutiny of his chin-length hair and leather headband, the deerskin leggings below his cotton breeches.

"I do not apologize for helping my family these years." Tse clambered back over the fence and landed with a thud in front of Willis. "But you need help now. So do I. You know I can do the work. I ask that you give me a chance."

Willis studied Tse a moment longer, then scanned the barnyard.

Tse followed his gaze—the fence bulging outward in spots, the weeds just beyond reach of the goats. One doe grabbed a mouthful of hay and tossed her head, scattering dry leaves and stems.

The reverend sighed. "Monday morning. Six o'clock sharp."

"Thank you." Tse extended his hand.

Willis grasped it, the blue of his eyes deepening. "It'll be good to have you back, Peter."

Tse heard the unspoken question—*Are you really back?*

He nodded. "It's Tse, now."

Willis withdrew his hand, an invisible wall coming between them yet again. He studied Tse for a moment. "There's one more thing you should know. We're currently under examination by the mission board. They're considering shutting this station down due to low enrollment." His jaw worked.

"Then why would you—the new teacher? Me?"

"Best way to build up the school. Be on time Monday." Willis spun on his heel and headed back toward the mission.

Tse leaned against the barnyard fence and stroked the head that butted through the rails. *Lord, what have I done?*

Tse tugged open the gate of his family's corral and stepped back to let the sheep stream inside. One of the family dogs yipped and nipped at their fleecy tails. Tse scanned for any stragglers and shut the flock in, distributing a few pats on his tongue-wagging friend before sending him off.

The sun sank toward the horizon, a fiery medallion flaming layers of cloud with deep orange and gold.

At hoof beats, Tse turned to see his father ride in.

"All in safe?" The older man slid off the horse and unbridled it, then set it free to find the roaming herd.

Tse nodded. How would his father manage the sheep once he started work at the mission? At least he seemed to have accepted Tse's new position. His mother on the other hand—Tse still needed to tell her. Tonight.

"They'll miss you to scratch their bellies and sing them to sleep." His father approached and placed one foot on the corral's lowest rail.

Tse chuckled. "I'll still take them out pretty often. Many days they will only need me at the mission morning and night."

"We'll manage all right." His father reached out his hand for an old ewe to sniff.

"Where were you, *Shizhé'é?*"

"Hataałii Chee's. Asked him to hold a sing for your mother."

The medicine man. Tse chewed the inside of his cheek. "When?"

"Next week." His father turned toward him, his forehead creasing. "You think I am wrong." Not a question, not an accusation. Merely an observation.

Tse studied his father, his straight shoulders, graying hair rolled and bound with buckskin at the nape of his neck, the lines of kindness about his eyes. Tse turned back to the corral.

"When she hurts, my son, I hurt."

"I know. Me too. I wish…" Tse sighed, the breath like wind through the junipers. "I pray for her. But I pray to Creator, in Jesus' name."

His father nodded, a slight, deliberate motion. He scanned the flock of sheep, huddled in wooly bunches for the night under the falling darkness. "You have honored your mother and me, even while following the missionaries' God. We see that, we know. But I don't see that He has done better for you than the old ways. I will hold to them until I see different."

"You men going to stand there until the *ch'iidiis* come out?" Firelight beamed from their hogan as his mother held back the rug covering the door.

"Trouble with her fingers doesn't hurt her tongue." His father lightly punched Tse's shoulder. "Come."

But Tse lingered longer, gripping the twisted juniper wood of the corral, his heart weighted by his father's words, his mother's ever-present fear of the *ch'iidii* spirits thought to roam once darkness fell. He gazed at the few streaks of turquoise in the western sky, all that remained of the sun's brilliance. So many times, he had tried to tell his family of Jesus. But only his younger sister, Dólii, believed.

Sometimes he wasn't even sure about her. Had his light faded like the sunset? Could Rev. Abernathy be right?

He sighed and turned for the hogan. Ducking through the door, he let the thick rug fall behind him. Warmth embraced him with the scent of coffee and hominy stew. He crouched by the fire in the center of their home, blew on his hands and held them to the heat.

"Come, come eat." Beaming now that her family was gathered, his mother braced herself and lifted the pot of stew off the fire. When her swollen wrists shook, his father reached to lower it to the ground.

Tse's chest tightened. She tried so hard. He dipped his head for a silent grace and dug into the stew, savoring the warming mingle of chile, hominy corn, and lamb.

His mother handed him a hot corn griddlecake, the pucker between her eyes that always appeared when she saw him pray.

Sitting back on his heels, Tse let the fire's warmth soak into his muscles and replayed in his mind the morning's encounter at the mission, Willis's reaction. It had been so long.

"My lambs were worth more than that. And we have my father to think of."

His mother's voice dragged Tse's thoughts to the present.

"Wool and stock go cheap right now." His father set down his coffee cup. "It's rugs Trader Hawkins wants, to fill orders from the *bilagáanas* back East."

"And how am I supposed to weave with these hands?" His mother clenched her fingers together.

Tse winced at the pain he knew the gesture brought, saw it echoed in Dólii's eyes before his sister dropped her gaze to her food. *Shimá* used to make the finest rugs this side of Canyon de Chelly. Dólii was learning, but eleven years stolen by boarding school could not be made up in the few months since she graduated from Hebron.

16

His father glanced at Tse, quirking an eyebrow as he popped a bit of meat into his mouth.

"*Shimá*." Tse drew a breath. "I've taken a job at the mission. To help us."

"What?" She halted her hand in the midst of dipping a griddle-cake in the stew.

"We need the wages. *Shizhé'é* agrees."

His father narrowed his eyes at him. Perhaps Tse wasn't supposed to mention that.

"Why not keep hiring on at the ranches, as you have been?"

"That work is not steady enough for what we need anymore." Only seasonal at best. "This is a good job." Or would be as long as the mission stayed open. He wouldn't mention that either.

His mother dropped the cake unheeded into the stew and sat back on her heels, her swollen knuckles tightening as she rubbed her hands between the folds of her skirt, one over the other, over and over. She stared into the fire.

Her silence spoke louder than her tongue. Tse shifted. "*Shimá*—"

"You've done what you want." She flapped her hand before her face as if waving away the smoke of the fire. "Eat your meal."

Tse bit into his corn cake, the food settling hard in his stomach. His mother was no fool—she knew their need as well as he. She might tolerate his working at the mission for a time, but she would never like it. Would never share his faith. Not after what happened seven winters ago. Wind whistled around the hogan, carrying whispers of the past despite his efforts to forget.

Lord, if only... Tse began silently, then halted. Why did he always switch to English when he prayed, even if it wasn't aloud?

Stupid question. He knew why, but he couldn't seem to do anything about it.

CHAPTER THREE

"You're bright and early this morning." Pastor Jensen beamed at Caroline and rocked on his toes atop the church steps, his bald head gleaming in the rare November sunshine.

With a smile, Caroline tried to hurry past, but the pastor's hand on her arm intervened.

"How is your father? And the new Mrs. Haynes, such a lovely woman. How are you all getting along?"

His kind eyes peered too keenly, and Caroline pulled away.

"Everyone is well, thank you." She slipped into the cool mustiness of the church narthex before he could ask more. She didn't want to talk about her family right now.

Caroline hurried down the short hallway of Sunday school classrooms to her own, where she taught kindergarten through second grade. Closing the door behind her, she leaned against it, letting the years-old odors of chalk dust and peppermint drops soothe her soul. Here at least, away from the strangely foreign Sunday morning bustle at home, she still belonged.

The little chairs rested, preparing for the swarm of giggles and chatter, pigtails and hobnailed boots to descend in an hour. Caroline moved between the rows, straightening chair backs, and set her bag on the bookcase where the faded world globe stood sentinel. Often she let the children spin it, praying together for wherever a chubby finger landed.

She cracked the window to let in autumn sunshine and crisp air, then pulled her new book, just purchased from the bookstore, from her satchel. Flipping through the pages, she paused to examine the photographs. The children would love them: an Apache camp, warriors on horseback, intricate sand paintings. So many tribes without the Gospel, right here in their own nation. She paused at a Navajo hogan like those described in the *Home Mission Monthly* article. Had they received her letter? Had she been entirely foolish to even inquire? She hadn't mentioned the advertisement to Father, much less her impulsive response. But she might never hear from them anyway.

Pushing away the thought, she turned the page to a hairy-masked dancer with painted bare chest. A shocked voice at her shoulder nearly made her jump out of her skin.

"Good gracious, this is not part of the assigned curriculum, is it?" Mrs. Thwaite, self-appointed Sunday school superintendent, peered scandalized at the photograph over her wire-framed glasses.

Caroline snapped the book shut and flushed. *Not again.* "No, ma'am. But it's necessary for the children to learn about the mission field, don't you think? They loved hearing about Miss Moon's work in China."

Mrs. Thwaite opened her notebook with pointed deliberation. Why did she always have to do that? Caroline knew the monthly lesson plans as well as she did.

"The lesson for today is on Jesus feeding the five thousand."

"I plan to cover that as well. But most of the children could teach that story themselves. Shouldn't we also give them the chance to learn about those who haven't heard of Jesus? With Thanksgiving this week, I thought the Indians . . ."

Mrs. Thwaite put on her patient expression. "You mean well, but as Sunday school teacher you are responsible to follow the curriculum. You will please stick to the assigned lesson plan."

The superintendent's stout shoes clipped out and down the hall. Caroline sighed and shoved the book back into her satchel.

Familiar Thanksgiving aromas of roast fowl and Mama's pecan pie hung in the air that Thursday, along with whiffs of Lillian's sweet potato pudding.

Caroline hesitated in the kitchen doorway and cleared her throat slightly. "Can I help you?"

Lillian looked up from cutting the pies, surprise lighting her eyes.

Guilt stabbed Caroline's middle. Had her disgruntlement been that obvious? She needed to try harder. Like she'd been trying every day the past few weeks.

"Thank you. Here, serve the pie while I dish up the pudding."

"Your pudding smells delicious." Caroline lifted nutty slices onto Mama's china dessert plates.

"An old Carolina recipe." Lillian dolloped whipped cream atop golden piles.

"I'm sure the Taft children will enjoy it." Caroline swallowed. "I haven't seen them so happy since their father died."

She had yielded to Lillian's hospitable suggestion for the holiday—how could she not? And she was glad she had, truly. Lillian was right, Thanksgiving was a time to give. Still, rebellious thoughts had crept in all morning as they prepared the multitude of delicacies. Though Lillian asked her guidance in finding the measuring spoons or the nutmeg, inner whispers of *Mama wouldn't do it that way... but I've never done it like that* hummed tension through her veins beneath their conversation.

Once Widow Taft arrived with her brood, though, and shy smiles brightened the sad little faces that had grieved Caroline's heart Sunday after Sunday, the tightness in her middle began to melt. The children received the bags of nuts, raisins, and candy Lillian had made for them as if Santa Claus had come early, then followed Benji as a modern Pied Piper.

"Let's see if there is any room left in those bellies." Caroline lifted the plates and offered Lillian a smile.

"Goodness, men can always find room for pie." Lillian cocked her head. "Your mama made the best pecan pie in Pennsylvania."

Caroline's throat tightened. "She did."

Their gazes met. Then Lillian exited with a swish of skirts and the coffee tray.

With a deep breath, Caroline followed.

In the fire-cheered sitting room, Anne Taft, widowed only a year ago, leaned her rounded shoulders against the padded back of Mama's rocker. She chuckled at one of Father's stories, the lines smoothing from her forehead, while her three small children sat a rapt audience for Toby and Benji's display of marble-shooting prowess.

Caroline sat on the couch with her plate and closed her eyes at the first bite of nutty sweetness.

When her toddler began to fuss, Anne gathered her brood to leave. Father had provided a carriage from his livery to take them home.

"That was a lovely Thanksgiving, Lillian," Father said, shutting the door behind their guests. "Thank you." He drew his wife close for a kiss.

Caroline turned away and headed into the deserted sitting room. She blinked at the burning in her eyes as she gathered syrup-smeared plates and scattered napkins. It *had* been nice. But she suddenly ached with memories of Mama reading William Bradford's account of the first Thanksgiving aloud after supper, Toby snug on Father's lap, she herself cuddled beside Mama on the Chesterfield, the crackling fire making everything safe and warm, like it would never change. But things changed. She should know that by now.

Benji entered, yawning.

"Put away your marbles, Benji-man. Then it's off to bed."

"I don't want to."

He was whining now, a certain sign of overtiredness. "Benji."

He plunked on the floor with a whimper but obeyed.

"I'll help you." Lillian came in and lowered herself to a stool beside him.

After taking the plates to the kitchen, Caroline came back to find Lillian and Benji dropping the last marbles in their drawstring bag.

"That's my boy." Caroline smiled and held out her hand. "Come now."

"I want Mother Lillian to put me to bed." Benji turned his head away and slipped his hand into Lillian's.

Caroline's arm fell to her side like a stone. Benji never asked anyone to put him to bed but her. Never. Not since Mama entrusted her newborn brother to Caroline's care before she died. He'd been her baby more than anyone else's.

"Now, why don't you go with your sister?" Lillian stroked Benji's curly head with a glance at Father, who now stood in the doorway.

"I want you to!"

"Never mind," Caroline managed. "Good night." She turned, ignoring Father and Toby's sympathetic looks, and fled upstairs.

Safe in her room, Caroline shut her door and threw herself on the bed, heedless of rumpling her Thanksgiving best. Hot tears wet her pillow. She didn't know if she was angry with Lillian, Benji, or herself. She didn't know anything anymore. Pressing her fists to her cheeks, she wept.

At last the sobs spent themselves, and her breathing slowed. She sat up in her room, dark but for the dim glow from the street lamp outside. Silly, running off to cry like this. The memory of Benji's little face turning away still pinched her heart, but he hadn't meant to hurt her. He had every right to want his new mother to put him to bed. But...

She lit the lamp and tried to push damp tendrils of hair back into her softly upswept bun. A strand caught on the thin chain of her locket, and she closed her fingers around the silver heart. Sitting down on the bed, she worked open the clasp. Mama's sweet face smiled up, her arm curved around a familiar flaxen-haired little girl.

"Mama," she whispered. "At least when you left us, I knew what I was supposed to do." The tiny photograph blurred, and Caroline slid to her knees by her bed, clutching the locket closed. She leaned one arm on the mattress and buried her face in the crook of her elbow. *What's the matter with me, Lord? Show me how to find my place here again, or show me something else. Just please show me what to do.*

She didn't know how long she knelt there, tears seeping into her sleeve. At last she drew a long, quivering breath and rested her damp cheek on her hand, rubbing the crick in her neck with the other. Surely God had a plan, though she couldn't see it.

At a soft tapping on the door, she lifted her head. *Please, not Lillian.*

"Caroline?"

Father. She rose and sat back on the bed. "Come in."

"Are you all right?" He creaked open the door, his gray eyes troubled.

She sniffed and shrugged, giving him a tiny smile.

"Lillian seems to think you'd rather talk to me." He came and sat in the chair by her bed, where he had so often told her stories years ago.

Caroline worked the trim on her skirt between her fingers.

"Benji will always need you, Caroline." Father leaned forward, creaking the chair. "Lillian doesn't change that."

But she had changed it. She couldn't help but change it.

Father lifted Caroline's chin, raising her eyes to his. "Are you unhappy about Lillian's presence here?"

She lowered her gaze. How to answer that?

"I see." Her father let go her chin and sat back.

Caroline flinched at the pain in his voice. She twisted her locket. "It's not that I'm not glad for you. I am, truly. But for me ... " The tears threatened again, prickling behind her eyelids as she looked up at him. "She's not Mama."

"Of course, she's not." The rims of his eyes reddened. "No one will ever take your mother's place. Not for you and your brothers, nor for me, either. Lillian is her own person. And as I've found, and I think you can too, a very wonderful person. Can you not accept her for who she is?"

"I'm sorry." Caroline bit her lip.

"One reason I felt God's blessing on pursuing Lillian was for your sake—that you might have a chance to be free." Father leaned forward again and laid his hand on her knee. "You've given some of your best years to caring for your brothers and me, and I and the Lord will never forget it. But I want you to have your own life, a home and family of your own."

Caroline's cheeks heated. She rubbed her thumbnail.

Father crossed one leg over the other. "Lillian has mentioned a young man, son of some woman in the Aid Society—"

"Father." Caroline lifted her head. "I did something—foolish, perhaps." She drew a deep breath. "I wrote to a mission school out west, in the Territory of New Mexico. They are in need of a new teacher and—I applied for the job. I doubt I'll get the position, but I should have told you sooner. I'm sorry." She braced herself for his response. Why was he staring at her so oddly?

Father shifted and cleared his throat. "New Mexico Territory, you say?"

Caroline nodded.

He patted his jacket pockets, then stood and ducked out of the room before Caroline could form a question. He returned with a slightly bent envelope in his hand. "Found this among my business letters in the mail yesterday—thought it was just an appeal or some such from one of those mission societies. Then I forgot...you and Lillian were so busy with Thanksgiving and all."

Caroline took the letter and read the postmark. *Shiprock. Territory of New Mexico.* She fumbled with the seal, finally tearing it open to withdraw the neatly penned note within. She scanned the lines, trying to take in their meaning, then reached one hand to steady herself on the bed. It was a moment before she could look up into Father's bewildered face.

Caroline drew a shaky breath. "They want me to come."

CHAPTER FOUR

"You're late."

Tse slid off his horse and looped the reins onto the mission corral fencepost. Willis—he still had trouble thinking of him as Rev. Abernathy—stood in the barn doorway, arms akimbo. Not a good start to the day.

"I had to find our horses. My family's hauling water today."

"If you would keep them corralled, they would not wander so far."

"And they would grow fat from no exercise."

Willis sighed, his breath clouding in the frosty air. "The goats have been bleating to be milked for near an hour. If you're going to work here, we need you to be punctual."

"Sorry." Tse strode past Willis into the barn, grabbed a pail, and let a doe into the milking stall, quieting her with a handful of grain while he brushed off her udder.

"I've got to be able to count on you." Willis followed him in. "With my aunt's health, I'm up to my ears just trying to handle both groups of students."

Tse squeezed the first warm, white streams into the pail. "How is Miss Spencer today?"

"I think the respite from the schoolroom is helping." Willis shoved his hands in his pockets. "Not sure how happy she is about the new teacher coming, though."

"You had a response?" Tse kept up the hissing rhythm of milking.

"Woman from Pennsylvania. Arrives in six weeks." He turned to go. "Make sure the stalls get mucked out today."

"Rev. Abernathy." Tse stripped the last milk from the goat's udder and stood with the foaming pail. Willis turned in the doorway, shadowed against the early morning light. Tse shifted his feet in the straw. He shouldn't ask—surely he knew the answer. "If you need assistance to teach in the meantime, I would be glad to help." He bit his tongue, hating the way he had stumbled over the English words. He hardly ever did that anymore.

"No."

Tse's insides flinched at the speed of the response.

"That won't be necessary." Willis's footsteps faded across the barnyard.

Tse blew out a breath through his nose and let the goat out of the stall. The next in line squeezed her way in, nose nuzzling at his hand for grain.

"Patience, little one." His father might laugh at him for talking to the animals, but they were God's creatures too. Tse leaned his head against the doe's warm side as he milked, the low rumble of her belly comforting beneath his ear.

Willis needn't worry about being able to count on him. If family obligation should delay Tse past the time the reverend's pocket watch prescribed, he'd never fail to stay at the mission as long as needed to complete his tasks. As his father liked to say, the white men might have the pocket watches, but they, the *Diné*—the Spaniards christened them Navajo—had the time. He remembered Willis's laugh when Tse told him that years ago, when they were boys. He doubted the *Reverend* Abernathy would laugh now.

Tse finished milking and tossed hay to the goats and feed to the chickens, falling easily into tasks familiar from his boyhood. He carried the brimming milk pails across the yard toward the low building that housed the mission's living quarters, lifting his face to the welcome sunlight. It sparkled on the frosted earth and lit the sandstone mesas in the distance with gold. The sky arced rich blue overhead, like the turquoise his grandfather fashioned into jewelry. Tse breathed the biting air deep into his lungs, the crisp cleanness of this land, this *Dinétah* of his people.

Perhaps this job would not be so bad after all. With Miss Spencer's failing health and his own family's need, the idea seemed an answer for both sides—as long as he and Willis could co-exist.

"Good morning, Peter." Miss Spencer met him on the porch, frail shoulders swathed in a thick shawl as she leaned on a cane, eyes smiling behind her spectacles.

She still favored his old school name. Willis, though, had switched to Tse. Did he think him no longer deserving of a "Christian" moniker?

Tse pushed the thought away. "Morning, Miss Spencer. Feeling better?"

"A bit. Take the milk right into the kitchen, please."

After straining the milk, Tse scoured the pails and set them upside down on a cloth to dry for evening milking. The morning bustle of schoolchildren echoed through the building from the dormitories. Crossing the still empty, sun-striped dining room toward the front door, he nodded to Miss Spencer.

"Will we see you at Sunday service?" Her voice halted him on the threshold.

He turned his head to meet the slight pucker between her thinning eyebrows and nodded. "I'll try to make it." He pushed through the door into the winter sunshine again. Somehow it didn't seem as bright as before.

"Going to the *bilagáanas'* church this morning?"

Tse looked up from reading his Bible in the gray dawn outside his family's hogan. His mother stood in the doorway, holding back the thick blanket that kept warmth in and wind out.

"Church is not just for white people, *Shimá*." Closing the book, Tse rubbed his nose. "It is for all God's people."

His mother sighed, but without comment raised her face toward the east. Lifting her hands, she softly chanted her morning prayers as the fiery sliver of sun crested the mesas, chasing the shadows of night away. She turned then to the south, the west, and the north, inviting the harmony brought by the sun from all four directions. "*Hózhǫ́ nahasdlii … hózhǫ́ nahasdlii …* " The amber light glinted on her hair, the black barely touched with silver, neatly coiled and tied with white wool in a *tsiiyééł* on the back of her head.

Tse rubbed his thumbs over the Bible on his knees. Rev. Abernathy saw the *Diné* orientation toward the east as purely pagan, but surely the Creator had embedded it in their culture for a reason. Didn't Ezekiel speak of the glory of the Lord coming from the east?

"I'll see if Dólii wants to go." Tse rose and stepped toward the hogan door.

"No, she has her monthly bleeding. Let your sister sleep."

His neck heating slightly, Tse tiptoed clockwise across the packed dirt floor, stepping past the low-burning fire and his father and grandfather's sleeping forms, stretched on the men's side across from where Dólii curled.

Tse sank down on his sheepskin and slid the Bible into his satchel, then leaned his head against the log wall. *Have I hurt my mother, Lord? How will she come to know You if she only sees You as the white man's God?* He reached for the cornmeal-filled pouch beneath his pallet, withdrew the necklace his grandfather had crafted for him, and rubbed the smooth, brown-flecked blue stone set in finely worked silver. Dared he wear it to church? God had created the turquoise, the silver. He clenched the necklace in his hand, trying not to think about the last time he had tried to attend services. Today would be different. He would make it so.

He stepped outside where his mother squatted by the fire to check the heating coffeepot. The rich, roasted scent made his stomach growl. He crouched beside her.

"Eat before you leave." She handed him a steaming cup before stirring blue cornmeal into the water boiling with a touch of juniper ash. Her fingers, joints swollen with the arthritis she seemed too young for, twined around the stirring sticks.

"I'll take frybread with me."

She shook her head at him, but her mouth softened with a smile when she saw his necklace.

Tse drained his coffee and stood. His horse, waiting saddled and tethered to the corral post, whinnied and stamped beneath the sunrise-gilded blanket of cloud. Tse swung up on his back and nudged him into a slow gallop. He must get chores done before the service started.

Two hours later, Tse slid into an empty seat in the back of the schoolroom. There were plenty to choose from. Uniformed schoolchildren filled the front rows, while a few head-scarved older women scattered across the other benches like milkweed down in fall.

> "Blessed Assurance, Jesus is mine
> Oh, what a foretaste of glory divine!
> Heir of salvation, purchase of God
> Born of His spirit, washed in His blood."

Tse joined in the singing, letting the familiar words soothe his soul. When Willis rose to preach, Tse let his gaze slip to the schoolroom windows. The sky now hung heavy with a rare gray blanket of clouds, heralding sleet or even snow.

The hymn's words circled through Tse's mind. If only his parents could understand that God meant this assurance for all peoples, not just *bilagáanas*. He played with translating the words in his head, but when he imagined them sung, the musical pitch jumbled the Navajo tones, rendering the words unintelligible. Some of the phrases didn't translate very well either. The hymn hadn't been written with his people in mind.

Willis cleared his throat, jerking Tse's attention back to the service.

A young mother slipped into the seat in front of Tse, settling her toddler beside her. The little one giggled and grabbed at her mother's shawl. Willis waited until the child quieted and then, with a glance at his pocket watch, resumed his sermon.

Tse sat straighter and tried to listen.

After the service, he visited with one of the older women and learned she came from his mother's clan. So someone from his family was here after all.

The toddler staggered between the rows of desks, grabbing seats and people's legs for security as she went. Just as she passed Tse, she turned her head to look for her mother, twisted one foot in front of the other, and sprawled on the planked floor.

"There, little one." Tse scooped her up, soothing her in Navajo. "You're all right."

She stared at him. Tears trembled in her wide eyes, not yet decided to fall. She reached for his necklace.

"What do you think you're doing?"

Tse lifted his head to meet Willis's cold blue gaze.

Tse lowered the little girl to the floor and sent her toward her mother with a pat, then straightened. "What do you mean?"

"Speaking Navajo—here?" Willis's whisper stung. "Wearing these?" With a sharp gesture he encompassed Tse's jewelry, his moccasins, the red band securing his hair.

Tse's scalp burned. Clamping his arms across his velvet shirt, he lowered his gaze.

"There are impressionable boys here, just learning to walk in God's ways. If you persist in walking in those of the devil, I must ask you to stay away lest you influence them."

Of the devil? Tse glanced at a huddle of boys in the corner, their hair shorn short above their high collars and buttoned jackets. One of them looked back soberly at him. So much like him they were. Or like he had been. The pressure in his throat mounted.

Tse spun around and left the schoolroom. He strode blindly across the yard, his feet scattering the sleet pellets now dotting the road. Swinging onto his horse, he touched it into a run toward home.

What a fool he was.

The sun broke through the clouds by the time Tse reached his family camp. Dólii stepped from the hogan, shading her eyes from the light, her smile easing his heart as always.

"How was church?"

Tse snorted and slid from his horse. "Be glad you didn't come."

"That bad?"

He patted the horse's roan side and unbuckled the saddle. It was time this mount ranged for a while again.

"Trying to please everyone?" Dólii reached to touch his necklace.

Tse pulled away. That wasn't it at all. He lifted the chain over his head and stuffed it in his pocket. "Where is *Shizhé'é?*"

"Cutting firewood with the other men."

Tse groaned. "I forgot that was today. Was he angry?" He should have been here to help his father. No, he should have been at church. Where should he have been?

"Not him. *Shimá* hasn't said much."

But their mother had known where he was going. Why didn't she say anything before he left? Tse strapped the saddle in place again and swung onto the broad back. Touching his horse lightly with his quirt, he headed for the juniper thicket where he guessed his father and the others would be gathered. His mount would just have to wait a bit longer to range.

The sharp crack of splitting wood alerted Tse to the men's whereabouts before he saw them. He crested a desert rise to see his father sawing, chopping, and hauling with several of his relatives. Felled junipers, cedar, and some pinon already lay axed on the ground for trimming.

"I'm sorry I was not here earlier." Tse slid from his mount and tethered it to a nearby piñon tree.

His father waved Tse's apology into the frosty air and nodded toward the end of the dead tree he had just felled.

Tse grabbed the heavier end and helped drag it into the clearing to be split.

"Too busy with the *bilagáanas* to help your family, boy?" His uncle's eyes glinted hard beneath knit brows. He shoved an ax toward Tse. "Make yourself useful."

Tse bit his lip, gripped the handle and swung, cracking clean through the twisted trunk. He chopped the length into smaller logs, squinting against the flying bits of wood.

"He works at the mission to help us, my brother." His father straightened.

His uncle just grunted and heaved an armload of wood into the wagon.

Crouching, Tse gathered the thick logs into his arms.

The thwack and crack of his cousins' axes echoed off the nearby rock cliffs.

"Get enough stores from trading your lambs?" That was his uncle again.

Tse dumped the wood in their wagon and glanced at his father.

Shizhé'é nodded. "We kept back some sheep for mutton, and there are corn, squash, and beans from the garden." He clapped Tse on the back and climbed into the wagon to pile the wood. "With that and our good son's job, we won't starve."

Tse heaved the ax over his shoulder and headed for another juniper to topple. Willis's accusing gaze from that morning flashed through his mind, followed by his mother's twisted hands, the meager sacks of flour, cornmeal, and salt stored in the hogan.

Tse aimed his ax at the root of the lifeless tree and swung. He would apologize to Willis tomorrow—though for what he wasn't exactly sure.

He must keep his job.

CHAPTER FIVE

Christmas Eve.

Caroline dropped into Mama's rocking chair by the fire and leaned her head against the cushion. She breathed deep the piney scent from the boughs over the mantle, the smell that said *Christmas* like no other. Firelight flickered on the waiting candles and bright balls on the tree, on the gaily wrapped gifts beneath it.

Caroline curled herself in the chair. Tomorrow would dawn the bustle of Christmas Day, the trying to let Lillian incorporate her Christmas traditions without forgetting Mama's. But with the house asleep and silent flakes blanketing the sleeping world outside, tonight was hers ... a time to say goodbye. In only a week, she would board the train. Where would she be next Christmas—celebrating with the "children of the hogans"? How many of those children did not know about the Baby in the manger, and that He came for them?

The fire burned low. Caroline gazed around the room, trying to imprint every fir branch, picture frame, and clock tick in her memory. She reached a finger to caress the crèche Father had carved before she was born, sitting expectant on the lamp table beside her, empty manger awaiting the tiny figure to be nestled there come morn.

"Caroline?"

Caroline uncurled from the chair, twisting to see Lillian standing in the doorway, a small parcel in her hands. "I thought you had gone to bed."

"A few more packages to wrap, you know. Mothers stay up late Christmas Eve."

Caroline glanced at the hand-knit stockings festooning the mantle. Certainly Mama always had.

"Am I disturbing you?" Still Lillian hesitated.

The wariness in her voice smote Caroline's conscience. "Please come in."

"I wanted to give you this tonight, without all the commotion there'll be tomorrow." Lillian stepped near and sat in the armchair nearest Caroline.

Caroline took the package and undid the red ribbon, the rustling paper. She lifted the lid of the music box, freeing tinkling strains of "Silent Night."

"Your mama gave it to me, years ago. I thought you might like to take it with you."

"Thank you." Caroline's eyes stung.

Lillian sighed and twisted the wedding ring on her left hand. "I can't help feeling it is my fault you are leaving us."

A charred log broke in the fire with a soft ka-thud.

Caroline traced the painted holly atop the music box lid with a finger. "It's not, it's only—" Her throat tightened. "I'm sorry." The last words came out a whisper, pitiful.

"I know I'm not your mother, Caroline." Lillian leaned forward. "I'm not trying to be."

Caroline's gaze flew to Lillian's face. But she found no condemnation in the brown eyes. She looked to her lap and closed the music box lid. "I suppose I simply don't belong here anymore."

"Belonging isn't a place, Caroline. I hope you learn that. But it is something you can find, with God's help." Lillian leaned forward and enveloped her in a hug that smelled of cinnamon and ginger. "Merry Christmas."

Still clutching the music box, Caroline blinked hard in the momentary darkness of Lillian's embrace. Then, with her free arm, she returned it. "Merry Christmas."

Long after Lillian's footsteps padded upstairs, Caroline rocked. When the clock struck twelve, she rose, retrieved the tiny figure of the Baby from its hiding place, and nestled it in the manger. Then slowly, as if it were made of crystal, she opened Mama's music box once more, her mind matching the words to the tune.

"Christ the Savior is born ... Christ the Savior is born."

The train blew a warning whistle, puffing steam into the frigid January air.

Caroline coughed on sooty clouds as she made her way back from the ticket office.

"They've loaded your trunk." Father stepped from the bundled and scarved clump that was her family. His hands clasped each other, as if otherwise they might reach out and stop her from leaving.

A man doesn't fancy sending his little girl off to snakes and sandstorms and savages and who knows what. His words weeks ago as he tried to convince her to reconsider echoed through her mind. Was it just the soot that made it so hard to breathe?

"'Bye, Carrie." Toby submitted to a hug and kiss before squirming away. "Write us about all the cowboys and Indians and everything."

"I'll try." A laugh stuck in Caroline's throat.

Benji pressed against Lillian, his face turned away. He'd hardly spoken to Caroline for the last two days. Lillian tried to turn him around to say his farewell.

"Please, Benji." Caroline knelt and touched his mittened hand.

With a sudden whirl that nearly knocked her off her heels, Benji flung himself into her arms. "Don't go, Carrie. Why do you hafta go?"

Caroline pressed his quivering little body close. Dear Lord, how could she do this? "To tell the Indian children about Jesus, remember, Benji-man?"

"I don't want you to."

Caroline rocked him back and forth.

The train whistled. The conductor's black boots stopped next to her. "You on this train, miss?"

"Let your sister go." Father's hand held her shoulder, the other prying her little brother—her baby—away.

With Benji's clinging arms transferred to his stepmother's skirts, Lillian gave Caroline a quick kiss. "We will be praying for you."

And then she was in Father's arms, squeezing her eyes against the rough weave of his coat, his beard scratching her ear once more.

"Father—I don't know what I'm doing."

"God does." Father held her back from him and looked into her eyes, his own holding a sheen she hadn't seen since Mama died. He cleared his throat and released her. "Go, my little girl. Go, and God bless you."

The conductor took her satchel, helping her up the steps. The whistle blew again, the train rumbled, moving, beneath her feet. Caroline stumbled, and a wave of other passengers carried her until she found herself in an empty seat by a window. She pressed her gloved palms to the glass as she strained to see her family, their hands fluttering through the smoke and coal dust. She waved back, hardly feeling the tears spilling down her cheeks. The train rounded a bend. They were gone.

She was off.

After her train change in Chicago, the miles clicked away beneath the steaming Santa Fe engine, through the snowy fields of Illinois, Missouri, and Kansas, into the craggy peaks of eastern Colorado— and, at last, across the border into New Mexico Territory.

Caroline shifted her cramping feet and tried to concentrate on *The North American Indian* amid the fussing of the toddler in the seat across from her. At last she closed her book and gave the worn-looking mother a sympathetic smile. "Would you like me to take a turn with him?"

"If you've a mind to, I won't say no. Could use the necessary." Pushing a strand of stringy blonde hair off her face, the woman plunked the runny-nosed child in Caroline's lap and headed down the aisle for the water closet. The little boy reached after his mother and howled.

Caroline jiggled him on her knee and tried to remember her tricks from Benji's babyhood. She pulled out her handkerchief to wipe the child's streaming eyes and nose. Poor baby, no wonder he had a cold in this drafty railcar. The night before, the train had been stuck in Raton Pass for hours until the snowplows could clear the tracks.

The handkerchief gave her an idea, and she tugged a clean one from her reticule to tie into a rabbit, then a mouse. Toby used to keep Benji entertained for hours with handkerchief puppets.

The little boy's sobs softened into hiccups as he watched her fold the soft linen. He grabbed at the mouse as Caroline made it jump on his knee.

"Got a knack with young'uns, have you?" The mother thumped back on her seat.

"I have two younger brothers." As the woman made no move to retrieve her child, Caroline crept the mouse under his chin, earning a snuffly chortle. She looked up at her traveling companion. "Where are you headed?"

"Someplace north of Gallup. My man took a notion to come out here last year and take up ranching. Thought he'd make his fortune, he did. Now he's sent for us to come out too. Says he doesn't want the boy to grow up without him."

"How nice for you to be together again." The curl in the woman's lip indicated the opposite, but Caroline didn't know what else to say.

"Well, he weren't of a mind to send no more money unless we came, so what choice did I have?" She squinted out the window.

Caroline searched for another topic. "Gallup will be my stop as well."

"What brings a pretty young thing like you out to this God-forsaken country? Couldn't find a man back east?"

Caroline's ears burned. "I am to teach at a Navajo mission school."

"Indians?" The woman huffed a laugh. "Seems a waste of precious time and money to school savages. Better to get rid of the whole lot, I say. That *Saturday Pioneer* editor had the right idea."

Caroline stiffened, her ears burning. "They are God's children too."

The woman snorted.

"Excuse me." Caroline stood and handed the toddler back. "I need a drink of water." She intended to sail pointedly down the aisle, but a particularly hard jolt nearly sent her flying into a plump gentleman's lap instead. Face flaming, she made her way to the little water tap in the back of the car, grasping seatbacks all the way, and downed a tin cupful nearly in one gulp. She set the cup back with a thunk. Honestly, how could God stand some people? The nerve of that woman. The children's faces from the photograph filled her mind again, softening the blaze in her middle to a warm crackle. Soon, she would meet them.

After disembarking at the two boxcars that formed the Gallup depot, Caroline caught a ride with a freight wagon driver delivering goods to trading posts as far north as Shiprock.

Four bone-jarring days later, the freighter pulled into the dusty town. The icy desert wind blasted Caroline as she clambered from the freight wagon. She gripped the rough-boarded side until her numbed feet remembered their role.

"Someone coming to meet you, miss?" The driver thumped her trunk beside her.

"I think so." She glanced around. *I hope so.* Dust blew in irregular clouds, catching amber rays of the lowering sun. Navajos and white settlers crisscrossed the street in the falling dusk, a few sending curious glances her way. No territory version of kindly, balding Pastor Jensen back home appeared, but surely Rev. Abernathy would be here soon. He had telegraphed he would meet the freighter at its scheduled stop in Shiprock.

Caroline tried not to stare as a Navajo family emerged from the Shiprock Trading Post across the street, arms laden with bundles, and climbed into a red-wheeled covered wagon. She caught the glint of silver jewelry at the mother's neck and even in the little boy's ears. He looked about Benji's age.

"I'll be goin' then." The driver spat a stream of tobacco juice. "Got one more post to deliver to before dark."

"Do you think I should—"

His "Hup!" to the team and the jingle of harness swallowed her question, and Caroline watched the freight wagon jolt away. Teeth chattering, she shivered beneath a bare-branched tree as the sun sank toward the mesas and the temperature dropped. Where was Reverend Abernathy? She glanced around the emptied street. Light gleamed in the windows of the trading post. Perhaps she could inquire there. Her trunk would be all right for a moment. She started across the road.

Near the corner of the building, movement caught her eye. A grizzled man with a scruffy beard—rancher? another freight driver?—stepped from the shadows. Even in the waning light, Caroline did not miss the leer he sent her. Hooking his thumbs in his belt, he winked.

Caroline averted her gaze and backed toward her trunk, numbed fingers clutching her satchel handle. *Help, Lord.* She searched the street again, sensing the man's eyes on her every move.

CHAPTER SIX

"You up next, Tse?"

Tse smiled and shook his head, watching his old schoolmate Nezwood Chee cling to the back of a rearing and plunging gray horse. The other young men gathered round called out mingled jeers and encouragement until Nezwood at last subdued the animal and slid from its back.

Leaning against his family's wagon, Tse joined in the cheers, then glanced around the camp forming for the *Yeibichai* dance.

His mother visited with a group of women while Dólii laughed and chattered with other bright-skirted girls. The scent of roasting mutton mingled with the spicy fragrance of the juniper scrubs dotting the desert around the Begay camp. This healing ceremony for a cousin of his mother's doubled as a welcome social gathering—and a chance for young men to show off for the girls.

Lord, use me here tonight. Though what Willis would say if he knew Tse had finished work early to attend a Yeibichai, he'd rather not think about. But Willis had left the mission before Tse today, bound for Shiprock to fetch the new teacher.

"Come on, Tse." Nezwood sauntered over, grinning. "You didn't used to stink too bad on the back of a horse."

Tse made a shooing motion with his hand, but as the calls intensified, he uncrossed his arms and pushed away from the wagon.

His peers cheered, and a barely broken black horse was unleashed.

Tse ran alongside it before grasping its mane, swinging up on its back in one smooth motion. One arm high in the air, he clung with his knees as the horse twisted and bucked, riding with the animal. At last he brought him under control and galloped twice around the circle before swinging to the ground.

At a burst of clapping, he looked over his shoulder to a group of girls with laughing faces. Tse's neck heated at the look Glenbah slipped him beneath her black lashes. He shifted his gaze to Dólii, but after a sisterly smile, she looked back at Nezwood. Was the new shine in her eyes more than admiration for their old schoolmate?

"Haven't lost your touch." Nezwood bumped Tse's shoulder with his.

"Looked all right up there yourself." Tse bumped back.

"You always could outride me." Nezwood shot him a glance. "Didn't think I'd see you here today."

Tse wiped his sleeve across his brow and resettled his broad-brimmed felt hat. His father's call to help make camp saved him from answering.

The men finished circling the wagons around the ceremonial shelter while the women supervised the food. Chatter and woodsmoke rose with the scent of coffee in the evening air.

"Thank you." Kai Begay, his mother's cousin, patted his arm when he finished lighting their campfire. "Such a good boy you are."

"How is Dezbah today?"

Lines pulled around Kai's eyes as she looked back toward the ceremonial hogan where her mother lay. "The singers finished the last sand painting. Maybe tonight will help."

Dezbah's lungs had been weak since young womanhood, and they grew worse when the weather turned cold, or in summer, wet.

Yet the *Yeibichai*, or Nightway, could only be performed after the first frost in fall—a ceremony for winter, the Season When Thunder Sleeps.

Tse's chest ached to speak of the true Healer, but he just gave Kai's shoulder a brief squeeze.

"Tse!" Kai's small son, Shashyáázh, hurled himself at Tse's legs.

Tse grabbed him and turned him upside down. When his shrieks of laughter became pleas for mercy, Tse set Shashyáázh—his name meant "Little Bear"—on his feet and tousled his shock of black hair. "You're getting too big for me, little brother."

"I looked through the *yei* mask this year." Shashyáázh nodded. "And I didn't cry."

The initiation. Tse remembered his terror as a child when it was his turn to have the heavy *yei* mask slipped over his head. Peering through the eyeholes was thought to protect *Yeibichai* attendees from blindness.

"And next term he will go to school." Kai smiled proudly.

Shashyáázh's grin faded. He ran to cling to his mother's shawl. "I don't want to."

"He is old enough?" Tse shifted his feet.

"This is his sixth winter." Kai lifted her son's chin high with a crooked finger. "He needs the *bilagáanas'* learning to do well in this new world, isn't that so, my son?"

Tse jammed his hands in his pockets. *But he's so small.* He pushed down the words with the memories. "Want to check on the meat with me, little brother?"

Shashyáázh's grin sprang back, and he tore ahead of Tse to the pits where mutton roasted. The smell reminded Tse of this family's staggering sacrifice for the *Yeibichai*—sheep to feed for nine days the *Hatáálii*—medicine men—and teams of *yei* dancers, not to mention dozens of clansmen and friends. His own mother had given four of their sheep to help. It was all done gladly, of course, in hope of healing for the elderly woman wheezing in the fragrant-branched shelter.

After sunset, families gathered by their wagons in the falling darkness, chatter falling to whispers, then silence. The moon rose over the mesas.

An eerie cry from the ceremonial hogan where Dezbah lay lifted the hair on Tse's arms. He caught Dólii's eye, her faint smile in the firelight mirroring his trepidation. His pulse thudded in his ears. *Be with us, Lord. Protect us. Help us shine Your light here somehow.*

Twelve masked figures emerged from the shelter of poles and cedar branches, stepping in time with the rattle of the gourds they carried in one hand, eagle feathers in the other. Their blue masks glowed white in the darkness, representing the *yei*, the Holy People who centered Navajo spirituality. Concho belts jingled above short kilts and clay-painted legs. Led by "Talking God," maternal grandfather and spokesperson of the spirits, they stamped in unified rhythm, dancing to the four directions, silhouetted against the leaping flames of the ceremonial fires under the moonlit sky.

Tse glanced at Shashyáázh. The child gazed in fascination at the sight he believed would have dazzled his eyes blind before his view through the mask.

One dancer turned in Tse's direction, and darkness crept toward him, powers recognizing the Spirit within him and rebelling.

"Jesus," he whispered. "Greater are You who are in me than he who is in the world." The tight rope in his stomach relaxed, his heart thudding back to normal.

The dancer turned away.

Tse drew a long breath. If only his people's dances, with all their mystery and beauty, could be used for the Creator's glory, for the One who could touch physical and spiritual eyes and make them see. The true Talking God who did communicate with mankind.

Who actually cared about them, in contrast to the detached regard of the *yei*.

He watched as the *Hatáálii* helped Dezbah from the hogan to sprinkle corn meal on the *yei*. The age-old chanting, the rattling gourds and jingling bells round the dancers' ankles filled Tse's ears till he couldn't hear himself think. He pushed himself up, hoping no one would notice, and slipped out of the circle of wagons and firelight.

Out in the quiet of junipers and rocky sand, Tse drew a deep breath and relaxed his shoulders. Above him stretched the stars, mica strewn across an obsidian sky.

"Creator God, marvelous are Your works." Tse leaned against a rock and tipped his hat back for a better view of the glittering heavens. A coyote yipped, answered by others. How long until his people really knew the One who created all these? It didn't take nine gods to do what One could.

He slid to the ground, his back against the rock, and sagged his clasped hands between his knees. Had he been right to come to the *Yeibichai*? He rubbed his nose, growing numb in the bitter air. He had wrestled the same way over attending the sing for his mother. And he knew what Willis and Miss Spencer's answer would be. But how could he witness to his people if he stayed away from them? He didn't see this part of his family much—Kai and her mother, Shashyáázh and his sister. Their winter camp was some miles south of his family's.

Tse plucked a nearby twig of juniper and rubbed the spicy-scented needles between his fingers. Some witness he'd been so far. Couldn't he have said anything when Kai shared about Dezbah, said he'd pray for her—something?

A rustle in a nearby thicket jerked his attention.

He eased himself up, resisting old fears of the wolf-man who wandered the desert after dark. Still, he had rather not meet a mountain lion or even coyote alone at night. His gun was back at camp. Tse's hands tensed.

With a crash, a figure stumbled out from the junipers.

Peering through the dark, Tse breathed again. "Nezwood?"

His friend lurched toward him, grasping at the rock. Nezwood stared a moment, then laughed strangely. "Well, if it isn't two old school buddies playing hooky again. Demon-dancing get too much for you?"

Moonlight glinted off glass.

Tse yanked the bottle from Nezwood's hand. "Where did you get this?"

"Someone got it off Trader Hawkins. We were passing around a quiet sip or two, but one of the elders got wind of it."

"So you snuck out to finish it off yourself?" Tse emptied the bottle into the bushes, then turned on Nezwood. "You want to bring shame on your mother, on your clan? On our whole people before the *bilagáanas*?" Unlike many other tribes, the *Diné* had not been much affected by the grip of the white man's whiskey. Not yet.

Nezwood gazed round as if he had misplaced something, then plopped to the ground.

His anger seeping away, Tse sank beside him. He dug a stick into the ground. It caught on a rock. "Why, Nezwood?"

"Would think you could use a drop yourself." Nezwood wiped his nose on his sleeve. "Bet that's why you snuck out here. Bothering you, isn't it? People who go to heathen ceremonies go to hell. Wasn't that beat into us enough at school?"

Tse broke the stick into bits. After a moment he turned, studying his friend's face in the moonlight. "How come you don't believe anymore?"

"Don't know that I ever did, really. Don't know if I believe nothing anymore. Maybe not Changing Woman or the *yei*. For sure not some *bilagáana* God who hates everything about us."

"That's not true." Tse's nails dug into his palms.

"Don't preach to me." Nezwood staggered to his feet and crashed off into the bushes.

Tse leapt up and reached Nezwood as the drunk man paused, reeling. Tse caught his arm. Feeling the path through his moccasins, he guided his friend back toward the distant chanting and odor of woodsmoke. A night wind rose, stinging dust into his eyes and chapping his hands.

"Why did you come to the *Yeibichai*, anyway?" Nezwood stumbled in the darkness, and he paused to steady himself against the nearby rock wall.

Tse shivered, clenching his jaw to keep his teeth from chattering. "Why did you?"

"Same reason as you, I bet. Girls."

"That so?" A laugh burst from Tse's chest as he guided Nezwood through a narrow passage in the rocks. It sheltered them from the wind.

"I saw you looking at Glenbah."

"Shut up." Tse's numbed ears now tingled with heat. His mind drifted again to the girl's shapely form and laughing eyes. She was pretty, all right. But he didn't really know her. He didn't even know if she was a believer.

"And your sister." Nezwood chuckled.

"Dólii?" Tse loosened his grip. What about her?

"She's grown into something of a beauty. I'd like to … " Nezwood mumbled something Tse didn't fully hear, but what he did grasp sent sizzling from his soles to his scalp.

He slammed Nezwood against the rocky wall, his knee in the man's belly and his arm across his throat. "What did you say?"

Nezwood choked and wheezed, plucking at Tse's sleeve.

Tse loosened the pressure a hair. "What—did—you—say?"

"Nothing! I didn't mean nothing."

Tse let go.

Nezwood sprawled to the ground, gasping, clutching his neck.

Tse's hand went to his own throat in a familiar gesture. What had he done? He reached to help Nezwood up. "Sorry. You all right?"

"What do you care?" Cursing, Nezwood shook him off. He hauled himself to his feet and stumbled back toward camp.

Tse hurried behind until he saw Nezwood safely with his family, then skirted the wagons back to his own family's fire, ignoring his mother's frown as he rejoined them. Half shielded behind the corner of their wagon, Tse sat, rubbing his knees, hardly feeling the warmth creep back into his hands.

He had seen Dólii's gaze go again to Nezwood's handsome face as he reentered the circle of firelight. Was she too innocent to realize he had been drinking? His beautiful little sister, as different from his troubled schoolmate as the sky from the canyons. *Don't, Shideezhi. He's not good enough for you.*

Nezwood's last question circled through his mind again. But Tse did care. He cared a whole lot. Couldn't the man see that? Tse raked his fingers through his hair. What good had he done, though—for Nezwood, or anybody? Why couldn't he be the shining light of Christ he desperately wanted to be?

Within the fire-lit circle, the dancers' chanting drummed on.

CHAPTER SEVEN

"Miss Haynes?"

Caroline whirled at the male voice, her heart pounding. A lean young man in a brown overcoat stood near her in the darkening street, a team snorting at the buckboard wagon behind him.

"Willis Abernathy." He removed his hat, the wind wreaking instant havoc on his combed blond hair.

Caroline's knees went wobbly with relief. "Rev. Abernathy. How do you do?" She reached her hand to be clasped in his strong one.

"I apologize for not being here sooner." The reverend followed her glance to the man on the corner. His jaw tightened. "Had a problem with a wheel on the way here. This your trunk?"

"Yes." Caroline sneaked another peek over her shoulder and exhaled to see the man had disappeared. Into the trading post, probably—or perhaps the saloon, if there was one. She shuddered. *Thank You, Lord.*

"How was your journey?"

"Long—especially the last bit by freight wagon. But I shouldn't complain about days when it took months a generation ago. And such beautiful country... the prairies, the mountains, the rock formations."

"See Shiprock?" He hoisted her trunk onto the wagon bed.

She nodded. The monolith that christened the town rose from the desert like the clipper ship that lent its name. She had felt smaller than a jackrabbit as the freighter lumbered through the rock's spreading shadow.

Rev. Abernathy helped her into the wagon and swung up beside her. Caroline clamped her gloved hands together, trying to control her shivering as another gust of wind blasted them.

"Nippy, isn't it? Wind should die down once the sun sets." Rev. Abernathy reached behind them to grab a shaggy pelt. "Here. Buffalo robe."

Caroline forced herself not to cringe as the hairy weight settled over her lap. No doubt she must get accustomed to close proximity with wild animal skins. Her shaking did stop almost immediately.

"We'll catch the sunset on the way to the mission." Lifting the reins, Rev. Abernathy turned to her. "Your everyday sundown out here puts the finest eastern skies to shame."

His eyes shone blue and crinkled at the corners when he smiled. A dimple in his chin gave him a boyish look.

Caroline turned her gaze straight ahead, her stomach fluttering a little as the wagon lurched forward. A smile tugged at her mouth. Certainly Rev. Willis Abernathy was no frontier mimeograph of Pastor Jensen.

Only a soft aqua glow on the horizon remained after the sunset, glorious as the reverend had promised. Now stars winked one by one through the darkening blue.

"I didn't realize it was a boarding school." Caroline gripped the wagon seat as they jolted along the rutted road.

"It's the only way to keep attendance steady." Rev. Abernathy shifted the reins between his hands. "Otherwise students would be constantly pulled out to help with the sheepherding, especially when the families move camp for better pasture. Boarding schools are one of the best ways to advance the government's assimilation program."

"What program is that?"

"Trying to help the children break with their savage past and assimilate into civilized society. 'Kill the Indian, save the man,' General Richard Pratt calls it. His school in Carlisle, Pennsylvania, has been a model for many like ours. Ever hear of it?"

"I might have." An image of Benji and Toby being taken from home to live with strangers flitted through her mind. "Is it hard for the children to be separated from their parents?"

"I'd say more parents are seeing the advantages of learning the white man's ways." Rev. Abernathy shrugged. "Few Navajo have responded to the Gospel yet, though. It's as tough a field as many a foreign one." He guided the team over a narrow bridge spanning an arroyo.

Caroline clamped her teeth on the inside of her lip until the wheels touched rocky dirt once more.

"I probably should have included this in my letter, Miss Haynes." Rev. Abernathy drew a breath, then let it out with a sigh. "But our mission board is actually considering closing this school."

"What—why?"

"Our numbers have stayed pretty low—still not enough parents in compliance with sending their children to school, plus we have competition with the government school in Shiprock proper. The board isn't convinced continued investment in Hebron is worth it."

"I see." Caroline's head spun. Had she come all this way for nothing?

They lurched into a gouge in the road, and she grabbed for the wagon side at the snap of breaking wood.

"Dratted wheel." With a groan, Rev. Abernathy stopped the horses. He jumped down and rounded the wagon to crouch at the corner nearest Caroline. "Thought I'd fixed it."

"Should I get out?"

"Guess so. And grab those extra spokes under the seat, would you?"

She fumbled in the darkness till her fingers closed around the stout dowels, then clambered down to hand them to him.

"Thanks."

Shivering without the buffalo robe's protection, she hugged herself and looked up again at the stars. How many miles were they from any civilization? Pennsylvania seemed on another planet entirely.

Sooner than she'd expected, Rev. Abernathy sighed and straightened beside her. "That should hold it till we get to the mission. I'll have our hired man fix it tomorrow." He touched her shoulder. "Sorry about this, Miss Haynes."

For the briefest moment, as they stood there in silent darkness together, his hand resting lightly on her arm, a chill of a quite different sort—and not altogether unpleasant—ran from Caroline's head to her toes.

Then Rev. Abernathy stepped back and offered his hand to help her into the wagon.

As they started down the road once more, Caroline folded her hands together under the buffalo robe and tried to gather her thoughts. "The school. If it is in danger of closing…"

"That's where you come in." Rev. Abernathy cleared his throat. "I'm confident hiring a new teacher will bring fresh life and order to our school. Next week we'll be taking wagons around to collect the children for the spring term."

"Your aunt founded the mission?" She tried to remember all his letter had said—now that she could picture him writing it, not a middle-aged preacher.

"She did, along with her brother. It was through their example that God called me into the ministry. But since a slight stroke a few months ago, she can't fulfill her duties as she used to—as the children need." He turned slightly on the seat. "Your response to our advertisement was a true answer to prayer."

His gaze warmed her through the darkness. Trying to settle the odd skipping of her pulse, Caroline glanced up. The sparkling span above caught her breath. Were there so many more stars out here? Or could she just see them better?

The Milky Way swooped across the blackness, glittering and dancing, thousands upon thousands of pinpricks of light.

Dizzy, she lowered her gaze. Around them, dark desert spread, a hump here and there indicating a bush or boulder. The lantern swinging from the wagon shone the only light, save the stars.

"You've taught Sunday school?" Rev. Abernathy was saying.

"Yes. And I have two younger brothers." Whom she'd practically raised, but that didn't qualify one to teach. "But I've never met any Indian children. I hope they will like me."

She felt, rather than saw, him glance toward her and smile.

"I wouldn't worry."

An hour later, lamplight gleamed from a low building as the wagon pulled into the mission yard. Other dark shapes hulked off to the left—outbuildings? Rev. Abernathy whoa-ed the horses and helped Caroline down.

The door creaked, spilling a pathway of light toward them and shadowing an angular shape in the doorway.

"There you are. I was beginning to worry."

"Long drive, Aunt." Rev. Abernathy hefted Caroline's trunk and mounted the steps to disappear inside.

Caroline followed on numb feet.

"Aunt Mariah, may I present Miss Caroline Haynes." Rev. Abernathy reappeared, his shoulders blocking the light a moment. "Miss Haynes—my aunt, Miss Spencer."

"Won't you come in?" Miss Spencer held the door.

Caroline stepped inside the mission, shuddering as the warmth enveloped her, melting hours of chill. She faced the elderly missionary. "Thank you, Miss Spencer. I am honored to meet you."

Awe tied her tongue. Was this how it would have felt to meet Lottie Moon or Ann Judson?

"Glad you made it here safely." The woman smiled, but it didn't quite reach her eyes. She wore her thin gray hair pulled back, her collar high. The eyes behind her spectacles, keen with the sagacity of many years, examined Caroline with a hint of frost.

"Thank you." She glanced around what must be the school dining room.

Two plank tables stretched across the bare floor, a dozen or so chairs marching along each one. A clock atop the mantle and framed Lord's Prayer on the wall added the only adornment. A little stark for children—but perhaps her weariness clouded her perception.

Miss Spencer turned. "Your room is right through that door. No doubt you will find us a bit rustic compared to the East, but I trust we have provided comfortably. Willis will take your trunk in."

"Thank you." Couldn't she say anything else? She sounded like a stuck Victrola.

"You must be tired, Aunt. I'll show Miss Haynes to her room." Rev. Abernathy stepped to Caroline's side, her carpetbag in hand.

"I'm perfectly well." Miss Spencer snapped, then brought her voice back to decorum. "But as you wish. Good night." Her cane and the slight favoring of her left side—the stroke her nephew had mentioned, no doubt—did not hinder Miss Spencer's sweeping from the room.

Caroline risked a glance at Rev. Abernathy.

"This way." He shifted his jaw, avoiding her eyes.

She followed him down a dim hallway until he pushed open a door.

"The girls' dormitory. Your room is just off it, here." He opened another door. "That way you can hear if one of them needs something in the night."

Caroline nodded, though she doubted he could see her.

"Should've grabbed a lamp." Rev. Abernathy fumbled in the darkness, then struck a match and lit one on the tiny bedside table. The space was hardly big enough to be called a room, more an enclosed alcove. He glanced around. "Used it for a sickroom in the past, but we thought it would be advisable for the girls to have you close by once they arrive."

She nodded again.

"Anything else you need?" Rev. Abernathy set her carpetbag by the bed.

She shook her head. Where had her vocabulary gone? "No, thank you. This is fine."

He stepped to the doorway, then turned, jamming his hands in his pockets. "My aunt is used to being the only woman here. Having her own way. But she'll come around."

"I understand." Caroline tried to sound as if she meant it.

"I'm glad you're here." He met her eyes with a smile. "Good night."

"Good night, Rev. Abernathy."

The door clicked shut. Caroline sank onto the narrow bed, squeaking the springs. A sickroom . . . well, hopefully no contagions remained. She was almost too tired to care.

At least the young minister was glad she was here. Perhaps tomorrow she would be too, but right now she merely wanted two things: a good cry and the next train back to Pennsylvania. Instead, she unpacked her Bible and unbuttoned her coat.

So much sky.

Caroline stepped onto the porch of the main mission building the next morning and drew a deep breath. The air fairly sparkled, pearly clear and clean to the horizon where the sun peeked above distant sandstone mesas. Frost glimmered on the rough porch railing, on the sparse dead grass in the yard, on the rocky dirt. She rubbed her arms through her shawl. How strange for it to be so cold with no snow.

A rooster crowed, and Caroline glanced toward the barn, whose shape she had guessed in the darkness the night before. A Navajo man bent in the small corral, feeling the sides of some animal. A sheep? It didn't look wooly enough.

Caroline hesitated, then stepped off the porch. Hugging her shawl about her shoulders, she crossed the yard toward the barn.

The man spoke low to the animals—goats, she could now see— then grasped a pitchfork and tossed hay into a bin, his movements quiet and sure. He wore a woven blanket tossed over one broad shoulder, a faded red velvet shirt beneath, breeches tucked into high leather moccasins.

Was that the glint of silver earrings in his ears? Caroline halted, nibbling her lip. Perhaps she shouldn't be so bold.

The man turned to set the pitchfork aside and glanced up at Caroline.

Why, he was young—perhaps only a year or two older than she.

His eyes unreadable, he passed the back of his wrist over the soft leather headband holding his chin-length hair in place, then nodded to her.

"Good morning. I am—Caroline Haynes." Careful to speak slowly, she laid her hand on her chest in emphasis.

The young man stared at her. Then his face lit with a grin, and he stepped to the gate. "And I am Tse, keeper of the mission goat herd. Welcome to our *Dinétah*."

"Thank you." Heat crept up Caroline's ears. His English was clearer than hers.

He tugged the gate open inward, letting out a flood of lop-eared goats.

"Where are they going?" Caroline jumped aside from the pattering hooves.

"Out to graze." Tse stepped from the pen and latched the gate, despite the piteous bleats of two wide-bellied goats left in the corral. He rubbed their noses, thrust pleadingly through the fence. "These friends do not understand they are due to kid soon."

"Kid?" Caroline wrapped her shawl tighter.

"Have their young. These two bred early this year, before we took the males away."

Caroline's ears flamed still hotter, but the herdsman seemed not to notice.

"It may be a few days yet, but I think it best they stay here." He nodded. "Good day, Miss Haynes."

He strode off, calling the goats with a low breath between his teeth, hardly a whistle.

"I see you've met Tse." Rev. Abernathy stood at her shoulder, following her gaze with a pucker between his eyes.

"He's the goatherd?"

"General overseer of the mission livestock and crops." He held out her coat. "Thought you might want this."

"I didn't expect the desert to be this cold." Caroline let him help her into the wrap, warmth flushing her cheeks. What was the matter with her?

"Few people do." Rev. Abernathy reached to scratch the forlorn goats' ears.

"So you farm here, as well?" Caroline held out her hand for one of the animals to sniff, jerking it back when the goat sneezed.

"We try to be as self-sufficient as possible—dairy goats, chickens, garden, fruit trees." Rev. Abernathy straightened. "Want to see around a bit before breakfast?"

He led her through the barnyard, past the dormant garden, and into a small orchard of bare-twigged trees. "Peach, plum, apple, apricot. The apricots bloom so early a frost often takes them, but I'm hoping for a crop this year."

"Who tends them all?"

"The older children all work shifts—girls with domestic duties, boys with outdoor tasks. We want to provide them with practical skills as well as academic and religious training."

"But they went home for Christmas?"

"Yes—not that the Navajo celebrate as we do, but my aunt needed time to recover. So we gave them an extended winter break. Now you are here, we can start fresh with the spring term."

A fresh start indeed. Glancing back, Caroline shaded her eyes to watch the goatherd heading into the rising sun with the herd, their shadows dark in the golden rays.

"Tse was educated here at Hebron." Rev. Abernathy followed her gaze. "We had high hopes for him—he's a smart lad."

Caroline turned to look at him. Did she hear a "but"?

"Since his graduation several years ago, though, he's returned to the old ways. Perhaps you guessed as much from his appearance. He refused to pursue college, though he could have done well."

"How sad." Caroline rubbed her arms.

"I wouldn't choose to have him around the school so much, but I don't know his equal with the animals." Rev. Abernathy ran his hand over a peach sapling's bare branch, then broke off a dead twig. "I'd advise you to be careful around him, though."

Caroline glanced once more after the shepherd and his flock, then lifted her face to the rose and gold of sunrise turning to pristine, cloud-studded blue. "So beautiful."

"Sunrise is significant to the Navajo. They always build their hogans facing east, toward the rising sun."

Caroline had seen a number of the six-sided log homes on the journey up from Gallup, squatting near the earth as if part of it, usually beside a rough corral. Seldom had she spotted more than two or three within miles of each other.

"The skies here are something, though. Sometimes I think God made the landscape barren so we'd look up more." Rev. Abernathy craned his neck to scan the brightening blue bowl above, then tossed the twig aside. "Want to see our church site?"

Caroline followed him up a trail winding faintly over junipered desert, then clung to his hand as he helped her clamber the rocky slope to the top of a butte overlooking the valley. Catching her breath, she tried to smooth her wind-whipped hair back into place. Below spread the sparse landscape, sand and clay dotted with junipers and sagebrush.

Rev. Abernathy pointed out the blur of leafless trees marking the San Juan River not far away.

"A bit inaccessible as yet, but feel that rock." He stamped the ground. "Talk about a firm foundation."

"Where do you hold services now?" Caroline pressed the solid footing with the toe of her boot.

"The school. We're hoping attendance will improve once we have a real church building."

"How large a gathering do you normally see?"

"Depends." Rev. Abernathy rubbed the back of his neck. "The schoolchildren, of course. Sometimes a few families, a grandmother or two. But those often don't show up until the service is practically over. Navajos have little concept of time."

Bleating turned their attention below, where Tse passed with the herd, goats clambering and dancing across the rocks like light-footed deer. The herder glanced up at them with an odd look, then moved on, whistling his peculiar call to the flock.

Caroline stepped along the edge of the outcropping, watching Rev. Abernathy.

"I often come up here to pray." He scanned the valley, a distant look in his eyes. "I think of what Jesus said, that the fields are white for the harvest. And I think, 'Lord, I want to be one of the harvesters.'" He dropped his arms and sighed. "Someday."

Caroline saw the passion, the determination in his eyes. Her heart did an odd little flip.

She stepped backward, and a rock beneath her right foot shifted, wrenching her ankle. Her feet slipped from under her. She tumbled down the slope, grabbing at anything to stop sliding, rocks grating her palms. Halfway down her feet struck a ledge. She landed with a wincing thud.

"Miss Haynes!" Rev. Abernathy scrambled down toward her, then stopped, his gaze locked on the rock where Caroline lay.

Caroline rolled over to push herself up with scratched hands, lifted her head and froze.

Not two feet away from her face, basking in the morning sunshine, a snake lifted its triangular head from tawny coils. It tasted the air with a flickering tongue.

CHAPTER EIGHT

No concept of time, huh? Tse kicked at a rock, startling one of the goats. Willis's words to the new teacher rankled. His people, the *Diné*, did have a concept of time—it was just different from the white man's. Of course that necessarily rendered it inferior.

Calm down, Tsosie. He wouldn't last long at this job if he got riled at every little thing.

The goats grazed content for the moment, having discovered a nice quarry of sagebrush near Willis's prized church site. Hay and grain made up most of their winter's diet, but Tse still liked to get them out in the fresh air a short while, even if grazing proved slim until spring. He leaned against a rock, alert to the movements of the herd leader, a bony old doe with twisted horns. Goats had far more a mind of their own than his father's sheep, and that one could lead him on a chase after the whole lot if she chose.

Yázhí trotted over and nosed his hand.

"You don't care about clocks, do you, little one?" Tse rubbed her sleek brown sides, rounding with her first pregnancy. "Not as long as I give all the time you need."

A shout brought him to his feet.

"Tse! Your gun!" Willis galloped toward him, panting.

"What's wrong?" Tse ran to meet him.

"Rattler." Skidding to a stop, Willis grabbed for the shotgun slung over Tse's shoulder.

Tse yanked from his friend's grasp and sprinted up the rocky outcropping where the reverend and Miss Haynes had stood a few moments before. A rattlesnake? This time of year? In a glance he took in the scene below, Miss Haynes cowering on the rocky ledge, the reptile lazing in the sun. The warmth must have coaxed the snake from its winter sleep, but it was not angry—not yet.

"Give me the gun," Willis hissed, climbing.

Ignoring him, Tse crept down the slope. With one motion, he grasped the head of the sleepy rattler and flung it down the side of the mesa. After a surprised flip, it slithered away, tail disappearing into a crevice.

Tse released his breath and wiped his palms on his breeches. He held out his hand. "You all right, Miss Haynes?"

With a minor avalanche of pebbles and dirt, Willis landed beside them. Pushing in front of Tse, he helped Miss Haynes to her feet and then turned on Tse. "Will you give up your stupid superstitions?"

"It was not angry." Tse braced himself against the rock in the narrow space left him. "But if you missed ... "

Willis just huffed and glared at him until Tse looked away. Pain twisted his gut. How had they come to this?

He looked back to see Willis helping Miss Haynes clamber down the rest of the slope, just a few feet to the ground. Dirt dusted the young woman's tailored coat, and she clung to the reverend's arm.

How long would she last out here, after today? How she had blushed at his mention of the goats' pregnancies. He'd been away from *bilagáanas* long enough to forget their squeamishness about such things.

The goats. Tse struck his thigh. They might have strayed clear to the river by now. He leapt to the ground and ran, feet chuffing up puffs of dust. His steps slowed as he reached the sagebrush again, where the goats still munched, raising their heads as if to ask where he'd been.

Thank You, Lord. And thank You that no one was hurt just now. Warmth spread through his chest at the reminder. God had not forgotten him … even if Willis thought Tse had forsaken God.

Fertile, pungent stench filled Tse's nostrils as he spread aged manure and bedding over the garden plot that afternoon. Here it would break down further, enriching the earth and readying it for spring planting. Sure did smell, though. Tse sneezed into his sleeve.

"Last load." Willis wheeled another barrow of manure from the barnyard and dumped it on the earth. He pulled off his work gloves and rubbed his thumb across the other palm, wincing. "I've got winter hands."

"Should try milking goats and herding horses year round. Won't go soft then." Tse dug the pitchfork into the pile and tossed rich matter over the soil. At times like this, working together, he could almost imagine he and Willis were boys again. Almost think they were still friends.

"What's this I hear about you being at a *Yeibichai?*" Willis tugged his gloves back on.

Tse halted, pitchfork poised midair. Slowly he lowered it to the ground.

"I saw Tom Chee on the way to Shiprock to fetch Miss Haynes. He mentioned it."

It took Tse a moment to recognize the English name. *Nezwood.* "It was for my family. I felt I should be there for them. I wasn't—"

"I don't pretend to have any say over the state of your soul anymore." Willis held up his hand. "But we cannot have the mission linked with heathen customs. Not in any fashion." He stepped closer. "I don't want to hear of you attending such ceremonies again. Not while you're working here."

Or you won't be working here. Tse heard the unsaid.

He lowered his gaze to Willis's narrow-toed boots. "Yes, sir." He turned and dug the fork into the manure, feeling the reverend's eyes still on him. Tse pitched until his arms burned and the sun sank orange toward the western horizon. When at last he straightened to wipe his forehead, beaded with sweat in the icy air, Willis was gone.

Tse rubbed his nose, fighting the burning in his eyes. How long was he supposed to keep it up, this balance between the tug of two worlds?

That evening, murmuring voices and children's laughter greeted him as he lifted the rug to enter his family's hogan.

"Tse!" Shashyáázh sprang up from beside the fire and grabbed Tse around the knees.

Tse steadied himself against the log wall, running his hand over his cousin's head. "What brings you here, little brother?" He glanced around the fire.

Kai and Sháńdíín smiled at him.

"They came for one last visit to your grandfather before the school term starts." His mother's voice sang with the joy of hospitality, having her cousin here. "Come, Tse. Eat. The *bilagáanas* should not keep you at the mission after dark. *Ch'iidiis* are about."

"I am not afraid of *ch'iidiis, Shimá.*"

"Sit." She pushed the pot of mutton stew toward him.

Inhaling the aroma of rich broth and potatoes, Tse let Shashyáázh pull him to the fire and sank down cross-legged, scooting near its warmth.

"He is telling about the turkey's tail feathers." Shashyáázh plopped beside him and turned his face up to Tse's father, who smiled down at him and continued the story.

"So, as Water Monster continued to show the *Diné* his beautiful underwater home, Coyote snuck through a passageway into another room. And there, he found Water Monster's baby. Well, when Coyote saw that baby, he wanted nothing more than to steal it from Water Monster. So he picked up that baby and stuck it right inside his coat."

"Coyote is a bad fellow." Shashyáázh glanced at Tse.

"That he is. And when the *Diné* had left Water Monster's home, it wasn't long before he discovered his baby was missing. And was he angry! He churned up waves and whirlpools and spewed out torrents of water, so the whole earth began to be flooded."

After bowing his head in silent prayer, Tse slurped a spoonful of steaming stew. The warmth curled down to his middle, relaxing his stomach as the familiar tale soothed his mind. He scooped another bite and smiled at his mother across the fire.

He listened as his father finished the coyote story, telling how the *Diné* and all the animals tried to flee from the flood of Water Monster's wrath, how even when someone finally thought to throw the baby back to its home, the waters still rose high, and how the people and animals at last found refuge in a reed shelter above the water. Tse's grandfather, propped on rolled blankets by the fire, his eyes cloudy with age, interjected occasionally to correct his son-in-law or elaborate a detail.

Tse drained his bowl and set it on the floor, musing on the story's parallels to Noah's biblical flood precipitated by sin. Long ago, had his people known that history and adapted it over the ages?

"Turkey was the last one inside," his father concluded, "and his tail feathers got caught in the door and washed in the water. So that is why they are white tipped today."

The children clamored for more stories, and his father began on Coyote's role in forming the canyons central to *Diné* history. Sháńdíín and Shashyáázh played a string game together, fingers weaving in and out in the firelight as they listened. In winter came the season of string games and telling stories, from the time of the first snow to the first thunder in spring.

Tse sat on his heels, lulled by his full belly, the smell of coffee and woodsmoke, the presence of his family.

"There is to be another Nightway next week." Kai leaned near, quirking a smile. "All the girls will wish to watch you on horseback again."

Tse scratched his ear, resisting the heat creeping up it. "I don't think I will be there."

"Nonsense." His mother gave a sharp nod. "Soon you should be building a hogan for a wife of your own."

"*Shimá*..." Tse uncrossed and re-crossed his legs, then sighed. "Rev. Abernathy does not wish me to attend the ceremonies."

The story must have ended just before he spoke, for now only the fire crackled in the stillness. Shándíín glanced from Tse to her mother, then back to Tse. His mother opened her mouth, then pressed her lips together.

"Your grandfather has fallen asleep," his father said at last. "We should sleep also."

Everyone moved to sheepskin pallets with murmured goodnights.

Tse watched his mother, still kneeling by the fire, examine her twisted fingers in the flickering light. Pain lined her face. He knew what she was thinking: that if not for her arthritis, she could sell enough rugs that he would not need to work at the mission at all, that he could be free to collect horses for a bride and set up his own sheep camp. He wished she wouldn't blame herself.

Perhaps Willis was right, though. Perhaps he should not attend the ceremonies, regardless of keeping his job. Perhaps being set apart did mean rejecting all that was Navajo and taking on the white man's ways. But where was that ordained in Scripture? Not like the people of ancient Israel were European, after all.

Tse slid under his blankets, watching the firelight flicker and fade until his eyelids dropped closed.

Smoke and flames of the *Yeibichai* fire leaped toward the sky, swirling before him. The *yei* dancers circled, closing in, feet stamping, gourds rattling, bells jingling, hair-tufted masks drawing nearer, nearer.

"Go away!" Tse tried to shout. "I worship only Creator now." But his words came out a whisper.

"You cannot approach Creator yourself." The mask of the lead dancer loomed in his face, its tubular mouth speaking. "That is what we are for. Who do you think you are? The *bilagáanas'* God will not accept you unless you change who you are. You are *Diné*. You cannot change that. Come back to us."

"No." Tse cried. He clapped his palms over his ears, but the ghostly blue faces pressed in.

Then the tallest *yei*'s face whitened, pinked, grew a beard. Rev. Spencer, Miss Spencer's now-deceased older brother, gazed at Tse from behind his desk, fingering a long, slim measuring stick.

"I do not wish to do this, Peter." Rev. Spencer's voice always had a nasal timbre. He might have proved adept at the complex tones of Navajo had he ever tried. "But we must break your obsession with this barbaric tongue."

It is not barbaric. It is beautiful. It is my language, and you will not take it from me. But Tse just stared mutely at the polished stick, watched it rise in the air.

Then he was running, tearing across the desert, leaping junipers, cutting through a sandy arroyo. And water was rushing, chasing behind him as if in league with Rev. Spencer, filling the arroyo, washing away his footing, rising to his chest. Someone must have stolen Water Monster's baby again. Fighting to keep his head above the waves, he tried to cry out to God, but English words would not come, only jumbled syllables. The water swept over his head. He couldn't breathe.

Tse sat upright on his sheepskin, gasping, terror searing his scalp. His family slumbered around him. The fire's coals glowed orange in the darkness. He pressed the heels of his hands to his eyes as the dream swirled back through his mind.

"Jesus... help me." The foreign words he had fought for in sleep now came automatically. "Help me."

His thundering pulse slowed. He let out a long, shuddering breath. It was deep in the night, yet moonlight still shone through the smoke hole in the roof. Tse stared at the silver beam.

"Why, Lord?" His breath caught on something nearer a sob than he wanted to admit. "They always say You love us. But sometimes I don't think You like us very well."

Tse flopped back on his stomach and buried his face in his folded arms.

CHAPTER NINE

Shivering head to foot, Caroline slipped back inside the mission from her midnight trip to the outhouse and latched the door behind her.

She scurried on tiptoe back to her room off the empty girls' dormitory and dove under the covers. Still wearing her wrapper, she tugged the blankets under her chin with shaking hands. Why hadn't she asked Miss Spencer for a chamber pot? And why hadn't they provided her one in the first place? Perhaps because the woman didn't want her here in the first place.

In spite of her resolve, tears pooled and threatened to spill. Caroline pressed her fist to her mouth, squelching the sobs. She wanted Benji—she wanted Father and Toby. Even Lillian would be familiar and comforting, compared to anyone within hundreds of miles. She wanted her own bed and the bathroom down the hall. Childish, but she did. What was she doing here, anyway, following a girlish fantasy to a remote mission outpost in the wilderness? Who did she think she was? Why had Father even let her come, if he were as worried as he claimed about savages and snakes and such? Maybe he and Lillian did want her out of the way.

Caroline squeezed her lids shut as the beady eyes of the rattler gleamed in her mind again. To think the creature still slithered alive somewhere, thanks to that goatherd. Caroline shuddered and curled into a tighter ball. What had been the backslidden Indian's name? Sounded something like a sneeze.

Lord, help me. She had to find her place here somehow—had to at least try. The mission had asked her to come after all. They needed her, wasn't that what the notice had said? Very well, then she must show Miss Spencer she could meet that need.

Huddling under the quilts, she tried to pray. Bit by bit, warmth crept back into her limbs, and she slept until wakened by the gentle touch of winter sunlight on her face. She dressed quickly and tied on an apron, glancing out the window at the ever-changing palette of shifting clouds. A new day, a new start.

"I hear you had quite a welcome to our church site." Miss Spencer shook out clean sheets in the girls' dormitory an hour later.

Sweeping the corners of the room, Caroline shuddered.

"We don't tend to see rattlers in winter. But you must learn to watch for them. We've only had one snakebite in the eleven years of the mission, and that was because my brother stepped in a rattlesnake's nest."

Caroline whirled, clutching the broom handle. "Was that—"

"No. Thank the Lord, that isn't how he died."

"What did you do?"

"Peter knew how to draw out the poison, though he was only a boy then."

Peter? Who was Peter? Caroline cocked her head.

"I keep forgetting." Miss Spencer lifted a frail hand to adjust her spectacles. "He goes by Tse now."

Tse—that was it.

Miss Spencer bent to tuck the sheets under the mattress, grunting slightly as she pushed with her weak left arm.

"Can I do that for you?" Caroline hurried to her side.

"No, thank you."

She crept back to her sweeping. Was this how Lillian felt when she arrived in the Haynes household? Caroline attacked a cobweb. Now there lay an uncomfortable thought.

Lowering her broom to catch her breath, Caroline glanced out the window. No sign of the Navajo herder today. "May I ask you a question?"

Miss Spencer straightened, rubbing the small of her back.

Perhaps that meant yes. "Why didn't Tse want to kill the snake?"

"The Navajo believe snakes hold power over death and share the secrets of rebirth with dormant seeds and roots. They believe killing them would anger the snake spirit and bring bad luck to the land."

"Tse still believes this?" Caroline's scalp prickled.

"The old ways die hard." Miss Spencer gripped the headboard of one of the narrow beds, her breathing labored.

Caroline stepped toward her, then hesitated, twisting her fingers together. "Please, sit and rest. I can finish—that is why I am here, after all."

The older woman opened her mouth as if to protest, then sighed and waved her hand. "Oh, very well. I suppose I haven't a chance with you and Willis allied against me." She sank onto a straight-backed chair with a sigh and watched Caroline unfold the blankets. A moment passed before she spoke again. "I've been girls' matron since my brother and I started the school in 1899. Before that, we worked among the Pottawatomie in Indiana."

"I truly admire your giving of your life to the Lord's work." Kneeling between two beds, Caroline looked up. She hoped the woman could tell how much she meant it.

"Well." Miss Spencer gazed in Caroline's direction, seeming to scan years past. "I wouldn't have wanted to spend it any other way." She blinked. "I'll admit my bones are getting a bit old to be on call all night. Though do not tell my nephew I said that."

Was that a glint of humor behind the spectacles?

"How long has Rev. Abernathy worked here?" Caroline tucked the blankets, fighting a ridiculous heat creeping up her cheeks. "He is your brother's son?"

"No. Willis is the son of our youngest sister."

Of course—his last name wasn't Spencer. Stupid question.

"His father owns a railroad manufacturing company in Chicago, quite successful. When Willis was sixteen, his parents sent him here while they went on a European tour. Hebron became home to him, so much that he came back to stay after attending college and seminary. He's practically run the mission since my brother passed away."

After spreading the last coverlet, Caroline stepped back to survey their work. Eighteen beds in two neat rows, each blanketed and tucked just so. Eighteen pillows soon to cradle small heads. Six freshly dusted dressers for uniforms and nightgowns.

Caroline wiped dusty hands on her apron, forcing back the ache tugging at her heart. Three days until the students would arrive. Surely then she wouldn't miss her brothers so desperately.

"'Bout ready?" Rev. Abernathy's voice echoed through the near-empty mission. Empty no longer, after today.

"One moment." Caroline peered into the tiny mirror over her washbasin, trying to finish pinning her hair into place. If only her fingers wouldn't jitter so. There. She stood back to inspect herself, adjusting her stylish fur hat. No doubt the wind would send it tumbling the moment she climbed into the wagon. Perhaps a scarf to secure it? She tied one on and checked her reflection again. Silly. The children wouldn't care how she looked.

But Rev. Abernathy might. She squelched the impertinent voice and slid her arms into her coat sleeves.

"Miss Haynes?" Rev. Abernathy's call hailed from outside now.

"Coming." Caroline snatched her gloves and flew from her room and out the mission door, buttoning her coat as she went. The morning air smacked her face, crisp and cold as a winter apple.

The twenty-third of January, start of the spring term at Hebron Navajo Mission School. Beginning of Miss Haynes, missionary schoolmarm. Could she do this?

It's time ... dear Lord, it's really time.

CHAPTER TEN

"Tse, I'll need you to drive today."

"I'd rather not." Balancing the milk pails he lugged, Tse halted beside the wagon where Willis stood harnessing one of the teams.

"You what?"

Tse's fingers clenched around the pails' cold metal handles. "I'd rather not help tear these children from their families." There, he had said it. "Is there something else I could do?"

"No, there isn't." Willis yanked at a harness strap. "We need two wagons to hold them all. You think I'm going to ask my aunt or Miss Haynes to drive?"

Tse stared at the hinges that locked the wagon bed together.

"Listen. I'm trying to be patient, but if you want to keep your job, get over and hitch up that other wagon. Take the western route, and we'll circle round and meet up. Got it?"

Tse met Willis's eyes, then turned on his heel, sloshing a slop of milk from the pail onto the reverend's boot. He heard Willis muttering behind him as he headed for the mission to strain the milk. Tse tramped up the steps and nearly collided with Miss Haynes, who came flying out the door. He bit his tongue and stepped aside.

The first wagon rumbled away just as he emerged from the mission. Feet heavy, Tse trudged to the barn. He rubbed the horses' noses and gave them a few oats, postponing the inevitable as long as he could. At last he backed the harnessed team into place and fastened the traces. He hauled himself onto the wagon seat and hunched forward, thinking of his family, the dwindling stores in the hogan. *Lord … I don't want to do this.*

Tse slapped the reins and clucked to the team, trying to ignore the rock settling in his stomach.

Hogan after hogan. Family after family. Stoic mothers. Children's tears.

Tse gripped the reins, the leather welded to his palms. He tried to distract the children as they drove, pointing out a flock of geese heading for the river, a hawk circling overhead. But inside he was twelve years old again, keeping chin high and jaw tight as Dólii clung to his hand the day Rev. Spencer first came, resisting the shameful tears blurring his vision as his parents and their hogan disappeared in a cloud of dust. His little sister had quivered against his shoulder as they crouched in a corner of the wagon, crammed in like sheep with the other children. Like those behind him now.

As Tse circled south and the shadows lengthened, the rock in his belly grew heavier. The horses plodded on, nearer and nearer to the Begay family camp. If only Willis and Miss Haynes would reach there first. He didn't want to be the one to take Shashyáázh and Shándíín away.

Tse sat up and breathed deeper as a wagon full of children came into view, already parked by the two hogans and corral. He pulled up the team and waited.

Kai emerged from the main hogan, guiding her children before her. The rounding under her velvet tunic indicated another child to join the family's circle. Perhaps the coming little one would be a comfort, with these two gone—especially after the baby they'd lost last year.

"Shashyáázh too, this year." Her husband placed his hand on the boy's head.

Willis crouched down to Shashyáázh's level. "Hello there, little fellow. Ready for school?"

Shashyáázh stared for a moment at the lanky white man, then buried his face in his mother's skirt, clinging with both hands.

Tse heard his pleading, though he couldn't discern the words from here. His throat tightened.

Shándíín tried to take her brother's hand, but he pulled away. Suddenly the rug covering the doorway of the other, smaller hogan jerked aside, and Dezbah hobbled out. Shaking her stick and pursing her lips at Willis and Miss Haynes, she ranted at her son-in-law, who had the grace to avert his eyes, deferring to the ancient taboo against a man looking his wife's mother in the eye.

When her tirade paused, however, the father spoke firmly. "Shashyáázh. You need to go with Rev. Abernathy now."

Kai gave Shashyáázh a tight squeeze, then placed his hand in his sister's. Shándíín towed him toward the wagon, with only one glance back to her parents.

Suddenly Shashyáázh's head shot up, and he yanked away from his sister. "Tse!"

Tse groaned inwardly as Shashyáázh pelted toward him. He jumped from the wagon to catch the small body.

"Easy there, little brother." Kneeling, he set his cousin on his feet.

"Don't let them take me. I want to stay and help *Shizhé'é* with the sheep." Shashyáázh hiccupped a sob, his arms clinging around Tse's neck.

Willis was approaching.

"I will be at the school often, little brother." Tse grasped Shashyáázh's shoulders and gently held him away. "I will see you there."

The hurt of betrayal in Shashyáázh's eyes smote Tse's heart.

Willis's dusty boots stopped beside them. The missionary hoisted the child, all the fight gone out of his small arms and legs.

Tse stood slowly and watched Shashyáázh tucked beside his sister in the wagon. The little boy clung to the backboard, straining to see his parents through the dust as the wagon jolted away.

I'm sorry, little brother. I'm sorry.

The goats bellowed to be fed by the time the wagons rattled into the mission yard. After helping shepherd the children inside, Tse unharnessed the team and led them into the barn, where the goats offered forgiving nuzzles and the other horses welcoming whickers. He clipped open a bale of hay and distributed it among the animals, sneezing on the chaff. Around his feet, chickens pecked at grain spilled by the greedy head doe as she bolted into place for milking. Tse nudged her over with his knee and squatted, feeling her flaccid udder. She would be one of the last to dry up, since she wouldn't kid until May. Her milk supply was decreasing fast, though. Maybe she carried triplets this year.

She stomped her foot as he began to milk, and he patted her rounding side.

Good thing they'd carried over two does without breeding them this year, so there would be plenty of milk for the children. Not that the *Diné* valued milk much as a food, but the *bilagáanas* sure did. He had gotten to like it all right during his student days.

Tse stripped the last meager drops from this doe and sent her back to the pen, one of the other goats trotting out to take her place. He would have milked this one first, the way her udder bulged, if the leader wouldn't have had three kinds of fits. Goats clung to their hierarchy, that was sure. A bit like people.

He thought of the look on Miss Spencer's face when Willis had insisted she let Caroline undertake the day's journey in her place. Had the new teacher's slim figure and eager gray eyes influenced the reverend's decision as much as concern for his aunt's health?

Tse leaned his head against the doe's side, breathing in the sweet scents of hay and animal breath. The rock in his stomach gradually dissolved. School was not altogether bad for the children, after all. Didn't they need to learn to survive in the white man's world? And here they would learn of Jesus, if only they could hear and understand.

As he let the goats out of the barn the next morning, a panicked wail sliced the air.

CHAPTER ELEVEN

Was that a child's cry outside?

Braiding a little girl's hair amid the first-morning dormitory pandemonium, Caroline froze. The little girl twisted to look up at her, and Caroline smiled into the heart-shaped face. Hearing no more, she resumed braiding. She wished she could communicate with these little ones. At least many of the older girls were returning students and already spoke English.

There it came again. Caroline dropped the braid and ran from the room, one of the older girls darting ahead of her. They burst out on the porch and halted.

Rev. Abernathy had set up a makeshift barber station at one end of the veranda with chair, sheet, comb and scissors. One group of boys stood at the opposite end, their hair shorn short above starched shirts and dark blue jackets and trousers. The others, hair still traditionally long, clustered near the barbering chair where the reverend attempted to confine a small, flailing figure.

"Shashyáázh!" The girl squeezed past the crowd of boys. As Rev. Abernathy looked up, the child pulled away and flung himself at his sister.

Of course—the siblings picked up yesterday. The little boy who had clung to his mother so.

The girl murmured to her brother in Navajo, her hand smoothing his heavy locks of black hair. He shook his head, pressing his face against her school dress, the same deep blue as the boys' uniforms.

"Esther," Rev. Abernathy rebuked. He laid down the scissors and moved near the pair. "No Navajo. You are back at school now."

"He doesn't understand English, Rev. Abernathy." The girl clasped her brother tight.

"What seems to be the matter?" Caroline stepped closer.

"He's putting up a fuss about getting his hair cut. I've seen it before." Rev. Abernathy laid his hand on the girl's shoulder. "Go. He'll be all right."

"He's afraid." Esther kept her arms about her brother and bravely raised her gaze to the reverend's. "Cutting hair means mourning death of family for us. He remembers from when our baby sister died."

"This has nothing to do with anyone dying. Tell him so."

Esther spoke to her brother in Navajo. He clung tighter, looking pleadingly into her face.

"You know the rules." With a hand on each shoulder, Rev. Abernathy pulled the children apart. Esther turned, brushing past Caroline to reenter the mission, chin high.

The child reached after his sister with a sob.

"Come on, little fellow." Rev. Abernathy lifted the child back onto the chair, but he shrieked and catapulted off the seat. Hanging onto his arms, Rev. Abernathy glanced at Caroline. "Miss Haynes? Hold him, please."

Caroline hesitated. Was this really necessary right now? The look on the girl's face... But Rev. Abernathy was waiting. She stepped to the chair, drew small Shashyáázh onto her lap, and wrapped her arms around his unyielding little body. He couldn't be any older than Benji.

As Rev. Abernathy swept a sheet over both of them, she felt the little boy's heart fluttering beneath his ribcage, his muscles quivering. "Rev. Abernathy..."

The reverend paused, scissors poised.

"Must this be done now? Perhaps another time—"

"He'll be fine. Hold him steady."

The scissors snipped. Shashyáázh jerked at the first few cuts, then seemed to shrink into himself. As soon as Rev. Abernathy removed the sheet, he sprang from Caroline's lap to seek refuge among the other boys. He turned to look back at her, feeling the shorn ends of his hair.

"Thank you. Next?" Rev. Abernathy beckoned to a teenaged young man who must have been new to the school, his hair traditionally bound on the back of his head. The boy advanced warily.

"Miss Haynes?"

At the reverend's voice, Caroline realized she still sat in the chair. "I'm sorry." She brushed the snippets of hair from her skirt and stood. Heading for the mission door, she avoided the eyes of the surrounding boys.

A sound beside the steps turned her to see Tse standing near, watching the scene. He glanced at her, and their eyes met for a moment. Then he looked away, yet she felt somehow exposed, ashamed. Of what?

Caroline hurried inside. She closed the door and leaned against it, hardly seeing the curious girls clustered around until Miss Spencer's voice broke through her fog.

"Girls, what are you gawking at? Those of you prepared for the day, you may set the table for breakfast. The rest of you, to the washroom. Off you go."

Caroline didn't miss the glance Miss Spencer sent her before returning to the kitchen, the glance that said, *If this is the best you can do as matron, it appears I won't be retiring after all.*

Tightening her lips, Caroline followed the subdued line of girls into the washroom. She and the older ones finished helping the younger girls comb and plait their hair, smiling at their reactions to the two mirrors hung over the basins. The little ones stared wide eyed, then broke into giggles making faces at each other.

At least they were laughing. Caroline glanced around the wash-room. Where was Esther, the little boy's sister?

She didn't appear in the dining room when Caroline herded the girls in for breakfast, the boys filing in to sit at the opposite table. Shashyáázh—was that his name?—shuffled at the end of the line, his little face still puffy from tears.

Caroline's heart twisted. She must befriend him, and soon. She knew about little boys, after all. After Rev. Abernathy asked the blessing, she slipped out while spoons clinked in bowls of cornmeal mush.

She found Esther in the girls' dormitory, sitting on the corner bed under one of the two windows and fingering some sort of jew-elry. The girl started and clamped her hands over it, looking up like a frightened deer.

"Is that a necklace?" Caroline eased the door shut and sat on the bed across.

Esther watched her, keeping her hands closed tight.

"It looked lovely. May I see?"

"You are not angry?"

"Why would I be?"

Esther ducked her head. "We're not supposed to have our jew-elry at school." She uncurled her fingers, letting the sunlight touch delicately curved silver and turquoise buds.

Caroline caught her breath. "That is beautiful. Where did you get it?"

"My grandfather made it for my mother. She gave it to me be-fore I came to school this time."

"Your grandfather made this?" Caroline reached a finger to the blossoming pendant.

Esther nodded.

"This belonged to my mama." Caroline touched the chain about her own neck, then pressed open the locket's clasp. "See? A picture of her with me, when I was younger than you."

"Where does she live?" Esther peered at the picture.

"In heaven now, with Jesus and the angels." Caroline tucked her chin to see the tiny portrait, then clicked the locket closed.

"Oh." Esther returned to fiddling with her own necklace.

Caroline tried again. "Such a pretty name you have, Esther. Rev. Abernathy told me you often pick Bible names."

"Miss Spencer gave it to me." Esther shot her a glance. "It is not my real name."

"Do you know the story of Esther in the Bible?"

"Esther was a beautiful maiden who married the headman of the tribe who captured her people." Nibbling her thumbnail, the girl tapped her boot on the floor. "Then she saved her tribe from those who wanted to destroy them."

"Did Miss Spencer tell it to you that way?" Caroline sat straighter.

"No. But I understood."

Esther gazed out the window, still tapping her boot. A bell rang, signaling the end of breakfast.

"Esther." Caroline laid her hand on the girl's arm and waited until she met her eyes. "Your brother will be all right."

The girl withdrew from Caroline's touch. She slipped the necklace into a pouch and under her bed, then rose and hurried out of the room without a backward glance.

Slowly, Caroline got down on her knees and reached for the pouch. If the children weren't allowed to have their jewelry at school, she had a responsibility. But then she stopped, thinking of the girl's wary eyes, how she pulled away when Caroline touched her. Something about Esther tugged at her, made her wonder what it might have been like to have a little sister, much as she loved Toby and Benji.

Hesitant, as if she were intruding upon something secret and precious, she drew one end of the necklace from the pouch and examined the beading. The intricate silver, the soft blue gleam of turquoise—how did the Navajo craft such things?

What could be the harm in a necklace, after all? And were Caroline to breach a fragile trust now, she might never regain it.

She pushed the pouch farther under the bed and headed back to breakfast.

The weeks passed in a blur of lessons and schedules, of cooking meals and comforting homesick children. Of lines of boys in dark suits and girls in navy blue dresses with white pinafores, marching in and out of the dining room, in and out of the schoolhouse, in and out from work shifts. Caroline's head ached from the bells— bells to wake up, to eat meals, to start school, to go to bed. If she sickened of them, how much more did the children, accustomed only to sunrise and sunset marking their days?

Sometimes, tangling her fingers in her hair, she wondered what had possessed her to leave the picket fences, maple trees, and red-headed Sunday school scamps of Pennsylvania for this land, where wind chapped her hands and Navajo children wept for their mothers at night and stared uncomprehendingly at her English lessons on the blackboard.

At least that's what little Shashyáázh did—Samuel, Rev. Abernathy had christened him.

But there were other times—moments, really, snippets of color and clarity in the fog of those early weeks—when she caught her breath at a sunset flaming magenta and gold from north to south, or a little hand slipped into hers and a shy smile lit a warm glow in her heart. Those carried her through when she couldn't think of another way to explain the alphabet to children who had never seen letters before. Or when she collapsed into bed with homesick tears—only to be awakened by a little girl with nightmares, who would then insist on sleeping on the floor as she was used to rather than in her bed.

Caroline eased the dormitory door shut with a sigh. At last, all the children settled for the night. With Rev. Abernathy gone to the trading post, she realized anew how much he did.

In the sitting room, she sank into what had become her favorite chair, drawn near the fire, and reached in her apron pocket for the crackling paper that had tantalized her all day. She withdrew the envelope and ran her thumb over the Pennsylvania postmark. So far away … a lifetime away.

She pulled out the letter. Disappointment nipped that the finely looped script was Lillian's, not Father's. Still, she drank in the news of Toby's late penchant for giving sled rides on the ice—and charging a penny each—and of Benji already outgrowing his winter boots. The ache in her throat sharpened. *Heavenly Father, how I miss them.*

She cleared her eyes with a knuckle to read Lillian's closing.

We miss you most earnestly, yet remain thankful for this opportunity for you and the good you can accomplish where God has placed you. Your father and I are grateful you are with such experienced missionaries as Miss Spencer and Rev. Abernathy. Their presence and years of wisdom must be a great comfort to you.

Caroline's ears warmed. Somehow she hadn't mentioned in her letters home that Rev. Abernathy was only a few years older than she. She would, of course—soon.

A sudden pounding at the door sent the letter skittering to the floor.

CHAPTER TWELVE

"Rev. Abernathy!" A man's voice, hushed but urgent.

Caroline looked at the clock. Nearly eleven—what in the world? The pounding came again, and she hurried to unbar the door lest the children wake.

"Tse?"

"Where is Rev. Abernathy?" The herdsman leaned one hand on the doorframe, wiping the other on his breeches.

"He isn't back from the trading post yet. What's wrong?"

"A goat is having trouble kidding. I need another pair of hands." His gaze swept her. "Will you come?"

"Me?" Caroline gaped at him.

Tse brushed the air with his hand. "Never mind. I'll get one of the boys." He pushed past her into the mission.

"Wait." Caroline caught his arm. "They're all settled for the night." If the smaller boys wakened through fetching one of the older ones, she might deal with chaos for an hour.

Tse blew out a breath. "I need help one way or the other."

"What would I do?" Caroline twisted her fingers together.

"Just hold her still." Tse shifted his feet, glancing out the open door toward the barn. The early March wind blew in, though mellowed from the gale before sundown.

"Let me get my boots." Surely "holding her" couldn't be too hard. After tugging on her galoshes, she threw her woolen shawl about her shoulders and followed Tse.

The light from Tse's lantern danced crazily as they hurried across the barnyard, Caroline half running to keep up with his strides.

A miserable bleating came from the barn. Caroline swallowed. "What's happening?"

"She delivered one kid some time ago, but she's been pushing ever since with nothing." The barn door creaked a complaint as Tse shoved it open. "The second kid must be turned wrong, but she won't hold still for me to tell."

This isn't Mama. This is just a goat. But Caroline couldn't stop her legs from trembling.

Within the barn's warm mustiness, Tse led the way to a back stall. He hung the lantern on a nail, illuminating a goat on her knees in the straw, bleating unhappily.

"The first kid." Tse jerked his head at a rag-wrapped bundle squirming in the corner.

Murmuring low to the goat, Tse squatted at the animal's side and nodded to Caroline. "Hold her head and talk to her. It's her first time. She's frightened."

Caroline lowered herself to the straw, tucking her skirts out of the way. Reaching for the doe's head, she started when the goat jerked away, long ears flapping. Caroline bit her lip and reached again, placing her hand gingerly on the doe's neck. "What's her name?"

Tse, rolling his sleeves above the elbow, looked up. "I call her Yázhí."

"There, Yázhí, it's all right, girl." Awkwardly, Caroline stroked the smoothly haired head, the drooping ears, as the goat bleated and strained.

"Hold her, now. She'll likely buck when I reach in." Tse finished scrubbing his arms in a bucket of water.

Caroline gulped. Was he really going to— She looked away and was nearly bowled over as Yázhí lunged to her feet.

"Hold her!" His voice sharp, Tse scooted after the goat on his knees.

Caroline fought to grip Yázhí's neck, murmuring whatever came to mind, hoping it sounded reassuring.

After a moment, Tse withdrew his hand with a frustrated breath and wiped it on a rag.

"What's wrong?"

"I can feel the problem but can't fix it. She's too small—my hands are too big."

"What can we do?"

Tse reached to stroke Yázhí's ears, his hand brushing Caroline's. His gaze rested on her fingers, small and slender next to his large brown ones.

"Will you try?"

Caroline stared. Surely he wasn't serious.

"We could lose the kid. Yázhí too. You just need to bring the front feet forward." His eyes met hers, dark and earnest.

Caroline's insides trembled. She couldn't do this. She had barely touched a goat before tonight, let alone reached inside of one. But... Yázhí's glazed eyes, her heavy breathing.

Caroline drew a shaky breath. "Tell me how."

Under Tse's direction, she scrubbed her hands and arms. She knelt by Yázhí's tail and pinched her fingers into the cone shape Tse showed her.

Tse's strong arms held the little goat down.

Lord, help me. Caroline squeezed her eyes shut and reached into the birth canal. Panic rose in her throat. "Now what?"

"Follow the neck down past the shoulder until you feel a hoof."

His steady voice calmed her slightly. Squeezing her eyes shut, she obeyed by feel.

"Now bring the foot forward. Cup your hand around it so it doesn't tear her."

Horrified, Caroline did so.

"Now the same with the other foot."

She maneuvered another moment, hardly daring to breathe. "They're both forward." She withdrew her hand, blessed oxygen rushing into her lungs.

Yázhí bleated and started to push.

Her limbs shaking, Caroline scooted away so Tse could take her place. She held Yázhí's head while Tse helped pull the kid out.

It lay limp in his hands.

"No." Caroline pressed her clean fist to her mouth. *Please, God, no.*

Snatching a rag, Tse wiped the kid's mouth and nose. He turned it upside down and slapped its side hard once, then again. The kid jerked and sneezed.

Tse laughed and exclaimed in Navajo, a grin lighting his face.

Caroline felt an answering smile spread over hers. "Thank the Lord."

Tse held the kid under Yázhí's nose as Caroline wiped her arm with a rag. The doe sniffed the wet bundle and began to lick it vigorously all over. Tse brought the other kid near and cuddled both against their mother. Reaching to touch the tiny heads, Caroline found them soft as velvet. The newest kid had one crooked ear, folded so it stuck out like a little girl's pigtail.

"Well done." Tse glanced up at her with a grin. The approval in his eyes curled warmth through her middle.

An hour later, Caroline leaned against the stall door watching the newborns.

Already wobbling on spindly legs, they butted and nuzzled at Yázhí's udder. Tse brought a bucket of warm molasses water for the new mother, and the doe gulped, turning her head every half minute to sniff at the flickering little tails.

"So beautiful." Caroline blinked sudden mist from her eyes.

Tse looked up, still holding the pail for the guzzling goat. "Have you not seen new ones come into the world before?"

"My father owns a livery stable, and he took me to see the foals a few times when I was a little girl. But I was never there when they were born." Nor had she been in the room for either of her brothers' births. "I suppose you've seen it all your life."

"Growing up with my father's herds, lambing and kidding were part of spring like wind and new leaves." Tse stood. Setting the bucket aside, he pitched clean straw over the soiled bedding. "But it never loses its wonder. Birth is one of God's greatest miracles."

Caroline looked up sharply.

"What?" Tse quirked an eyebrow. He left the stall to put the pitchfork in the tack room, coming back with a scoop of grain to pour into a trough for Yázhí. Tse scratched the doe's head in silence for a moment. "You are surprised to hear me speak of God? Rev. Abernathy has told you I have gone back to my heathen ways?"

Caroline plucked at a stem of straw stuck in her shawl.

Tse leaned his hands on the low stall door. "I am trying to be who God made me—*Diné*—Navajo." Yázhí crunched her grain. "That doesn't mean I've abandoned my Lord."

He looked up, his coffee-colored eyes holding hers a moment before Caroline looked away. She stared unseeing at the goats, questions tumbling through her mind.

One of the kids, the doeling she had helped birth, tried a wobbly step-jump and went sprawling, her legs spread-eagled in the straw, face bright-eyed with astonishment.

Caroline and Tse laughed.

Yázhí ambled close and nuzzled her little one until the kid scrambled to her feet.

"She looks to be a good mama. You never know the first time." Tse took the lantern off the hook and nodded toward the barn door.

"Come in the mission to wash up and get warm before you go," Caroline said, following him. "I'll heat some coffee."

Tse looked down at her, his face softened with surprise in the lantern light. "Thank you."

After scrubbing her hands and arms nearly raw in the mission mudroom, Caroline put the coffee pot on while Tse washed up. She leaned against the kitchen counter, a smile tugging at her lips. She hadn't been near a birth since Benji arrived … and Mama left. This time, though, mother and baby had lived. Babies, that is.

The coffee bubbled. Caroline carried steaming cups into the dining room just as Tse appeared in the doorway, wiping his hands.

"I'll take mine outside. My shoes—"

"Leave them at the door. That's what I did." Caroline set the cups before two chairs across from each other.

Tse hesitated, then drew off his leather moccasins and padded across the floorboards. He waited for Caroline to sit and slowly pulled out the other chair. Sitting down, he cupped his hands around the steaming brew. His knuckles were chapped, his fingers roughened and strong.

And big. Caroline hid a smile. Hence her recruitment into goat midwifery.

Silence fell. The hot liquid trailed warmth through to Caroline's middle, but somehow their easy conversation in the barn fled here in the sleeping mission. Lamplight flickered on the walls. Only the clock ticking toward one punctuated the building's slumber.

"I've never seen it so still," Caroline finally said. "At mealtime this room is a madhouse."

Tse nodded, his gaze shifting around the shadowed room. "I haven't sat here since my last year of school. Meals were the only time I saw my little sister. Not at the same table, of course, but we smiled across the room."

"I've seen Esther and her brother do that. Samuel is new this year, the one who cried when … " She halted, remembering the look on Tse's face after she helped with the barbering.

"Sháńdíín and Shashyáázh. We are family, through my mother's clan."

So Tse was a blood relative to these children—would be considered their older brother, according to Rev. Abernathy's explanation of the matrilineal clan system. Samuel's sad eyes filled Caroline's mind. "Was it hard for your little sister, being separated from you?"

"She once told me mealtimes were the only thing that got her through her first term."

"Miss Spencer says it's important to keep the boys and girls separate."

"She does not understand." Tse's cup came down with a sharp clink. "For us, family is who you are. If that is broken apart, you are lost, stripped of identity, without security."

Caroline swallowed. The pain in his eyes took her aback.

Tse looked into his cup, letting out a long breath. "I should not speak so to you. Wil—Rev. Abernathy wouldn't like it."

Caroline rubbed a scratch on the wooden tabletop. "Was Rev. Abernathy here when you started at Hebron?"

"We grew up together, he and I—he is only two years older." Tse took a sip. "His parents sent him here to live when he was sixteen."

"Miss Spencer told me that." Caroline tilted her head. "But I never would have guessed you knew each other as boys."

"Yes, well, you've seen that we do not agree too much, now. But he led me to Christ."

Caroline stared. That was a new morsel of information.

"They wanted me to go to college, he and Miss Spencer. Thought I could be a success in the white man's world. But…" He shrugged. "My family, my people, are here."

They both jumped as the front door banged and Willis pushed in, bundled to the ears, arms laden with parcels. Tse bolted up, nearly knocking his chair over. Willis stared at them.

Caroline rose quickly.

"Yázhí had trouble kidding." Tse snatched his hat off the table. "Miss Haynes had to help me."

Willis pulled his muffler down to speak. "Everything all right?"

"Two healthy kids."

"Good." Willis shot Caroline a glance and dumped the packages on the table. "Give me a hand unloading, Tse?"

Tse shrugged on his coat and followed Willis out the door. It clicked shut behind them, muting the rising wind.

Caroline rested her hands on the chair back before her and stared at Tse's coffee cup.

"Fifteen minutes, children." Caroline stood behind her desk the next day, the recess bell's clanging quickly lost in the stampede toward the classroom door.

Samuel trailed out last, boots shuffling on the floorboards.

Caroline reached to touch his shoulder, but he sidled away.

Outside a stiff breeze tossed the little girls' braids like the ball the boys passed back and forth. The wind lacked the chill of past months, though, and Caroline lifted her face to it, breathing the scent of freshly turned earth in the garden, the sweetness of rosy blossoms budding on peach saplings. Bees hummed a spring overture, and overhead dangled fuzzy catkins from the big cottonwood.

Samuel huddled on the bottom step, picking at a button on his jacket cuff.

Caroline glanced to see the other children occupied, then sat beside him.

"Don't you want to play, Samuel?" She cupped her hand and pantomimed throwing a ball. "Play ball?" If only he could understand her—or she him. All these weeks, and he still hadn't said a word in English.

Finally he looked up at her, that perpetual pinch between his eyes. "Sháńdíín?" The dark pools pleaded.

"I know you miss your sister, but you will see her at dinner." Caroline touched his cheek. The older children's classroom, taught by Rev. Abernathy, was on the other side of the building, their recess isolated from this one. "Don't you want to play?"

Samuel turned his face, hunching his shoulders away from her.

Caroline sighed and rose to her feet.

Across the yard, Tse emerged from the barn, Yázhí bleating behind him, the new kids dangling from his arms. He bent to set them in the barnyard.

Caroline glanced down at the little figure scuffing his boot heels in the dirt. "Samuel." No response. "Samuel!"

He looked up.

She held out her hand. "Want to see the baby goats?" She pointed to the barnyard. "See Tse?" Perhaps, being a relative, he would perk up the child.

Samuel looked, then rose and slipped his hand into hers.

Caroline squeezed his cold fingers. He didn't squeeze back. "I'll return in a moment, children."

They crossed the yard, sunshine warming her hair as the breeze lifted it.

"*Ya'at'eeh abini.*" Tse straightened from forking manure and smiled.

Samuel responded to the morning greeting in Navajo, holding out his hand for the kids to sniff. Tiny muzzles quivered at his fingers, and one sneezed. Yázhí nosed ahead of her babies, searching Samuel's hand for a treat.

"You are not out with the herd today?" Caroline leaned her arms on the fence.

Tse heaved a forkful of soiled straw into a wheelbarrow. "Isaiah took the other goats out." The lanky teen, nearing graduation, often helped Tse with the animals. "The barnyard needs cleaning, and these little ones need sunshine."

The kids tested skips and jumps on wobbly legs. Yázhí bleated a scolding when they bounced too far from her.

A chuckle filled Caroline's nose. "They are so darling."

Tse paused to glance at the kids, then at Samuel, who stroked Yázhí's head, sober faced.

"He misses his sister." Following Tse's gaze, Caroline hugged her elbows.

"And his mother, and father, and grandparents." Tse returned to digging with swift, hard strokes.

Could that be why Tse had gone back to his native customs? Anger at being taken from his family as a child?

"Why did you—" Her tongue caught at her boldness. "That is, did you have a good experience growing up at Hebron?"

Tse glanced sharply at Caroline and opened his mouth, then closed it. He sank the pitchfork tines deep in the matted layer of straw and waste and crossed to the opposite corner of the barnyard.

Now she'd offended him. Why couldn't she keep her thoughts to herself?

Then he was back, breaking chunks off a carrot for Samuel. The little boy offered them flat-palmed to Yázhí, who lipped them up with a crunch and gulp. The corners of Samuel's mouth turned upwards.

Caroline risked a peek at Tse and found a slight smile matching hers on his face as he gazed at his cousin.

"I was a boy of twelve winters when I first came to the school, almost a man." Tse did not look at her, but he didn't seem upset.

"My sister was seven." He handed Samuel the last carrot stub and resumed forking. "I was always getting in trouble for speaking Navajo instead of English."

She needed to get back to the schoolroom. Just another moment while Samuel finished feeding Yázhí. "It must have been difficult for you. But ... it makes sense, don't you agree, the requirement of English? All the immigrants who come to America have to give up their own languages and learn that of the land."

"Immigrants?" Tse stood upright. "Shouldn't you be learning our language, then?"

His words dashed icy cold. "I'm sorry—"

A bell clanged.

"Recess is over." Tse nodded toward the school, lifted the wheelbarrow handles, and headed for the manure pile behind the barn.

Her mind swirling, Caroline took Samuel's hand and turned back toward the school building.

Rev. Abernathy stood near her door, watching them.

She hurried across the yard, Samuel trotting to keep up. "I'm sorry. We went to see the new kids—I lost track of time."

"Desert globemallow." He held out a sprig of delicate poppy-like blooms, several orange cuplets on a stem. "One of the first signs of spring in this territory."

"Thank you." Caroline's cheeks warmed as she took the flowering sprigs.

Hands behind his back, Rev. Abernathy nodded and rose slightly on his toes. "Better get back to class."

Caroline drew a steadying breath and beckoned to the children.

Two boys chattering in Navajo galloped toward her. Heading round the corner of the building to his own class, Rev. Abernathy paused and glanced from the pair to Caroline.

She touched the nearer child on the shoulder, halting him. "Speak English, boys."

The silenced children filed past her into the schoolroom. Samuel pulled his hand from hers and disappeared inside.

Before closing the door, Caroline glanced back at the barnyard. Tse was gone.

CHAPTER THIRTEEN

"Mighty dense product there." Trader Hawkins squinted at the sack of wool Tse swung onto the low scales. "Sure you got no rocks tipping up the weight?"

Tse's jaw tightened. *Diné* and traders alike from miles around knew his father as an honest man. But he forced a deferential smile. "See for yourself."

The trader dug briefly through the wool, then waved his hand at Tse. "Just funnin' you." He hawked and spit, then named his price—lower than Tse had hoped, but fair enough for the current market. "Got anything else today?"

"Three rugs."

"Bring 'em in." The trader ducked out from the wool weighing and cleaning shed behind the trading post and headed for the main building.

Dólii climbed from the wagon parked beneath a new-leafed cottonwood to help him unload the rugs.

"Coming in?" He took the last rug from her. Usually *Shimá* sold the rugs, but she hadn't felt up to the wagon ride today. And Dólii had woven this one.

She shook her head and glanced over to the wool shed, then up at the fluttering leaves. "Not today."

Tse shrugged and followed Trader Hawkins inside. The scent of leather, kerosene, and lard greeted him before his eyes adjusted to the dim interior. Harnesses, ropes, and lanterns hung overhead, while canned goods and rainbow bolts of cotton and velveteen lined the walls behind the counter. At his feet, sacks of cornmeal and flour leaned against barrels of crackers, candy, dried peaches, and nails.

Tse spread the first rug on the counter. The bell on the door jangled as he rubbed a buckled spot *Shimá*'s twisted hands had vainly tried to smooth. Dólii, while progressing, wasn't very skilled yet. Tse's roughened fingers caught on the wool.

"*Yá'át'eeh*, Tse."

Tse turned at the greeting to find Glenbah at his elbow. He suddenly found it hard to swallow, perhaps because his heart seemed to have lodged in his throat. He coughed and returned the greeting. "*Oo yá'át'eeh*." He fought to keep his gaze on her face, on her dimpled brown cheeks and flashing eyes.

"What brings you to trade today?" She cocked her head.

"These." Tse dragged his focus to the rugs on the countertop. "And wool. We are shearing now." *Shizhé'é* liked to shear before the wool lost its peak condition as the weather warmed.

"I brought my winter's weaving too. See?" Glenbah unfurled a rug from under her arm. It swept from her hands to the floor. Rich reds and grays marched in symmetry, the triangles, zigzags, and crosses tightly woven and perfectly smooth.

Tse's heart sank. Trader Hawkins would be sure to give less for *Shimá* and Dólii's after seeing Glenbah's creation. He nodded. "Very nice."

"Right with you, Tsosie!" Trader Hawkins hollered from the back room. Tse dipped his head at Glenbah and strolled to the other side of the store, examining the new stock of hunting rifles. After a few minutes, he felt her presence beside him again.

"I didn't see you at the last ceremony."

He tried to speak, then stopped to clear his throat. What was the matter with him today? One would think he'd eaten wool instead of trading it. "I, uh, couldn't go."

"Will you be at the next Enemyway?"

Despite the name, that ceremony, called a Squaw Dance by *bilagáanas*, served as prime courting ground as girls selected young men to dance with. Tse tried to think of a response.

"Tsosie?"

Tse turned at the trader's rescuing call and nearly leapt across the room to the counter. Sure enough, Trader Hawkins had caught sight of Glenbah's rug and offered far less for his family's than *Shimá* was hoping for. But in his eagerness to be gone, Tse cared less than he had half an hour ago. He collected the supplies the trade credit entitled him to, all the while trying not to stare at the flouncing of Glenbah's rose-colored sateen skirt. How could she be everywhere in the trading post at once?

He breathed a sigh of relief as he emerged into the spring sunshine. He tossed the bags of beans, flour, salt, and coffee into the wagon bed.

"Dólii?" He glanced around. Dust blew and chickens pecked in the yard. Another red-wheeled wagon rattled up with a load of wool to trade. Where was his sister?

He followed the murmur of voices to the wool shed.

Dólii perched on the rail of the low fence that sometimes corralled sheep, Nezwood leaning beside her. They looked up as Tse's shadow fell through the doorway.

"Tse." Nezwood straightened.

Tse nodded. "Dólii, you ready?"

With a glance at the young man beside her, Dólii slipped off the fence and past Tse into the yard. Settling his hat, Tse leveled a look at his old schoolmate, then turned to follow.

The wagon jolted through their silence on the drive homeward. Dólii gazed at the frosting of spring green lining the river, hands folded on her newest turquoise blue skirt.

Had she worn it on purpose to the trading post, on chance of meeting Nezwood? Surely Tse was making something out of nothing.

"You seen much of Nezwood since the winter?"

"Not much." Dólii's moccasins shifted.

"Seems to like talking to you." Tse sneaked a glance from the corner of his eye. Were her cheeks darkening?

"We're all old friends."

"Yes, but—" Tse's sigh blew on the stiff breeze. "Be careful, *Shideezhi.*"

Dólii tossed her head, dancing her earrings. "And what about you? I saw Glenbah following you around like a new-weaned lamb."

"Hush." Tse's neck burned.

"Why? *Shimá* thinks well of her. And she is a fine weaver."

She was that. Any man who wed her would surely prosper. So why wasn't his heart drawn to her, even if his eyes were? And what about her faith? While Glenbah had gone through all the motions at school, he believed she still held to the old fears and tenets.

Tse transferred the reins from one hand to the other. Why did things have to be so difficult?

Late the next afternoon, Tse threw a sheep on its side and, holding it down with his knee, clipped the fleece away from its chest with sure strokes. "How many more?"

"Too many." His father glanced up from the yearling he was shearing and surveyed the milling herd, counting. "Won't finish today."

Tse snipped the wool from the animal's shoulders and hind legs, then at last let it spring up to run free. He tossed the fleece to Dólii and *Shimá* to bundle. Some would be for the trading post, some cleaned, carded, spun, and finally woven into rugs.

Readying his lasso for another sheep, Tse cast a glance at the reddening western sky. He had to get to the mission for evening chores. He almost laughed at himself, getting to be like a white man, breaking into a sweat over the time of day. But Willis—Rev. Abernathy—would have his neck.

Tse threw the rope's loop around the neck of a sturdy old ram and threw him, murmuring reassurance as he sheared. Soon the sheep would be glad of lighter coats, little as they appreciated the indignity now. His back ached as he loosed the ram and stood.

"I will finish for today, my son." His father clapped a hand on his shoulder.

"It's too much, *Shizhé'é*."

"You're saying I'm old? I still got my arms and legs. And Dólii can help. Go. They'll be wondering at the mission."

"Thank you." Guilt and gratitude pressed on his shoulders. Tse sprang over the fence and ran for his horse, touching it into a lope almost as soon as his seat hit the saddle. He'd have to forget about supper for now.

Willis and one of the older boys were already distributing hay to the animals when Tse burst into the barn.

Willis turned, brushing alfalfa dust from his sleeves. "Where've you been?"

"Shearing. I'm sorry—I left my father to finish as it was."

"Well, the stock wish you'd left sooner. Better get milking. Isaiah, wash for supper."

The boy finished pouring grain into the horses' feed troughs and headed for the main building.

Tse started after him, intending to fetch the milk pails, but Willis gripped his elbow.

"We pay you to be here on time. It's not fair for the boys to have to do your job."

Tse jerked his arm away. "I told you—"

"I'm tired of your excuses." Willis let go and strode across the barnyard, his shadow stalking like a leggy rooster in the waning golden light.

Tse stared after him, pain compressing his chest. Truth be told, he was late very rarely. But Willis's weariness went far deeper, as did his own, over their severed friendship. He didn't know what to do about it, save pray. And he hadn't been getting many answers these days.

Miss Haynes emerged onto the porch to ring the supper bell, Willis passing her with a nod and a word. Had the spark Tse'd sensed between his old friend and the new teacher begun to burn into anything of substance?

Tse waited until she disappeared back inside, then climbed the steps and slipped through the dining room chorus of clattering dishes and hungry children. He glimpsed Miss Haynes's head bent near the girls' table, her hair catching the lamplight like golden brown silk on ripe corn as she served plates.

He stepped out of view into the kitchen for the milk pails. What had possessed him to speak so freely to a white woman those weeks ago? Surely she and Willis had spent many a good conversation on him, shaking their heads over his waywardness. That night of the kidding, though, she had seemed different, somehow—like she actually wanted to listen.

Tse didn't look at Miss Haynes as he crossed back through the edge of the dining room on his way to milk. He did sneak a glance to Shashyáázh, though. His cousin drooped on one of the benches along the boys' table, poking at his plate with a fork.

Tse averted his eyes. It would only make things harder on Shashyáázh to interrupt his evening routine. Usually Tse had completed chores before suppertime.

A girlish stream of Navajo caught his ear as he turned the doorknob. Miss Haynes's voice, gentle but automatic, interrupted.

"Speak English, girls."

Tse pushed out through the door, letting it slam shut on its own. No. She wasn't different at all.

CHAPTER FOURTEEN

The click of a latch wakened Caroline in the darkness.

She slipped out of bed and eased open the door between her room and the girls' dormitory, running her gaze over the rows humped with sleeping forms.

The moon highlighted Esther's bed at the end, the rumpled sheets and empty pillow.

Perhaps she had only gone to the outhouse, but instinct propelled Caroline out into the hallway, following the murmur of voices. She halted before the bend that led toward the boys' dormitory—a corner the girls were forbidden to turn.

"You must forget this superstitious fear, Esther." That was Rev. Abernathy.

"But Shashyáázh—"

"Your brother is fine. You know you're breaking the rules."

Silence.

"If sneaking off like this continues, there will be consequences. Understand?"

Caroline resisted the urge to peek.

"All right. Now back to bed."

She waited until the hurried padding of footsteps came near, then stepped away from the wall.

"Esther." Caroline caught the girl's shoulders as she startled away. "It's me, don't be afraid." She felt the child's trembling through the flannel nightshift. "Precious girl, what's wrong?"

"I heard an owl." Esther turned her face away, but a shaft of moonlight from the dining room window caught the tears quivering on her lashes.

Caroline guided the girl back to the dormitory and tucked her in, then sat on the edge of her bed, listening.

"Because you heard an owl, you were afraid for your brother?"

"An owl's call warns of death." Esther shifted, bringing one arm above the blankets. "Maybe it was for someone else."

Caroline covered Esther's hand with her own. "The owl was just calling to its friends, perhaps saying, 'What a beautiful night.' It has nothing to do with death, unless you're a mouse."

"When my baby sister died, an owl hooted over our hogan just before, though it was day. And when my mother was birthing me, she heard an owl. That night, my grandfather died." She lifted her gaze to Caroline's, fear tightening her eyes.

"Esther…" A prickle teased Caroline's spine. No wonder the child was haunted so. "I am so sorry for the losses in your family. It might seem like those deaths were related to the owls, but they're not. Owls are beautiful birds, God's creatures. You needn't be afraid."

Esther glanced out the window once more, then shivered and rolled away from it, curling on her side, hair tumbling over her face.

Caroline brushed it back, then, when Esther did not protest, sat stroking the silky strands until the girl's breathing slowed and evened.

A muffled hoot outdoors paused Caroline at the door to her own little room. At the creak of bedsprings, she turned to see Esther's head disappear under the bedcovers.

"David Manygoats is quite the essay writer." Rev. Abernathy pushed his spectacles up his nose and peered at Caroline over the kerosene lamp a few days later. Its amber light flickered on the table between them as they sat in the mission sitting room, grading papers.

"Manygoats?" Caroline lifted her eyebrows. "Is that really his name?"

Rev. Abernathy chuckled. "Or the translation of it. If you think about it, some English names aren't much better: Tallman, Whitehead, Lightfoot."

Caroline laughed. "True."

"Some schools give students two new names when they enroll, first and last. Pick two out of a hat and done. Get some odd combinations that way, though." He sobered. "Just don't laugh during roll call like I did my first year here. Took me months to win their trust back."

Was there something she had done to lose Samuel's trust? Probably she had never yet obtained it in the first place. She still wanted to ask Rev. Abernathy about the encounter with Esther the other night, if she could find the words.

The clock ticked. Miss Spencer dozed by the fire.

The elderly missionary could have gone to bed, but Caroline had an idea Miss Spencer didn't want to leave her and Rev. Abernathy unchaperoned. The thought warmed her ears, and she focused on little Anna's roundly penned responses to the reader questions: *The first setalment in north Amarica was Jamestown. Wite men kild many of the Indians.*

Caroline bit her bottom lip and corrected the spelling. She had never thought much about that part of American history until now.

"David, though." Still scanning the essay, Rev. Abernathy tapped his pencil on the paper. "Have to see about sending him to college when he's old enough."

"Does he want to go?" She thought of what Tse had said that night after the kidding.

"Why wouldn't he? He's a smart young man."

Caroline marked a few more papers. "May I ask you something?"

"Sure." He stacked the graded essays.

He always finished before she did. Maddening. "Why did you decide to come back here instead of joining your father's railroad company?"

"My aunt likes to talk, huh?" With a sharp glance over his glasses, he scooted back his chair and headed for the bookshelf.

Oh dear, now she had offended him too.

But Rev. Abernathy returned, thumping a concordance on the table, no doubt to prepare his sermon for Sunday.

No matter that there would likely be few listeners save the children.

"I can't stand ledgers or account books, that's why." He turned the pages, peering at the fine print. "Give me Luther or Calvin any day."

Silent, Caroline watched him.

After a moment, Rev. Abernathy looked up at her and closed the book. "No, that's not the real reason. Part of it, but not all."

"What, then?"

He leaned his elbows on the table, steepling his fingers above the concordance. "Tse."

"Tse?" Caroline didn't know what she had expected to hear, but it wasn't that.

"I saw the difference Christ made in his life. He was so angry before, so rebellious. But we were friends, he and I." He cleared his throat. "God saw fit to use me in leading Tse to Himself. I thought I'd never known greater joy." He paused, Adam's apple working.

Caroline dropped her gaze to a row of tipsy alphabet letters.

"When I went back to visit my parents in Chicago the summer after graduation, my father talked of nothing but sales and bottom lines and making a success of myself. I had found a different sort of success, a sort that mattered for eternity. So I went off to Moody and never looked back."

"Moody Bible Institute?"

Rev. Abernathy nodded. "I determined to show my father my own brand of success." He rubbed one hand within the other. "But now—"

Caroline studied him, the worried lines creasing his forehead. She clenched her fingers at a sudden urge to brush back a lock of sandy hair above his eye. "Have you heard anything new from the mission board?"

He shook his head and flipped open the concordance again. "So. How have these early weeks been for you?"

"I don't know, exactly." Why was she never sure of herself anymore? "I love the children. And I enjoy teaching, though I'm feeling my way much of the time. But I don't know how to reach Samuel. He seems closed to me, whatever I try. And his sister..." Here was her chance. "I woke when Esther got up last night and heard you speaking with her. I tried to comfort her when she came back, but I don't know that I did any good."

"Superstitions, omens, taboos—these are some of the hardest to break out of the Navajo." Rev. Abernathy took his glasses off and rubbed his eyes. "They have hundreds of them—fear of coyotes, owls, muddy water. I don't know a tenth."

"So what do we do?"

"Patience, I guess. And time. The boarding schools help too—get the children away from their parents' influence and in a more ordered environment. Still, sometimes you wonder. I thought I'd never reach Tse—Peter, he was then." He replaced his spectacles and peered back at the page before him. "I guess I never really did."

"Are you certain Tse has turned his back on the Lord?"

"Has he talked to you?" The reverend looked up, frowning.

She pressed a crease out of a rumpled sheet with her thumb.

"I know this is all very new to you. But no man can serve two masters. Christ calls people to leave their old ways and become new."

"You mean, become like us." Yet in Acts, the Gentiles hadn't had to become Jewish to follow Jesus. She hadn't the courage to voice her questions.

Silence stretched. Miss Spencer's chin hit her chest, and she jerked her head upwards with a mild snort.

Caroline sorted her papers into alphabetical order for returning to the students tomorrow.

Rev. Abernathy scribbled a few notes, then yawned, stretching his shirt-sleeved arms above his head. "I'm going to turn in."

"Good night." Caroline lifted her head, an evasive longing tightening her throat.

Miss Spencer woke as if on cue and creaked out of the rocking chair to head for her own room.

"Miss Haynes." Rev. Abernathy stood paused in the doorway. "You'll find a way to reach Samuel. Children aren't that different, really, from Pennsylvania to Navajo territory. Pray about it."

He flashed a smile and was gone.

Too tired to rise yet, Caroline remained at the table, leaning her head on her hand.

Caroline set the music box on her desk and stood back to scan the classroom of wide-eyed children. She clasped her hands behind her. "I need one assistant to open the box. Who will help me?"

Hands shot into the air, but Caroline's gaze pulled to the little boy huddled on a side bench. "Samuel, do you want to?"

He shook his head, pressing his hands between his knees. So he did understand some English now.

Caroline bit her lip. "Nathan?"

Beaming, the stocky eight-year-old stepped up and lifted the lid.

"Silent Night" twinkled into the schoolroom.

"It's a *ch'iidii*!" Nathan jumped back as if stung and scurried to the back of the schoolroom. Several children shrieked.

"No!" Apalled, Caroline snapped the lid closed. "There is no ghost."

Samuel shrank even further into his seat, eyes dark and frightened.

"It won't hurt you, I promise." Perhaps this hadn't been an inspired idea after all.

The children stared at her from the corners where they had fled.

"It plays a song. It's—like a drum." Caroline picked up the music box. Did the Navajo use drums? She should have learned that by now.

The children looked from the music box to Caroline.

"Here." She opened the music box again. The Christmas carol tinkled forth, incongruous with Easter approaching—though the children might not know it.

"Come closer." She perched on the edge of her desk and held the box out invitingly. It played a few measures and stopped. "It needs to be wound. Look." She lifted it high.

A few brave souls stepped near, craning their necks to look underneath at the gears.

"Where I live, sometimes people have a party and dance to music like this." Caroline turned the crank and set the box back on her desk to play. Well, not exactly like this, but "Silent Night" did have a waltz rhythm.

"*Bilagáanas* dance?" Nathan tore his gaze from the rotating gears to stare at her.

Caroline laughed. "Yes, white people dance—some do anyway."

"How?"

Standing, Caroline held out her arms to an imaginary partner and began to waltz. The children erupted into giggles.

"You look like my baby sister at a song-and-dance." Anna bounced on her toes.

"That's because I don't have a partner." Caroline grabbed Nathan's hands and three-stepped with him until the music squeaked to a stop. She halted, flushed and breathless, and closed the music box. How long had it been since she had danced? Since Jeremiah, probably.

She turned to the circle of laughing faces, each one becoming dear to her. "How do you dance?"

Laughter faded. The children looked at each other.

"I'd like to see." She suddenly realized she would.

Another moment's hesitation. Then little Anna lifted her feet and began a brisk two-step. Other children fell in behind her, curving around the schoolroom as if playing Follow the Leader. Girls broke out of line to circle around the boys, all feet stepping in rhythm. Smiles spread as buttoned boots flew.

Caroline glanced to Samuel. He stood still by his seat, but he followed the dancers with eyes shining brighter than she'd yet seen.

"For mercy's sake!"

Miss Spencer stood in the doorway, lips white, one hand gripping the frame for support. The children froze, faces fading to blankness.

"In your seats immediately." Miss Spencer limped between the desks, leaning hard on her cane.

Caroline started toward her. Was she going to faint? Have another stroke?

But Miss Spencer held out her hand to hold Caroline back. "On second thought, children, you are dismissed for recess."

Caroline glanced at the clock. Not yet time for recess.

The children filed out the door. It clicked behind them. Silence.

Miss Spencer reached Caroline's desk and sank into the chair. She lifted a trembling hand to her spectacles and closed her eyes.

Caroline swallowed. "Would you like a drink of water?"

"What on earth were you thinking?" Miss Spencer opened her eyes.

"I—showed them my music box. I demonstrated a waltz, and then asked how they dance. I didn't mean … "

Miss Spencer shook her head, shuddering her whole body. "Dancing of any sort is not approved by our mission board. But Indian dances must be absolutely forbidden. Many are tied to pagan rituals." She scanned the empty schoolroom as if masked warriors might emerge from the walls.

"I'm sorry."

"You meant well." Miss Spencer met Caroline's eyes, censure replaced by weariness behind the wire-rimmed spectacles. "But this must never happen again."

Caroline nodded. She took the elderly missionary's elbow and helped her to her feet, matching her steps to Miss Spencer's shuffling ones as they made their way to the door.

Miss Spencer eased her way down the steps and headed for the main mission building. The children huddled in the schoolyard, their gazes analyzing. Two boys half-heartedly tossed a ball.

The wind teased Caroline's hair, failing to lift the heaviness in her chest. She should call them back in. She scanned the children, mentally taking roll.

Samuel. Where was Samuel? Caroline hurried down the steps, searching the corners of the schoolyard with her eyes. She caught a small boy's arm. "Asa, have you seen Samuel?"

He shook his head.

Caroline ran around the side of the building. No little boy, just a clump of desert globemallow springing from among the rocks.

She hurried back to the front and up the steps. Could he still be inside?

The schoolroom sat empty, floating chalk dust catching the sunlight through the windows.

Caroline halted in the aisle, twisting her locket. *Lord, where is he?* Panic pounded in her ears, as when she lost Benji once at the county fair. But this was silly—Samuel had been here only a few moments ago. How lost could he be on the school grounds?

She spun at a rustle from the cloak closet and flung open the door.

Samuel crouched in the corner, peering up like a frightened owlet. He clutched something in his hand.

She dropped to her knees, heart pounding with relief. Pulling him to his feet, she hugged him close. "What were you doing in there?"

But he pushed from her arms and ran outside.

Caroline stood and clamped her hands on her elbows, frustration rising in her throat.

Chapter Fifteen

"Nooo!" The shriek echoed through the mission at nightfall.

What on earth? Caroline dropped the tin cup she had been filling for Anna's bedtime drink of water and dashed from the kitchen into the hallway.

Left, toward the girls' dormitory, seemed quiet.

She hurried to the right, slowing at the corner. She had barely been in this section of the mission, what with the strict separation of the boys and girls outside the schoolroom.

After knocking on the door unheeded, she pushed into the ruckus inside.

Boys in various stages of dress and undress clustered around Rev. Abernathy, who seemed to be struggling with a small child.

"What's going on?" Caroline squeezed between the boys, who turned to stare at her.

"You shouldn't be in here." Rev. Abernathy straightened, holding a shrieking, flailing Samuel under the arms.

"I heard the shouting. Tell me what's wrong."

Rev. Abernathy plunked Samuel on the bed. The child sprang to his feet and hurled himself at the missionary's trousers' pocket. Rev. Abernathy held him off with one hand. "He's upset because I took away an arrowhead amulet his mother had given him. He'd been hiding it all this time."

What Samuel had been clutching in this hand the other day…

"Stop, Samuel." Rev. Abernathy hauled the little boy back onto the bed.

"Nooo!" Samuel's bare heels kicked a war dance on the footboard.

"You see he can speak English when he wants to." Rev. Abernathy turned, shooing the wide-eyed onlookers. "Boys, get ready for bed. Miss Haynes, I can handle this."

Oh, clearly.

Samuel scrunched near the headboard, hands over his ears, sobbing something in Navajo. "What's he saying?"

"I think he wants his mother."

Caroline stepped closer to listen.

"*Shimá...Shimá. Hágo.*"

She didn't know the words, but she heard their meaning.

Mama...Mama. Come.

Caroline gripped the bedpost against memory's tidal wave. "Let him have it back."

"What?" Rev. Abernathy spun to face her.

"At least for a little while. Till he calms down."

"You're asking me to let him keep a pagan fetish? I can't believe you." He stomped to the bedside and smacked Samuel's backside. "Samuel. Stop it now."

The little boy jerked, then squirmed to sit up, staring through eyes red and glazed with tears.

Something snapped inside Caroline. "For mercy's sake—" She shoved the reverend aside and knelt on the bed, gathering Samuel into her arms. "He just wants his mother!"

Samuel squirmed against her, but she held him firmly, murmuring low. Benji too, often fought being held when he needed it most.

Finally, squeaking a whimper, Samuel surrendered, the fight melting from his limbs.

He burrowed his face into her shoulder, sobs shuddering his little body and flooding her own eyes. She held him close and rocked, pressing her hand to his quivering back, shielding him from the rest of the room.

Only vaguely did she hear Rev. Abernathy hurrying the other boys toward bed, feel his touch on her shoulder urging her to leave. Caroline paid no attention. Finally the light from the kerosene lamps dimmed, and darkness fell around them. Still she held Samuel, until his sobs slowed into slumbering jerks and his arms relaxed around her neck. She laid him back on his pillow, smoothing his nightshirt over his knees, and ran her hand over his cropped, sweat-dampened hair.

Samuel's forehead furrowed, and he rolled over and buried his face in the pillow.

Caroline spread the covers over him. Slowly she stood, rubbing at a cramp in her back.

Boys slumbered around her. Rev. Abernathy's shadowed shape sat on a chair by the doorway, silent and disapproving.

She slipped past him, needing air.

Out on the mission front porch, she leaned her forearms on the railing. Night coolness played across her hot cheeks and her hair.

A coyote yipped. Another answered, howls lonesome across the desert.

Caroline felt at her neck for her locket. Her shirtwaist was still wrinkled and damp from holding Samuel. The arms of another little boy clung in her memory now, one she had clasped in her seventeen-year-old arms when he woke screaming for the mama who could never come back. Night after night she had rocked him, her own tears raining on Toby's curls. His cries filled her dreams even after he fell into restless sleep. *Mama—nooo! Mama . . . come back.*

She pressed the heels of her hands against her eyes.

The screen door squeaked, and Caroline turned.

"I finally settled the girls, when you didn't return." Moonlight glinted off Miss Spencer's glasses.

Caroline's hand came down on the railing with a soft thud. "I completely forgot. I'm sorry."

"What happened?" The question lay between them, an invitation with no condemnation.

"Samuel..." Caroline sighed. "Rev. Abernathy took away an arrowhead amulet Samuel's mother had given him. He was inconsolable."

"So it sounded." Miss Spencer stepped to the railing, looking out over the mission yard, painted silver and black in the moonlight. "He is asleep?"

"Finally. I held him until exhaustion won out." She glanced at the serene profile, the silvered hair. "Rev. Abernathy didn't think I should stay, but I had to."

Miss Spencer met her gaze for a long moment. Then she nodded, and the tightness that had hovered between them since the dancing altercation eased.

Caroline twisted Mama's locket between her fingers. Samuel had gripped it as she held him. "Toby used to cry like that." The words slipped out almost before she knew.

"Toby?"

"My little brother." She swallowed. "After my mother died. He was only six."

"How did it happen?"

"It was... when Benji, my youngest brother, was born."

"Ah." Miss Spencer laid her hand over Caroline's on the railing, her touch feather light and warm. "My mother too."

Caroline swiped at suddenly welling tears. "It's such a blur, the weeks after she passed—neighbors bringing food and trying to say something comforting, being up in the night to care for Benji. Trying to understand... she was gone."

And had she ever, really? Had she ever had time?

Caroline pinched the bridge of her nose.

Miss Spencer's hand stayed on hers, stroking ever so slightly back and forth.

At last Caroline sniffed hard. "I remember most just sitting on Toby's bed and rocking him, crying together. Like with Samuel tonight."

Miss Spencer moved her hand and held out a handkerchief. They stood silent at the rail together, the sleeping mission behind them. An owl hooted from a tree by the barnyard.

Caroline folded the handkerchief in half, then again, and again. Heaviness crept into her limbs, heavy as the thoughts churning in her mind, as the despair in Samuel's cries. How could it be right, to take children from their parents like this? To tear families apart and devastate a little boy in the name of a loving God?

She glanced up at footsteps. Rev. Abernathy emerged onto the porch, easing the door shut behind him. She couldn't read his expression in the darkness.

"You all right, Miss Haynes?"

Caroline hugged her elbows. "No." The word surprised her, but she wouldn't take it back. *And neither is Samuel.*

"He'll get past this."

As if she had spoken her thoughts. But would he? Did you ever truly get over missing your mama?

Caroline pushed away from the rail, past the reverend, and into the mission.

In her little alcove of a room, she shivered out of shirtwaist and skirt and into her nightgown. After lighting the kerosene lamp on her nightstand, she crept under the covers, plumping up her single pillow to lean against. She reached for her Bible and held it on her pushed-up knees, running her hands over the leather cover.

She hoped Samuel was still sleeping, without tears. Maybe he would dream of his mother. But that might only make matters worse.

If coming to this school is Your will for these children, Lord, why does it wreak such havoc on this child? Doesn't he matter? Don't You care?

Wrapping her arms around her knees, she laid her forehead on the closed Bible and squeezed her eyes shut.

CHAPTER SIXTEEN

"He's gone."

His mother's words stabbed Tse in the chest as she stepped from his grandfather's hogan into the sunlight.

"Just now?" He reached to steady her.

"A few moments ago." She ran the tips of her fingers under her eyes.

Tse wrapped his arms around her. She leaned into him, her bony shoulders jerking within his embrace. She wouldn't let herself weep too much, not openly—it wasn't their way. After a moment, she pulled away with a quick squeeze on Tse's arm.

"May I see him?" Tse swallowed against the burning in his throat.

His mother swiped at her cheeks and glanced at him, then flicked her gaze across the desert. Shadows sharpened on the rocks as the sun lowered toward the west. At last she released a shuddering breath and nodded. "His body is old and worn out. No *ch'iidiis* will want it."

Tse stooped to enter the low doorway and blinked until his eyes adjusted to the dimness inside the little hogan, where his grandfather had lived alongside their larger family hogan as long as Tse could remember—first with his wife, then alone. He had never really been sick, just grown weaker, his eyes cloudier, hair whiter, skin more papery. That was why his mother did not fear the *ch'iidiis* as usual...only the corpses of the very old and the very young were not dreaded, as evil spirits would not care to inhabit such weak vessels.

Tse's breath squeezed from his lungs as he knelt by his grandfather's body.

The old man seemed to be napping on his sheepskin near the fire, as he had so often these past months. Tse expected him to open his eyes and speak with that familiar twinkle, perhaps tell a coyote story. Except his fragile chest no longer rose and fell, his dark, thick-veined hands lay still. Already, his mother had put her father's moccasins on the wrong feet and a ring on his index finger, that he might be recognized if he came back from the dead.

Tse hesitated, then placed his hand on his grandfather's shoulder. Cold—already turning cold. A shudder racked Tse's frame. His vision blurred, and he couldn't stop his jaw from shaking.

"*Shi' cheii*...I wish I could have made you understand." He pressed his fist to his teeth to stop the tears.

Only last week he had tried to tell this now still and silent man about hope after death, about Jesus, who had conquered death. But his grandfather wanted nothing to do with the religion of those who had driven him from his land when he was Tse's age, who had taken so much.

"I know of the Creator, boy," he had said. "I have lived in harmony with the ways of the Holy People. That is enough for me."

Tse couldn't convince him it wasn't. And now it was too late. He squeezed his eyes shut and gulped, not wanting to frighten his mother with sobs.

Four days later, Tse returned from the unmarked grave on the hillside to find his grandfather's empty hogan crackling with flames, orange tongues of fire licking at the log sides and shooting through the smoke hole in the roof.

A short distance away stood his mother and Dólii, watching.

His limbs weak from fasting, Tse slid from his horse and let him loose into the corral. The breeze blew smoke and ashes into his eyes, and he squinted against the sting. *How long, O Lord?* How many hogans must burn and people die in darkness before God brought healing to the *Dinétah?*

But he heard no answers on the wind.

Gold touched the feathery tips of the junipers growing out of the rocks above the bluff where Tse perched. Hundreds of clouds, strands of milkweed down in the pearly dawn, pinked and gilded. A strip of light brightened at the eastern horizon. All at once the sun burst above the mesas, shooting its pure, dazzling radiance straight into his eyes.

Tse looked down at the pages of his Bible, momentarily blinded as birds chorused into song, announcing Easter morning. After a moment the tiny print cleared, and he ran his finger down the column, murmuring the story aloud. "'And very early in the morning, the first day of the week, they came unto the sepulchre at the rising of the sun ... '" His throat tightened, cutting off the words. His grandfather's unmarked tomb in the hillside slid through his mind.

Tse cleared his throat. "'And he saith unto them, Be not affrighted: Ye seek Jesus of Nazareth, which was crucified: he is risen; he is not here: behold the place where they laid him.'"

He glanced to the gleaming orb in the east, then up at the clouds, rosy wisps turning to serene puffs of white in the deepening blue. The Creator's church far surpassed any building Rev. Abernathy might plan here.

Below stretched the gold-bathed desert, down beyond the rocky ledge where Miss Haynes had encountered the rattlesnake. Still farther lay the river.

"He is not here; he is risen." Bittersweet longing mingled with joy within his chest. Laying aside his Bible, Tse lifted his face and hands—not to the sun, but to the Creator of the sun.

"Jesus Christ is risen today, Alleluia! Our triumphant holy day, Alleluia!"

Caroline swallowed back the lump in her throat and tried to sing, balancing the hymnal between herself and Esther. If she closed her eyes, she could be back in the pew in Pennsylvania, Toby and Benji fidgeting in their Sunday suits, Pastor Jensen beaming from the pulpit flanked with Easter lilies, Father smiling down at Lillian. Lillian? She jerked her eyes open.

Why had the joy she'd always known fled this Easter morning? She skimmed her eyes ahead in the hymnal. "But the pains which He endured...Our salvation have procured." She believed that as much as ever, didn't she? Yet her heart hung heavy beneath the lace-trimmed bodice of her leaf-green dress. Could it be because she didn't see what difference these words were making here in this territory? Perhaps she was just homesick. She tucked the thought under the last "Alleluia" and sat.

At a creak and click amid the between-hymns shuffle, Caroline sneaked a glance over her shoulder, past rows of boys in starched collars and girls with stiff white bows on black braids.

A figure slipped into the back of the room—the older pupils' schoolroom, converted to a church on Sundays. Seeming oblivious to Rev. Abernathy's lifted brow, Tse settled next to a grandmother in a colorful headscarf. Catching Caroline's eye, he nodded and sent her a small smile.

Somehow comforted, she faced front again, the tightness easing from her throat.

"He is risen!" Rev. Abernathy stepped to stand behind his teacher's desk, now spread with a white cloth and topped with a wooden cross and pitcher of apple blossoms.

Caroline joined in the response, thinking she heard Tse's strong rejoinder from the back: "He is risen, indeed."

After the service, Caroline helped Miss Spencer set out a luncheon in the sunny schoolyard. A brisk wind flapped the cloths spread over plank tables and sent rosy peach blossoms scattering across the dirt and into the children's hair. The few students with families able to make the trip clustered around their parents, sitting in close circles on the ground while the other children formed their own groups.

"Join me, Miss Haynes?" Rev. Abernathy spoke beside her shoulder as she dished up her plate.

Caroline hesitated, glancing at the wooden chairs he indicated under the big cottonwood's shade. She had avoided him the last few days, but she couldn't think of any reason to refuse. And it was Easter, after all, a time for forgiveness and new beginnings. She smiled. "Thank you."

Rev. Abernathy waited for her to sit, then drew his chair near hers. Caroline balanced her plate on her knees, focusing on the neat piles of chicken salad, ham, scalloped new potatoes, and young lettuce sprinkled with sugar and vinegar—first fruits of the garden's earliest planting.

"Fine spread you ladies prepared." Rev. Abernathy bit into a biscuit and leaned back in his chair. "You're quite the cook, Miss Haynes."

"Oh, bother." Caroline set her plate aside. "I forgot something to drink."

"Water or tea?" Rev. Abernathy sprang up.

"I—tea, please." She watched him stride to the tables. Why had he taken such a notion to be gallant? Was he attempting to smooth things over after their tiff about Samuel the other night? She'd prefer a simple apology. She nibbled her lip. Perhaps he considered her the one who should offer that and was trying to be magnanimous.

"Thank you." She accepted the cup he brought and took a sip. As Rev. Abernathy settled back, Caroline poked a fork at her food. She shouldn't have filled her plate so full. Across the yard Miss Spencer conversed with a mother, one of the older girls acting as interpreter. If only she would finish and come join them. If only Rev. Abernathy would say something.

"May I sit here?"

Caroline looked up to see Tse standing near with his plate. He glanced between them, hesitant.

She smiled and indicated the empty chair.

But Rev. Abernathy cleared his throat. "Miss Haynes and I have business to discuss."

Tse lifted his chin, nodded and stepped away.

Caroline's scalp burned. What call did Rev. Abernathy have to rebuff Tse so? She straightened her shoulders and turned to the man beside her, gripping the edge of her plate as she tried to keep her voice even. "What business?"

"I wondered what you thought of our Easter service." He threw her a smile.

"It was quite nice." She took a bite of chicken salad and made herself chew.

Tse found a spot with the boys, crouching on the ground.

"Nothing to what you're used to back East, I'm sure, but that will come, Lord willing."

Caroline let Rev. Abernathy talk while she whittled away at her lunch. At last she spied his aunt hobbling in their direction.

"Miss Spencer, won't you sit for a while?" Caroline rose.

"Thank you." She sank into Caroline's vacated chair with a sigh and rested her trembling hands in her lap. "I suppose I stayed on my feet too long."

Tossing the remainder of her tea on the yellow tulips pushing up by the mission porch, Caroline hurried up the steps and into the dim quietness of the mission. She took her dishes into the kitchen and stacked them on the others in the sink. Leaning her hands on the edge, she stared at the piles of dirty plates and cups.

She missed her family so much her chest hurt. She reached for Mama's locket, but her fingers touched only the lace on her bodice. Of course—she had traded the necklace for a cameo brooch in honor of the day. But now she had to hold it, to feel the familiar coolness of the silver engravings and touch Mama's face, if only the image of it. She pushed away from the basin and headed for her room.

Sinking onto her bed, Caroline slid open the drawer of her bedside table. She lifted the handkerchiefs and felt beneath them. A prickle tensed her spine, and she pulled the drawer out on the bed and emptied its contents. Two books, three hankies, her little sewing kit. No locket.

Had she left it on the dresser? Springing up, Caroline snatched the doily from atop the bureau. Nothing. She fell to her knees and peered under the bureau, then felt beneath the bed.

Tightness gripped her chest. Not her locket—she couldn't lose Mama's locket. Could it have caught on her shawl when she rushed out on her way to service this morning? Her door had stood open when she entered just now—could someone have taken it? Surely not. But—

She darted down the hallway and out the front door, nearly colliding with Rev. Abernathy.

"Something wrong?" He sidestepped, holding the door.

"I . . . " She stopped and swallowed, her hand feeling the empty space at her yoke. He might think her silly. "I can't seem to find my locket."

"What locket?"

"The one I wear every day." Had he never even noticed? She pushed her tongue against her teeth. "It was my mother's. I thought I'd left it in my room this morning, but it's gone."

Rev. Abernathy clamped his lips together. Stepping back onto the porch, he clapped his hands. "Attention, children."

Chatter silenced.

"Miss Haynes is missing a valuable locket."

Caroline twisted her fingers together. She hadn't meant to create a scene.

"Anyone who sees this necklace"—Rev. Abernathy leveled his gaze at each cluster of students in turn—"or who knows where it might be, must report to me or Miss Haynes immediately." With a nod, he turned and headed back into the mission. "I'll search inside."

"It's really not—"

The door slammed shut behind him.

What had she meant to say? That it wasn't important? Caroline touched her collar again. Yet it was important, to her.

The children stared at her, their faces sober.

She hated Rev. Abernathy's accusing tone. He didn't truly think one of these boys or girls could have taken it, did he? She scanned their faces. Anna, Nathan, Samuel, Dorcas, Isaiah, Esther. Surely not these—not her children.

The thought cramped her stomach more than the missing locket.

CHAPTER SEVENTEEN

Shashyáázh had Miss Haynes's locket.

Or he knew its location. Tse felt sure. Though he wasn't sure how much English his cousin understood yet, he'd seen Shashyáázh's guilty start at Willis's announcement, his studied indifference as the children around him whispered and he turned back to his game. Why the little boy would have anything to do with the teacher's missing jewelry, he couldn't imagine, but he intended to find out.

Tse waited until Rev. Abernathy disappeared inside the mission and Miss Haynes bent to search in the sparse grass near the steps with two of the older girls. Then he ambled over to the cluster of small boys playing in the dirt of the schoolyard.

He squatted beside them for a moment, then tickled Shashyáázh's elbow. "Come with me, little brother."

Shashyáázh pulled his arm away, keeping his eyes on the miniature corral he was fashioning from twigs. "We're playing." Like Tse, he murmured the Navajo words low.

"I know. Come."

Slowly, Shashyáázh dropped his sticks and let Tse pull him up by the hand.

Tse led him around the garden and into the shade of the orchard. New leaves mingled with the blossoms overhead, the bees' steady hum giving a natural buffer for their voices.

Tse crouched to his cousin's level—not that Shashyáázh met his eyes. "Where is Miss Haynes's locket?"

Shashyáázh clamped his arms across the buttons on his jacket. His foot jiggled.

"Do you know? I know you will not lie to me." Tse touched Shashyáázh's arm and waited.

At last his cousin's chin began to quiver, and his shoulders sagged. "I didn't think... she would mind."

"Mind what?" Tse dropped his hand to his knee.

"Rev. Abernathy took my arrowhead from *Shimá*, but I thought a *bilagáana* amulet might... I thought maybe she wouldn't mind." He scrubbed his eyes with dirty fists, streaking muddy tears across his cheeks.

Tse pulled off his bandana and wiped the little boy's face. "And what do you think your *amá* would say to hear her boy is a thief?" He waited until the sniffles quieted. "Where is it?"

Shashyáázh dug in his trousers pocket and held out his hand.

Tse took the engraved silver heart, fingered the delicate chain. Gently, he worked open the clasp to be sure nothing had been damaged.

"Is that her?" Shashyáázh craned his neck.

"The little girl is Miss Haynes, I think." Tse turned the locket so the tiny photograph caught the light. "The other must be her mother."

"Her mother?" Shashyáázh lifted his eyes to Tse's.

Tse nodded and clicked it shut. "You see, you took something that Miss Haynes's mother gave her. You did just what Rev. Abernathy did to you."

"I'm sorry." Shashyáázh picked at one of his jacket buttons.

"And you must tell Miss Haynes you are sorry." Tse stood. "Come."

"No!" Shashyáázh shot upright and reached for the locket, trying to pry it from Tse's hand.

"Little brother…" Tse held it away, aching at the fear in his cousin's eyes. He laid his hand on the small bony shoulder. "This is not an amulet. And amulets cannot protect you. But Jesus can, if you ask Him."

"But I'm bad at English." Shashyáázh looked at the ground, stubbing one boot toe in the dirt.

The words pierced Tse's chest, arrow-sharp. He opened his mouth, but no words came. Instead he pulled Shashyáázh to him, rubbing one hand over the little boy's hair. He glanced over his shoulder to see Miss Haynes heading their direction.

Tse drew a breath. "Come."

He tugged Shashyáázh forward like a reluctant young goat into the sunlight where Miss Haynes scanned the ground. The wind teased her skirt, soft green as young willow, about her ankles.

Caroline's nose burned. Her hair blew across her face, stinging her eyes. It was no use—either it would turn up or it wouldn't. Frivolous to spend Easter Sunday searching for jewelry. The orchard swam before her eyes in a pink and white blur. *Mama, I'm sorry. How could I be so careless?*

Two figures emerged from the blur. Caroline blinked and pushed back her hair. Tse—and Samuel. Catching her eye, Tse tipped his head toward the orchard.

What in the world? With a glance back toward the mission, Caroline followed.

Between the arching boughs of apple and plum blossoms, Tse halted and nudged the little boy, studying the ground beside him. "My cousin has something for you."

Samuel fidgeted, and Tse whispered to him in Navajo.

Caroline glanced over her shoulder and breathed easier to see neither Rev. Abernathy nor Miss Spencer close enough to hear.

Head still hanging, Samuel held out his hand to her, fingers clenched around something. She caught a glint of silver and gasped.

"Where did you find it?" Caroline snatched the locket from him and clutched it to her breast.

Tse nudged Samuel again, but the child shook his head and pressed his face against his older cousin's breeches.

Tse sighed. "He took it, Miss Haynes."

Took it? Samuel? Suddenly she remembered his little fingers clutching at her necklace that night as she held him close. He must have remembered it and snuck into her room during the flurry of luncheon preparations today.

"Samuel, why would you do that?" She crouched, trying to see his face, clenching the silver heart till the clasp dug into her palm. "This was my mother's. It means a great deal to me." She fought an awful urge to shake the child. "Look at me."

Samuel whimpered, strengthening his hold on Tse's leg. Caroline raised her eyes to Tse's and saw him flinch at whatever he read there.

"May I speak with you a moment, please, Miss Haynes?" Tight-lipped, Tse loosened the child's arms.

Caroline followed him deeper into the orchard, leaving Samuel crouched in the grass that sprouted between the young trunks. Her stomach churned worse than when she thought the locket lost. Horrid lies she'd heard, that Indians took naturally to thieving, stung her mind like bees, but she shoved them away. That wasn't true, she knew it wasn't. And Tse had made Samuel return it.

"Tse…" She clasped her hands together, still clutching the recovered locket. It was hard to talk to a man's back. "I'm sorry I spoke sharply to Samuel. I know he's your cousin. But I cannot excuse stealing."

"Nor do I." Tse seemed to be studying the graft on one of the apple saplings. "But he is not avoiding your eyes because he does not respect you. To us, it is rude to look directly at someone who is speaking."

Caroline's chest deflated. "I'm sorry. I didn't know."

"I know." He turned to face her. "Do you understand why my cousin's mother gave him that amulet?"

"No ... not exactly."

"For protection against *bilagáanas*. White people."

Caroline winced.

"I ask that you think before making him fear you more than he already does."

"Fear me?" Caroline's voice caught. "I've done nothing but try to love him. I defended him and held him that night his mother's gift was taken from him, even against Rev. Abernathy's wishes. Why should he have any reason to fear me?"

"Because of who you are." Tse's dark eyes held hers, uncondemning but steady. "And who he is."

She dropped her gaze to the locket in her hand.

"He took your necklace because he was afraid. He thought it was an amulet and it might protect him. He told me he didn't think you would mind. I do not excuse him, but that does show something of his regard for you."

Caroline rubbed her thumb around the edge of the silver heart. She didn't know what to say.

"Samuel?" called Rev. Abernathy. "What are you doing over there?"

Caroline spun to see the reverend approaching the orchard.

Samuel snapped upright and glanced back over his shoulder to Caroline and Tse. Rev. Abernathy followed the child's gaze. "What's happened? Miss Haynes, are you all right?"

Caroline drew a breath and hurried forward. "Tse found my locket." She held it out, the silver chain glinting in the light of the lowering sun. "I apologize for troubling everyone."

"Tse found it?" Rev. Abernathy frowned, looking from one to the other. "Where?"

Her mind blanked.

"My cousin helped me." Tse stepped up beside her.

"They make a good team." Caroline touched Samuel's shoulder.

"Well." Rev. Abernathy studied her, and Caroline fought to keep her gaze steady beneath his scrutiny. "I am thankful your property has been restored. Tse, the animals need tending, Easter or not. It's nearing chore time."

"Yes, sir."

Rev. Abernathy strode away.

"Samuel." Caroline knelt beside the child, staring at the grassy dirt beside her. Gently, she turned him to face her and touched his chin. "Thank you for returning my necklace." She didn't know if he understood or not, but at last he flicked his eyes up to meet hers. She smiled, and the fear in his gaze melted, replaced by something that almost—not quite—curved up his mouth.

But then he pulled away and ran to join the other boys.

Caroline stood, her legs suddenly aching with weariness. Would she never reach him? Had she pushed him away still further by her anger earlier?

"Thank you." Tse stood beside her.

For the first time she noticed his hair had been chopped short— from hanging near his shoulders, it now barely reached past his ears, though still held back with the same red leather band.

"What else could I have done, after what you said?" She poured the locket chain from one palm to the other.

"Many things." Ever so briefly, Tse touched her hand.

Her heart pounding a bit erratically, Caroline focused on the children across the yard. Samuel again sat in a circle of little boys. She didn't even know what game they were playing.

"I used to think I knew practically everything about children." She untangled the locket chain and reached to fasten it around her neck. "Now I'm not so sure." She fumbled with the clasp.

"There is no shame in needing to learn. Only in thinking you do not need to." Tse hesitated. "Do you need help?"

Caroline laughed, lowering her hands and rubbing at the crick in her neck. "I can't get this foolish clasp fastened." She tried again. Perhaps because she hardly ever took her locket off, the clasp stuck stubbornly.

"Can I—may I try?"

Caroline turned her back to him and relinquished the ends of the chain. His fingers tickled in the hair at the nape of her neck.

"There."

"Thank you." She turned, her gaze drawn to study him again.

"What? You want to fix my necklace now?"

She flushed. "No. But—your hair. You cut it for Easter?"

He fingered the cropped ends, the smile fading from his face. "No." He stepped away from her, pausing at the edge of the orchard to gaze toward the western horizon. "My grandfather. He died last week."

A memory pricked Caroline's mind—Esther's words from that first day. *Cutting hair is for mourning death of family in our way.* "I'm so sorry."

"So am I." He heaved a sigh and strode away, his shorn head bent.

Caroline watched him go, fingering the locket safe around her neck once more. She wanted to talk to him further, to ask about his grandfather. Had Tse been close to him? What did the Navajo believe about life after death? Had Tse ever tried to share the Gospel with him? But Tse had disappeared inside the barn.

Much to learn, indeed.

CHAPTER EIGHTEEN

Caroline's chalk squeaked on the blackboard, setting her teeth on edge. *First Reader: Study Period. Primer Class: English.*

She rubbed at the headache pounding behind her eyes. As if this weren't already the most dreaded hour of her day. She pasted on a smile and faced the children. "All right, First Readers, take out your books and move to the back seats, please. Primer class, come forward."

The smallest children, along with a handful of eight- and nine-year-olds who were new this year, settled in the front two rows.

Caroline pulled her chair close to them, automatically glancing toward the side seat where Samuel always huddled. His solemn eyes stared back at her. While he didn't shy away from her as at first, he had yet to participate.

"Repeat after me, children." Forcing herself to sit straight, Caroline opened the McGuffey's *Primer*. She pointed to the sketch on the page, which rather resembled the military-style caps of the boys' uniforms. "Cap."

"Cap." The children chorused.

Caroline glanced at Samuel. His lips stayed sealed tight as a jar of jam.

"Very good." She turned the page. "Now, 'fox.' Repeat, children. Fox."

"Fox."

She glanced over again. "Samuel, will you try?"

He shook his head, clamping his arms across his chest.

She turned back to the others and held up the sketch. "Jug."

"Jug."

"Very good." She flipped another page, and another. Her back ached. A little girl smothered a yawn. There must be a better way. No doubt excellent language learning techniques were taught in teacher training schools. Well, that was Hebron's own fault for not requiring that in their advertisement.

Caroline turned another page. "Samuel?"

He looked up, eyes big.

"It's a goat, like the kids outside. Can you say, 'goat'?"

Bending his shoulders inward, he examined the floor, digging his boot toes into it.

Caroline bit back a sigh. "Class?"

"Goat."

At least they responded, if with all the enthusiasm of Benji at bath time. The thought of her little brother clogged Caroline's throat. What was she doing so far from him, anyway? Nothing of much worth, it seemed today.

"Thank you, children." She closed the book and stood. "First readers, I will hear you recite one by one now."

A crash startled her from Nathan's painstaking reading. Children squealed, and Caroline jumped up to see Yázhí's doeling, the female kid with the crooked ear, dancing in a puddle of water near the open door—and the overturned water barrel.

Children darted toward the kid. Panicked, the little animal bolted into the schoolroom, skittering around the desks. Shrieking with glee, the students pelted after the scampering hooves.

How on earth did she get out of the barnyard? "Children— let me get her." Caroline ran after the careening group. Her foot slipped in the puddle and she tumbled to the floor, knocking her elbow on one of the desks. She scrambled to her feet. "Children!"

The little goat sprang onto the teacher's desk, hooves tapping out a nervous tune, then leapt into the air when she saw Caroline coming. The doeling landed in the corner between the desk and the coalscuttle and stuck at an awkward angle, bleating.

"In your seats." Caroline paused, catching her breath. "I'll get her." She took a step forward, then halted.

Samuel crept toward the little goat, holding out his palm and murmuring in Navajo.

Caroline caught something that sounded like "Yázhí."

The kid quieted and stretched her head toward Samuel's hand, nostrils quivering. Samuel scratched the soft fur around the stubby horn buds, then reached behind the scuttle and tugged the little goat out and into his arms.

"Thank you, Samuel." Caroline knelt as Samuel carried the kid toward her. She stroked the little animal's neck. "You like the baby goat?"

"*Tł'ízí-yázhí.*" Samuel rubbed his cheek on the soft head.

"Clizi—?" Caroline cocked her head.

"That's baby goat." Anna leaned forward from the desk where she had obediently returned. "*Tł'ízí-yázhí.*"

"Thli-zi ... yahzi?" Caroline tried to wrap her tongue around the syllables.

Samuel's eyes brightened. His lips parted over two front teeth. Could that be a smile?

An idea zipped through Caroline's mind like a lightning bug. She laid her hand on her chest. "I can say your word. Can you say, 'goat'? Thli-zi. Goat." She patted the kid.

Samuel stared at her.

She stared back, biting the inside of her lip. *Please, Lord.*

"Goat."

"Yes! Very good!" She squeezed her hands to keep from crushing the child to her, baby goat and all.

Samuel pursed his lips at her, then the kid.

"You want me to say it? Cli-zi yazzi."

He shook his head. "*Tł'ízí-yázhí.*"

"Th-l-izii-yázhí."

Mouth corners turning up, Samuel nodded.

"Now you." Caroline touched his shoulder.

"Goat," he said, and the kid butted Samuel's chin. He giggled, showing more teeth. "Goat!"

Caroline scrambled to her feet, snatched a reader off a nearby desk, and paged through it. She plunked onto a bench by where Samuel stood and pointed to a picture. "Mouse." She looked at him and cocked an eyebrow.

"*Na'asts'ǫǫsí,*" Samuel said, as the kid squirmed in his arms, and he adjusted his grip.

"Nahs-so-si?"

He shook his head.

"*Na'asts'ǫǫsí!*" Another child called from the back of the room.

Caroline repeated until Samuel approved, then nodded to him.

"Mouse," he pronounced.

Caroline flipped the page. "Horse." She glanced at her small instructor.

Setting the heavy kid on the floor, Samuel sat next to it, arms around its neck. "*Tłłii.*"

She blinked. "What?"

Samuel giggled. "*Tłłii!*"

Caroline tried to imitate the sound, but she couldn't even discern the consonants. How on earth might such a word be spelled? A squeak emitted from her lungs.

Giggles exploded around the room like popcorn. Samuel bounced on his bottom.

Anna jumped up and ran to touch the apple on Caroline's desk, miraculously unscathed by the kid's capers. "*Bilasáana.*"

That sounded a bit easier. "*Bilasáana.*" Caroline rose and scanned her beaming pupils. "Now you—in English."

"Apple," they chorused.

One of the smallest boys touched his eye. "*Anáá'.*"

"An-ah." Caroline repeated the word. "Eye."

"Eye." The children's voices swelled with their smiles.

"*Ajaa'.*" Samuel flapped the baby goat's ear.

"A-jah." Caroline tweaked her own ear. "Ear."

"Ear!"

The noon bell jangled.

Caroline glanced at the clock. When had the morning ever flown by so fast? "Excellent, children. You are dismissed for dinner."

The students clattered out of the schoolroom, trailing giggles and chatter. Samuel still sat on the floor, the kid now nestled in his lap.

Caroline knelt beside him. What Rev. Abernathy might say were he to enter at that moment flitted through her mind, but she pushed it away.

"Shall we take her back?" She gestured to the door, never knowing just how much English Samuel understood.

He nodded, and she helped him set the sleepy little goat on her feet.

Samuel led the kid through the schoolroom and across to the barnyard, where Yázhí trotted in circles, bleating herself hoarse. A board nibbled loose at the bottom of the fence told the little escapee's tale. Samuel slipped the little goat inside the gate, and the doeling ran to join her brother, both diving under their mother to butt and suckle. Though her offspring's enthusiasm nearly knocked her off her feet, Yázhí instantly quieted and chewed her cud.

Caroline and Samuel stood side by side at the fence, watching.

Samuel tilted his face up and grinned shyly. "Goat."

What a precious smile he had. She had never seen it until today. Caroline touched his nose. "*Thl'izii.*"

Samuel darted off after the other children toward the main building.

Caroline leaned against the fence, pressing steepled fingers to her lips. "Thank You, Lord."

At a sharp tug, she turned to find her apron string trapped in the teeth of Samuel's little friend. The kid leaned back on her haunches, cocking her head. Caroline pulled the sash away and tickled the little goat under the chin. "You rascal."

Samuel had responded. He had participated, smiled, even laughed. He had finally turned the corner, surely. But that night, Caroline heard him crying again. And Rev. Abernathy would not let her go to him.

The child was fine, Rev. Abernathy said, surrounded by older boys he knew. They would not let him feel alone. This was a stage he must get through, a learning and growing up. And he would learn, if he were not coddled too much.

Caroline paced in the hallway, unable to sleep as long as she could hear those distant sobs.

At last, merciful silence seeped through the mission.

Caroline sank into a chair by the window in the mission sitting room. She traced the moonlit windowsill with a finger and tried to pray—for Samuel, for Esther, for Rev. Abernathy, for herself. If only she could know for sure if she were really supposed to be here, whether she were doing any good, or how to make a difference if she wasn't.

Tse came to mind, and she prayed for him too, with the loss of his grandfather. How heartbreaking if he hadn't known the Lord. It was hard enough to lose family members who did. The grief in

Tse's eyes had pinched her heart that Easter Sunday in the orchard with Samuel.

Samuel. His tears tonight... his laughing little face that morning. Somehow, she had connected with him, even if briefly. There must be a way to do it again.

Chapter Nineteen

"Bilasáana. Naas—na'asts'ǫǫsí."

Tse paused on the mission front porch, listening to the words murmured through the open window into the night. Who would be speaking Navajo—such oddly accented Navajo—at this hour? And in the mission? He eased open the door.

Miss Haynes, sitting alone at a dining table in a circle of lamplight, looked up with a start and flipped over a slate she seemed to have been studying. "Oh—Tse."

"What are you doing?" He stepped closer, curiosity rising stronger than manners.

"I thought you were—never mind. Why are you still here?"

"I stayed late to mend the barnyard fence. I came to bring the lantern in before I head home." He reached for her slate and turned it over, staring at the roughly sketched syllables.

"I'm sure I spelled them wrong."

Tse swallowed. "I wouldn't know. Navajo is yet unwritten." He glanced into the shadowed corners of the room. "Why—how—what are you doing?" His voice cracked on the last word.

"You told me I should learn Navajo." Her mouth quirked.

"I didn't mean—that is…" His neck heated. He had only meant to make a point.

"Yesterday one of Yázhí's kids—the doeling—got out and nosed her way into our English lesson. She created quite the confusion, but Samuel caught her. Somehow I imitated his words for 'little goat,' and he smiled." She met his eyes, the gray of hers deepening. "I had never seen him smile before."

Ah, Shashyáázh. His smiles used to light up family gatherings.

"Then the children began telling me the Navajo words for various items, and I told them the English, and we repeated each other—even Samuel. He had never participated like that before. So..." She halted, staring down at the slate.

Tse followed her gaze, tracing the chalked letters with his eyes. Then he studied the woman before him, her head bowed as she turned the slate pencil between her fingers.

Tse cleared his throat. "Would you like help?"

Miss Haynes glanced up, hesitated, then nodded. "Yes, please."

Tse scooted a chair next to her, taking care not to squeak on the floor. He took the slate and rubbed out her attempts with the side of his hand.

"I will try to write them out phonetically." He paused, slate pencil poised above the smudged black surface. Could he do this? He glanced over his shoulder once more, then swallowed hard.

"Here is 'mouse.'" He shaped the letters, guessing as he went, inserting lines and spaces in an attempt to portray the complicated tones and stops.

"That's one of the words the children tried to teach me." She carefully sounded out the syllables. "*Na'asts'ǫǫsí.*"

"Be careful of your tones. In Navajo, you can say something completely different from what you mean by mixing up the tones." He sketched out another word. "Once, when I had hardly spoken our language for months because of school, I was trying to tell my mother about the way of salvation. Instead I told her to go out and get drunk. The wrong tone."

Miss Haynes choked, clapping her hand over her mouth. "What did she do?"

"Just as I told her." Tse kept a straight face until Miss Haynes's eyes widened to match an owl's. Then he chuckled and shook his head.

Her soft laugh warmed the air between them.

"Here." He pushed the slate toward her. "Try again."

She copied his pronunciation, repeating each word several times.

He nodded. "Better." He wrote "*tł'ízí*" on the slate.

"*Tł'ízí*. Goat." Miss Haynes leaned over his shoulder.

"Right." Tse smiled at her.

"Does Yázhí mean 'little'?"

He nodded. "I call her that because she is the smallest of the yearlings."

Miss Haynes beamed, evidently pleased with her detective skills. "How do you say, 'Hello'?"

"*Ya'at'eeh.*"

"Yaht-eh?"

How had he never realized how difficult his language would be for *bilagáanas*? Because he had never seen one try to learn it before, that's why.

"Close. Let the back of your tongue block off your throat between syllables. Listen." He demonstrated.

Miss Haynes tried and promptly coughed. Their laughter rose like steam from a coffeepot.

Tse sobered and glanced toward the darkened hallway. What were they doing? Any moment Willis would wake and come to investigate. His throat tightened, burning at the back.

"Are your family believers, then?" Miss Haynes leaned over his arm to read the chalked list.

He shook his head. "Just my sister." Resisting the tension in his shoulders, he traced out *shideezhi*. "Here is what I call her: 'my little sister.'"

"There's a different word for older sister?"

He nodded and wrote *shadi*, the slate pencil squeaking far too loudly.

"That's what my brothers would call me." A wistful smile touched her lips. "And what Samuel must call Esther." Her smile faded. "Not that he gets to see her now."

Shashyáázh's forlorn face swam through Tse's mind. Could their subterfuge somehow get his little cousin in trouble? The dark corners of the past pressed in on him, breathing down his neck. Any moment he would hear the ominous footsteps of Rev. Spencer, Miss Spencer's deceased brother—the thwack of his stick. The muscles in his legs tightened.

"How do you address God?"

Tse fought to bring his focus back to the present, to the circle of lamplight, the questioning lift of Miss Haynes's eyebrows. "I— what?"

"When you pray in Navajo."

He drew a breath. "I don't, generally." *Ever.* "In Navajo, I mean." The pencil snapped under his fingers. He shoved the slate away. "We shouldn't be doing this."

"Why not?"

"You know why not." Tse pushed back his chair and headed for the door. He had to get out.

"I know Miss Spencer and Rev. Abernathy are against the use of Navajo." Miss Haynes followed him. "But what we were doing before wasn't working with Samuel. Using his language is giving me a connection to him that I couldn't make before. They have to see that."

"You think?" Tse gripped the doorframe. "When I was a schoolboy here, I can't tell you how many times Rev. Spencer washed my mouth out with lye soap for saying those words on your slate. He beat me despite my little sister's wails." He looked at Miss Haynes's face, blanched but for her eyes. "I finally gave up for Dólii's sake, not for Rev. Spencer. But no, they do not have to see."

Miss Haynes pressed one hand to her throat.

Was she going to be ill, like he had many times after a soap treatment, retching out behind the barnyard, the lye burning his throat and tongue? Singeing those beautiful, familiar words of Navajo with shame. Tse massaged his neck at the memory. The goats had stuck their heads through the fence to him, offering comfort and acceptance. Soon he'd begun to assume their care.

"How can a school claim to preach Christ and treat children so?"

Her eyes made him think of a stunned rabbit. Was she really so naïve? Tse sighed. "Miss Spencer and Rev. Abernathy do not hold with cruelty now. But they would not like this. I must go." He paused at the door, then glanced around. Why had he come in here?

The lantern. He fetched it from the dining table and hung it on the hook beside the door. "Good night."

"Tse."

Her voice caught him just before he closed the door. He held it, waiting.

"Thank you." She stepped closer, into the moonlight spilling through the doorway.

He hesitated, then nodded. "You're welcome." With a click of the latch, he stood alone on the porch, only starlight easing the darkness surrounding him.

The moon rose, silvering the buttes and sharpening the shadows, as Tse's horse clopped across the desert toward home. Good thing his family didn't share Willis's obsession with time. Still, they might be wondering about him by now.

He slumped in the saddle, trusting his horse's direction, more weary from that hour in the dining room than the fence mending. He never should have gone in, never should have made it his business what she was doing.

Memories surfaced in the still night like scum on a pond. The acrid taste of soap, the dread of being discovered when he stole a few moments to talk with Dólii in their language—two rules broken there—his sister's cries whenever he was punished, her tears wounding him deeper than the reverend's rod.

Rev. Spencer, for all his sternness, had not been a vicious man, yet each blow tore away at Tse's boyish identity, whispering, "You Navajo—you no good—you nothing."

Then the silent days when he finally surrendered and so barely spoke at all, since he refused to use the white man's tongue. Until Willis arrived, a boy lonely and abandoned as Tse himself. Perhaps that was what finally made Tse willing to let Willis help him with English—after their fierce baseball matches in the evenings, that is.

He turned his horse down the faint path leading to his family's camp, where shorn sheep slumbered in the corral. The dogs lifted their heads at his approach, their silence a greeting.

He slid off his horse and patted its rough neck, a strange regret tugging at his throat. No good could come of the language lesson tonight. Perhaps even harm, if Willis found out.

Yet gentle warmth filled his soul as he remembered sitting in that circle of lamplight, etching out words in the language of his heart for someone who wanted to know, to learn. Her compassion for Shashyáázh touched him... and the pain in her eyes when he told her of the past.

But one thing was certain—they could never do that again.

Next morning, Tse woke to find his mother still sleeping and Dólii's blanket empty. He stepped outside the hogan into the cool gray dawn.

Birds twittered in the junipers as Dólii stirred mush over the fire. She glanced up at him, then back at the pot.

"Is *Shimá* all right?" He squatted beside her.

"Her knees were bad this morning. I told her to rest."

"Are you all right?" Tse held out his hands to the fire's warmth, examining his sister's face as she concentrated on the stirring sticks.

Dólii rose and fetched a long stick to poke the fire.

Was she avoiding his question on purpose?

At last she lowered to her haunches, wrapping her arms around her knees. The firelight played over her delicate features, the purple calico of her skirt. "You were out late last night."

"So?" Tse shifted.

"Of course, *Shimá* and *Shizhé'é* don't ask *you* questions about where you've been." Dólii cast him a glance.

Tse let it pass. "What happened, *Dóliibaa hózhǫ́*?" Maybe using her full name, meaning beautiful bluebird, would soften her.

His sister drew a breath. "You know I took the sheep out yesterday so *Shizhé'é* could haul water."

Tse nodded and poured himself coffee from the pot set in the coals.

"When he returned at sundown … " Dólii swallowed.

"What?"

"He came looking for me."

Tse quirked an eyebrow. His father would not have been pleased to be forced to venture out after dark.

"He found Nezwood and me. Together."

"What?" Tse sat up on his knees, his fists tightening. "What did he do to you?"

"He was very angry."

"No, Nezwood. What did he do?"

"Nothing."

But Tse saw the quick rise and fall beneath her velveteen blouse. "Dólii."

"He kissed me, that's all."

"He did what?"

"Why am I telling you this?" The mush boiled over, and Dólii sprang to her feet, snatching at the stirring sticks. "You don't understand."

"I understand enough." He clamped his arms across his chest. "What did *Shizhé'é* do?" His sister could be as stubborn as a goat.

"Told him not to come near me again without horses for a marriage price." Dólii stirred the thickening mush so hard a lump flew out and hit her hand. With a yelp she flicked it off and held her hand to her mouth.

Tse's anger faded slightly at the tears in her eyes. Were they from the burn or another kind of pain? He sighed and scrubbed his hand through his hair. Women. How to understand them?

"*Shideezhi.*" Awkwardly he touched his sister's sleeve. "If he loves you, he will do as our father wishes." He squinted into the rising sun. "Have you prayed about it?"

Dólii shrugged and stirred silently, turning her face away.

His little sister in love, Miss Haynes trying to learn Navajo, Shashyáázh pining away at school. Tse threw a stick into the fire and rubbed his hand across his eyes.

Chapter Twenty

"Miss Haynes, Miss Haynes, how does your garden grow?" Hoe in hand, Rev. Abernathy leaned on the fence separating the boys' garden plot from that of the girls, a boyish grin bringing out his dimple.

Caroline sat back on her heels from planting squash seeds and smiled at him, pushing back her straw hat in the late May sunshine. Springtime—and the lack of conflict between them the past few weeks—made it easy to warm to him today. As did the dimple.

"With pole beans, and collard greens, and ... " She glanced at the neat rows behind him, where the boys dropped kernels three at a time. "Sweet corn all in a row. I'd no idea gardening could be so delightful."

"Wait until you taste summer produce, freshly picked."

Potato and pea plants already waved green above the soil, but today marked planting for the warm-weather vegetables. Rev. Abernathy said they shouldn't have another frost now, with June drawing near.

Caroline leaned forward to press crumbling earth over pale squash seeds, breathing in the sweetness of sun-warmed earth. Around her the schoolgirls dug holes, dropped seeds, and tamped dirt, their movements far quicker and more graceful than hers. But then, they had no doubt planted gardens before. Here beneath the cloud-tufted blue sky, drinking in sunlight and robin-song, Caroline wondered why she never had.

"Would you like some flowers, along the sides or in the corners?" Rev. Abernathy shifted his boots. "I can ask my aunt if she has any seeds left."

"That would be lovely." Brushing dirt from her hands, Caroline stood. Her heart quickened at the look he gave her, and she stepped back. "I—should help Miss Spencer start supper."

He nodded. Was that a flicker of disappointment in his eyes? "We'll be finishing up soon."

She felt his gaze like the rays of the lowering sun, following her all the way back to the mission. It unsettled her.

An hour later, Caroline stepped onto the porch and tugged the bell rope, sending the supper call clanging across the grounds.

The girls had already followed her in to help with the meal, but now a flock of boys clattered past, faces and hands smudged with dirt.

"*Ya'at'eeh*, Samuel." She touched the little boy's shoulder as he shuffled by at the end of the line, eyes fixed on his feet.

"*Ya'at'eeh*, Miss Caro-line." He lifted his head, a smile lighting his face.

Warmth circled her heart as she watched him disappear inside. She turned back to ring the bell once more for any stragglers.

Rev. Abernathy mounted the steps, tugging off his work gloves. Patches of sweat dampened his shirt.

"Hungry?" She smiled.

He nodded, tapping his folded gloves on the porch railing. The evening light touched his hair with gold. "What did you say to Samuel?"

"I—greeted him." She let go the bell rope.

"In Navajo?"

Caroline swallowed. How could she have been so careless? "I didn't intend to go against the rules. But the other day when the goat got in the classroom—"

"What?"

Oh, dear. "It wasn't a problem, but somehow the children and I began a Navajo-English word game, and … " And a snuffed lamp had been re-lit within the child. "Please don't blame Samuel. It wasn't his fault." She wouldn't mention the late-night lesson with Tse.

Rev. Abernathy sighed and removed his hat, slapping the dust away on his thigh. "We have rules for a reason."

"I know." She hesitated. "But what would be so dreadful about having both languages here? Why must English reign supreme?"

"English is the language of our country."

"Of *our* country?"

Rev. Abernathy stared at her. After a moment, pain slashed through his eyes. Looking away, he stepped to the railing and laid his hat on it.

"I understand your point. Believe me, it breaks my heart what our government has done to these people. That's why I'm here." He faced her. "But things are as they are. These children have to learn to survive in civilized society. Their heathen language only binds them to the old ways. They must break with it, with them. They *have* to, if they're to survive."

He stepped closer and softened his voice. "You understand?"

No. Caroline nodded.

Rev. Abernathy briefly squeezed her elbow, then stepped back. "I better wash up."

She covered the spot on her arm where his hand had touched. Gripping the railing with her other hand, she stared out across the desert, pink and gold in the setting sunlight. Did she understand anything anymore?

Paring potatoes for supper the next evening, Caroline heard the stamp of Rev. Abernathy's boots on the porch as he returned from the trading post. She finished peeling, dropped the pale potatoes into bubbling water, and hurried out to help unload, wiping her hands on her apron.

A murmur of voices from the sitting room halted her. She tiptoed closer, wincing as a floorboard creaked under her feet.

"Come in for a moment, would you, Miss Haynes?" Rev. Abernathy stuck his head out, his voice stretched tight.

She stepped inside the sitting room, and Rev. Abernathy eased the door shut behind her. Miss Spencer looked up from the rocking chair, her eyes reddened, an open letter in her hands.

Caroline's heart thudded into her throat. Please, not from Pennsylvania—not her family.

"We've received a letter from our mission board." Rev. Abernathy indicated a chair.

Caroline sank into it. *Thank You, Lord.* But that was selfish. Evidently the letter had distressed the elderly missionary.

Miss Spencer pressed a handkerchief to her nose, then lifted her chin. "Our superiors have summoned us for a meeting to discuss the future of the school."

"You think they're planning to close it?" Caroline touched her fingers together.

"We hope to convince them otherwise." Rev. Abernathy laid his hand on Miss Spencer's frail shoulder. "But my aunt and I must leave for Farmington. Can you manage here for a week or so?"

On her own with thirty children? Caroline sucked a breath. "Certainly."

"I can ask Tse to sleep in the barn, should there be any emergency."

"I would appreciate that." God willing, they would have none of those.

Back in the kitchen, Caroline pushed the pot of dancing potatoes to the back of the stove, still slightly dizzy with relief that the letter had not been for her. But the school—surely the Lord wouldn't let the board close the school. She creaked open the oven door and slid a knife into the ham.

"Miss Haynes?"

She jumped, letting the oven door bang shut. Her knife skittered to the floor.

"Didn't mean to startle you." Rev. Abernathy picked the knife up and laid it in the sink.

"I didn't hear you come in." Her pulse settling back to almost normal, Caroline lifted a towel from a pan of cornbread and began cutting it into squares.

"I wanted to thank you for being willing to stay with the children." He stepped closer.

"Of course."

"This may seem like a crisis point for Hebron to my aunt. But I'm confident that, with God's help, we will prevail, perhaps even gain more funding through this meeting. Our attendance is up a bit, and—now we have you."

"You will be in my prayers." Caroline glanced up. A mistake—his face was too close, his eyes too earnest, too blue. She concentrated on slicing through the crumbly golden bread.

Rev. Abernathy made a sound as if to speak, then sighed.

Caroline risked another look. When had she ever seen him so awkward?

"Would you sit with me?" He rubbed the back of his neck and motioned to the worktable, flanked by two slat-backed chairs.

Caroline sat, clasping her hands in her aproned lap to hide their sudden trembling. What could he have to say?

Rev. Abernathy lowered himself into the chair across from her, touching his fingertips together on the table. "I am very grateful you came to Hebron."

Aware of her hair's disarray, Caroline tucked a loose wisp behind her ear. "So am I." She was, wasn't she?

"I realize we have had slight … disagreements at times, yet I believe these only stem from our mutual concern for the Indians, for these children. A concern we both fully share."

Caroline nodded and glanced toward the stove. She should check the potatoes. No, why was she thinking that now? Why wouldn't he get on with—whatever it was?

"Miss Haynes." He shifted and cleared his throat.

"Yes?" Caroline laid her folded hands on the table.

Suddenly meeting her eyes, he reached across and laid his hand over hers, sending her heart galloping into double-time. "I have long prayed the Lord would bring someone to me who had a passion for this work as I do, a heart that would beat for the harvest with mine."

She tried to pull her hand away. "Rev. Abernathy—"

"I know it is fast. But here on the frontier, we don't have time or opportunity for the formalities of the East. It could be that God would see fit to use our marriage to establish this mission on a truly firm foundation."

Marriage? She tried to swallow.

"I do not expect an immediate answer, but give it some thought." He gently squeezed her fingers before releasing them. "And prayer. Perhaps our absence will give you some time to reflect."

He rose and turned to leave, pausing in the doorway. "I will inform the board that I am waiting on your answer. They may put more confidence in a preacher with the prospect of being a married man."

Then he was gone, leaving her alone in the kitchen. The lowering sun gilded the window as the potatoes beat a tune on the lid of their pot.

Still feeling the pressure of his hand on hers, Caroline closed her eyes and tried to remember how to breathe.

Crickets squeaked from outside her open window, this night the warmest here yet. Caroline flipped her pillow to the cool side. Even so, the desert temperatures plummeted significantly at sundown. She didn't miss the nightlong mugginess of Pennsylvania.

Like the moving picture show she had once seen in Philadelphia, the evening played through her mind, her heart thudding with the beat of Rev. Abernathy's remembered words. Her first proposal. For Jeremiah had never really proposed, more assumed. Or perhaps it had been she who assumed. That final letter from China had seemed to indicate as much.

She turned over, and other images joined the picture show. Rev. Abernathy standing atop the rocky church site, speaking of the hoped-for harvest … staying up late marking his students' papers … giving her the delicate orange wildflowers. Rev. Abernathy cutting Samuel's hair, smacking him for crying for his mother. Giving orders to Tse. Mama always said to note how a man treated those weaker than he. Not that Tse was weaker—his shoulders stretched broader than the reverend's. But Rev. Abernathy clearly did not see him as an equal. Not now, anyway. How had their relationship differed in boyhood days?

If only she could talk to Mama.

Rev. Abernathy was a good man. Upright, passionate, spiritual. Devoted to eternal matters. Easy on the eyes, notwithstanding the spectacles. Her ears warmed, and she pulled up the covers.

Perhaps our marriage … Lord, he said marriage! *Is this part of why You brought me to this territory?*

Yet somehow her heart hit a snag.

CHAPTER

TWENTY-ONE

The sun's gleaming edge peeked over the mesas as Caroline helped assist Miss Spencer into the wagon.

Rev. Abernathy took the satchel Caroline handed up, settled it behind the seat, and gathered the reins.

"Thank you for being here. You and the children will be in our prayers." He reached down and gripped her hand. "I'm trusting you."

Unsure of the message in his blue gaze, Caroline nodded and withdrew her hand.

The wagon rumbled off, the dust cloud gradually blurring into the sunrise. She locked her arms over her middle and turned back to the mission, scanning the crowd of children gathered by the porch, awaiting instructions. From her. Her mind blanked. What should come first?

A patter of hooves echoed across the ground, and she turned to see Tse leaving the barnyard with the goats. Passing between her and the children, he lifted a hand and nodded, his steady brown eyes and slight smile easing the tension in her stomach a little. She kept her gaze on his broad shoulders until he disappeared behind a bluff.

Caroline lifted her chin and squared her own shoulders. Well, then. She could do this. Hadn't she become mother to two energetic boys at seventeen? Hadn't she handled over a dozen lively children each Sunday morning back home, and more than that each day in class since coming to Hebron? Perhaps a small speech would be appropriate—a formal reassurance to the pupils that all was in order, that everything would proceed smoothly as usual.

"Children…"

Thirty pairs of eyes swiveled toward her, expectant.

Caroline swallowed. "Let's eat breakfast."

At supper that first night, Caroline scurried between ladling bowls of soup, wiping spills, and filling milk glasses. How did the presence of just two more adults mark the difference between order and mayhem? If only Tse would join them for meals, but he had politely declined when she asked, taking his plate out to the tack room where he had settled for the week.

Caroline paused at the boys' table to refill emptied bowls.

Next to Isaiah's place, Samuel's soup cooled, his spoon lying untouched.

"Don't you want your supper?" She touched Samuel's hunched shoulder.

A shrug.

"He doesn't eat much." Isaiah paused in his race to rid the world of soup. "Rev. Abernathy says he'll eat when he's hungry."

"A growing boy should be hungry." She felt Samuel's forehead. Why was she only hearing this now? Because she never sat at the boys' table, of course. But Rev. Abernathy should have mentioned something. "Do you feel sick, Samuel?"

Another shrug.

"Try to eat a little." She brushed her hand over his short, blue-black hair. "Isaiah, keep an eye on him, please?"

Caroline hurried on, listing childhood ailments in her head. He hadn't felt warm. What had it signified when Toby or Benji wouldn't eat? Oh, why must this happen now?

Rounding the corner into the kitchen to start breakfast the next morning, Caroline's heart nearly stopped at the sight of a man bending over the sink.

At her stifled shriek, Tse spun to face her. "It's only me."

"Land sakes, you scared me." Caroline gripped the doorframe.

"Sorry. Just wanted to wash this, then I'll get out of your way."

For the first time she saw the red-stained cloth he pressed to his palm.

"What happened?" She darted to him and grabbed his hand, turning it to the window.

"It's nothing." He pulled away. "I was stringing new fence, and an old wire decided to battle with me."

"Rusty wire?" She lifted the cloth to examine the ugly cut, still seeping blood. "That's bad. Let me clean it."

"I washed it already. It's fine." He backed toward the doorway, his face reminding her of Toby's whenever she proposed cod liver oil.

"You want to get lockjaw?" Caroline pulled out a chair from the worktable and pointed to it. "Sit. I'll get the turpentine."

After hesitating another moment, Tse sat.

Caroline scrubbed her hands, filled a basin, and rummaged through the medicine cabinet. Sitting across from him, she laid his hand in her lap. She dipped a clean rag in the water and wiped the blood from the gash in his calloused palm.

"A birthing goat bothers you, but not blood and doctoring?" Tse quirked an eyebrow at her.

She gently squeezed his hand to make it bleed. "I couldn't raise two younger brothers without tending scores of cuts and scrapes. Sometimes they came home looking like they'd been ambushed by a war party." Her cheeks flamed at her slip of the tongue, but Tse didn't seem to notice. Or was too polite to say anything.

"You raised your brothers. Why?"

"My mother died. When my youngest brother was born."

She looked up to find Tse gazing just past her, his eyes gentle.

"The locket."

She nodded.

"No wonder you are so good with the children, then."

"What do you mean?"

"You know how it feels to miss a parent."

A lump rose in Caroline's throat, catching her by surprise. She focused again on his hand, trying to lighten her voice. "I suspect you didn't think that the first day."

"Think what?"

"About me being good with the children." Now she wished she hadn't spoken. "When I held your cousin for his haircut."

Tse sat quiet a moment. "But I've seen you with him since," he finally said. "And with the others. You love them."

His words crept into her heart and nestled there, albeit tinged with faint reproach. Keeping her gaze on his hand, Caroline lifted it toward the window's light. The bleeding had slowed.

"This will burn, I'm afraid." She dipped a corner of the rag in turpentine, wrinkling her nose as the smell singed her nostrils. "But I don't take chances with rusty wire."

"I can see that."

She caught a twinkle in his eyes. He barely twitched as she pressed the disinfecting cloth to the cut.

"You're far braver than my brothers." She bound his hand with a clean bandage and stood to search the cabinet again.

"What are you looking for?"

"Something to aid the healing. I don't know…"

"My mother has some salve. I can ride home for it later." He pushed back his chair and rose. "Thank you, Miss Haynes—or should I say, Doctor Haynes?"

Caroline laughed and turned, meeting merriment in his brown eyes. She glanced away, oddly shy. "You probably shouldn't be milking. It could reopen the wound."

"I can get one of the boys to help for a day or two." He hesitated, then backed toward the door. "Well, thanks."

"Just keep it clean." Caroline smiled and bent to gather the cloths and basin.

When she straightened, he was gone. The kitchen stood sunshiny, empty.

Well. Caroline drew a breath and turned her attention to breakfast. Tse had already strained the milk and poured some in pans for the cream to rise. A basket of fresh eggs adorned the counter also. He must have been up and working for hours to have chores done and be stringing fence already.

She glanced out the window to see Tse heading for the garden with a hoe. Not taking the goats out today, then. Hopefully weeding would prove cleaner work for his hand. And it was a comfort to have him close by, somehow.

A pleasant warmth simmered in her middle as she sliced bacon for frying, bringing a hymn to her lips. "When morning gilds the skies, my heart awakening cries..." Caroline cracked eggs into a pan, a smile awakening on her face. The day ahead seemed less daunting now.

Riding home to their summer camp midday, Tse found his mother weaving in the *chaha'oh* shelter. He stopped her with a lifted hand when she started to rise from the rolled sheepskin seat.

"You said you were staying at the mission these seven days." She settled back with a sigh.

"I am. I just came to get something." He crouched near her, tracing the beginning design of her rug with his eyes. "Is your pain better, *Shimá*?"

She flexed her hands and reached for her batten, running the slender stick in and out between the threads that stretched from top to bottom of the loom, creating a path for the next layer of yarn. A smile softened her face with the familiar motions. "The sun helps."

"One of the Creator's gifts to us, no?" The warm rays seemed to travel straight into his belly, easing the knot of worry he had carried so long he hardly noticed it anymore.

Did the incline of her head spell agreement?

"What brings you here, then, my son?" Her hands, so graceful despite their twisting, ran a length of wool between the separated threads, then tamped it down with the weaving fork.

He flexed his bandaged fist. "I got the worst of a fight with a fence. Miss Haynes cleaned it for me, but I need your salve." As she moved, he started to his feet. "I'll get it."

But his mother had already hauled herself up, stumbling slightly, yet barely leaning on the arm he held out to steady her. She took his hand, turning it over with a practiced eye. "Come." She started for the hogan.

"Miss Haynes wrapped it for you?" After unwinding the bandages and examining the wound, his mother smeared on the piñon pitch salve that soothed as much as the teacher's turpentine had smarted.

"Rev. Abernathy and Miss Spencer are away." His mother knew that—why did he feel the need to explain? "And she has doctored her brothers."

She clucked her tongue and reached for a clean bandage.

Tse forced himself to hold still, wishing she would say something more. But she stood silent, winding the linen around his hand.

"Thank you, *Shimá*." He leaned forward to land a kiss on her cheek. "I will be home in a few days."

She moved to the door of the hogan, lifting a hand as he untied his horse from the corral. "Be careful, my son."

Tse swung atop his horse and nudged him into a gentle lope, his mother's words niggling the back of his mind.

CHAPTER TWENTY-TWO

"Miss Caroline, will you help me with my thread again?"

Caroline looked up from her mending to smile at Dorcas, one of the older girls. "Of course." She picked at the knotted thread. Miss Spencer had frowned and Rev. Abernathy raised a brow at the students addressing her with any form of her given name. But "Miss Caroline" sounded so much softer, friendlier, than stiff "Miss Haynes."

"There." Caroline smoothed out the last knot.

"It's so different from weaving." With a sigh, Dorcas returned to the evening circle of older girls gathered in the sitting room, improving their needlework while the little ones slumbered in bed.

Caroline dug into the mending basket again and pulled out a small sock. Samuel's, perhaps? He seemed to have eaten a bit better tonight. She glanced to where his sister had sat at the start of the evening and frowned.

"Where is Esther?"

The girls looked at each other. "She said she had to go to the outhouse."

Caroline tipped her head to ease the crick in her neck, thinking back to Dorcas's remark. "Do you girls weave at home?"

"My aunt is teaching me." Dorcas focused on her sampler. "I was half through my second rug when school started. But it's hard to catch up between terms." She jumped in her seat and stuck a pricked finger in her mouth.

Caroline plied her needle in and out. Productive thinking ought to keep her eyes open. Why couldn't they have weaving at school? Wouldn't that be more practical than samplers anyway? The older girls could teach the younger. Perhaps a word to Miss Spencer some-day—if she could gather the courage after the dancing incident.

In and out, in and out. The boys grew holes in their stockings quicker than she could darn them. And how could little girls prove so destructive to white ruffled aprons? Her hands weighted with weariness like twin stones. Just three more days before Rev. Ab-ernathy and Miss Spencer returned. No, four, for they would not travel on the Sabbath.

She bit back a sigh and glanced up again. Still no Esther? It had been a good half hour. Caroline nibbled her lip, then laid her work aside and rose.

A search of the outhouse revealed no twelve-year-old girl. After circling outside the mission, Caroline found her huddled on her bed in the darkened dormitory.

"Esther, are you ill?" Caroline kept her voice to a whisper for the sleeping younger girls. "What's wrong?"

Esther sat up, her face wan in the half-moon's gleam. But she shook her head. "I am fine."

"You are not fine." Caroline stroked the girl's back.

Esther flinched from the touch. A shiver shuddered her frame, and her arms clamped over her belly.

Possibility flashed through Caroline's mind. She eased herself down on the bed, hesitated. "When you went to the outhouse, did you find bleeding?"

The dark head stayed bent. A tiny nod.

"You poor girl." Caroline reached to draw her close, and while Esther did not quite go willingly, she didn't resist. "It's nothing to be ashamed of. You are merely becoming a woman. I have cloths you can use."

"I am not ashamed."

"Well, then. Good." But why hide in the dark? Caroline drew back, almost missing the next words.

"Not of that."

"Then what?" Caroline cocked her head.

Silence.

"I can't help if you won't talk to me, dear one."

"My *kinaaldá*." Esther looked up, her face pinched. "What will I do about my *kinaaldá*?"

"Your what?"

"The ceremony, for when a girl changes. It's how you become a woman, when you become part of the tribe. But I can't have it at school." Esther rocked back and forth, back and forth. "I want my mother."

The whimper ached Caroline's heart. She ran her hand down the girl's silky braids. *Lord, help me here. I haven't dealt with this one before.* "Let me get you something."

After fetching the cloths, Caroline stopped by the sitting room to reassure the girls, then headed for the kitchen. Back in the dormitory, she settled Esther against a hot water bottle and two pillows propped together.

With a cup of tea in her hands, the girl's shivering eased.

"Better?"

Esther nodded.

Caroline smoothed the blankets over Esther's knees. "Tell me about this ... "

"*Kinaaldá*."

She nodded.

"It lasts four days." Esther sipped her tea and swallowed. "You go for long runs to build your strength. The older women help you make a special corn cake that bakes all night. We have songs and prayers." She pulled her knees up, staring into darkness. "All your family is there."

"Could you have it when you go home during the summer?"

Esther shrugged. "It's supposed to be before the next month."

"I see." Caroline rubbed her thumbnail. "I don't know what to do about your *kinaaldá*—I'm sorry. But we can pray here. Would you like that?"

When Esther did not protest, Caroline bowed her head. Never had she prayed over a girl's . . . over a woman's . . . she couldn't even form the thought in her head without blushing. Still she prayed, vaguely asking God to grant Esther His peace, to bless her and mold her into the woman He had created her to be. Feeling a woefully inadequate missionary, she lifted her head.

"Thank you."

"You're welcome." Her middle warmed, and she touched Esther's hand.

Reaching to fluff the pillows, Caroline felt a corner of rough cloth. She pulled it out and held it to the window. "Your sampler?"

Esther nodded, tracing the rim of her cup with a finger.

"It's beautiful." Even in the moonlight, Caroline could make out an embroidered river winding between thick trees with French-knotted foliage. She traced the verse partially stitched across the top: *For in the wilderness shall waters break out, and streams . . .*

"I love the river." Esther's whisper came like a breeze through cottonwood leaves.

"The San Juan?" Caroline ran her fingertips over the design.

"My mother would take my brother and me to gather wild asparagus there in spring. She filled her skirt while we chased each other in the water. My brother would sneak up and splash me. He'd laugh and laugh." A sigh almost stayed in the teacup.

An idea buzzed through Caroline's brain, but she couldn't speak it. Not to Esther, not yet. "Do you think you can sleep now?"

Esther handed the cup back and turned on her side.

Caroline tucked the hot water bottle closer and kissed the girl's smooth cheek. "Sweet dreams." She prayed it would be so.

Reentering the brightness of the lamp-lit sewing circle, Caroline glanced at the clock.

"It's late, girls. You had best come to bed." She ignored their curious glances as they folded needlework and wound thread. Surely it was Esther's prerogative to explain, if explanation were necessary. Her cheeks warmed again. Certainly such things had not been topics of conversation among her girlhood set back home.

After a round past the boys' wing to ensure all had retired for the night, Caroline sank into a chair in the sitting room, quiet at last. But excitement pricked away at her earlier weariness. She ran the idea through her mind like a skein of yarn, checking for soundness. Surely it would be good for all of them, especially the children. Particularly a certain young girl and her brother. She smiled to herself, squeezing her hands together.

Now she had only to approach Tse.

Tap, tap.

Alone in the tack room Friday morning, Tse stopped punching new holes in a mended harness and listened. Hearing nothing more, he resumed his work.

Tap, tap.

Tse dropped the tangle of leather and buckles onto the workbench and crossed to open the door that divided the small room from the barn.

"Miss Haynes." He squelched the odd jump of his heart at the sight of her. "Is something wrong?"

"No, not at all." She glanced past his shoulder at his meager quarters for the week—the cot spread with one of *Shimá's* blankets, the rough three-legged table with his Bible, the workbench. "Am I disturbing you?"

He shook his head and stepped into the main barn with her, drawing a breath of old hay and horse sweat. "How can I help you?"

"I wanted to ask." She locked her hands before her. "Could you drive us to the river tomorrow?"

He quirked an eyebrow. "Us?"

"I want to take the children on a picnic."

"A picnic?" Why was he repeating like a child of three winters?

"At the river." She smiled as if he were that child. "I think they could all do with a bit of fun."

"Why do you need me?" Tse shifted his feet.

"I can't drive a wagon. Not yet, anyway."

"Isaiah could."

"But we need two. Your cousins would love to spend time with you. Esther actually gave me the idea, though she doesn't know it. I thought it might be good for Samuel."

"Being with his sister?" Tse folded his arms. "Yes, but what would Rev. Abernathy say?"

Miss Haynes bit her lip. "Surely the rules could be relaxed for a pleasure outing."

A pleasure outing. Certainly had been a while since they'd had one of those. Tse rubbed the side of his nose. "Their uniforms?"

"What about them?"

"They'll play in the river, you know."

"I didn't think of that." Miss Haynes dropped her arms to her sides. "I suppose those are the only clothes they have."

Tse avoided her gaze, stuffing away the thought that nudged at his mind.

A horse whiffled and stamped in its stall. A magpie squawked from the barnyard.

"There must be some way." She sighed and turned to leave. "I will think on it further. Forgive me for bothering you."

He watched her go, head bowed, twitching her skirt away from a manure deposit. He pushed back into the tack room and picked up the awl again, pressing into the strip of leather, muscles bulging his sleeve. A rock weighted his chest at the thought of Miss Haynes's slumped shoulders. But he couldn't risk incurring Willis's ire again.

Willis. Why did everything have to circle back to him? Even when not physically present, he seemed to govern the mission from afar. Tse threw the awl down and leaned his hands on the workbench a moment, then strode to the doorway.

"Miss Haynes?" He jogged through the barn, splatting his foot into the same patch of manure she had avoided. He scraped off the sole of his moccasin in the straw. And he'd just cleaned out the barn this morning.

"Yes?" She peeked back in, the morning sunlight catching gold in her light brown hair.

Tse tipped his head back the way he had come, and she followed him past the stalls, this time into the tack room.

Kneeling before the trunk in the corner, Tse hesitated. What was he doing? And yet...

He yanked the horse blanket off and creaked up the lid.

With a quick intake of breath, Miss Haynes knelt close beside him. Leaning over the piles of velveteen blouses and small tiered skirts, cotton breeches and soft moccasins, she touched a silver buckle.

"I didn't know they kept these." She lifted a calico skirt and smoothed the soft folds across her lap.

"Most schools don't." Tse rested his hands on his knees. "Perhaps I shouldn't have shown you, but ... "

She pressed a finger to her chin. "I don't know what Miss Spencer or Rev. Abernathy would say, but it seems only sensible." She glanced at him. "What do you think?"

"I think ... " He cupped one of the moccasins in his hand. "The children might like to be themselves for a day."

"Then you'll take us?"

A grin tugging at his cheeks, Tse rubbed his thumb over the soft deerskin shoe and nodded.

CHAPTER TWENTY-THREE

"Tse!" Shashyáázh pelted across the mission yard toward him, beaming bright as the sun peeking over the mesas.

Tse straightened from fastening the wagon's harness traces to the team, caught his cousin and swung him around. The grin stretching Shashyáázh's thin little face lightened Tse's heart.

"Look at you." He set the boy on his feet and ruffled his cropped hair.

"Miss Caroline found my clothes." Shashyáázh smoothed the front of his velveteen tunic. "She said we can wear them to the river."

"I see." Tse watched his cousin hop from one moccasined foot to the other. Except for his hair and thinness, he might have been the same happy little boy who tugged Tse inside for a coyote story last winter.

The mission door banged, and Tse looked up.

Nearly hidden behind an enormous picnic basket on each arm, Miss Haynes felt her way down the porch steps.

He loped across the yard toward her. "You should watch where you are going." He took one basket. "Might step on another rattlesnake."

Her gaze shot to the ground at her feet. Then she laughed, looking up at him from beneath her straw hat. The eyelet yoke of her trim white blouse framed her face, heightening the gray of her eyes.

"Thank you, kind sir." She dipped her knees, catching the edge of her blue checked skirt with one hand.

Her smile caught him in the throat. Tse shifted the basket to his other arm. "You—" He coughed and swallowed hard. What had he been about to say—"You look beautiful"? *Get a hold of yourself, Tsosie.* Willing his heart not to jump like a scared rabbit, he swept his arm toward the wagons and grinned. "Let's go before the sun beats us to the river."

The students streamed out of the mission, boys and girls, big ones and little, in a swirl of red and purple skirts, patter of moccasins, blur of deerskin leggings and cotton breeches. They halted before the two wagons, turning uncertainly to look at their teacher.

Shándíín finally spoke for them, fingering the squash blossom necklace around her neck. "Where should we sit?"

Tse knew what Willis's answer would be. Boys in one wagon, girls in another.

By the way Miss Haynes nibbled her lip, she knew it too. She studied Shándíín, then glanced to Shashyáázh, sidling nearer his sister than he had been allowed for weeks.

"Sit wherever you like." Miss Haynes pushed back her hat and sent the group a smile.

With squeals and shouts, the children swarmed into the wagons. Shándíín boosted her brother into the end of one and clambered in after him. The look on Shashyáázh's face as he slipped his hand inside his sister's squeezed Tse's chest.

"Tse, where shall we put the picnic baskets?"

He turned to meet Miss Haynes's uncertain gaze. He stepped to the nearest wagon and slid his hamper under the seat, then reached for hers.

"There is still room." Shoving the basket into place behind the chattering children, Tse glanced to the other wagon where Isaiah perched in the driver's seat, waiting for the signal to start. "Want to ride with me?" Tse's neck heated at how the words blurted out. But the smile in her eyes as he held out his hand snuffed any thoughts that she considered him presumptuous. He helped her up, then climbed to sit beside her.

With a slap of the reins, he started the procession off, his heart light as the summer breeze.

Caroline gripped a sapling for security as she stood on the uneven riverbank and gazed up at a leafy canopy. Sunlight dappled through heart-shaped cottonwood leaves, dancing elm sprays, and silver spears of Russian olive. So beautiful, and so close to the mission— why had they never come here before?

A horse snorted, and she looked down to see Tse at the river's edge, watering one of the teams near the splashing, shouting children. After a moment, he gently tugged the horses back up the bank, pausing to let them snatch at the lush grass.

"Have to watch they don't bloat on this stuff." He glanced up at her.

Caroline leaned away from the sapling, still hanging on with one hand. "I haven't seen this much green since Pennsylvania. I didn't know how weary my eyes had grown for it."

"Water brings life in the desert."

Streams in the desert. Caroline thought of Esther's sampler, the unfinished verse.

Children's laughter rose above the water, sparkling like the sunshine on the river. Boys clambered in trees, their deerskin leggings shielding shins from the rough bark, while the girls, like wildflowers in their bright skirts, darted through clusters of willow or dabbled at the river's edge. The smallest boys dug in the gravelly mud with sticks.

Thank the Lord for Tse's suggestion regarding clothing. She could only imagine Rev. Abernathy's face if he came home to muddied uniforms.

Caroline pushed away thoughts of the reverend. She didn't want to think about him, or the school closing, or—what he had asked her to think about. Not today.

She glanced at Tse instead.

He stood gazing at the river, one hand ruffling the near horse's mane, the other holding their bridles firm. What might he be thinking of? So much she didn't know of this man. Yet she wanted to, somehow.

As if he felt her study, his eyes shifted to hers, then away quickly as the dragonflies that darted above the water.

"There aren't any snakes around here, are there?" Caroline stepped onto a boulder, teetered, and gripped another branch.

"Just water snakes."

She shuddered and clutched her skirts closer with her free hand. "Is it taboo to kill them too?"

"Why would you want to? They are not dangerous." He tugged the horses' heads up. They jerked in protest, straining toward the grass, but Tse won out. "Come now. You want to end up with a bellyache?" He led them up toward the parked wagons.

"Rattlesnakes are." Caroline followed him. "Dangerous."

"Not unprovoked." He glanced back at her, a glint of humor in his dark eyes. "I am not afraid of angering the snake spirit, Miss Haynes."

Caroline's stomach squirmed. How did he know?

"But I think many of my people's ways have wisdom. Why kill one of God's creatures if there is no need?"

"I suppose you have a point." The gentleness in his glance unsettled her.

Little running feet demanded her attention. "Miss Caroline, can we eat now?"

"It's that time, isn't it?" She glanced at Tse on the bank above them, feeling oddly shy. "Join us?"

He hesitated, then grinned and nodded. "Let me tether the horses."

Tse helped her unload the luncheon baskets, and Caroline smiled to see the children cluster in sibling groups like happy bees on the blankets she had brought. She hadn't even realized before that Isaiah and Anna were brother and sister. As for Samuel, he stuck to Esther like a sand burr, opening his mouth for bites of ham sandwich. Why couldn't Caroline get him to eat like that at school?

She and Tse lingered after the children darted off to play again, Caroline nibbling a cookie while he crunched one of the apples left from the winter stores. They should have apricots and peaches before long, judging by the laden trees skirting the schoolyard and lining the orchard back at the mission.

"So." Tse spit out an apple seed. "Tell me more of your family, in this green land of Pennsylvania."

"Toby is eleven, and Benji is going on six. My father remarried last fall." She brushed cookie crumbs off her skirt.

"Was that difficult for you?"

Caroline shot him a glance. How did he know? And how had no one ever asked her that before? She nodded and looked down, pinching a blade of grass from beside the picnic blanket. "What about you? Have you just the one sister?"

Tse hesitated. "Yes."

"And she attended Hebron too?"

"She was seven when we came." He twisted the stem of his apple. "I think, in some ways, it was harder on her than me. She was so young."

Like Samuel. She still heard him crying at night now and then. "Does she follow the native ways like you do?"

"I don't know just what you mean." A furrow creased between his dark brows.

"I want to understand . . . " She twisted the grass between her fingers. "Why did you go back to Navajo ways?"

Tse turned the apple core in his hands a moment without replying.

Perhaps she should have held her tongue.

"I wanted to honor my father, my mother. And the Creator who made us who we are." He glanced at Caroline as if he expected her to disagree, to contradict him.

"Do your parents object to you being a Christian?" She slit the grass blade into two slivers with her thumbnail.

Tse tossed the core aside and gazed across the river. The horses, tethered to a cottonwood nearby, stomped and swished at flies, nibbling the sparser grass farther from the water. Children's laughter drifted up from the bank.

"I will never forget my father's face when I came home after graduation in my short hair and white man's clothes. 'So,' he said, 'they have taken you as well, they and their God.'"

Caroline studied his profile, his strong nose and chin, his firm cheekbones. He did not look at her. The breeze sighed in the trees, wisping her hair around her face.

"At school, I often borrowed a book to read while out with the herd. My favorite was by a man named Hudson Taylor."

Caroline drew a quick breath. "The missionary to China." He had been one of Jeremiah's heroes.

"Mr. Taylor put on Chinese dress and a pigtail, and God used him. And Paul became all things to all men—including his own people. So . . . " Tse shrugged. "Miss Spencer and Rev. Abernathy do not understand. I do not think they want to. But I no longer see shame in my father's eyes when he looks at me. And he no longer frowns when I pray. I hope someday he may pray to our Creator in the name of Jesus too."

If so, would that be in his own language? Or would his father be kept from that, as Tse seemed to be? Caroline brushed the grass bits from her fingers. So many questions.

A shriek sounded from the river. Esther stood dripping, hands on hips as she faced her dancing little brother, the smile on her face belying the scolding tone of her voice. Samuel dove into the river and splashed her again, and Esther chased after him, then caught and tickled him until he screamed with glee.

Caroline smiled and hugged her knees. When had she ever heard him laugh like that?

Released, Samuel tore after his sister, heels churning up waves behind him. Tse pushed to his feet and crept toward the river, holding his finger to his lips. Then with a yell he plunged into the water and sent a wave splashing toward Samuel. The child turned and pelted after Tse, laughing so hard he had to pick himself up twice. The other boys joined forces in drenching Tse, their shouts startling a pair of birds into the air.

Caroline rose and picked her way down the bank, stepping over the muddiest spots. She found Dorcas and two other girls clustered around a clump of feathery green near the water's edge.

"Look, Miss Caroline. There is still some wild asparagus." Anna extended a handful of tender spears. "Can we have it for supper?"

"If you tell me what to do with it." Caroline fingered one of the nubbly stalks.

"I will show you." Breathless, Esther joined the group.

"You're all wet." Caroline squeezed one of her sopping braids.

"Shashyáázh is a naughty boy." Esther smiled and shook her head. She crouched beside the lacy plants with Dorcas, murmuring with her in Navajo.

Rev. Abernathy's parting words flitted through Caroline's mind, but she hadn't the heart to correct the girls into English—not today. Instead, she knelt beside them, fingering the lacy fronds. She glanced between the bright faces. "You girls are together so much, you might be sisters."

"We are," Esther said. "Our mothers are from the same clan."

Samuel's laughter shrieked through the air again, and Caroline glanced behind to see Tse swinging him above the water by his ankles. Other small boys leaped around them, pleading to be next.

She smiled at Esther. "I love hearing your brother laugh."

"He was the laughingest baby." Esther sat back on her heels. "My mother says he had his laughing party earlier than any other child she knows."

"Laughing party?"

"When a baby laughs for the first time, you have a party and invite your family and friends to celebrate life's joys." Dorcas gathered asparagus into the calico folds of her skirt. "The baby gives salt to everyone who comes. It teaches him to be generous and share."

"Remember, at your little sister's laughing party, how she spilled the salt?" Esther looked up.

Dorcas rolled her lips together and nodded.

"You have a little sister?" If so, she must be too young for school. Caroline would have noticed that relationship, with all the girls in the same dormitory.

"She died last term." Dorcas rose, holding her laden skirt together like a pocket.

Caroline stilled. "Last term? At school?"

But Dorcas headed up the bank, pushing through the thickly growing willow. Caroline glanced at Esther, but she stared at her lap, picking loose asparagus fronds from her skirt.

Why had this never come up before?

"Miss Caro-line, *hágo.*" Samuel scampered toward her. He grabbed Caroline's hand and tugged, chattering in Navajo.

"He found a mother duck and her babies," Esther translated.

"*Hágo,*" Samuel insisted.

Caroline laughed and let him pull her to her feet, half running to keep up with him. She skidded to a stop at the edge of the river. "Samuel, I can't cross that."

He let go her hand and padded onto the mossy fallen tree spanning the river, then turned and beckoned, beaming.

Caroline bit her lip and put one foot on the end of the log. It shifted, and she took it off. The time she had climbed a tree to rescue a stranded Benji flashed dizzily through her mind. She'd thought they'd never both make it down alive.

"I'll help you." Tse bounded onto the log and held out his hand.

"I'm afraid not." She shook her head.

Samuel, bouncing on his toes atop the log—how could he do that and not fall off?—beckoned again. "Pl—ease."

Speaking English, for her? Her heart melted.

Tse reached toward her again. She grasped his hand, rough and warm from the sun, and let him help her onto the log.

One step . . . two steps. She kept her eyes on the gray bark splotched with green fuzz. Three steps . . . four. She glanced at the flowing brown water. Her feet froze.

"I'm going back."

"You're halfway across." Tse tugged her forward.

Step . . . step . . . step. She lifted her skirt with her free hand and increased her pace. She could do this, perhaps even make her way back unassisted. Step—step—

Something slithered from among the tangled branches near the bank, and a greenish-gray coil slipped into the water right beneath her foot.

Caroline screamed, lost her balance, and plunged backwards into the river, yanking Tse with her.

She popped up from muddy swirls, gasping and coughing, and struggled to her feet in the knee-deep water.

"Where is it? Where's the snake?" Clutching her skirts about her legs lest the creature slither its way underneath, she tripped and plunked down again.

Children squealed and splashed in her direction. Tse lurched toward her, sputtering, and grabbed for her hand.

She pulled herself up by his steady grip, then splashed after him to the river's edge. She collapsed to her knees in the pebbly shallows, and Tse plunked beside her, both panting to catch their breath.

Tse swiped his wet hair off his face and glanced at her, then shook with a laugh that began in his chest.

Caroline stared at him a moment, then his rumbling chuckle elicited hers, and she laughed until she sat back on her heels in the water and wiped her eyes with the back of her wet hand. "Oh, mercy—I'm sorry, Tse."

"Feels good." Tse sloshed to his feet. "We could all take a dip, now that you scared any snakes beyond the next bend."

Caroline laughed again. Several children, giggling and chattering in Navajo, reached for her hands and helped her up the other bank. Her shoes squished and her hair dripped muddy water down her lace-trimmed collar.

At a tug on her hand, she looked down into Samuel's insistent face. She squeezed back. "Show me."

Together they crouched by the nest in the reeds, where the mottled brown mama duck huddled into the shadows, trying to keep the downy little heads from peeking out beneath her wings.

Samuel held his finger to his lips, his eyes bright. Caroline imitated the gesture, and his teeth peeked out in that grin again.

The river softened to silver as the day waned, golden sunshine still highlighting the mesas beyond. Caroline and Tse sat on the bank, watching the children have one last game.

"We should head back soon." She glanced at Tse.

He nodded but didn't move, rubbing a twig between his fingers.

Caroline followed his gaze to Esther, tossing pebbles into the rippled water as she perched on a boulder near the river's edge.

Suddenly Tse chuckled.

"What?"

He shook his head and plastered on a sober expression, but his gaze flicked toward their water-stained shoes, the hem of her skirt still muddied from the dunking.

"Stop it." Caroline's cheeks warmed, though a smile tugged at her mouth.

Tse focused obediently on the river.

A moment later, something crept through the grass toward her skirt. Caroline gasped and snatched her feet away—until the crooked stick in Tse's hand registered.

"You!" She seized the twig.

He held it fast and laughed, his eyes dancing.

Caroline braced herself and tugged.

Tse clambered onto his knees and nearly yanked it from her.

She dug her boot heels into the bank, pulling until the stick broke in two. Their laughter swelled till her cheeks ached. At last she groaned a sigh and tossed her piece away. She lifted a hand to feel her hair, the loosened strands stiff from dried muddy water.

"This was a good thing, coming to the river."

Glancing up at Tse's words, she caught an odd look in his eyes.

He looked away and pushed himself to his feet. "Ready to go?"

She nodded and grasped the hand he extended to help her up. As she straightened, their eyes met. She stood still, her hand clasped in his.

His eyes searched hers. Something fluttered in her middle, something frightening and sweet.

"I will hitch the team." Tse stepped back, releasing her hand.

Caroline watched him go, gripping her fingers together at her waist, her heart skipping like the stones the children skimmed across the water.

The wagons jolted homeward toward the mission. Some of the children sang softly, Navajo tunes Caroline had never heard, and once "Jesus Loves Me." Others curled in corners and nodded off. In the back of their wagon, Esther hummed, one hand stroking her brother's head pillowed on her shoulder.

Once Caroline glanced at Tse, at his strong, quiet profile.

He did not turn his head.

She looked back at her hands, keeping her gaze down until the wagon turned the corner onto the mission's lane, the horses clopping under the familiar signpost.

"Whoa." Tse pulled the team up short.

An empty buckboard sat in front of the barn. The mission door stood open. Children scrambled out of Isaiah's wagon, which had pulled in just ahead of theirs.

And Rev. Abernathy strode toward them, his mouth set in a grim line.

CHAPTER TWENTY-FOUR

"Where in tarnation have you been?" The reverend's words snapped sparks.

Caroline slid from the wagon without waiting for Tse's help. She hit the ground hard and hurried toward Rev. Abernathy. "We didn't expect you back until Monday. We took the children to the river."

"We?" His gaze shot to Tse, and he strode to the wagon. "This was your idea."

"No." Caroline ran to catch up with him. "It was mine."

Rev. Abernathy circled to the back of the wagon. His gaze first nailed Tse, then Caroline. "And this?" He pointed to the children's clothing. They shrank against the sideboards, eyes wide. "This was your idea too?"

"We didn't want them to soil their uniforms." If only her voice didn't sound like a guilty ten-year-old.

"Children, inside and back in your proper clothes." Rev. Abernathy gripped the side of the wagon, a muscle working in his jaw.

They tumbled silently from the wagon, moccasins pattering across the yard.

"Rev. Abernathy, for pity's sake—"

"I trusted you." He pointed toward the mission, where Caroline noticed Miss Spencer for the first time, leaning against a porch post, her face gray. "You close to gave my aunt another stroke!"

"I'm sorry." She twisted her fingers together. "You said you wouldn't return until after the Sabbath."

"So you thought you could do whatever you pleased? Throw aside all decorum, all propriety, all mission rules?"

Tse swung to the ground with a thud. "Rev. Abernathy—"

"Stay out of this, Tse." He stepped closer to Caroline. "I've tried to be patient, Miss Haynes. But time and again, you've sought to undermine our goals here at Hebron. My aunt told me about the dancing. If that had happened when someone from the board was here, we would have been shut down immediately, no appeals. If you wish to continue as teacher here, there must be no more of this."

"You'd send me away? For letting the children wear their own clothes on a picnic?" Where was the romantic-eyed preacher of a week ago?

"Willis!" Tse grabbed his arm. "It was my idea about the clothes. Miss Haynes did not even know you had them. You—" He swallowed and released Rev. Abernathy's arm. "You are behaving neither as a gentleman nor as a Christian."

"You're one to talk." Willis barked a laugh. "We give you second chances, and third chances, and you just try to drag these children after you, to turn their hearts away from God."

Tse slammed the side of his fist into the wagon. "That's not true."

"Oh no? Then what do you call that?" He pointed at the children clustering up the mission steps. A few halted and turned back at his voice, the little ones wide eyed. Esther flinched and pulled Samuel against her tiered skirt.

Tse stepped back. His chest rose and fell, once, twice. When he finally spoke, his voice was raw. "You are teaching as doctrine the precepts of men."

"If you still think you know how to run this mission better than I, maybe you should just leave." Rev. Abernathy shoved his hands into his pockets.

Caroline caught her breath. *No. Please, no.*

Tse stood very still, only his jaw shifting slightly. "You mean that?"

"I might have known this wouldn't work." Rev. Abernathy kicked a rock.

Caroline clenched her fingers. Tse couldn't lose his job, his family needed the income, he had told her so. "Rev. Abernathy, please—"

But Tse stopped her with a lifted hand. "Go ahead, then, Willis. Burn their clothes, as other schools do. Take away their language. Tell them God made a mistake in creating them, but you are going to fix it. Then see if they will believe He loved them enough to die for them." He spun on his heel and strode toward the barn.

"Tse!" Caroline ran a few steps after him.

"Let him go."

She whirled back to face Rev. Abernathy.

He shook his head. "It's better this way."

Better? A gust of wind flapped Caroline's skirt, driving dust into her eyes.

A movement on the mission porch caught her eye. Samuel, still in his breeches and velveteen blouse, clung alone to the railing, his face pinched.

How was this better?

At the clop of hooves, Caroline turned to see Tse leading his horse out of the barn. He swung onto its back and galloped away without a backward glance.

"Good riddance."

At Rev. Abernathy's mutter, she spun around to see him heading for the mission. "Wait!"

He halted, turned.

"What happened at the meeting?"

"They're giving us one more year." He shifted his jaw. "If things don't improve, we'll be closed before next summer." He turned and disappeared into the mission.

Improve how? More students? More converts?

One less Navajo herder?

Caroline hugged herself, her eyes stinging from tears or the wind, she didn't know.

Isaiah clattered down the mission steps, military sharp once more in cap, jacket, and trousers. He began unhitching the teams from the wagons.

The porch stood empty now. Samuel must have gone in when Rev. Abernathy did. Blindly, Caroline mounted the steps and pushed through the door.

Back in their uniforms, the children moved like silent little soldiers, wiping tables, placing plates and forks. They would not look at her.

She wanted to smash something. Instead, she found Miss Spencer in the kitchen, rolling and cutting biscuit dough, her right hand compensating for the left, both seeming to work independently from the rest of her. She did not turn at Caroline's step.

Anna rushed in with a basket of peas from the garden.

Caroline took it, and the girl darted away like a frightened bird.

So much for wild asparagus. Her chest tight, Caroline crossed to the sink and rinsed the peas, then began slitting the pods and flicking the insides into a pan. For several moments only the slap of biscuit dough and the ping of peas sounded in the kitchen.

At last Caroline drew a breath. "Miss Spencer—I don't know what to say."

Miss Spencer lined the biscuits on a pan, slid them into the oven, and creaked the door closed. She stood before the stove a moment, rubbing one wrinkled hand over the other. Finally she sighed.

"My nephew is young and passionate. Give him a few days to cool off. No doubt he'll see in time you meant well and merely didn't think."

Caroline drove her thumb through a pod so hard the peas sprang to the floor.

"I'm sorry." She clamped her teeth on her lip and chased the rolling peas into a corner. *Tse, I'm sorry.* Didn't think—no, she hadn't. Hadn't thought what the consequences might be, here in this place where little boys weren't allowed to see their sisters and saying hello in the wrong language brought censure and a weekend picnic cost someone his job. What would she do if Rev. Abernathy carried through on his threat to send her away as well? She blocked the thought. Surely he wouldn't. He was merely upset, as Miss Spencer had said. Hadn't he proposed marriage to her only a week ago?

A crash of thunder shook the mission. Caroline jumped.

"We usually get these afternoon storms more toward July and August." Miss Spencer stepped to the window frame and tugged on it.

Caroline helped pull the window closed, then lifted the pan of peas onto the stove.

"We can't cook the peas when the potatoes aren't even peeled." Miss Spencer's snap tensed Caroline's spine. "I must have sent Esther for them half an hour ago. Where is that girl?"

"I'll go look." Glad for an escape, Caroline wiped her hands and hurried out the door, nearly crashing into a wide-eyed Isaiah.

"I can't find Samuel." The boy caught himself on the doorframe.

"What do you mean?"

"After I stabled the horses, I went to check on the younger boys, and he wasn't there. Not in the schoolroom, either." His lean young face creased.

Caroline's heartbeat quickened, but the child had to be around somewhere. She touched Isaiah's shoulder. "Perhaps he's with Esther—I was going to look for her. Come on."

Outside, the wind tossed tree branches, scattering green peaches across the schoolyard as she searched for the children. Looming closer by the second, dark thunderheads built in the west.

"Esther? Samuel?" Shielding her face with her arms, Caroline pushed against the wind toward the garden. She continued to call for them, but the gale only shrank their names.

Her foot hit something, and she snatched up an abandoned basket, half filled with dirty potatoes. Esther's basket. "Isaiah, check the barn!"

Squinting into the blowing dust, she scanned the mission grounds.

Foot-high corn stalks nearly flattened in the wind. A lone chicken skidded along the ground, squawking, feathers bent backwards. Isaiah snatched it up mid-stride and clambered over the barnyard fence with it.

Caroline jumped out of the way of a tumbleweed bowling across the yard. *Lord, where are they?*

The cloakroom. She darted into her schoolroom and flung open the closet door.

No Samuel.

She ran to the other side and searched the older pupils' room. Empty. Stepping back outside, she tugged the door shut behind her against the wind.

"Miss Haynes!" Rev. Abernathy jogged toward her from the main building.

She ran to meet him. "We can't find Samuel and Esther."

"So I hear." He slowed, catching his breath. "They're nowhere in the mission."

"Then where?" She couldn't quite breathe. "They can't have just run off!"

"Couldn't they?"

"Where would they go?"

"Toward home, probably. It happens. But they mustn't get far in this storm. Isaiah! Tell one of the other boys to start chores. Then help me get a couple of horses saddled." Rev. Abernathy loped toward the barn.

Caroline squeezed the basket handle, fighting nausea. Lightning flicked over the mesas. *Dear Lord, help*. Was this all her fault?

She dropped the basket and ran for the mission. Ignoring the children's stares, she yanked a shawl around her shoulders and tied another over her head. Racing back out and down the steps, she met Rev. Abernathy and Isaiah leading saddled horses out of the barn.

Caroline trotted up to the reverend, her breath coming in gasps. "Let me come too."

"No."

"Please. We can go in different directions." The first drops of rain, heavy as pebbles, pelted her hair through the shawl and darkened dots on Rev. Abernathy's hat.

"It's not safe." He glanced up at the charcoal clouds scudding in. "Stay here with the children and pray."

Caroline hugged her shawl to her as they rode away, trying to quell the panic rising in her throat. *O Lord, guide them—help them. Please.*

Tse's blood pounded in time with his horse's hooves, chuffing up clouds of dust behind him. Thunderclouds thickened and rushed nearer, darkening the sky.

His outburst to Willis had been foolish, maybe, but he didn't regret it. How would Willis's ancestors have felt if missionaries had stripped away their kilts, their bagpipes, their Scottish tongue? Would they have taken away the wooden shoes of those Dutch missionaries down in Gallup? But no, the *bilagáanas* were always right—government officials, Indian agents, or missionaries. No matter how many broken treaties, broken promises, broken families. Broken children's hearts.

Thunder growled. Tse slowed his horse and squinted at the roiling horizon. He let out a breath and nudged his horse's flank with the quirt.

Pretty early in summer for a storm. His father might need help bringing in the sheep. Flocks spooked easily in thunder and lightning. Probably, though, *Shizhé'é* had sensed the storm well ahead and already had them safe.

Just in case, Tse circled back toward the mission, heading for the farthest point their flock usually grazed, letting his horse pick his way around the sage and rabbit brush. The fire in his belly burned lower as weariness settled over his shoulders. Tending the sheep might be the only work he'd have for a while. But he'd have to find another job, if Willis were really serious about dismissing him. The railroad no doubt still sought strong arms and willing backs, but that might mean traveling hundreds of miles. Could he go that distance from his family? *Lord...*

A crack nearly split his eardrums, a flash lighting the desert around him as his horse reared high in the air. Tse clung with his knees until his mount's front hooves hit the earth again. He patted the shaggy neck, murmuring comfort while his heart thudded back to normal. A roar filled his ears as the rain swept in, a gray sheet pelting through his clothes.

Sliding to the ground, he yanked a blanket from behind his saddle and covered his shoulders. The tightly woven wool would have kept the wet out, had he thought to don it sooner. His horse snorted, and Tse grabbed his bridle. He'd lead him from here rather than risk a spooked throw. He squinted through the torrent, picking his way along the rim of an arroyo, steering clear of the edge. The wash could surge with foaming runoff without warning. Head down, he trudged on through the rain.

The children's laughter of that afternoon, the rippling river, trickled through his mind. He couldn't remember any such outings from his schooldays. Had he just blocked them from his memory? Or was Miss Haynes the first at Hebron to realize how much it would mean to the children? He stumbled in the mud, his heart galloping at the thought of her.

What had come over him to hold her hand like that—to look into her eyes? She would never think of him, not in the way a woman did of a man. The startle in her face had reminded him of that with brutal reality. And he could not, must not, think of her.

"Tse!"

He jerked to a halt at the shout. Who—? Tugging his horse around, he squinted through the rain.

A slim figure stumbled toward him through the downpour.

"Sháńdíín?" He started toward her. "What are you doing out here?" He caught her shoulders as she fell toward him.

"Shashyáázh," she gasped. "He's gone."

"What do you mean, gone?" Tse's heart skipped.

She was shaking, crying, so she could hardly speak.

"What happened?" Tse knelt beside his cousin in the mud and rubbed his hands along her arms, forcing his voice steady. "Tell me, *Shideezhi*."

"The owl—Miss Spencer sent me for potatoes, and an owl flew right over me. I ran to find Shashyáázh, and he wasn't anywhere—he was gone!"

"Did you tell Rev. Abernathy? Miss Haynes?"

"They wouldn't understand." She shook her head, wet braids flying, and looked up pleading, her face so like Dólii's. "Shashyáázh needs *Shimá*. He needs to be home."

Tse stood, his heart thudding dully. Thunder crashed overhead, and Sháńdíín flinched against him, her teeth chattering.

He had run away too, more than once during his schooldays. Always thinking he could outsmart them, that this time they wouldn't find him. But he had been older, had known the land well. Not like Shashyáázh, so small to be stumbling alone through a storm.

"We'll find him." He yanked off his blanket and wrapped it around Sháńdíín, then boosted her onto his horse. *Please, God.*

CHAPTER TWENTY-FIVE

This would be the way Shashyáázh would have come. If he were well enough oriented to head the right direction.

Tse scanned the ground and surrounding brush with each step, praying the rain wouldn't keep him from finding the trail.

There. Beside a sagebrush.

He crouched and traced the slight indentation in the mud with his fingers. The shelter of the plant had kept it from being fully washed away.

"Is it him?" Sháńdíín slid from the horse.

"I think so." A child's imprint, made by a small moccasin. So Shashyáázh had not followed Willis's orders to change his clothes. Somehow it comforted Tse, though *bilagáana* boot prints were easier to follow.

Tse pressed on, Sháńdíín beside him now, following bits of broken sumac and disturbed clumps of snakeweed. No more moccasin marks. Had he lost the trail? Or had the rain merely obliterated it?

He swiped back his dripping hair. *Please, Lord.*

"Is this one?" Sháńdíín crouched a short ways ahead of him, nearing the edge of the arroyo.

He knelt beside her. She was right. But why would Shashyáázh head for the wash in the midst of a storm? Didn't he know…

Tse left his horse for Sháńdíín to lead and moved faster, crashing through the wet sagebrush. At the rim of the gorge, he cupped his hands to his mouth. "Shashyáázh!"

Nothing.

He crept along the rim, peering down. The rain was gentling, but dusk rapidly darkened the air. Could he have misread the signs? Had Shashyáázh gone another way?

"Tse!"

He turned back at Sháńdíín's call, wiping the rain from his eyes with his sleeve.

She tugged the horse toward him. "I thought I heard something—from over there." She pointed her lips toward a rocky outcropping shielded by a clump of junipers.

Tse set off at a run, leaping over boulders in his way. He ducked under a juniper and pushed back the wet, sweet-scented branches. "Shashyáázh?"

A cry like a frightened baby goat rejoiced his ears, and there his cousin was, huddled under the rocky ledge like any wise Navajo boy would do when caught in a storm.

Tse fell to his knees, Shashyáázh burrowing close into his arms, with only small sniffles to show he'd been trying to be brave.

Tse called to Sháńdíín and sat against the rock, pulling his cousin onto his lap.

"You gave us a scare, little brother." Tse's throat closed. He hugged Shashyáázh hard.

Sháńdíín poked her face, pinched and hopeful, through the curtain of juniper. She fell upon Shashyáázh with a cry.

Tse let the child go to his sister and leaned his elbows on his knees, his face in his hands. *Thank You, Lord.* For a while he'd been afraid that—but no, he wouldn't think that way.

"Will you take us home, now?"

Tse lifted his head to meet two pleading pairs of eyes. For an instant he wavered. Was it possible? Then slowly, he shook his head. "Children—"

"Rev. Abernathy wouldn't know." Sháńdíín clutched his hand. "Since you're not going to work at the mission anymore."

The words thudded dull in his stomach. But Willis hadn't fired him, not really. Not yet. He had only been angry. Hadn't he?

"Rev. Abernathy and Miss Haynes will be looking for you, be worried." The words came heavy. "It's too far to your family camp now, with you all wet. And even if I took you there, they will find you anyway and take you back to school." He ought to know.

Shashyáázh pressed his fists to his eyes and gave way to sobs.

"Little brother, don't." He touched the small shoulder, but Shashyáázh shrank away. Tse swallowed, the pressure in his throat threatening to choke him.

"Come, Shashyáázh." Sháńdíín stood, her shoulders slumped.

"Nooo!"

"Tse is right, you know he is right." Her voice sharpened, and she hugged herself. "I could have told you the same thing if you had asked me before running off like this."

Shashyáázh stared at his sister, then crumpled into a ball.

"Hágo." Sháńdíín took her brother's hand and tugged him to his feet. She did not look at Tse.

Feeling like the Enemy Navajo who had allied with Spaniards and white Americans in the past, Tse pushed to his feet and led the silent children out of the sheltering branches. He boosted them onto his horse, tugged its head around, and headed for the mission.

The rain had stopped. Clouds scudded away from the rising moon.

Once he glanced back at the children, but Shashyáázh only lowered his eyes.

"Where did you find them?" Her hands still shaking with relief, Caroline stripped off Esther's soaked stockings and started on Samuel's deerskin leggings.

The children huddled together in the rocking chair near the sitting room fire, wrapped in Tse's wool blanket. The blaze crackled in near silence, as the other students had been hustled off to bed as soon as the search party returned.

"Shándíín came after me to tell me her brother was missing." Tse spoke from the corner. "We found him taking shelter under a rocky outcropping near the wash."

"Whatever possessed you to be out there in the first place?" Rev. Abernathy crouched beside the children, gripping the chair's arm. "You know better."

They shrank together into the chair and said nothing.

"Esther!"

"Please," Caroline broke in. "We just need to get them to bed." Not that she didn't want answers as much as the reverend did, but this was no way to get them.

"We will discuss your behavior in the morning." Rev. Abernathy slapped his hands on the chair arm and stood.

Samuel shuddered, his teeth chattering.

"Heat some water." Caroline wrapped his cold hands in hers, the fingers icy and unresponsive. "They need hot baths."

The reverend blew out a breath and left the room.

"I will go now." Tse stepped from the darkness into the firelight. Samuel whimpered and reached out to him. Tse encircled the children in his arms, murmuring to them in Navajo, then straightened and nodded to Caroline.

"Shouldn't you spend the night?" She glanced at the blackened window. The rain had passed, but wind still lashed branches against the sides of the mission.

Tse flicked a look to Rev. Abernathy, reentering with an armload of nightclothes, and shook his head. "The storm is over."

Esther tugged the blanket from behind them and held it out to Tse.

"Keep it, *Shideezhi*." He placed his hat on his head, wet strands of hair clinging to his neck below it, and strode to the door.

"Tse." Caroline stood.

He turned, meeting her eyes with his dark ones.

I'm so sorry ... about your job, about everything. And the children—surely Tse knew why they had run off, though she had her own suspicions. But she couldn't speak and ask as she wished, not with Rev. Abernathy here.

"Thank you." She hugged her elbows.

Tse nodded and left, the door clicking softly behind him.

Caroline turned back to the children, avoiding Rev. Abernathy's gaze. "Is the water hot?"

"Will be soon. Come on, Samuel." The little boy shrank against his sister, but Rev. Abernathy pried him away and led him down the hall toward the boys' washroom.

Caroline sighed. "Esther, I'll help you bathe."

The girl slipped from the chair and followed her silently.

After the bath, Caroline tucked Esther in bed with a hot water bottle, just as she had a few days earlier. How long ago that seemed. "Lie down, dear one."

"Miss Caroline ... " Esther hugged her knees.

"Yes?"

"I'm sorry."

"You went after your brother, then?" Caroline sank onto the bed beside her.

A tiny nod.

"Why didn't you tell us?"

Esther shrugged.

Surely there was more to this. Caroline leaned to hug the girl's stiff shoulders. "Thank the Lord you're both home safe."

But this wasn't home to these children, was it? No more than it was to her as yet. Home was the reason they had run off.

With no more information forthcoming, she kissed Esther's cheek and rose.

She closed the door of the girls' dormitory, her legs suddenly weak as a newborn goat's. Stumbling into the sitting room, she sank into the rocking chair and pressed the heels of her hands to her eyes.

Rev. Abernathy's step jolted her out of a near-doze, and she straightened. "Is he asleep?"

"Hope so." He sagged into another chair and leaned his elbows on his knees. "I know you hate to see the children punished, but there must be consequences for a stunt like this."

Caroline swallowed. "If you had not frightened them, I doubt they would have run off."

"If you had not taken them on that fool picnic, none of this would have happened."

Her lips tightened. Clamping her hands on her elbows, she rocked hard.

"Thank God for Tse, anyhow." Rev. Abernathy rubbed the back of his neck.

"Yet you sent him away." She halted the rocker and gripped the arms. "He needs this job."

"I haven't decided to fire him. I don't know yet." He slapped his hand down on his thigh. "Why should you care so much, anyway?"

Caroline stared at the tips of her muddy boots. Because it wasn't fair, nor just. Because Willis had affronted Tse's dignity and integrity, and did so nearly every day. Because Tse was a good and godly man. Because… She couldn't analyze her other reasons. Not now.

All she managed was a whispered, "Shall you dismiss me, as well?"

"No." Rev. Abernathy rubbed his forehead. "Nothing in me wants you to leave us. The children love you, and I…"

His words a week ago hung heavily in the air between them. Caroline stared at her fingers, twisting in her skirt.

"I frankly don't know how the school would survive without you." He cleared his throat. "But neither can I allow God's work to be undermined."

God's work… or his?

"Of course not." She fought the lump in her throat and pushed to her feet. "Good night."

He still sat by the fire, leaning his head on his hand.

In her little room, leaving the lamp lit for now, Caroline pulled the sheet up to her chin and gazed at the dancing flame within the slender glass shade.

How long ago she and Tse had loaded baskets into wagons, picnic bound, with bright-eyed boys and girls in velvet, calico, and deerskin, their chatter and song joining with the birds. Was it truly only that morning? The flame wavered and blurred, and she swiped her eyes with the back of her hand. The girls mustn't hear her cry.

Returning to the mission had jolted them all back to earth, that was certain. The confrontation with Rev. Abernathy… the storm… finding Esther and Samuel missing. The agonizing wait at the mission, then Tse's form emerging through the darkness, the children bundled on his horse's back. She shuddered, burrowing deeper under the covers. This night might well have ended in tragedy. Thank God for Tse, indeed.

Warmth curled through her middle as it had when they stood by the river, her hand clasped in his strong calloused one, his face so near she could hear his breathing. And the look in his coffee-hued eyes ... A tingle ran clear to her toes.

Caroline bolted upright, blew out the lamp, and lay down stiff, hugging her arms across her stomach. She couldn't be thinking this way about ... Tse. Her limbs trembled, and she rolled over, burying her face in the pillow. *Lord, it could never—we could never—no.*

She must have imagined that look in his eyes.

Someone was knocking, calling her, stealing her from a dream where Tse led her on his horse's back through a storm.

"Miss Haynes. We need you."

She rolled to her feet in the darkness and fumbled the door open, blinking at the sudden candlelight.

Rev. Abernathy shielded the flame with his hand, his face grave. "Samuel has taken ill."

CHAPTER TWENTY-SIX

Caroline hurried down the darkened hallway, following the flicker of Rev. Abernathy's candle and fumbling with the sash of her wrapper. They cut across the silent dining room, then through the sitting-room entrance into the reverend's own suite off the boys' dormitory.

Samuel's wheezing filled her ears as soon as she stepped through the door.

Still unsteady from sleep, Caroline knelt by the child's bedside and brushed back his damp hair. He lifted his head for paroxysmal coughing, his whole body jerking. She propped him up to breathe better. How could this have come on so quickly? Could it be croup?

Miss Spencer touched her shoulder. "We need boiling water for steam. Help me."

"When did it start?" Caroline followed the older woman into the kitchen, shivering despite the summer night. She pumped water into the kettle.

"Willis woke me half an hour ago. I believe Isaiah alerted him."

Caroline felt a rush of protectiveness. "He should have fetched me first."

"I am still headmistress of this school." Miss Spencer's tartness softened with her next words. "But I told him you would want to be wakened too."

Caroline lugged the kettle into Rev. Abernathy's room. She lifted it onto the small wood stove in the corner, usually only fired up in winter, then she dropped back by Samuel's side.

"What else should we do?" She enfolded his hands in hers. So cold they had been a few hours ago, now hot and dry. "We need a cool cloth to bring his fever down."

"My aunt is fetching her special cough syrup." Rev. Abernathy shifted the kettle toward the center of the stove and stepped nearer the bed, thrusting his hands in his dressing gown pockets. "A dose of that, some good steam to clear his breathing, and he should be on the mend."

Somehow his hearty tone rang hollow.

Samuel's head drooped on the pillow, eyes half open, his only movement the struggling rise and fall of his chest.

"It's my fault." Caroline touched his cheek. "If only he hadn't gotten so wet and chilled."

"Yes, well—he may be better by morning. These childhood night scares can reverse fast." He turned. "I'll get the wet cloth."

Caroline stroked Samuel's forehead, her own chest tightening. Despite her words, she doubted a swim in the river would have caused this, had it not been for getting caught in the storm afterwards. And that was Rev. Abernathy's fault for his harshness.

She pushed back the braid that had fallen over her shoulder and drew a steadying breath. The reverend was right on one thing, at least. She couldn't count the midnight scares she'd had with Benji or Toby, from croup to vomiting to high fevers. And as he'd said, most improved by morning.

Please God, let it be so.

Samuel did fall into a deep sleep before dawn. Though he breathed only a bit easier, his fever lowered, and Caroline sent Miss Spencer to bed while Rev. Abernathy caught a few winks on the sitting room sofa. Once the sun rose, the older boys fumbled through the chores. Tse did not appear.

Caroline sat with Samuel while the reverend led what she imagined to be a rather subdued Sunday service. She rocked beside the slumbering child, the soft wheeze in his chest keeping her alert as she tried to read her Bible.

"Miss Caro-line?"

"Yes, dear one?" She closed the book and reached for Samuel's hand.

A tight, barking cough jerked him up off the pillow. She settled him back after the hacking eased. "Let me fetch you a drink."

He sipped tea with honey, then lay back with a sigh that caught halfway on another cough.

"Can I get you anything else?" She laid her hand on his cheek. Warmer than it had been first thing that morning, though not as hot as in the night.

He fingered her sleeve. "*Shimá?*"

Her heart constricted, and she smoothed the backs of her fingers over his hot forehead. "Of course you want your mama." If only she could get her for him.

School lessons dragged the next two days. Caroline and Rev. Abernathy took turns moving between the classrooms and relieving Miss Spencer at Samuel's bedside. If he didn't exactly get worse, neither did he get better.

Caroline stared out the window of her own schoolroom late afternoon, turning a pencil between her fingers as she sat at her desk. She couldn't seem to sit completely still, despite the heat. Flies buzzed through the open windows, and the high collar of her shirtwaist stuck to her neck. Only a few more weeks of term, and the children would go home for the summer. Samuel would be well by then. Surely.

"Miss Caroline?"

Caroline shook her head slightly. "Yes, Anna?"

"Is it time for class dismissed?"

She glanced at the clock. The hands had ticked well past time—Willis must have forgotten to ring the bell. "I'm sorry, children. You may go."

Books shut, pencils clattered, boots padded out the door, and the usual chatter subdued. Pushing a damp strand of hair from her forehead, Caroline rose and crossed the floor to retrieve a dropped slate pencil here, an abandoned reader there. She paused by Samuel's empty seat. How could such a quiet little boy leave such a gap in the classroom? Rather like Tse left at the mission. Where was he, anyway? Had he taken Rev. Abernathy seriously? Picking up another reader, she flipped to the picture of the goat, tracing the sprightly line drawing with her finger.

"*Tł'ízí*," she whispered.

Please, Lord, make him well.

"What's troubling you, my son?"

Avoiding his father's gaze, Tse hefted another barrel of river water onto the bed of their wagon where his father stood. He took his hat off and wiped his brow, breathing hard.

"You've not gone to the mission now three days." His father settled the barrel into place, then climbed down beside Tse.

Tse sat against a barrel still on the ground to catch his breath and stared at the river. A dragonfly buzzed his nose. Every ripple of the water, every log, every quivering green leaf, was a punch in his gut, a reminder of the picnic, of Caroline—*Miss Haynes. Stop it.*

He stood and turned to lift another barrel.

"Tse." His father gripped his shoulder. "Tell me."

"Willis told me to leave."

"Why?"

"Because … " Because he and Miss Haynes had let the children wear Navajo clothes? Because he and Miss Haynes had been together at all? Because Tse offended him by his very existence these days? "He was angry. I do not know if he meant it."

Together they lifted the barrel and rolled it into place. Neither said more as they loaded the remainder of their water supply for the week.

"So, why don't you go back?" His father snapped the tailgate back into place.

"*Shizhé'é*—"

"Find out if he did mean it. Would that not be the thing to do?"

Tse glanced at his father, then back at the river. He was right, of course. Tse, as one who claimed to follow the true God, should have figured that out. But …

He gave the tailgate a final slap and rounded the corner of the wagon as his father climbed aboard. The lowering sun slanted between the trees, the mesas casting long shadows.

Tse swung onto the wagon seat beside his father. He clucked to the horses, keeping his gaze straight ahead.

Willis could have taken his words back when Tse had returned the children, if he had really wanted to. Of course, Tse hadn't lingered any longer than necessary. The look in Shashyáázh's eyes when he left him, like a puppy kicked by a beloved owner, wounded him still. Was that the real reason Tse hadn't gone back? Or was it pride, as his father seemed to think?

Or was it Miss Haynes?

He stomped that thought as soon as it formed.

Tse glanced at his father, now gazing ahead at the orange-streaked sky above the mesas. The lines drawing his forehead and eyes smote Tse in the chest. *Lord, forgive me. Let not my stubbornness cause my family more pain.*

He shifted the reins between his hands. "I will go back in the morning."

CHAPTER TWENTY-SEVEN

She couldn't get Samuel's fever down.

Caroline dipped her cloth in the bowl of cool water again and squeezed it out. After laying it on Samuel's forehead, she lifted the watch pinned to her bodice and leaned near the lamp to see the nickel-framed face. Nearly two in the morning.

She sponged the child's face, his neck, his hands. The heat from his body warmed the cloth within minutes, and she dunked it in the water again. Pushing up his nightshirt sleeves, she wiped his arms.

Samuel shivered but didn't waken. He hadn't opened his eyes since late yesterday afternoon.

Caroline shook down the thermometer and slid it under his tongue. Praying he wouldn't bite down on it, she waited, watching the mercury creep higher. She withdrew the thermometer and examined the reading under the lamplight. Her fingers tightened on the slender glass cylinder. Only once had Benji had a fever this high—three years ago, and it had sent him into a convulsion.

Caroline wrung out the cloth again. She pulled back the covers and unbuttoned Samuel's nightshirt to sponge his chest.

His skin held a sickly pallor beneath the brown. He shuddered at the cold touch and curled onto his side, his whole body spasming with coughs.

Caroline held the bowl close in case he vomited, but nothing came up. She almost wished it would. If only the phlegm would loosen.

Samuel rolled onto his back, and his eyes fluttered open, glassy and frightened.

Caroline redid his buttons, then laid her hand on his forehead and smiled at him. "Would you like a drink, sweet boy?" His skin almost burned her palm.

He moved his head slightly. Taking that as a nod, she lifted him higher on the pillows and held a cup of water to his lips.

One sip, and paroxysmal coughs ensued, with gasping, choking, and wheezing.

Caroline held him up against her, her heart thudding against his jerking ribcage. Dear Lord, was the child going to choke to death?

At last the hacking subsided into labored breaths, and Caroline laid him back on the pillow.

He lay still and limp, his eyes closed.

"I'll be right back." Caroline rose on trembling legs. Did he even hear? She smoothed back his damp hair, the whistling rattle of his lungs her only answer.

She slipped out into the sitting room, where Rev. Abernathy dozed in a chair by the darkened fireplace, one lamp dimly lighting the room.

At the door's click, he jerked awake with a snort, rubbing his hand across his eyes. "Ready for a break?"

"I'm going to fix another mustard plaster." Taking the lamp, she hurried past him and down the dark hallway to the kitchen.

The inside of her nose burned, watering her eyes as she mixed the ground mustard with flour and water and added vinegar. She spread it on a thin cloth and folded the edges over, then placed the whole mess in a bowl. Stepping to the sink, she pumped a little water to rinse her hands.

"How is he?" Rev. Abernathy's voice came from the doorway.

Caroline let go the pump handle and gripped the edge of the sink.

"You're exhausted. I'll take over for a while." He stepped up behind her and gently laid his hands on her shoulders.

Caroline pulled away. Clenching her upper arms, she shook her head. "He..." She pressed her lips together. "He doesn't sound good."

Rev. Abernathy rubbed the back of his neck and sighed. "I'll take a look at him."

Back in the sickroom, the reverend bent over Samuel, his ear to the boy's chest. After a moment he straightened and pulled the covers back over him. He laid his hand on Samuel's head, then stepped back.

"What do you think?" Caroline worried her lower lip.

"Go ahead with the mustard plaster." He left the room.

Was that all he was going to say? Caroline wanted to run after him, scream at him. Instead she clamped her jaw and sat on the bed beside Samuel. She undid his shirt again and laid the plaster on his chest, her own lungs tightening at the hollows around his collarbone every time he breathed. She covered the plaster with a piece of flannel and laid her hands atop it. *Please, Lord...* She bowed her head, unable to form more words.

"Miss Haynes."

She looked up to see Rev. Abernathy peeking his head in the doorway.

He beckoned.

With another glance at Samuel, she rose and slipped from the room.

He sat on the bench by the front door in the darkened dining room, tugging on his boots. "I'm going to Shiprock."

"He's bad, isn't he?"

"I've seen worse." Rev. Abernathy stood and settled his hat on his head. "But maybe I can catch the doctor before he leaves on his morning rounds. Worth a try, anyway."

He lit a lantern. "Don't worry about lessons. The children can do chores and study on their own for this one morning."

Departing from schedule? Rev. Abernathy?

He unlatched the door and pushed it open, spilling summer moonlight into the room. He hesitated, and Caroline sensed his eyes seeking hers.

"He's in God's hands." With one last glance, Willis clicked the door shut.

She shivered. The darkness pressed around her, full of night sounds through the open windows. Crickets chirped, frogs peeped. Rev. Abernathy's boot steps faded across the yard. The barn door creaked open. After a few minutes, hoof beats clopped, picking up speed as they turned onto the road.

A long ride, to Shiprock.

Caroline turned back into the lamplight of the sitting room. She straightened a chair, adjusted the lamp wick. Then bracing herself, she slipped back into the sickroom. Her stomach relaxed a bit at the sight of Samuel sleeping quietly. She lifted the mustard plaster to see the skin reddening underneath, showing it had done its job. Removing the remedy, she wiped Samuel down again and rubbed his chest with camphorated oil.

Deep in a feverish stupor, he did not stir.

She slumped into the bedside chair and rested her head in her hands. Miss Spencer had said to wake her for a shift before morning, but Caroline wouldn't be able to sleep anyway. The elderly lady might as well rest.

Caroline rubbed her palms across her eyes. At least the doctor was coming, Lord willing. He would be able to help. Of course he would. She steepled her fingers against her lips.

The tiny hands on her watch ticked away the night, hours of cold cloths and burning skin and Samuel's agonizing hacking that jerked her guiltily from half-dozing dreams.

At last, gray dawn crept over the mission grounds beyond the bedroom window. A lone bird chirped, then another. And the doctor's motorcar clattered into the yard.

Caroline drew what felt like her first deep breath in days.

The doctor, a tired-faced man with a short gray beard and kind eyes, shut himself in the sickroom with Samuel and Miss Spencer.

Caroline wandered the sitting room for what seemed like hours, twisting her hands. A rooster crowed from the barnyard. Rev. Abernathy sat at his desk in the corner, staring at a pile of school papers.

What could be taking so long?

The door opened. Rev. Abernathy stood, and Caroline stopped pacing.

The doctor eased the door shut behind him. He set his bag on a side table, rearranging the contents.

Caroline gripped her elbows. "How is he?"

"Got a sick little fellow on your hands." The doctor clicked his bag shut and glanced between them. "He been failing before this?"

"No." Rev. Abernathy's reply came quickly.

Caroline shot him a glance. "He hasn't been eating well for some time. I only found out a week ago."

"Never adjusted, eh?"

Rev. Abernathy folded his arms.

"I've left some medicine with Miss Spencer. Hard to know how much good it'll do." The doctor put on his hat. "Got to get back to town, got a young mother due with twins. Keep doing what you're doing. I'll try to get back sometime next week, but the turning point will probably come before then, one way or the other." He headed for the door.

"But what else can we do?" Caroline followed him. "What about the hospital in Farmington?"

"I wouldn't move him. Nope, worst thing you could do."

"Should we send for his parents?" Caroline twisted her locket.

The doctor sighed. "That'd be up to the reverend."

"I don't think that will be necessary." Rev. Abernathy stepped forward. "Thanks for coming, doctor."

"Best of luck to you folks." The doctor pushed open the door. "From past experience with these boarding school young ones, you're going to need it."

The door shut. The doctor's footsteps tramped down the porch steps, then the rumble of his motorcar set the chickens to squawking.

Caroline stared at the closed door, clenching her locket so hard she had to force her fingers to loosen lest she break the chain.

"Well." Rev. Abernathy spoke from behind her. "Guess I'll see if my aunt has given him any of that medicine yet."

"Why won't you send for his parents?"

He sighed.

"You hear how he keeps crying for his mother." She faced him. "She would want to know. This isn't right."

"I'll tell you what wouldn't be right." Rev. Abernathy's face hardened. "To hand this child over to his parents, who would only take him to their heathen medicine man and make him worse. That wouldn't be right."

He stepped closer to her. "Don't pretend you understand these people better than I, no matter what Tse may have told you. I know what I'm doing, and my word stands." He spun on his heel and strode away, closing the sickroom door behind him.

Caroline pressed her fingers to the bridge of her nose and squeezed her eyes shut. Tse . . . if only she could talk to him, see the gentleness in his eyes, hear his steady voice. Maybe he would know what to do.

A squeak of floorboards jerked her back to reality, and she looked up to see a slender figure slip away down the hall.

"Esther?" Caroline hurried after her, catching up almost at the door of the dormitory. Gently taking hold of the girl's shoulders, she turned Esther to face her. Her heart broke at the tears tracking down the young cheeks.

"He's dying, isn't he?" Esther's voice cracked. "My brother is dying."

"No!" Caroline tightened her hands on the girl's shoulders. "No. We are doing all we can for him. The doctor says he may start to get better soon." She wouldn't think about the other possibility behind "turning point."

"But he won't. I know he won't." Wresting away from Caroline, Esther tore open the dormitory door.

"Esther—"

The door slammed.

Caroline let her hands fall to her sides. So much for her comforting skills.

"What happened?"

She turned to see Rev. Abernathy, shadowed in the sunlight at the end of the hallway.

"Esther. She thinks … "

"Thinks what?"

"That her brother is dying."

The reverend's shoulders sagged slightly. Running his hand along the doorway lintel, he turned back.

"Rev. Abernathy." Caroline followed him through the dining room and into the sitting room.

"Yes?" He sat down at his desk and rummaged through papers.

"What did the doctor mean, 'from past experience'?"

Rev. Abernathy kept stacking the pages, lesson plans for that day.

"Tell me!"

He sighed. "We usually lose a few children each year. Some just never manage to adjust."

"What?" Caroline gripped the back of a chair.

"Government schools lose far more, with their high occupancies. Our rate isn't too bad."

Not too bad? Caroline had never excelled at arithmetic, but she ran the figures in her head. A few—so three children out of thirty students? Ten percent a year?

The conversation with the girls at the river seared her memory. Dorcas's little sister in the fall... that was one.

And now Samuel. Who would be next?

Her stomach roiled. She turned and ran.

"Miss Haynes—we need to start classes."

But she didn't look back.

The buckling nibbled her fingers, perhaps tasting the tears on them. Crouching behind the goat pen outside the barn, where she couldn't be seen from the main mission building, Caroline framed the comical little face between her hands and rubbed the silky ears. The kid lipped the cuff of her sleeve, turning the trim green with moist alfalfa dust.

Caroline sniffed hard, but still the tears ran. She couldn't seem to halt them. Once again, someone she loved was slipping away, and there was nothing she could do to stop it. Nothing at all.

A sob ripped through her throat, and she tried to muffle it with the back of her hand.

The buckling cocked his head and stared at her. Beside him, his sister nosed through the fence and gently nuzzled the front of Caroline's dress.

She laid her cheek against the soft nose. This was the one who had broken into the classroom that day, who made Samuel smile and gave her the key to the boy's heart. Now that little boy lay fighting for every breath, without even the comfort of his mother's arms.

Caroline smacked a wooden fence slat, skittering the kids away and sending a splinter into her finger.

In God's hands. Why did people only say that when they seemed to have given up hope?

The mission door slapped, and Caroline looked up to see the children filing out, down the steps and across the yard to the school building. She and Rev. Abernathy had combined classes the last few days so just one of them could teach, the other taking turns with Samuel.

How ironic for Esther to still be kept from her brother, even now that the older and younger students were mixed.

Caroline stayed huddled low as the children, followed by Willis, disappeared inside the schoolroom doors. Then she stood and drew a shuddering breath.

She should go inside, see if Miss Spencer needed anything, though Caroline had sat with Samuel half the night. But she couldn't, yet. Couldn't go back in that room where Samuel tossed in delirium. Couldn't face Miss Spencer or Willis, who knew children came to this school and died and did nothing to make it stop.

She rubbed her wrist across her eyes.

"Miss Haynes?"

She started and turned.

"Tse?" With a glad little leap of her heart, she stepped toward him, standing there behind her with a frown between his eyes. "What are you doing here?"

"I . . ." He shook his head slightly. "I came to talk with Rev. Abernathy." He stepped near and brushed her elbow with his fingertips. "What's wrong?"

The tenderness in his voice, the gentle touch, blurred her eyes yet again. "He's so sick." She pressed her knuckle to her lips.

"Who? Willis?"

"No." She sniffed. "Your cousin, Samuel." She tasted shame that she couldn't remember the little boy's Navajo name.

"What—when?" Tse dropped his hand to his side.

"He fell ill the night after the storm. Chilled, I suppose, though I don't think he'd been well for weeks." She twisted her fingers together. "Now he can barely breathe. And Rev. Abernathy—he won't send for his parents."

Tse took a step back from her, a look in his eyes she'd never seen before.

"He says they would just take him to the medicine man. But I keep thinking … they would want to know."

Without a word, Tse spun around and took off across the yard.

CHAPTER TWENTY-EIGHT

Not Shashyáázh. Not his little brother.

Not again.

Tse's legs pumped faster until he broke into a run. *Dear God, please. If You have any pity on me, on my family, my people, please.* He leapt the porch steps and burst into the mission, the door banging against the wall. Breathing hard, he took in the dining room. Empty.

Miss Spencer hobbled from the sitting room, a medicine bottle in hand. She stared at him. "Peter? Mercy, you frightened me. Have you seen Miss Haynes?"

"Where's Willis?" He didn't care he wasn't supposed to call him that.

"I believe he's in the schoolroom. Why?"

Tse glanced past her, to the open doorway that must lead to Shashyáázh. Without asking permission, he stepped past the headmistress and into Willis's room, falling to trembling knees beside his cousin's bed.

Tse laid his hand on Shashyáázh's burning forehead. His throat closed at the child's pallor, his labored breathing. "There, little brother," he whispered, the words rasping. "I'm here." Shashyáázh lay still, too still, but for the labored rise and fall of his thin chest. He gave no sign he even heard Tse's voice.

Tse sat back on his heels and set his jaw. He ached to stay with his cousin, but—he wasn't who Shashyáázh really needed right now. And it might soon be too late, just as it had been nearly eight years ago. Every sign told him that.

Miss Spencer hovered near his shoulder. "Peter—"

"Excuse me." With one last squeeze to his cousin's small hand, Tse stood and wheeled out of the room, jogging out the door and down the steps, veering toward the schoolhouse. He halted before the closed door of the older children's schoolroom, catching his breath. Suddenly he couldn't lift his fist to rap. What would he do, just barge in there and expect Willis to listen to him? The memories pressed in, and he was a desperate boy again, pacing outside Rev. Spencer's door, trying to work up the courage to knock, to plead with him.

It hadn't worked.

Tse squeezed his eyes shut. *Lord, please.* He wiped his palms on his breeches and knocked.

He couldn't fail again.

At no response, Tse squeaked open the front door, then that of the cloakroom, and stepped into the class area.

Willis looked up from his desk and raised his eyebrows. The children, squeezed two or three to a desk in the one room, turned to stare.

Willis rose, his gaze locked on Tse. "Eyes on your work, students. I'll be right back."

Tse followed Willis into the little cloakroom.

Shutting the door behind them, Willis faced him. "So, I thought you would be Miss Haynes. Glad to see you here, though. Ready to apologize and move on?"

"I heard about my cousin." Tse clenched his jaw. "And I just saw him."

Something flickered in Willis's eyes. "He's getting the best of care here."

"So you have learned nothing from the past?" Tse's voice shook, but he couldn't help it. "You do not think he has the right to be held by his mother, his father? You do not think they have the right to know?"

"Listen." Willis stepped closer.

"That's the trouble with you *bilagáanas*. You never remember!"

"Hold it." Willis grasped his shoulders, as they used to do to each other as boys, in fun or when trying to make a point in an argument. "Listen, Tse. This has nothing to do with what happened back then."

"Yes, it does." Tse put a hand on Willis's chest and shoved him away. "Are you going to just let this child die like my brother?"

Willis froze. Their eyes locked.

Tse's hands trembled. He could only hear their heavy breathing.

Willis shook his head. "Listen—"

Tse slapped the wall. "No, you listen for a change! Why do you never listen? When will anyone ever listen to my people?"

"Stop it." Willis's voice sliced the air. "You'll frighten the children."

After a moment, the reverend stepped nearer and laid his hand on Tse's shoulder. "Believe me, I'm acting solely in your cousin's best interests. Anything you might try to do would only harm him. That is why I must forbid it."

Tse shrugged Willis's hand off. He read the warning in his old friend's eyes.

"Now." Willis stepped back. "If you want to head down to the barn, there's plenty that could use your attention."

So that's what Willis thought, then? Just pretend nothing had happened, give him his job back, and he would be happy?

Turning, he fumbled for the doorknob. The door crashed open into the sunlight.

With a stifled shriek, Miss Haynes jumped out of the way.

Tse charged down the steps without looking at her. He didn't even care if she had heard them.

"There you are, Miss Haynes." Willis's voice faded behind him as Tse headed for the barn. He thought he heard Willis ask her to check on Samuel.

Shashyáázh.

Tse flung open the barn door and felt his way through the musty dimness to the tack room. Sinking down on the cot where he had slept the week before, he buried his face in his hands. He stayed there a long time, unable to even form the words to pray.

The door creaked. Tse lifted his head to see Miss Haynes peering in, her forehead pinched.

His gut twisted, and he looked away. He didn't want her pity.

"May I come in?"

But neither could he refuse her entry. He was too Navajo for that, hospitality too ingrained in his blood.

He tipped his head.

She stepped inside, her footfalls hesitant, and sat on the edge of the trunk where they had found the children's clothing before the trip to the river.

Was that really less than a week ago?

"I never knew you had a brother."

He dropped his hands between his knees and stared at them. So, she had heard.

"What happened?"

She didn't want to know. They never really wanted to know—they might ask questions, but usually only when they thought they already knew the answers.

A mouse scratched in the barn wall. A goat bleated from the barnyard.

At last Tse looked up at her, into those gray eyes.

She did want to know.

He let out a long, shuddering sigh and rubbed his hand across his eyes. "He was the youngest in our family." His throat threatened to close, and he swallowed hard. "He first came to school several years after Dólii and I started. Then he never adjusted. Rev. Spencer caned him for speaking our language and he..." Tse shifted his jaw, fighting the burning in his eyes, in his throat. "He never talked much after that. When a diphtheria epidemic came through the area, he was one of the first to get it."

The mouse scratched again, then silence hung in the hay-dusted air.

"Rev. Spencer would not send for our parents. He would not even let me see him, though I forced my way in once. Miss Spencer might have relented, I think, but she always yielded to her brother. I finally ran away to get my parents myself, but Willis..." He clenched and unclenched his fists. "Willis came after me, found me, made me come back." He gave a humorless half laugh. "I'd taught him to track too well. Then it was too late." He caught his tongue between his teeth.

"What was his name?"

He glanced up at Miss Haynes. A tear tracked down her face.

He swallowed. "Nataani." He drew a long breath, rubbing his hands on his knees. "It's not that I think the *Hatááłii*'s chants would have helped him, though they use herbal remedies too. But I still wonder if my mother might have, somehow. She knows much of healing, but mostly, she just would have been there. You know?"

Miss Haynes looked down and nodded.

Tse's gaze fell on her locket. She did know. She had lost her mother. She knew what it meant to grieve the loss of one dearly loved. No wonder she always seemed to care more than Willis did.

"I don't mean to trouble you." Or maybe he did. Past time someone was troubled about what went on around here. Tse pressed his hands on his knees and stood.

"I wanted to know." She wiped her cheeks, then pressed her fingers together beneath her chin. "Tse … I'm so sorry."

He looked away from the tears in her eyes. Had a white person ever spoken those words to him before? But what difference did it make?

Tse began to gather the few items he had left in the tack room the week before, bundling them together.

"Where are you going?" Miss Haynes stood slowly.

"It is too late for my brother." After smoothing the blanket over the cot, Tse stepped to the door. "But it may not be too late for Shashyáázh."

He glanced to meet Miss Haynes's eyes and saw understanding dawn.

"This will mean the end of your job for sure." She stepped closer to him.

Her nearness constricted his chest. He took a step back. "I think that has already come. But it doesn't matter. We must obey God rather than men." The tightness that had clenched his middle since that night he brought the children back—no, since he drove the wagon to help gather them at the beginning of term—eased even as he spoke. Yes, this was what he must do. This was right, let the consequences be what they may. *Thank You, Lord.*

Miss Haynes drew a breath and lifted her chin. "Then I'm going with you."

CHAPTER TWENTY-NINE

Caroline handed Tse a bridle. He worked swiftly, silently, in the dimness of the stall, saddling a mare for her, cinching the girth, buckling the straps. His horse stood ready outside.

Her nose still clogged, but her eyes were dry. At last, she had something to do. If only Rev. Abernathy wouldn't come out, wouldn't see them, before they were gone. She had failed Samuel already— failed to find out what was really wrong, failed to realize he was distressed enough to run away. She couldn't do it again. *Hurry, Tse.*

He led the horse into the main barn and checked the saddle girth, then lifted each hoof, his movements sure yet gentle.

How could he even stand to be at the mission, to work for Rev. Abernathy? His little brother... sickened by being separated from all that he knew and exposed to foreign food and surroundings, deprived of even the comfort of his mother's arms for his last breaths. A shiver shook her despite the stuffy heat. What kind of Christ's love was that?

Tse finished examining the last hoof and let it down. Shifting, the horse tossed her head. Tse ran his hand down her mane and took the bridle.

"Are you sure you want to do this, Miss Haynes?" He glanced at her. "You may not have a job come morning either."

"Caroline."

"What?" He frowned.

"It's not right for me to call you by your first name while you call me Miss Haynes. It has bothered me for some time." She realized that as she spoke. "Would you rather I called you Mr. Tsosie?"

Tse coughed a laugh. "I wouldn't know who you were talking to."

"Then please."

Tse tipped his head. "Are you sure then—Caroline?"

She nodded. The gentleness in his voice nearly started the tears again. But she was sure. It would be better if one of the *bilagáana* missionaries invited Samuel's parents too, wouldn't it?

They said no more as Tse led the mare out through the narrow back door of the barn. He bent for her to mount with a foot on his clasped hands, then swung onto his own horse.

He touched it into a brisk lope, crouching low over its neck like a *Diné* warrior of old.

Caroline cantered behind, a little thrill tickling her spine as they rounded a bluff. They had done it. *Samuel—Shashyáázh.* In her mind, she tasted the Navajo syllables Tse had spoken, the child's name. *We will get your* Shimá *for you after all.*

Tse did not slow for some time. At last, well beyond sight or sound of the mission, he pulled his horse back to a walk and let both mounts catch their breath.

Overhead the sky arched deep blue, clouds building in pristine piles that could turn to thunderheads late in the day.

How could the world be so beautiful, when a child lay fighting for his life? Caroline urged her mare on.

The sun beat down as they rode south, circling rock formations, skirting arroyos, once pausing to rest beneath a lone piñon tree. How long had it been—an hour? Two? Stray tendrils of hair stuck to Caroline's neck as they headed back into the sunshine. Her unshielded face scorched.

Tse nudged his horse nearer hers. Removing his own hat, he held it out.

Her throat closed at the kindness in his eyes, but she gently pushed away the stiff felt brim. "I am all right."

"Your face looks like a ripe peach." He leaned over the space between their mounts and plunked the hat atop her head.

Her cheeks warmer than ever despite the brim's shade, Caroline adjusted the hat. "Thank you." The scent of his hair, embedded in the wool, teased her nose. "And thank you for letting me come."

"Why did you?" He scanned the desert around them.

"I thought if one of the missionaries … perhaps that Willis … "

"No. Here, to the *Dinétah*. Why did you come?"

Caroline swallowed. How to answer that?

Birds rose in a black cloud, dipping toward the green smudge of trees that marked the river to their right.

She watched them swoop and rise. "I'm afraid wanting to get away from home was part of it. And a childish fantasy, perhaps, wanting to be a heroine, to bring the light of the Gospel to the *heathens*. She shook her head. "Lately I've been feeling any benefit the Gospel might bring here is thwarted by how we carry it."

"Not fully." Tse blew out a breath. "Human mistakes may hinder the light, yes, but they cannot completely block it. God is bigger than that."

Then why did He allow so much hurt? She tried to squelch the thought, but it was there.

"Why do you still believe, after all this?" She did not explain, but by the glance Tse gave her, he knew what she meant.

Tse rode quiet a moment, then rubbed the side of his nose. "The night after Nataani died, I ran out to the desert. I threw myself on the ground, raging, shouting at God, that if He would do this, I wanted no part of Him." He swallowed. "But I … it may sound strange, but I met Jesus there. It was a bit like the vision quests my father told me of, but I saw Him, suffering on the cross, taking my griefs and sorrows on Himself as well as my sin. And I saw Him, alive, and holding Nataani's hand in His pierced one."

Caroline couldn't take her eyes from Tse's face. Emotion clogged her throat.

He glanced at her with a half smile. "I couldn't turn my back on Jesus. Not after encountering Him like that."

She sat quiet a moment. "I understand." Even if so many questions remained.

A breeze gentled the heat's fierceness as they turned west. The sun had begun its journey down the sky by the time they came in sight of the Begay family camp, two hogans huddled near a corral and a garden patch green with cornstalks and pumpkin vines.

Tse pulled his horse up and scanned the land.

"What's wrong?" Caroline halted her mount beside his.

"Wagon's gone."

She hadn't thought what they would do if no one was home.

Tse loped his horse up to the corral and swung off.

Caroline guided her mount after him, her stomach tensing now that they had actually arrived. Perhaps she should have let Tse come alone.

He caught her horse's bridle and tethered it to the corral fence along with his horse, then caught her as she slid down.

For an instant he stood, his strong hands still encircling her ribcage, a strange look on his face as he stared down at her. Then, with a quick movement, he released her and turned to head for the hogan.

Her heart skittering, Caroline stood by her horse, unsure whether to follow or wait. At a call, she glanced over her shoulder.

A young woman—Caroline recognized her as the children's mother—emerged from the cornfield. She wore a cradleboard on her back.

Had Esther and Samuel gained a new sibling since the start of term? Caroline tried to remember whether the mother had appeared with child back in January.

"*Ya'at'eeh.*" The woman glanced from Tse to Caroline, then back again.

Stepping near her, Tse spoke to her in Navajo. They both glanced back at Caroline, then the mother spoke to Tse.

Caroline nibbled her lip.

The mother ducked into the hogan with her basket. Tse walked back to Caroline.

"Kai's husband is cutting wood with my father." He fingered his headband. "I have not told her yet, but if they do not come soon, I will."

Suddenly remembering, Caroline lifted his hat from her head and held it out. "Here. Thank you."

Tse took it and absently turned the brim in his hands.

Caroline's chest tightened as Kai stepped from the hogan once more. A mother shouldn't have to hear such news alone...though by the pinch between her eyes, she had guessed something of it already.

At the rattle of wheels, Caroline spun to see a red-wheeled wagon laden with wood appear over a rocky crest, two men perched on the seat.

Tse said something under his breath and half ran to meet them.

Glancing at Kai, Caroline offered a tentative smile, but the woman stepped forward, keeping her gaze fixed on Tse. The baby on her back opened his eyes and blinked sleepily.

In spite of the twist in her heart, Caroline smiled at the little one. Did Samuel even know he had become a big brother?

The men clambered from the wagon. Tse spoke a few words to a gray-haired man who must be his father, then walked with the younger man toward them.

Samuel's father glanced from Tse to Caroline. He gripped his belt. "Something wrong? My children?" His English halted and stopped.

Tse drew a breath and glanced at Caroline.

The pain in his eyes made her wince. But she couldn't tell them for him.

So he did. Shadows darkened their faces. Kai stepped to her husband and gripped his arm, though otherwise they showed no outer sign of alarm.

But Caroline had seen that look in a mother's eyes before—the same look Mama had worn when Toby developed a horrible case of croup at age two. The look of a mother afraid for her child's life.

The parents spoke now, quietly together, then to Tse. After a few moments, Tse stepped to Caroline's side, his face drained.

"His father will come." He still turned his hat in his hands, as if he didn't know he held it. "But the grandmother is ill also, in that hogan there." He indicated the smaller dwelling with his head. "Kai cannot leave her."

"But she has to. Samuel has been crying for her so. He..." She clenched her fingers together. "If she doesn't come..."

"I know." Tse rubbed his hand through his hair. "I offered to stay, but she says Dezbah needs a woman. At least his father will come."

And hopefully Willis will let him in. The understanding lay between them, unspoken.

Caroline swallowed a thought, but it bobbed up again. She glanced to Samuel's mother, who stood twisting her thumb between the fingers of her other hand. How could even Willis turn a distressed mother away?

Well, perhaps he would, but they must try, whatever it took.

Caroline drew a breath. "Perhaps I could stay."

Tse stopped twisting his hat. His eyes widened.

"Ask him." She nodded toward Mr. Begay.

Tse opened his mouth as if to speak to her, but instead nodded and turned to Samuel's father.

They conferred a moment, while Caroline gazed out across the desert, turning bronze and golden green in the lowering sun. What had she done? But it would be worth it, if...

"Miss Hay—Caroline?"

She turned back.

Tse stepped close, a softness in his face. "They have agreed."

Her heart sped even as she drew a breath of relief. Samuel would have his *shimá* at last.

Samuel's father held out his hand and said something that must have meant thanks. Caroline blinked back a burning in her eyes as she grasped his work-roughened palm.

"They will tell Dezbah, then we will leave you. My father will drive us." Tse followed Caroline's gaze to the older man still standing by the wagon. With a hand to her elbow, he guided her forward. "Come and meet him."

Why did her insides explode into a swarm of butterflies?

Tse's father uncrossed his arms and stepped forward to meet them.

"*Shizhé'é*, this is..." Tse quirked an eyebrow at her, and Caroline gave a tiny nod. "Caroline. Caroline, my father."

The man grasped her hand in his, searching her face. "*Ya'at'eeh.*"

Though his dark eyes pierced, when she managed to meet them, she saw kindness there. The butterflies quieted a bit.

"*Ya'at'eeh.*" She hoped she got the tones right this time.

The man's eyes lightened with surprise, and he said something to Tse.

"He says he is glad to meet you." Tse scratched his neck. "He says I have spoken well of you."

He had? Heat flamed Caroline's face, then traveled down to curl gently through her middle. She squeezed the older man's hand before releasing it. "Please tell him I am honored to meet him as well. And that he has a fine son."

Did red darken Tse's neck too? It was hard to tell beneath the golden brown of his skin. But Tse met her eyes a moment, held them despite what he'd told her about eye contact in Navajo culture. And looking into their warm brown depths, Caroline found it hard to breathe.

At voices, she broke her gaze away and caught a keen look from Tse's father. Willing her cheeks to cool, she turned to see the parents hurrying toward them.

Samuel's father hoisted himself into the wagon while his wife spoke to Tse.

Tse turned to Caroline. "Kai will take you to her mother now."

Caroline's heartbeat quickened. "But how will I communicate with ... " She searched for the grandmother's name.

"Dezbah speaks English."

Caroline stared at him. At his gentle push, she followed Kai to the little hogan.

The young woman lifted the rug covering the doorway and tipped her head for Caroline to follow.

She drew a breath and ducked through the opening.

At first she blinked in the darkness. The only light came through a hole in the roof above a small wood stove. Gradually she made out wooden crates, baskets, and rolled bedding stacked neatly against the six chinked log walls.

Against the north side lay a figure on a sheepskin under a Navajo blanket. Kai knelt and spoke softly to her mother.

Dezbah lifted her head, and Caroline recognized the woman's lined face from when she had shaken her stick at the missionaries the day they collected the children. Now she pursed her lips at Caroline and spoke sharply to her daughter.

Kai replied, her voice insistent, and Dezbah at last waved her hand and fell back on her sheepskin. Samuel's mother rose, sent Caroline a slight smile, and slipped out of the hogan.

Dezbah lay on her side, facing the wall.

Caroline hugged herself. *Now what, Lord?*

A shaft of sunbeam shone in as someone lifted the rug door again.

Tse. She hurried to him. If only he could stay too.

"Someone will come to relieve you, probably tomorrow." He glanced at Dezbah, then touched Caroline's arm. "Thank you for doing this. You will be all right?"

She nodded. "Go with God."

"You too." With a gentle squeeze on her arm, he dropped the rug between them, snuffing the hogan into darkness once more. After a moment, wagon wheels rumbled, then faded.

Caroline turned to find Dezbah gazing at her. The soft wisps of white hair about her wrinkled cheeks contrasted with the accusation in her eyes.

Caroline stepped to the woman's pallet. "*Ya'at'eeh*, Dezbah. I am Caroline Haynes."

Dezbah studied Caroline's face, her nose pinching inward as if sensing a vile odor. After a moment, she shook her head and rolled over to face the wall once more.

Caroline swallowed and glanced up at the roof hole. Late golden sunshine still beamed through.

It would be a long night.

CHAPTER THIRTY

"What in heaven's name?"

"Watch your language, Willis." Tse jumped from the back of the covered wagon and stood aside to let Kai and her husband climb down. His gut tightened as he headed up the steps.

The reverend stood frozen on the porch, jaw jutting hard, eyes icy blue.

"Willis—"

"*Rev. Abernathy*," his friend ground out. "And did I not make myself extremely clear about..." He shot a glance at the couple standing below.

"Is my cousin still alive?" Tse gripped the railing.

Willis hesitated. "Yes."

Thank You, Lord.

A dark-blue blur darted past, nearly knocking Tse off the steps, and Shándíín flung herself at her parents. Tse's throat squeezed as the family held each other. Kai lowered the cradleboard for her daughter to see, and Shándíín caressed the baby's cheek, his fluff of dark hair.

Tse turned to Willis. "They have a right to be here." He met his gaze straight on, resisting the temptation to back up.

Willis's face didn't soften a morsel. He stepped to the railing and looked down at Shashyáázh's parents. "Mr. and Mrs. Begay, I regret you have made this unnecessary trip."

Tse stepped up behind him on the porch. Had he forgotten how limited their English was? Shándíín had taught them a little, but still.

"I'm afraid we cannot permit—"

"Willis."

Tse turned to see Miss Spencer standing in the doorway.

"Let them in."

"But, Aunt." Willis looked from her to the Begays and back again.

"Come in, Mr. and Mrs. Begay." Miss Spencer limped out onto the porch, holding the door wide.

Gently setting Shándíín aside, Kai and her husband mounted the steps, not looking at Willis or even Tse.

Willis stepped after them, pausing for an instant beside Tse. "You're fired," he said under his breath.

The words, not unexpected, still hit deep in Tse's chest. The door slammed behind the group.

Tse inhaled through his nose. So. That was that.

He trudged down the steps. Shándíín stood at the bottom, wide eyed. He touched her shoulder briefly, not looking at his father, still perched on the wagon seat. The horses tossed their heads and snorted. They would need water, in this heat. No telling how long they might be here.

Tse approached the team, patted their necks, and began unhitching them to lead to the watering trough.

His father clambered down, and they worked at the harness in silence for a moment.

At last his father spoke. "They let the parents go in. That's good."

The Navajo soothed Tse's ears.

Unhooking the wagon tongue from the team, his father lowered it to the ground, then straightened, standing between the horses.

"What did Rev. Abernathy say to you, my son?"

Tse let the horse closest to him nibble the front of his tunic, then rubbed its velvety muzzle between his hands. "I'm sorry." His throat tightened. "I lost my job." Regained and lost again, all in one day.

His father said nothing as they led the team to the trough, as the horses ducked their noses into the water and drank, lifting their heads to blow and spray water droplets. The lowering sun shimmered on the water's rippled surface.

As they turned to lead the horses back, his father reached out and clasped Tse's shoulder, his grip warm and firm. "You did right."

The weight lightened in Tse's chest.

"Ouch." The hot lid burned Caroline's fingers as she tried to snatch it off the boiling-over pot. Letting the lid clatter onto the hogan's dirt floor, she held her hand to her mouth, fighting the stinging in her eyes. How was she supposed to cook on an old metal tub turned over a fire, anyway? At least that was what Dezbah's stove looked like to her. No doubt she should be glad it wasn't an open fire.

"Can't you *bilagáanas* do anything?" A muttering from the figure on the sheepskin.

Caroline gritted her teeth, shielding her hand with her skirt to set the lid back on the pot of boiling mutton. Perhaps leaving it ajar would help. She pushed the pan to what she guessed might be a cooler part of the stove and set about cutting the potatoes she had found to add to the stew.

At last the white chunks bobbed with the meat. Caroline wiped her hands on her skirt and pasted on a smile before turning to Dezbah. "The stew won't be ready for a while. Can I do anything for you until then?"

"You and your kind have already done more than we can ever recover from." The elderly woman shook with coughing, a deep, dryer cough than her grandson's.

She should be propped up. Caroline knelt and reached for the woman's shoulder.

"Don't touch me." Dezbah threw her arm out, nearly striking Caroline in the face.

Caroline fell back on her rear, then scrambled to her feet, her face burning. "I only meant to help you."

Dezbah hacked into a scrap of cloth, then rolled to face the wall again.

Caroline turned and stirred the stew hard. If the woman didn't want help, she wouldn't get it. Why did she think Caroline had offered to stay with her, anyway? To rob her or something? Broth splattered onto the stovetop, the droplets hissing. She halted her stirring and rubbed her forehead. What was she doing? Not turning the other cheek, that seemed certain.

She twirled the spoon a moment, then laid it down. "Dezbah." She turned, smoothing her skirt with her fingers. "Have I done something to upset you?"

"Weren't you with them that took my grandson away?" Dezbah spoke without turning her head.

"But I love your grandson. And we've been caring for him as best we can." She stepped closer to the sheepskin pallet. "I don't understand why you're so angry at me."

Silence hung a moment. Then Dezbah rolled over with a thump. "You have taken my mother, my son—now my grandson. And you don't understand?"

"What?" Caroline's fingers clenched her skirt. What was she talking about?

Dezbah gave a half laugh. "You understand nothing." She turned her face away, her frail shoulders trembling.

Shaken, Caroline turned back to the stove and stared at the jiggling pot lid.

Dezbah refused to eat supper that evening. Crouching on the ground near the stove, Caroline forced a few mouthfuls herself and then pushed her bowl aside. She hadn't cooked the mutton right, rendering it tough and slimy. She hugged her arms around her knees and gazed at the flickering yellow light of a kerosene lamp set on a wooden crate.

Dezbah coughed again, her breathing wheezy. Caroline glanced back at her and chewed her lip. Surely broth would help the woman, if she could just get a little in her. Rising, Caroline dipped some into a bowl and made her way to the pallet.

"Will you try a little—?"

"No." Dezbah turned her face from the spoon. "I don't want it."

"And I don't want your family to think I didn't even try to feed you." Caroline sighed and clinked the spoon back in the bowl.

The two of them sat in the near darkness, so close yet so distant, Dezbah's back a barrier between them. The fire crackled faintly within the stove. Far away, coyotes yipped.

"Will you tell me what you were speaking of earlier?" Caroline almost wished to bite the words back. Yet part of her yearned to know. "About your mother, and your son?"

Dezbah lay so still that Caroline wondered if she had fallen asleep.

Then, with a rattling sigh, the woman lifted a hand to the side of her face, shifting the fire-lit shadows. "You really don't know?"

Caroline shook her head.

"You heard of Kit Carson?"

"Wasn't he—a soldier, or colonel? A scout?"

Dezbah rolled half toward her and lay silent a moment, staring at the ceiling. "I was young like you when your government decided the Navajo needed to be subdued once for all. They blamed the raiding parties of some *Diné* on all of us, and their allies, the Utes, were our enemies. So Kit Carson—Red Shirt, we called him—and his blue soldiers began raiding our camps, burning our hogans, our cornfields."

"That's terrible."

"Well, they didn't hurt us, you know—not yet." Dezbah's mouth twisted in the lamplight. "We just had no place to live, no food to eat. Many of our people took refuge in Canyon de Chelly, where they held out for some time. But by winter, most of us realized we would not survive. My family surrendered to the soldiers, along with many others."

Caroline swallowed. "What did they do to you?"

"Marched us south—far from our *Dinétah* and our four sacred mountains, to Fort Sumner. How you think I learned English? More than 400 miles in winter, on foot, through mountains and snowstorms. The food they gave us made us sick. I have fought this lung evil ever since, what keeps me even now from my grandson's bedside." Her hands, clenching the blanket, shook convulsively.

Caroline reached out to her, then held back at the fire in Dezbah's eyes.

"They kept us there like animals, for years. Bad food, no shelter but what we could dig into the ground. My little son couldn't take it. He was too small—only his fourth winter when they took us. His *ch'iidii* passed from his body one night as I huddled by the fire, trying to keep him warm." Tears tracked unheeded through the wrinkles of her face. "My mother fell sick on the march there. We tried to help her, but when she fell and could not get up, the soldiers shot her where she lay, her blood spattering the snow. They did that to everyone who couldn't keep up—the sick, the old, the pregnant mothers."

Caroline pressed her hand to her mouth. Nausea swept her.

"What?" Dezbah turned her face fully toward her at last. "You think your great U.S. government would not do such things? You think you come to help the poor Indians, with your mission and your school and your ways—what you think are the only right ways. I know you think you're better than us. I know you think Creator smiles on your ways and frowns on ours. You say your Jesus loves us, then you take our children and destroy everything that makes them who they are. Shame to you! Shame, shame!"

A fit of coughing jerked Dezbah from her pillow, but she pushed Caroline's hand away with a strength that belied her frailty.

"You want to help? Leave us alone so we can someday recover." She coughed again, her wheezing deepened, then fell back on her mat.

Caroline drew back and rose on shaking legs. Stumbling to the doorway, she pushed out through the hanging rug and leaned against the side of the hogan. She slid to the ground, her back scraping against the rough logs.

"Oh, God." She clenched trembling arms around her knees.

Yes, some things about the mission troubled her... she'd thought some of Rev. Abernathy's methods not quite right. But he was a minister of the Gospel, Miss Spencer an experienced missionary. Surely they knew best—or so she had thought until this crisis with Samuel.

But this—this tore at the root of everything she believed in.

She didn't know how long she sat there, numb but for the beating pain in her heart, as the night air cooled around her and the late dusk turned to darkness. Slowly, relentlessly, faces marched through her mind. Samuel... Esther... Dezbah... Tse. The mothers and children torn apart that first day of term. Her own arms tightening around a quivering Shashyáázh as Rev. Abernathy's scissors turned him into an unwilling Samuel. Her voice telling the children to speak English, over and over.

Tse's anguished voice, crying, "When will anyone ever listen to my people?"

Tears wet her fingers. *Oh, God, have I been so blind? Have we not been doing Your work here at all?*

She pulled her knees close and buried her face in her arms, dismay and shame burning deep in her belly.

CHAPTER
THIRTY-ONE

A muffled sound startled Tse out of a doze.

Rubbing his hand across his eyes, he shook his head and glanced around. His father sat above him on the mission steps, head nodding, hands sagged between his knees. Tse stood from his crouch on the bottom step and arched his back, leaning his head from side to side to ease the kinks. The moon rose over the mesas.

What had he heard? The Begays were still inside with the missionaries and Shashyáázh. All the schoolchildren should be abed by now. Miss Spencer had emerged once, bringing Tse and his father supper plates after they finished the barn chores together. She hadn't invited them in, but he wouldn't expect her to.

There the sound came again. Tse cocked his head, then plunged into the shadows, rounding the corner of the mission.

Moonlight, dappled by peach tree branches, illuminated a slender figure huddled against the side of the building.

"Sháńdíín?" Tse crouched beside his cousin. "*Shideezhi,* what is wrong?"

She swiped at her cheeks.

"Is it your brother?" Tse touched her arm. "I think he will do better now that your parents are here." At least he hoped.

"No, he won't, he won't." Sháńdíín shook her head violently.

"Why do you say that?"

"The owl." She rocked back and forth. "Remember, I told you, the owl before we ran away. Always, the owl brings death to my family—it took my little sister, now it chases Shashyáázh. I went after him, I thought maybe we could escape, but it is too strong. It is always too strong." She buried her face in her arms and wept.

Tse's throat ached. Gently, he pried one of her hands from clinging to her knees and drew her to her feet. "Come. Let's sit on the porch."

Sniffing up little gasping sobs, Sháńdíín let him lead her to the steps. She sank beside him with an exhausted hiccup.

Rubbing his knees, Tse sat in silence a moment. Far out on the desert, a coyote howled, and Sháńdíín scooted closer to him. Coyotes were said to portend death too.

"I used to be afraid of owls and *ch'iidiis* too." Tse spoke softly so as not to wake his father. "But I heard a story that helped me not to fear them. Would you like to hear it?"

Hugging herself, Sháńdíín nodded.

Tse drew a deep breath. "Long ago, across the sea in another land, there was a man who had thousands of *ch'iidiis* living inside him. They made him so wild that he lived in the burial places, screaming and cutting himself with stones."

Sháńdíín shivered. No Navajo would venture near a burial ground.

"But one day, Jesus came to the burial places where this man stayed. He wasn't afraid of the *ch'iidiis*, like everyone else. He told the evil spirits to leave the man—and they did. The man was made well and told everyone what Jesus had done for him."

Sháńdíín sat still, staring out across the desert.

"You and I know evil spirits are real." Tse hesitated. "Even if Rev. Abernathy doesn't always seem to." He laid his hand on her knee. "But Jesus is stronger. If we have Him living inside of us, we don't need to fear *ch'iidiis*. Jesus is stronger than they are—stronger than sickness, stronger than death."

"But Shashyáázh." Shándíín looked down and pinched the fabric of her skirt, folding it over. "Can Jesus make him well?"

"He can." Tse sucked a breath and removed his hand from her knee. "I'm asking Him to. But He doesn't always, Shándíín. My little brother died here." He swallowed hard.

His cousin clenched her skirt, her fingers trembling.

"But my brother trusted in Jesus." Tse pressed his hands together. "So I finally realized that nothing could really harm him—not even death."

"No." Turning away from Tse, Shándíín covered her ears with her hands and broke into fresh sobs.

"There, *Shideezhi*." Tse ran one hand through his hair and stroked his cousin's back with the other, as he used to comfort Dólii when she was little. His own chest squeezed, and he closed his eyes, mental gears shifting to English. "Lord Jesus, please comfort Shándíín. Please touch Shashyáázh with Your hand—"

Shándíín's sobs tore at his heart afresh. He opened his eyes, slipping back into his native tongue. "*Shideezhi,* what is wrong?"

"What's the use of praying, when God doesn't even know our language?" She had buried her face in her arms again, muffling her voice. "He only listens to the *bilagáanas*."

"That's not true." Tse pulled his hand away to massage his neck, the old burning tightening his throat. "God knows all languages." He did, didn't He? "The Bible says someday people of all tongues and nations will sing around Him in heaven."

But did he himself really believe that? Cold trembled through him.

Shándíín lifted her head, loose tendrils of hair sticking to her wet cheeks. "Then why can't we talk to Him in it?"

At her raised voice, Tse's father stirred on the top step.

Tse glanced back at him, waiting until he settled back into a sleepy slouch.

Shándíín sat still, her fists clenched on her lap, her face taut toward Tse's.

He gripped one hand within the other beneath his chin, trying to control their shaking. Why, indeed? People prayed in English, in Swedish, in German and Italian, didn't they? In the Bible they prayed in Hebrew, Aramaic, and Greek. And the Holy Spirit spoke through many languages at Pentecost.

"I guess because…" He forced the words from his closing throat. "We've been told for so long that we can't."

Shándíín laid her head back on her knees, a huddle of despair.

Lord… she'll never trust You if she doesn't believe You listen and care.

Tse's heart pounded. He worked his mouth. How to even begin? *Help me.* He opened his mouth. His tongue stuck as Rev. Spencer's voice slashed his mind in rhythm with the switch. *We must break your obsession with this barbaric tongue… it has no place in the Christian life.*

A shudder racked his body. Why didn't God like their language? Had He not created it? Had He not created them? He pressed clenched fists to his eyes. *I can't do this, Lord.* His chest heaved. *I can't.*

He huddled there shaking like a little boy, the memories, the pain, the beatings, and the belittlings pounding him from every direction.

And then he heard it.

"T'áadoo nił yé'í,
háálá nik'é niná'níshdlá;
nízhi' bee níízhi'; shíí' nílį́."

Tse caught his breath. Only his heart kept beating, thumping harder than ever, as the words, spoken silent yet so loudly, reverberated through his mind. The verse he had read many times in Isaiah, but the words ... a trembling started in his middle and spread to his limbs. The words ...

The words he heard in his own language.

"Fear not: for I have redeemed thee, I have called thee by thy name; thou art mine."

I have called thee by name, Tse ... thou art mine.

"Doodatsaahii," Tse choked. *"ShiDiyin* God ... *Bóhólníihii."* My Holy God ... the Lord, the Creator, the holy, living One ... the One who had conquered death, hell, and the grave. For the world, and for him ... for Tse Tsosie. Because He loved him. He loved and accepted him, not for being conformed into the image of some other human culture, but for who he was, who He had made him to be, the son He saw through Jesus.

The tears came then, wetting his fists and dripping onto his breeches. And he prayed, the words spilling out brokenly, beautifully, in his native tongue, hurt and praise and thanks and supplication, for Shashyáázh, for Shándíín, for himself, for his people. The tears washed away the hardness from his stomach and chest, the tightness from his throat.

He raised his head to see Shándíín staring at him, her gaze stunned.

Tse lifted one corner of his mouth and brushed his knuckles across her damp cheek. "God does speak our language, *Shideezhi.*"

Caroline lifted her head from her knees and rubbed at the crick in her neck. Above her, stars winked in blackness. She shivered. How long had she slept huddled here outside the hogan, reluctant to go back inside and face Dezbah? Caroline hugged her knees. She'd never known what it was to be hated before, never thought anyone had reason to hate her. Until tonight.

Then she stiffened. From within the hogan, Dezbah was coughing—and coughing. It sounded like she could barely breathe. Caroline scrambled to her feet and stumbled through the rug-covered doorway, her feet still half asleep.

"Dezbah?" Caroline knelt by the sheepskin.

The older woman rolled toward her, caught in a paroxysm.

Caroline tried to support her shoulders, but it didn't help.

Dezbah coughed until it seemed she had no breath left. Finally she hacked into her bit of cloth and lay back. Her wheezing whistled through the hogan.

Caroline's heart pounded in her ears. Dezbah sounded nearly as bad as Samuel, but she had no fever, though her skin was damp with sweat. From what she had said, this was a chronic lung sickness. Perhaps her agitation that evening had brought on such a severe attack. So was this Caroline's fault too?

Dezbah jerked with another spell of dry coughs.

Croup. Caroline pressed her fingers to her temples. It couldn't be, of course, but that was what this reminded her of. No fever, just the desperate fighting to breathe in the middle of the night.

Maybe steam would help, as it always had the boys. She added to the fire in the stove and dipped water from the barrel's dwindling supply into a pot, then pushed it to the center of the stove. When she bent to lift Dezbah higher on her pillow, the woman twisted away.

"I will . . . do it," said Dezbah.

Caroline held back as Dezbah braced on bony arms and hauled herself slightly more upright. She fell back with a gasp that became another cough.

"What can I do for you?" Caroline steeled herself for a rebuff.

But Dezbah didn't respond, her eyes sagging shut.

Steam billowed from the pot for what seemed hours, though Caroline couldn't track the time. Still Dezbah coughed and struggled to breathe, once spitting blood into her cloth.

At last Caroline slid her arm under Dezbah's bony shoulders. "I'm going to take you outside."

"At night?" The woman stiffened. "You are a crazy *bilagáana*."

"Only just outside the hogan." Tse had told her of the fear *ch'ii-diis* brought to any who ventured abroad after dark. "Night air used to help my little brothers when they had trouble breathing." Only God knew if it would help Dezbah's ailment or make it worse, but she had to try something.

"No." Dezbah rolled away.

"I want you to see your grandchildren again." Caroline set her teeth, rolled the woman back, and lifted her to a sitting position.

Dezbah struggled, but Caroline hauled her to her feet. Slinging the elderly woman's arm over her shoulder, she half carried her outside, easing her down on the ground against the hogan wall where she herself had sat earlier. She ducked inside for blankets, popping back out to tuck one around Dezbah and slip another behind her back, then collapsed on the ground beside her.

Caroline closed her eyes, catching her breath. The children's grandmother proved heavier than she looked.

"You're a stubborn one."

Caroline opened her eyes. Was that a glint of humor in Dezbah's gaze? The woman turned her face away before she could be sure, coughing again.

For some time, Dezbah's respiration seemed as agonized as ever. Then she drew a slightly longer breath. Then a longer one. And didn't cough. With a sigh, the woman closed her eyes and relaxed against the blanket between her and the log wall of the hogan.

"Better?" Hesitant, Caroline reached out and pulled the blanket over Dezbah's shoulders. The slightest motion hinted a nod, and the tightness in Caroline's stomach eased a bit. *Thank You, Lord.*

The elderly woman adjusted herself beneath the blanket, brushing her shoulder against Caroline's. Dezbah shifted away from her.

Caroline bit her lip. There it was again—that wall she had come against time and again in past months. Between her and Samuel, her and Esther. Sometimes between her and Tse. Rock-hardened between her and Dezbah.

Only tonight had she really begun to understand what it was made of.

America. The land of the free and home of the brave, a Christian nation blessed by God ... so she had always thought. Now the flag of her country, even of her church, seemed lifted to expose heinous, festering sores underneath. Sores she found even in her own heart, lesions of blindness, of prejudice. Of thinking her way the right way, for no better reason than it was what she knew.

The tightness in her throat nearly choked her. No wonder hardly any Navajo came to the mission church services. So much hurt, so much damage, and in Jesus' name. How could He stand by and let it be? Why had He even let her come?

She drew a breath and studied Dezbah's profile, wizened in the moonlight, the strong cheekbones, sagging chin, closed eyes. What anguish she had seen, yet survived, with an inner strength and abiding love for her family. Yet Caroline had judged her for the type of stove she had. *God forgive me.*

"Dezbah." Caroline swallowed, her mouth suddenly dry.

Dezbah shot her a glance, then looked away again.

Caroline's heart thudded, but something pressed her forward. "I want to tell you I'm sorry." Her voice trembled. "I'm so sorry for how my people have treated yours. We have claimed to represent the Lord Jesus, while often defying His commands and acting contrary to who He is." She twisted her fingers together. "I have no right to your forgiveness, but... I'm sorry. And for my own part in the harm that has been done to your grandson." Tears blurred her eyes. Her last words came out a whispered sob. "I'm so sorry."

They sat in silence for some time. Finally Caroline risked a glance at the woman beside her.

Dezbah sat gazing at the night sky. The moon dipped below the mesas, leaving the stars a glittering blanket overhead.

Caroline shivered, still unused to the chill of summer nights in the desert. Would Dezbah say anything? She shouldn't expect her to. Letting out a quivering sigh, Caroline wrapped her arms across her middle and leaned her head against the logs.

Dezbah sighed too, soft and low like a dying fire. "Why did you come here, to our *Dinétah*?"

The same question Tse had asked her. Yet more than ever, she didn't know the answer. "I thought it was... what God wanted me to do. I had always wished to go somewhere, to teach children about His love." She fingered her locket. "But I'm beginning to see I have more to learn than to teach."

Another long moment passed. Dezbah shifted, her shoulder brushing Caroline's again. This time she didn't pull away, just gazed across the darkened desert. "And what is there between you and the Tsosie boy?"

Caroline's heart stopped, skipped, then thudded into double-time. "What do you mean?" She swallowed, smoothing her skirt over her knees with shaking hands. "That is—there is nothing."

Dezbah tipped her head, the moonlight glinting her hair silver. "Good."

Caroline clasped her hands around her knees, but still they trembled.

CHAPTER THIRTY-TWO

On eagle's wings he soared, high over the *Dinétah*. Above mesas and arroyos, the river flanked with green. Into the sunrise Tse flew, through rays of gold, orange, and pink, light so bright it dazzled his eyes and shone straight into his heart. He dipped and wheeled, laughing for joy in the Creator. The God who was with them—not far off like the yei, and not looking down on them with disapproval like the missionaries often seemed to. With them in suffering and in joy, closer than their very skin, their breath.

Then he sailed lower, catching an updraft on the edge of a valley and gliding downward over junipers and sagebrush. A flock of sheep grazed below. He landed on his feet among them, the ewes and lambs nudging against his legs, an old ram lifting a horned head to inspect him before he returned to nibbling brush.

The wind lifted Tse's hair, breezing a holy whisper in his native tongue. "Tse, *shiye'*—my son. Shepherd My sheep."

The creak of the mission door startled Tse awake. He stretched his arms before him, shifting his legs on the mission steps. The eastern horizon paled toward dawn. He turned his head to look toward the sound, wincing at the stiffness.

Miss Spencer stood in the doorway. She met Tse's eyes and lifted a trembling hand to her mouth.

Tse shot to his feet. *No. Please God, no.*

Sháńdíín uncurled from her spot on the porch beside her father, who had joined them sometime in the night, and sat up, her eyes wide. Her father stood stiffly, as did Tse's.

Please, Lord ... whatever the news is, please ... He wasn't even sure what he was praying for.

"The fever has broken." Miss Spencer lowered her hand and smiled through tears. "He's breathing more easily. Thanks be to God!"

With a cry, Sháńdíín flung her arms about her father's waist. Stumbling to the porch railing, the man half sat on it, one hand over his eyes, the other stroking his daughter's hair.

Tse's knees quivered. He nodded at Miss Spencer. "Thanks be to God, indeed."

Sháńdíín and her father followed the elderly missionary inside. The door clicked shut.

Tse stepped to the porch railing beside his father. Gray clouds skimmed over the horizon, fluffy like lambs' tails, brightened with pink and edged with yellow.

His father placed his arm about Tse's shoulders, gladness passing between them without words. Tse blinked the blur from his eyes. *O Lord, You are merciful ... You are good.* He sniffed hard. *Thank You.*

"Tse."

He turned.

Willis stood behind him, his weary face and tousled hair showing the night's toll. His shirt was wrinkled like he'd slept in it, his suspenders awry. He shoved his hands into his back pockets. "I'll thank you to leave the mission property now."

He turned on his heel. The door shut.

Tse swallowed. He felt his father's gaze, grieved and somehow understanding, though he wouldn't have comprehended the words.

Tse rubbed his nose and stepped to the edge of the porch. A glowing sliver glimmered over the horizon, shooting fire over the mesas, gilding gray clouds into gold.

But unto you that fear my name shall the Sun of righteousness arise with healing in his wings...

Willis couldn't take that away, nor what God had done here last night. No one could.

"May I take a horse?" At his father's nod, Tse pelted down the steps, taking the last three in one leap. He untied one of the team, swung onto it bareback, and touched it into a lope, crouching low over its neck as they flew down the lane.

Out of earshot of the mission, he slid off his horse and ran like a little boy, leaping over sagebrush and snakeweed, startling a jackrabbit and covey of quail, finally falling to his knees in the rocky dirt, his face lifted to the rising sun. He flung out his arms and yelled, a shout of joy and victory, a warrior's cry of triumph. Christ's triumph.

He bowed his head, the tears falling as sudden as the joy. Gripping a clump of *Dinétah* earth in his fist, he let it trickle through his fingers.

He looked up at the sky, snowy clouds still edged with gray and gold in the turquoise blue. "*Ahe'hee', shiDiyin God,*" he whispered. "Thank You."

His horse clopped up behind him and snuffled his head. Reaching to caress the whiskery nose, Tse wiped his sleeve across his face and stood.

He knew nothing of what was ahead, what he was to do now. What would become of him or his family. But Creator had heard, had spoken. Was mighty, and powerful, and Healer of body and soul.

And for today, that was enough.

The sun, well above the horizon now, warmed Tse's shoulders as he turned his horse toward his cousins' camp. No smoke wisped through the hole in the hogan's roof. Could they still be asleep? He slowed his horse and swung down, looping the reins to the corral.

"Caroline?" He stepped nearer the hogan, then softly called again.

A stir from within, and she lifted the rug, blinking in the sunlight, hair wisped messily about her pale face. Her eyes widened at the sight of him, and she let the rug fall behind her and hurried forward.

"Tse?" Hope and anguish mingled in her tone.

"*Ya'at'eeh.*" He almost reached for her hands, then caught himself.

"How is he?"

"He is better." The sweet rush of gladness filled his lungs again. "The fever broke at dawn."

"Oh, thank God." Caroline covered her face with her hands, swaying slightly. "Thank God."

"Easy." Tse reached a hand to steady her.

"Rev. Abernathy let them in?" She lowered her hands and looked up at him, the brightness of tears in her gray eyes.

"Miss Spencer did."

"And Esther? How is she?"

"Well, I think." The hope on his cousin's face when she heard the good news flashed through Tse's mind again. How much to tell Caroline now? "I prayed—"

"So did I. So hard. I was so afraid..." She curled her hands together.

Tse's chest tightened. "Me too. But God is merciful." Hesitant, he laid his hands on either side of her shoulders. "And my cousin is better, Caroline, truly."

"You saw him?"

"Well, no." If only he could have. "But Miss Spencer said so, and she would know."

She nodded and sniffed.

"How is Dezbah?" Tse glanced at the hogan.

"She had a bad night." Caroline shifted from his touch.

Tse's arms fell to his sides, oddly empty. "I am sorry."

"She's better now." Caroline twisted her fingers together.

He swallowed. "I have more to tell you." What would she say, to hear he had lost his job once and for all? Or to hear he'd prayed in Navajo?

A hacking fit of coughing erupted and hung on the breeze. Caroline glanced back toward the rug covered door. "Dezbah's wakened, I must see to her. But thank you—Tse, thank you for coming to tell me." She reached out as if to touch him, then pulled her hand back and started toward the hogan.

"Wait."

She halted but did not turn.

"One of the family will come to relieve you before tonight." He ran his tongue over his teeth. Why did everything feel so wrong? "You will be all right?"

At last she glanced back at him, with a wisp of a smile that somehow hurt him more than her tears. Then she nodded and ducked inside the hogan. The rug flapped down, hiding her from his sight.

He stood staring at the silent doorway a moment, then blew out a breath. His horse answered with a nicker, and he turned for the corral. Absently he rubbed the inquiring muzzle. In place of the glory of an hour ago came a dull burden that weighted his legs. Even the sun seemed dimmer.

Now what, Lord? He rested his forearm against the warm, sturdy shoulder of his horse and bent his head into it.

CHAPTER THIRTY-THREE

Caroline hadn't thought it would be hard to say good-bye. Yet tears stung her eyes as she knelt by Dezbah's sheepskin once more and clasped her gnarled hand.

The old woman flicked her sharp gaze over Caroline, then nodded ever so slightly before pulling her hand away.

Caroline stood, turning to step between the stove and the boxes of supplies.

Another woman, niece to Dezbah, stood at the door and held the rug aside for Caroline to slip through. Mr. Begay waited on the seat of his red-wheeled covered wagon to drive her back.

To the mission. To Rev. Abernathy, and the children, and the rules, and all she no longer knew for sure she believed in.

Caroline climbed up on the wagon seat and clasped her hands in her lap. Perhaps things would be clearer back at the school.

The red wheels jolted and turned to head away from the lowering sun. Shadows stretched across the desert. Mr. Begay urged the horses on, no doubt eager to get back home before full darkness fell.

They rode in silence until the wagon turned into the lane leading to the mission.

"Miss Haynes." The man beside her shifted on the seat.

Caroline half turned to look at him, remembering just in time what Tse had said, that Navajos did not look directly at someone speaking. She averted her eyes and twisted the cuff of her sleeve. This man hardly spoke English. Did he wish to chastise her, like his mother-in-law, for endangering the life of his child?

"*Ahe'hee'*—thank you." Mr. Begay cleared his throat. "My son."

"You needn't thank me." She shook her head. "Thank Tse."

The man nodded. "But you with Tse."

Caroline swallowed. "Then you are welcome." The words felt ironic, somehow.

The wagon pulled into the mission yard. She climbed down and thanked Mr. Begay. As he drove away, she scanned the mission grounds, so familiar yet somehow foreign, though she'd only been absent a day and a half.

Several of the older girls still knelt in the garden, getting a bit more weeding done in the long summer twilight. One stood, then pushed through the garden gate and flew toward her.

"Miss Caroline!" Esther threw her arms around her, nearly knocking Caroline off balance. "Did you know my brother is better?"

"I know." Caroline hugged her close, laying her cheek on the girl's smoothly parted hair. Her head reached Caroline's chin—had she grown in a day?

Esther stepped back and lifted a shy gaze. "Tse prayed for him. I think—Jesus heard."

Caroline's throat tightened. She squeezed Esther's hand.

Light beamed on them as the mission door opened, and Rev. Abernathy clattered down the steps. "Welcome back."

"Rev. Abernathy." Caroline tensed her hands behind her.

"Do you have a…" He peered as if for a satchel to take from her, then stepped back. "No, of course not." Glancing at Esther, he cleared his throat pointedly. "Is the garden finished?"

"Almost." Esther looked down.

"Go help the other girls finish up, then all of you, off to bed."

After the girl darted away, Rev. Abernathy looked at the ground, then back to Caroline, shoving his hands in his pockets. "I feel I should apologize."

"For what?" She hadn't meant the words to come out so sharply.

"I'm afraid I overreacted a bit." He hesitated, rubbing the back of his neck. "About the river outing. I'm sure you meant no harm."

Caroline stared at a button on his shirt. Was that all, then? And was she to apologize in turn, for going against his wishes?

She raised her gaze to his face. The sincerity in his blue eyes made her swallow—and step back. She nodded, glancing aside and giving the automatic reply. "You are forgiven."

He reached toward her and squeezed her hand briefly.

The last time his fingers had held hers flashed through her memory, and she pulled her hand away. Blindly she mounted the steps and pushed through the mission door. His question before he and Miss Spencer left for the board meeting—his proposal. He would be expecting an answer.

What am I supposed to do, Lord?

"Miss Haynes." Miss Spencer folded Caroline in a rare embrace. "It is good to have you back, my dear. Would you like to see our patient?"

Her breath caught. "Oh, yes, please."

Miss Spencer led her through the sitting room and eased open the sickroom door. Holding her finger to her lips, she stepped aside to let Caroline peek in.

Samuel lay curled on his side against the pillows, his shoulder rising and falling with a whiffling snore, one hand tucked securely in his mother's. She dozed in the chair beside the bed, baby at her breast, her head bent toward her son even in sleep.

"She has barely left his side since they arrived." Miss Spencer spoke just above a whisper.

Caroline nodded. The backs of her eyes pricked.

"Of course, we can't allow her to stay more than another day or two." Softly, Miss Spencer closed the door.

"Why?" Caroline snapped her gaze up to the older missionary's face.

"Surely you know the answer to that." Miss Spencer quirked a thinning brow. "While you should not have gone against Willis's authority, I believe the Lord may have used it for the best. But we cannot continue the home influence here at school—the children will begin to question all we have taught."

… You say your Jesus loves us, then you take our children and destroy everything that makes them who they are. Shame to you! Shame, shame!

Caroline bit her lip and lowered her gaze.

Miss Spencer sighed. "Come and have a bite of supper. We saved you a plate."

Caroline followed the elderly missionary with her eyes as she disappeared toward the kitchen. Miss Spencer didn't limp as much as she used to. Something to be thankful for.

And Samuel. She mustn't forget to be grateful, for his easy breathing, his natural sleep. But would he just fall ill once more, when his mother was taken away? At least the children would be going home soon for the remainder of the summer. Surely he would have time to get truly well again, before fall.

She stepped out onto the porch and let the evening breeze cool her hot eyes.

Rev. Abernathy emerged from the barn with a milk pail in each hand. He looked up as he neared the porch and flashed a grin. "It's good to see you back, Miss Haynes. We missed you."

"Why are you doing the milking?" Caroline took a step down toward him.

"What do you mean?" His grin faded.

"Where is Tse?"

"Take these in." Rev. Abernathy handed the pails to Isaiah, who had appeared behind her.

After the door shut behind the boy, Rev. Abernathy stepped up to stand level with Caroline. "I thought you knew."

"You let him go?" Caroline's chest tightened.

"You knew that was a possibility."

"But I thought... after—"

"He went against my orders?" He huffed a laugh.

"I went for Samuel's parents too." Caroline gripped the railing, the rough wood biting into her fingers.

Rev. Abernathy lifted a brow. "All the more reason for me to protect you from misguided influence." He stepped still closer and took her hands in his. "I care about you, Caroline." He rubbed his thumbs over the backs of her hands. "May I call you that?"

She pulled from his grasp and hurried inside. Safe in her room, she shut the door and sat on her bed.

A splash of orange caught her eye—a teacup with a few sprigs of desert globemallow, sitting on her bedside table. Caroline reached to turn it toward her. Rev. Abernathy's doing, no doubt.

She shoved the teacup back, splashing water out onto the table, then dabbed at the spill with her handkerchief, blinking back angry tears. How could he do it? Tse's family needed his income from that job—as Rev. Abernathy knew full well. How *could* he?

Caroline leaned forward, elbows on knees, and rested her head in her hands. "Willis." Her first taste of his given name came on a breath of frustration. Why did she ruffle so at his use of her first name, yet not when Tse used it?

No doubt many would call her foolish, say the reverend must have had his reasons for Tse's dismissal. Willis did care for her—the orange blossoms stood as mute testimony. Here the Lord was offering her a good and godly man, for all his faults, who wanted to make her his wife, give her a place to make a home and a difference.

But what sort of difference? Dezbah's words stabbed her memory like hot needles.

And Tse. How would the mission manage without him? How would ... she?

Perhaps Rev. Abernathy—Willis—would let him come by to help out now and then. He still lived in the area, after all. She would see Tse, still. Surely.

The niggling doubt threatened a hole to her heart she didn't dare contemplate.

CHAPTER THIRTY-FOUR

"Nothin' to trade today?" Trader Hawkins spat a stream of tobacco juice toward the spittoon he kept convenient to his post behind the counter. He missed.

"Not today." Tse leaned against the counter. "I want to ask you—"

The trading post door creaked open, admitting a rancher Tse had worked a summer for, back a year or so ago.

"Need some feed, Hawkins." The man strode up and flicked distaste over Tse with a glance.

"Comin' right up." The trader moved to fill the man's order.

Tse shifted his jaw and waited. He should be used to taking second place by now. He glanced out the window to the wagon where Dólii still sat. Had she indeed asked to go along for more time with him, as she said? Or was she hoping to see Nezwood? Tse hadn't seen his old schoolmate in some weeks. Perhaps he had taken *Shizhé'é*'s advice and backed off.

"So what didja want, Tsosie?"

"I am ... " He hesitated and leaned closer. "Do you know how I can get work on the railroad?"

"Railroad, eh?" Trader Hawkins rubbed a hand over his graying red beard. "Thought you was working up at the mission."

Tse shifted his feet and shook his head.

"Well. I know a fella with the Topeka-Santa Fe. He told me if I knew any strong Navajos willing to work, let him know." The trader squinted at Tse. "Might mean going to Colorado, Kansas, who knows."

Tse swallowed. "That far?"

"You go wherever the tracks go." Trader Hawkins turned as another customer entered. "I'll send him a telegram if you want. Maybe see if I can round up a few more to go with you."

"Thank you." Tse stood unseeing a moment, then drew a deep breath of the coffee beans and dried peaches filling the barrels along the counter. He crossed the creaking wooden floor and pushed out the door into blinding sunlight. *Kansas.* How could he go so far from his family, from the *Dinétah*?

Easy. Because he had to.

A giggle caught his attention, and he glanced at the wagon.

Dólii still perched on the seat, but Nezwood now leaned on the corner, his hat tipped back as he laughed.

Tse fought a hot rising in his throat. There was that sparkle in his sister's eyes. How did Nezwood always find her?

"Dólii, time to go." He strode to the wagon.

"*Ya'at'eeh.*" Nezwood stepped back with a grin.

"*Ya'at'eeh.*" Tse clipped the word. "You here to trade?"

"Sure. And to see your pretty sister." He flashed another smile at Dólii. She lowered her eyes, a smile tugging at her mouth.

She *was* pretty. Too pretty, as far as Tse was concerned. He swung up onto the wagon seat and released the brake.

And here he was going only the Lord knew how many miles away from her.

Last day of term.

Caroline stood on the mission porch as Samuel and Esther clambered into the covered wagon behind their parents.

Samuel poked his head back out through the opening in the canvas and grinned at her.

She held back the ache in her throat with a smile and wave. She would not, must not cry—at least until they left. Was his thin little face filling out more? Or was it just that he was smiling?

Mr. Begay took up the reins and nodded to Willis, who stood on the ground to see this last wagon off.

Caroline pressed her tongue against her teeth to keep the smile in place.

Summer evening sunshine stretched the wagon's jolting black shadow across the yard as the team started.

The Begays had been the last to come for their children, sending Willis to his pocket-watch every quarter hour as the afternoon wore on. Miss Spencer had finally gone in to lie down, once Samuel and Esther were the only two left.

Caroline had been glad for every extra minute.

Still in the yard, the wagon halted, and Esther scrambled out the back, her ruffled calico skirt catching on a board. She raced back toward the mission.

"Miss Caroline!" She scampered up the steps. "*Shimá* said I could ask you to my *kinaaldá*. It is to be in two weeks. Can you come?"

"I should love to. Thank you." Caroline pulled the girl close and squeezed her eyes tight as Esther's arms encircled her once more, then placed a kiss on the shiny hair, warm from the sun. "Your family is waiting," she whispered in her ear.

And Esther was off, darting swiftly as a bird. The darkness of fear had been lifted, somehow, from the girl's eyes, her spirit. Caroline hadn't been able to puzzle out why, and she hesitated to ask.

She waved until the wagon faded to a jolting miniature, then pressed a knuckle to her lips to stem the tears. They were all gone, now—her children.

Willis blew out a breath and ran his hand through his sandy hair. "Finally." He turned and mounted the steps. "Sometimes I think it would be more efficient to just drop the students off the way we pick them up."

Without a glance at Caroline, he pushed into the mission. The door slapped behind him.

Caroline leaned on the railing. Perhaps she should have asked Willis for permission about the *kinaaldá*. But it had happened so fast, she hadn't thought—or perhaps she had, unconsciously, and hadn't wanted him to say no. She sighed.

The day's heat was gentling already, a slight breeze cooling her face, rustling the thick leaves on the peach trees, and skimming over the empty mission schoolyard.

So quiet. Only a slight cackle or muffled bleat from the barnyard.

Caroline straightened and hugged her elbows. She would be glad for the ceremony, for something to break up the summer. How was she ever to fill the next two months?

Miss Spencer had plenty of ideas for filling them, as it happened—and the dozens, no, hundreds of glass jars Caroline found herself lugging from the cellar the next day. The apricots were ripe, and the best crop in years already going to waste—according to Hebron's headmistress, who took charge like a veteran of the Spanish-American War.

Apricot preserves, apricot jam, apricots halved, peeled, canned in syrup or laid out in the sun to dry. Apricots for breakfast, fresh with cream for dessert, golden rounds juicy with sunshine and sweetness she'd never found back in Pennsylvania. Apricots overflowing from baskets on the porch, lining trays in the kitchen. Caroline began to see them in her sleep.

"No matter how many we pick, they never seem to lessen," she said to Willis one afternoon in the orchard.

"Yes, well." The leafy branches where his ladder reached rustled. "That's what you get when you're spared a late frost." He eased his way down the ladder with a bushel basket. "Haven't seen a crop—"

"Like this in years." Caroline straightened from sorting the bruised and bird-pecked fruit for jam from the perfect for plain canning. "So I've heard."

"I was going to say, since I came back to the mission." Willis landed on the sparse orchard grass and swung the basket to the ground with a gentle thud.

Caroline swiped her wrist across her forehead, bumping back her straw hat. How long ago would that have been—three years? Four? And she knew he feared this might be the last. He'd been staying up late every night, writing letters to supporters of the mission back East, trying to garner funding and enthusiasm for the school. A rumor around the San Juan region had already painted Hebron's doors closed by the fall—she'd heard him tell Miss Spencer so. Willis had asked Caroline for help, and after some hesitation, she had written to Pastor Jensen of her home church, asking if they could spare any funds to support the mission—she knew they supported Jeremiah and his mission overseas, after all.

She'd hardly known what to write, at first, but then her pen had started to flow—telling of Isaiah and Anna and Nathan and Dorcas, of Shashyáázh and Sháńdíín—Samuel and Esther, as she'd made herself write. When had she started thinking of them by their Navajo names?

She even wrote of Dezbah, of the suffering she'd endured as a young woman at the hands of the United States, in what Caroline had since learned was called the Long Walk. Enacted under the "Great Emancipator" Abraham Lincoln, no less.

Trouble was, she wasn't sure the stories she wrote really reflected that well on the mission or would generate much for its support. But they were true.

Caroline crossed to fetch an empty basket from the pile under another apricot tree, picking her way around the spoiled, slimy fruit scattering the ground. They missed the children's help to clean up. "Are you glad you did?"

Willis quirked a brow. "Did what?"

"Came back. Here."

He stepped closer and took hold of the other side of her basket. "I know I would be, if you would tell me what I'm waiting to hear."

Why had she turned their light conversation deeper? She stared at his hands gripping the basket, irrationally thinking of Tse's hands the night of the kidding, so long ago. Willis's were narrower, whiter of course, softer—the fingers less calloused.

She looked up into his eyes, their blue properly pleading, yet with a twinkle of—was it confidence? She shook her head. "Willis…"

The corners of his mouth tipped up, bringing the hint of the dimple at her use of his name.

Not quite what she had intended. "I can't give you an answer yet." She swallowed as his smile faded. "I'm sorry."

"Very well, then." His jaw tightening slightly, he took the basket from her and strode up a little rise to the next row of apricot trees.

Now she had hurt him. She sighed and picked up a new basket.

At a yell, she looked up to see her would-be suitor spread-eagled on the slope.

"Willis!" She ran to his side, jumping over the fallen fruit.

"I slipped." He sat up dazedly and examined the orange pulp on his hands.

A giggle rose in her throat. She rolled her lips together, rendering it a snort. "I'm sorry." The mess, the look on his face—he reminded her of Benji caught in a mud puddle.

"Fool fruit." Willis pushed to his feet and wiped his hands on his trousers. "More trouble than they're worth." He stomped off toward the mission.

Caroline's laugh died on her lips as she watched his orange-blotched, white-shirted back disappear through the orchard. Why did he have to take everything so seriously? Clothes would wash. And *he* wouldn't have to be the one to scrub them.

She turned back to the squashed pile where Willis had splatted, and the chuckle bubbled up again. She pressed her fist to her mouth to squelch it. She hadn't wanted to laugh so since—since she and Tse fell into the river.

If Tse had slipped in the apricots, he wouldn't have gone off in a huff. He would have shaken his head and laughed too, perhaps even teased her, as he had with the stick in the grass at the river at sundown, before he had taken her hands and pulled her to her feet, and looked into her eyes ...

Her stomach flipped. She clenched the edge of the basket and squeezed her eyes shut. *Caroline Mary Haynes, what has come over you?*

CHAPTER THIRTY-FIVE

"Miss Caroline!" Esther broke away from the circle of women gathered around the pit where her *kinaaldá* corn cake had baked all night. Beaming, she halted in front of Caroline in her traditional woven rug dress, buckskin-tied hair loosened from her long morning run. "I am about to cut my corn cake."

And then she would be a woman, a full-fledged member of the tribe. Caroline smiled. "I can hardly wait to taste it." She glanced around the unfamiliar crowd. "Is—Tse here?"

"Somewhere around, I think." Esther darted away, tossing one more smile over her shoulder as she ran.

Caroline meandered about the perimeter of the festivities, conspicuous in her dress of white summer lawn amid the reds and purples of the other women's skirts and blouses.

Children flashed past, chasing each other or a stray dog or lamb. The scent of roasting mutton mingled with woodsmoke. Grandmothers sat in the shade of the *chaha'oh* shelter, visiting and watching babies in cradleboards. The people worked together, old and young, men and women.

Now and then someone glanced her way, but Caroline hung back—especially when she caught sight of Dezbah in the circle of women. As the morning sun gained strength, Caroline stepped into the shade of the main hogan and fiddled with her locket. Perhaps it had been a mistake to come.

"Caroline Haynes?"

"Yes?" She looked up into the smiling eyes and broad-boned face of a young Navajo woman.

"I am Dólii." The girl reached out her hand and tipped her head in a way somehow familiar. "Sister to Tse."

"Oh, of course!" Caroline clasped Dólii's hand in hers. "I am so glad to meet you."

Dólii withdrew her hand but smiled. "Will you join us for some corn cake?"

"Is—would it be all right?"

"Shándíín wants you to come." Dólii lightly touched Caroline's elbow and turned for her to follow.

Caroline trailed her to the circle where Esther and her women relatives passed out warm wedges of the thick mass filling the corn-husk-lined baking pit.

Caroline crouched hesitantly on the outskirts with a soft "*Ya'at'eeh.*"

A few returned the greeting, while others glanced at her in silence and then turned back to their conversations.

Caroline caught Dezbah's eye. Was that a nod of acknowledgement? She couldn't tell. Dólii squatted beside her and handed her a slice of the thick corn cake. Caroline nodded her thanks. If only she and Dólii could be friends someday—she missed having women friends her own age.

After the corn cake distribution, everyone scattered and grouped for general celebration and socializing.

Caroline sat on the ground to watch. Tse's mother came to sit nearby, Dólii helping her ease onto the ground as well. The older woman glanced at Caroline, then pursed her lips and looked away.

Caroline swallowed and searched the crowd for Tse again. He was here, wasn't he?

"*Ya'at'eeh*, Miss Caroline." Samuel ran up, beaming.

She reached out for his hug, suddenly missing Benji. If only her family could come for a visit, but she doubted they'd make the trip, not this year anyway. She gently pinched Samuel's nose to make him laugh. His cheeks were indeed filling out. *Thank You, Lord.*

A shadow fell over them, and Samuel jumped from her arms with a squeal to throw himself at someone behind her.

"Easy, little brother."

At the familiar voice, Caroline scrambled to her feet. She straightened beside Tse, oddly shy to look into his face. Had he always been so tall?

"*Ya'at'eeh*, Tse." She studied his crisply buttoned velveteen shirt, the turquoise and silver of his necklace, no doubt worn specially in Esther's honor.

"*Ya'at'eeh*." He tousled Samuel's hair, already growing out now that he was home. "Has this young rascal given you a good welcome to his sister's ceremony?"

"He certainly has." Caroline laughed shakily. She met Tse's eyes for an instant, then glanced away, her heart skittering. "It is so good to see him better."

"It is."

Silence, strangely awkward.

She hugged her elbows. "How are you?"

"All right." He studied her. "And you?"

"Well, thank you." As well as could be expected, at least, with all the last few weeks had held. Why could she not think of something more to say?

"Tse!" Esther ran up and threw her arms about Tse's waist, hugging tight. She leaned back her head to look at him. "*Shimá* says you must come and eat with us once more next week, before you leave."

"I will." Tse brushed his knuckles against her hair, and Esther flew off again. He watched her go. "She is a little magpie today." His smile faded as he looked back to Caroline, seeming to read the question in her eyes.

"Leave?"

"I am joining a track team on the Santa Fe railroad."

She could only form one word. "Where?"

"A few of us are catching a wagon to Gallup. From there we may go to eastern New Mexico, Colorado, maybe farther—I don't know."

"I see." A sudden welling choked her.

Tse moved to answer a gesture from his mother.

Caroline stared unseeing at the scampering children, hugging her middle as if to hold in the terrible ache. When Tse straightened from speaking with his mother and made as if to turn back, Caroline hurried away, eyes on the ground as if searching for something. Once away from the crowd, she ducked around the smaller hogan and leaned against one of the log walls, on the side that faced only junipers and sandstone.

Oh, Lord… She pressed clenched knuckles to her lips, the desert shimmering and blurring with tears, the devastating truth crashing over her in wave after wave until she could no longer stand. She slid to the ground and rested her head against the rough logs.

She loved Tse Tsosie.

She had tried to ignore it, been terrified to even think of acknowledging it. But now she knew, with the piercing clarity of spear-sharp pain, why she could not imagine marrying Willis … why she had felt happier, safer, with this quiet man than she had since before Mama died … why every kid goat, Navajo greeting, and mention of a snake reminded her of him.

And soon, she might never see him again.

"Caroline?"

She startled and swiped at her cheeks.

Tse crouched beside her.

"I'm sorry. This is a celebration day for your family." She twisted the damp handkerchief between her hands.

"What's wrong?"

His voice, so gentle, nearly undid her. So much she wanted to say—how sorry she was for Willis's dismissal, the unfairness of it. How sorry for her own blindness, in so many ways. But all that blurted out was, "I wish you didn't have to go."

"But I do." He eased forward and leaned his hands on his knees, his voice low, earnest. "For my family—my mother and father, my sister. Even Kai and her family—with the new baby and all, and their herd has been struggling. We help and support each other. They need me. It is our way."

The *Diné* way. It was who Tse was—who God had made him, who he would always be.

And Caroline wasn't.

She lowered her head, ashamed to meet his gaze, to let him see what he could surely read plainly in her eyes.

A roughened finger brushed her cheek. "Caroline."

She looked up, startled, into his eyes, and saw the sheen of tears there. And she knew—knew with a rush of sweetness followed by pain that racked her—that he cared too. That after all these years of waiting, there was a man who loved her as she had longed to be loved.

And that he knew, as she did, that it could not be.

"I'm sorry. I wish ... " He dropped his hand from her face, rubbed his nose and blinked hard.

"So do I." The words scratched out in a whisper. She rolled the handkerchief's hem tight, then unrolled it.

Silence hung between them, heavy and pulsing.

Tse brushed his fingertips against hers, sending a shiver through her spine and to her toes. She clung, twining her fingers in his strong ones, his calloused thumb stroking ever so gently over the back of her hand.

Only a moment, then he pulled away.

"I should go." He drew a ragged breath, then pushed to his feet.

And she was alone again, hugging her knees, the back of her waist damp against the logs from the day's heat. Against this same hogan she had sat, the night she stayed with Dezbah. When the older woman had asked what was between her and the "Tsosie boy."

Caroline rested her forehead on her lawn-skirted knees and let the tears flow, dampening the delicate fabric. Her answer rang true now, if it hadn't then. For it did not matter what there was, but what there could be.

There could be nothing. Nothing at all.

Why, Lord? Tse's legs weighted like waterlogged wood as he headed back toward the festivities, his steps pacing his prayer, the Navajo coming more naturally now. *Could You not at least have kept her from caring, if not me?*

But she did—her tears, tearing at his heart, had told him that. And every inch of his being had sung at her nearness, wanted to catch her in his arms, to soothe away her tears and kiss her ripened corn-silk hair and—

He passed a hand over his eyes. *God help me.*

Was this somehow his fault? Should he never have allowed her to go with him for Shashyáázh's parents? Something had changed since then. Yet her argument had made sense at the time.

His father rose from a cluster of elders and waved him over. "We must head for home, my son. Your mother's knees are paining her, though she thinks she hides it from me."

Tse fell into step beside his father, letting the comfort of *Shizhé'é*'s presence salve the ache in his heart. So little time he had left, with his family. He could not even think what it might do to his parents, should they learn their son had fallen for, not just a Christian, which they might have expected, but a *bilagáana*.

Perhaps Rev. Abernathy's dismissal was God's blessing, after all. For now all he could do was get as far away from her as possible.

And pray that by God's mercy, his heart—and hers—might someday be set free.

CHAPTER THIRTY-SIX

Caroline sat on the porch snapping green beans with Miss Spencer one August evening, as dusk settled around them and mosquitoes, though far fewer than in Pennsylvania, buzzed inquiringly about the kerosene lamp. The peeper frogs that seemed to have taken up residence in the well raised their evening chorus.

The lazy days of summer didn't seem to apply at Hebron Mission. She'd thought the canning over with the last of the apricots, but then came the tomatoes, and the beans, and soon the peaches would be ripe. The days seemed an unending circle of picking and snapping and chopping and boiling, of steaming kettles and wiping faces with apron hems, of jars gleaming red and green and golden, ready to line the pantry and cellar for winter.

She didn't mind, really. Working till she fell into bed at night, she thought less about the soreness in her heart, less about the children, less about Tse, laboring on a train track however many hundreds of miles away.

At least a little less.

"Penny for your thoughts." Miss Spencer creaked her rocking chair as she reached for more beans.

"I, ah . . ." Caroline's fingers sped with her scrambling brain. "How did you know God had called you to be a missionary?" There. That should be a safe topic.

"My. A long time ago." Miss Spencer pushed her spectacles up her nose with a fragile finger.

"But how?" Suddenly she actually wanted to know. Why had she never asked before?

"For me, it was rather simple." The older woman set her chair to rocking again. "No lightning from heaven or such like. My brother was going to minister to the Pottawatomie. He needed someone to help him, to keep house for him. So I went. Then when the Lord opened up a door in New Mexico Territory, we came here."

"Did you…" Caroline hesitated and fingered a bean. Snip. Snap. "Did you never wish for marriage, a family?"

"Certainly that desire was there, once." Miss Spencer waved a hand before her face, whether shooing a mosquito or past dreams, Caroline couldn't tell. "But I came to see this as my calling. And when the Lord calls, He also equips."

Seemed sound, certainly. But had He called *her*? Last night Caroline had begun another letter to Pastor Jensen, this time asking if he knew of any teaching positions back home—she'd asked him to keep it confidential, said this was only a contingency plan should the mission close. But she knew that wasn't it, not all of it, anyway. Even if the mission stayed open, she no longer knew if she would stay. She had little heart left for the coming of the next school year now. Was that because she had begun to question their work? Or because Tse wouldn't be here?

"But, my dear, God's calling and that of wife and motherhood aren't always mutually exclusive."

Caroline lifted her head, suddenly aware Miss Spencer had continued their conversation. She nodded, trying to look as if she'd been paying attention all along.

"Many women have followed His call alongside their husbands. Ann Judson, for example." Miss Spencer gave a significant nod.

"Evening, ladies." Willis mounted the steps, his lantern light dancing over the porch floorboards and his face beneath his hat. He must have been in the barn.

Caroline focused on the beans in her lap, her ears warming. *Lord, this isn't the answer I was looking for.*

"Do you want to?"

She looked up to see Willis staring at her expectantly. "I beg your pardon?"

"Go with me to the trading post tomorrow. I need to pick up supplies, check for mail. Could use some company."

Mail? *The letter.* She had wondered, if she decided to send it, how she would get around asking Willis to mail it for her. "I should like that, yes."

"Fine, then." Willis snuffed the lantern and hung it on a nail. "We'll leave first thing. 'Night." He stepped inside, shutting the screen door behind him.

Caroline glanced at Miss Spencer.

A smile played at the corners of the elderly lady's mouth.

Oh, dear. Did Willis intend more by his invitation than seemed on the surface? Caroline snapped a bean extra hard, sending one half flying across the porch. Clamping her lips together, she went after it.

Why must everything be so complicated?

Her first time in a trading post.

Caroline breathed in the scents of wax, kerosene, and tobacco as Willis made his way ahead of her to talk with the trader. She would wait until Willis moved on to making his selections, then give her letter to Mr.—Hawkins, was it?

Two Navajo women stood at the counter, their heads bent over a bolt of turquoise sateen. Two rolled rugs leaned beside them.

Caroline wished they would unfurl one. She'd never had the chance to study Navajo weaving up close, except in Dezbah's hogan, and that hadn't been the best of timings. But no doubt they had already been priced, the women now making their selections on credit.

She wandered over to examine a display of turquoise and silver jewelry. There lay a necklace like Esther's—squash blossom, she had called it. Caroline glanced back over her shoulder. Willis still chatted with the trader.

"Good day, Miss Haynes."

"Dólii?" Of course—the women at the counter must have been Tse's sister and mother. She hadn't recognized them from the back. "How lovely to see you. And please, call me Caroline."

"How are things at the school?"

"Quiet, now." Caroline chuckled. "But not for long—the fall term starts in a few weeks."

Dólii nodded, but the smile faded from her eyes.

Caroline's middle squirmed. No doubt the beginning of school term had never been a happy time for the Tsosie family. She wasn't at all certain how she felt about it herself.

Silence held between them a moment.

Did she dare ask? "Have you—heard from Tse lately?"

"Just a note saying he is working on a track team somewhere east of Gallup. He may be going north soon."

"You must miss him dreadfully." Caroline fought the ache in her throat.

Dólii glanced away with a slight nod.

Willis approached, his boots creaking the floorboards. "I'm going to look at some supplies that just came in by freighter, not unloaded yet. I'll be out back."

"Very well."

He nodded, then strode out.

Surely he knew Dólii—Tse had said his sister only graduated last year. Yet Willis didn't acknowledge her. But perhaps he'd merely been distracted, hadn't meant to be impolite.

And now was her chance.

"Excuse me a moment, Dólii." Drawing the letter from her handbag, Caroline headed toward the trader, bent over the counter as he tallied up figures. She hesitated a few steps away, her fingers tightening on the envelope. *Oh, Lord, should I really send it?*

The bell on the door jangled, and a man with a jutting jaw and bushy eyebrows stalked in. "Need some more feed, Hawkins."

"Your stock been goin' through the feed mighty fast lately." The trader headed back into a storeroom.

"Yeah, well—if them lazy Navajos didn't let their cattle and sheep roam all over ravaging the landscape things might be different." He glared at Tse's mother, who still stood fingering the blue sateen. Her shoulders stiffened, and she lifted her chin before stepping away.

Her cheeks hot and prickling, Caroline turned and stared into a barrel of crackers. Mindlessly she picked one up, then another, and put them back.

At a thud, she spun to see one of the rugs fallen and unfurling across the floor, spilling intricate inter-weavings of triangles, zigzags, and stair-step patterns.

The rancher glared at the floor—he must have knocked it over. "Well, pick up your rug, girl!" he barked.

Dólii knelt to roll it.

"Should know better than to leave it in the way." He took a pinch of tobacco from the dish on the trader's counter.

Caroline could stand it no longer. She crossed the floor, sending a glare at the rancher, and helped Dólii finish rolling the rug.

Dólii said nothing, just moved both the rugs to a corner and joined her mother in selecting bags of flour and coffee.

"Anything else for you?" The trader thunked a bag of feed on the counter.

The bell on the door danced wildly as a plump woman with a toddler on her hip thrust it open. "Hiram! You forgot my list—again." She shoved it under the rancher's nose.

"Don't need a list. Got it all in my head."

"And then we'll blamed well end up without salt for a week like last time." She slapped it on the counter. "Can't trust a man."

She turned, jiggling the child. Her eyes narrowed when she saw Caroline. "Ain't you that schoolteacher we sat with on the train comin' out here?"

The stringy blonde hair... the runny-nosed little boy... "Of course. How nice to see you again." *Forgive the lie, Lord, it slipped before I thought.*

"So you actually stuck it out." The woman sniffed. "And just how *nice* have you found Injun-teaching to be?"

"Please, ma'am." Caroline's teeth clenched, and she glanced at Dólii. "I would ask you not to use such language around my friends."

The woman's left nostril flickered. "Well, perhaps you can ask your *friends* not to let their mangy livestock get out of control and overgraze our land. The waste they make of resources is simply shameful, my Hiram says."

"Are they grazing your land?" Caroline gripped the envelope tighter. "Or are you grazing theirs?"

The woman stared at her, mouth half open, then laughed slightly and turned away.

Her hands and middle trembling, Caroline turned back to the barrels, studying pickles and candy until the ranching family concluded their purchases—not without much arguing betwixt master and mistress—and the door shut behind them.

"Rancher, ha," Trader Hawkins muttered. "If he'd just rotate his pasture, he might not feel so much call to blame Navajos for his trouble."

Caroline turned and stepped toward him, then halted, fingering the envelope in her hands. Willis was still gone, but should she?

"Help you, miss?" He glanced up, scratching his gray-sprinkled red beard.

"I—" She glanced down.

"Aha, letter to mail." He reached over the counter and plucked the envelope from her. "That'll be two cents."

Caroline dug out the change and handed it over, her stomach tightening. It was just an inquiry, nothing binding. Yet part of her cried to snatch the letter back. She thanked Trader Hawkins and turned away.

Willis stood in the doorway.

Caroline started. Had he seen? Well, if he had, she had done nothing wrong. But how would she explain, should he ask?

But he only held the door open for her. "Ready to go?"

She stepped into the sunshine and stood still for her eyes to adjust after the dimness.

Under a cottonwood tree a few dozen yards away, Dólii climbed into a covered wagon. Her mother already waited on the seat.

"Dólii!" Caroline ignored Willis's odd look and hurried toward the wagon.

Dólii peered down at her, the reins already gathered in her hands.

"It was good to see you today." Caroline twisted her fingers together. "That man, that woman—they were horrid. I'm so sorry."

Dólii sighed and looked away. "There are good and bad of every kind of people, I suppose."

Generous of her to say so, since it must seem the latter abounded far more among *bilagáanas*. Yet Caroline sensed much remained unsaid. Dólii didn't trust her yet—not that she could blame her. She touched the corner of the wagon. "You are all right?"

Dólii's mother murmured something to her in Navajo, and Dólii lifted the reins.

"Of course." Her polite smile returned. "Thank you for helping me roll up the rug, Miss Haynes."

"Please call me Caroline."

But the horses had already started, the wagon rumbling away.

She and Willis said little on the ride home. Until he suddenly turned off the road.

"What—where are we going?"

"Thought we'd take the scenic route."

Caroline held onto the seat as they jounced over rocks and clumps of grass, as the terrain gradually greened until she glimpsed silvery-brown water glinting ahead.

Oh, Lord, not the river. Not today.

"My aunt's idea." Willis set the brake and pulled a picnic basket from under the seat. He shot her a grin, bringing out that exasperating dimple. "Will you join me for a luncheon, Miss Haynes?"

Well, what was she to say?

So they sat on the bank, eating Miss Spencer's egg sandwiches, gazing at the rippling water, fish zigzagging by now and then.

Surely it wasn't a very good sign if you couldn't think of a thing to say to a man who'd proposed marriage to you.

"Why so quiet today, Caroline?" Willis tossed a crust to a lone crow, who squawked and flapped away.

She pulled the stem off her peach and rolled it between her fingers. It shouldn't still rankle for him to call her that, surely. "Just thinking."

"Of?"

Laughing children in clothing that seemed to have grown on them. Splashing water and feathery wild asparagus. Eyes the color of rich coffee and a man's hand gripping hers on this very riverbank, a hand she now realized she'd wished would never let go.

"Caroline?"

"At the trading post today." She glanced up at him, then away. "A rancher and his wife—I don't know if you saw them, but it was awful, the way they spoke about the Navajo. Why must there be such walls, such prejudice between people?"

"Mmm." Willis popped the last of the dried apricot cookies into his mouth and chewed. "It's a puzzlement, all right. I suppose the ranchers do have some grievances."

"But this land was never theirs to begin with."

Willis did not elaborate. After a moment, he reached into his back pocket and held out a narrow envelope. "This was waiting at the post for you."

Caroline took it, addressed in a familiar bold hand. Her heart did a little leap. *Father.* It seemed so long since she'd heard from him directly—Lillian was more of a letter-writer than he.

"Ready to go?" Willis stood and brushed off his trousers.

She opened the letter as they bounced toward home, savoring the cracking of the seal, slipping out the thick stationery embossed with Father's livery-stable letterhead.

My dearest daughter…

Her throat tightened. She could almost hear Father's voice through the penned words. Though he treated the family news more sparsely than did Lillian, Caroline nearly seemed home again while reading it. She could see Toby's grin, hear Benji's chatter, smell the faint scent of lemon verbena that lingered in the cupboards from Mama's favorite soap. Homesickness gripped her chest, stronger than ever for its absence the past few months. Perhaps it was right she had mailed that letter to Pastor Jensen … perhaps the East was where she belonged after all.

As if he might read her thoughts, she shifted away from Willis and focused on the last paragraph.

I asked Lillian to let me write this letter to you. King David wrote in the Psalms that "weeping may endure for a night, but joy cometh in the morning." Truly this has come to pass for both Lillian and me, for the Lord has not only given us each other, but is now seeing fit to bless us with a child together, even in our "old age." I know, Daughter, you will share our joy...

Caroline folded the sheet and tucked it back within the envelope, heaviness creeping over her. Of course, she would be glad for Father and Lillian—must be. They were building a family together, a new family out of two, into which Toby and Benji were still young enough to be grafted.

But she wasn't. Caroline touched her locket. There was no place for her, back home, not a lasting one.

She wished she hadn't mailed that letter.

CHAPTER THIRTY-SEVEN

Central New Mexico, August 1911

"Huh!"

Tse pulled back his lining bar and thrust the chisel point into the gravel ballast beneath the rail again. In unison with four other men on the track gang, he lunged his full weight against it to shift the monstrous length of steel back into place, joining in the shout.

"Huh!"

By the time the noon whistle blew, his throat was caked with dust. Tse coughed and wiped his sleeve across his face as he stood in the dinner line. His shoulders and arms, the backs of his legs, burned. Worse was the ache of homesickness. But he must get used to it. He would.

"Not much like herding sheep, is it?" Kee, another Navajo worker with big ears and a boyish smile, held out a canteen.

"*Ahe'hee'.*" Tse drank gratefully, the water, warm but clean, washing the grime from his throat. He handed the canteen back. "Good thing we're tough."

"We Navajos are the best workers on the gang." Kee's eyes twinkled in his round face.

At a sudden scuffle behind them, Tse turned, craning his neck to see.

Two men, one Navajo and one Negro, wrestled together, arms locked, then tumbled to the ground and rolled, punching, shoving.

"Stop!" Tse ran over. He reached to grab the arm of the Navajo worker, who looked barely out of his teens, then ducked to dodge a kick.

"All right, all right, break it up, boys." The foreman, a *bilagáana* like all the supervisors, strode over, scowling. "You fight, you get no dinner. Got it?"

A final scuffle, then the men tumbled apart and stood, breathing heavily.

Tse met the young black man's eyes and was cut by the coldness there. He turned back to join the end of the line, an ache weighting his heart. Was it not enough that both groups suffered injustice from the *bilagáanas*, that they should hate each other as well? He had noticed early on the track gang the distance his people kept from the Negro workers. It troubled him.

As he stepped forward in line, Tse caught a look from an older worker standing near, a black man with a white beard and patient eyes that gave him pause. Did the tension trouble that man too?

"So where's your family, Tsosie?" Kee asked that night in their makeshift bunkhouse, converted from a railroad car and stacked with double-decker beds.

"Near *Tsé Bit'a'í*." Rock with Wings—the Navajo name for Shiprock sent a throb of homesickness through his chest. He breathed deep, trying to ignore the scent of sweat and unwashed bodies that permeated the bunk car, and propped himself on one elbow. "Yours?"

"Two Gray Hills." Stretched out on the bunk across from Tse's, Kee fingered his small pouch of corn pollen. Like many of the *Diné* workers, he carried it with him to ward off evil. "Got me a wife and new baby, a girl. My Kaibah, she worries I'll take up with some woman in one of the towns we pass through. Some of the men do, you know, being away from their families so long and all. But Kai-bah, she needn't worry about me." He flopped onto his back and stared at the dirty underside of the mattress above him.

Kee seemed so young—Tse had little thought him married with a child. And how he loved them. Tse could see it by the pinch drawing Kee's eyebrows together.

But after a moment, his new friend flashed his usual grin. "How about you? Got a girl back home?"

Tse studied the fresh blisters on his hands. "I—no."

"You sure?" Kee sat up and thunked his head on the bunk above. He lay back down, rubbing the top of his skull. "You don't sound too sure."

"I am." Tse rolled to face the wall. He closed his eyes, listening to the heavy breathing of men around him, a burst of raucous laughter from outside the car, the far-off howl of a coyote, a piercing reminder of home.

"Hey, Tsosie."

Tse rolled back.

Kee held out an arrowhead in his palm. "Got an extra one of these—had them blessed by a *Hatááłii* back home. I offer it to you, my friend. May it protect you until you can return home to your loved ones—*whoever* they may be." A teasing lilt entered his voice at the end.

Could he refuse without offending? "Thank you, my friend. But I do not need it."

"Got one already?"

"I trust in Creator to protect me." Tse shifted. "I am a—I follow the Jesus Way."

"You go to one of those mission schools?" Kee pulled his hand back and turned the arrowhead over.

Tse nodded.

"Me too. St. Michael's. Just for a year or so. I never really got all the Jesus talk. The old ways make more sense to me."

"It was not just the school teaching for me." Tse drew a breath. "It was when I met Jesus Himself."

"What do you mean?"

"Hey!" The bunk above Tse creaked, and a tousled head leaned down to glare. "Some of us trying to get some sleep."

"Sorry." Tse tugged the thin blanket over his shoulders, listening as Kee's breathing settled and evened. Odd, no one had complained of their talking until he mentioned Jesus. Maybe that fellow had just had enough for the night—or maybe he had been embittered by mission schools, like so many. Or perhaps there was more to it. Certainly there was a Power in this world who did not want Jesus shared with anyone.

Ahe'hee', Jesus, that You are greater. Your name will be exalted. And thank You for a friend here. Kee's grin, his teasing, eased Tse's heart. He let his weary muscles relax into the lumpy mattress. A bit of the *Dinétah* was Kee, here so far from home.

How about you . . . got a girl back home?

Caroline's eyes, gray and soothing as summer rain, swam through his mind, and he jerked. He pressed his fingertips against his eyelids, against the sweet memory of her face. *Diyin God, please—get her out of my head.*

Rain, on the first day of school.

Caroline stared at the wet, running panes, barely lightening with the gray of dawn. She cupped her hands around her cup of morning coffee, her mind still blurry from little sleep and the chaos of the previous night. Clouds had been already gathering yesterday morning, and she'd suggested to Willis that they wait on collecting the children, even a day or two, till the weather cleared. But he'd insisted they not disrupt the set calendar.

No surprise there.

"Odd, the amount of rain lately." Miss Spencer spoke from behind Caroline.

At the stirrings of thumping drawers and childish voices, Caroline turned and headed for the dormitories. *Lord, get us through this day. Especially these boys and girls.* She still needed to connect with Samuel—Willis had taken charge of the boys last night, and Caroline had barely managed to touch the child's hand in passing, though she thought his eyes lit slightly when she had.

At least she'd been able to convince Willis to delay the hair-cutting last night. The children had been soaked by the time they got them all back to the mission, and he'd acquiesced to warm baths and bed. Lord willing, they'd have no illness to start off the term. But there would be no putting off the barbering this morning. Her stomach clenched at the thought.

At breakfast, she tried to catch Samuel's gaze from the other table, but he kept his eyes on his mush every time she looked. At least he was eating, or seemed to be.

When Willis entered with scissors, bowl, and sheet, though, Samuel's head jerked up. He leaned his elbows on the table and pressed his thumbs together under his chin as Willis told the boys to follow him out on the porch, asking Isaiah to translate.

The boys filed out. Samuel stayed sitting.

Would he refuse? Disobey?

Willis waited, holding the door open. Slowly, Samuel slid from the bench and shuffled out the door.

The memory of him running and laughing at Esther's *kinaaldá* constricted Caroline's throat. She stood and began to clear the tables, ears straining for any sound from the porch as she stacked plates and bowls, folded napkins, gathered cups.

A child wailed outside.

Caroline jerked, sending dirty spoons clattering to the floor.

Miss Spencer rose from the head of the girls' table and cleared her throat. "Are you all right?"

Caroline nodded dumbly and knelt to gather the utensils. Her head pounded. Had that been Samuel? It hadn't sounded quite like him. Maybe one of the new small boys—poor little soul.

She should go out there, should do something. What?

After taking the dishes to the kitchen, she escaped to the washroom with the girls to comb and trim and braid their hair. Esther, seeming half a head taller than in July, helped.

Perhaps Samuel had resigned himself this year. Willis had not asked her to help this time, no doubt afraid she would refuse. But the new little boys—she was almost sure she heard more than one crying.

"Miss Caroline!" Anna twisted her head, her brows pinching together. "Water's dripping down my neck."

Caroline laid down the comb, with which she had apparently been continuously wetting Anna's hair. "I'm sorry." She grabbed a towel and dabbed the child's neck. "There. Better?"

The day passed in a blur of assigning seats, of learning names—names unfamiliar to both her and the children, as Willis doled out "Christian" ones. Of trying till her head ached to communicate with lost-looking, frightened-eyed little girls and boys.

The bell rang before she'd even finished assigning reader levels. She sat on the edge of her desk and rubbed her throbbing temples as the children filed out the door.

Samuel, hair cropped short once more, had sat quiet on his bench all day. Every time Caroline tried to catch his eye or passed near him, he studied his shoes. Amid the bustle with the new ones, she couldn't take the time to kneel beside him and see if she could get him to smile.

Did he resent her, for not being there for him this morning? More, should she even be participating in all this?

You say your Jesus loves us, then you take our children and destroy everything that makes them who they are.

She wanted to block her ears against the memory. The school policies weren't her idea—and the children did need some sort of modern education, didn't they, the world being what it was? Oh, if only she could talk to Tse.

Her throat aching, she tangled her fingers in her hair. *Lord, if you don't want me teaching at this school, I am willing to walk away. Just make it clear, I beseech Thee. I don't know what to do.*

CHAPTER THIRTY-EIGHT

Caroline stared at the tipsy numbers on the papers before her a few weeks later, the figures seeming to dance in the sitting-room lamp and firelight. She'd rather work arithmetic conundrums herself than correct them. Almost.

At a soft step in the doorway, she looked up, expecting to see Willis outlined in the darkness. Her breath caught in her throat. *Samuel.*

He stood blinking, small hands twisting his nightshirt like Benji when wakened with a nightmare, feet bare despite the late September night's chill.

"Can't you sleep, dear one?" She laid aside the papers.

He only looked at her. Did he still understand so little English? With several new and needy children, she'd still not had the time with him she wanted this term. One small boy—Absalom, of all names Willis could have picked—couldn't sit still for more than two minutes together, dancing in his seat, knocking his slate to the floor, pinching and pushing his classmates. Sorely as he tried her patience, she sensed much of his misbehavior had the same root as Samuel's withdrawnness the previous term. And a little slip of a girl, christened Deborah, barely would meet Caroline's eyes and flinched whenever spoken to.

But Samuel.

Caroline pushed back her chair and held out her arms.

He hesitated only a moment, then padded toward her and climbed onto her lap, snuggling his head against her shoulder.

Caroline leaned her cheek on his cropped, sweet-smelling hair. *Thank You, Lord.* She held him close, rocking back and forth, the snap of the fire and tick of the clock wrapping them in a gentle blanket.

Samuel shifted and nestled closer to her. He reached for her hand and played with her fingers.

Caroline ran her other hand over his hair and down to his ear. Gently, she tweaked it. "*Ajaa*'," she whispered.

"Ear." The corners of Samuel's mouth lifted.

Caroline touched her eyebrow. She didn't remember this one. "Eye?"

He twisted to see. "*Anáá*'."

"*Anáá*'?"

He grinned and nodded, those precious white teeth peeking out again. Next he taught her "nose" and "belly," sending them both into fits of muffled giggles.

Oh, how wonderful to hear him laugh. It eased a knot in her stomach she didn't know she had. Perhaps this term really would be different, better, than the last. She looked into his bright little face. If only she knew how to say, "I love you"—surely the children need-ed to hear that above all else, if they were ever to understand that the God the missionaries spoke of loved them too. For now, she just touched Samuel's nose with a gentle finger. "*Yá'át'ééh,* Shashyáázh."

"Caroline."

She looked up.

Willis stood just behind her chair, his mouth tight.

Samuel stiffened away from her.

She couldn't think of anything to say, just sat there, keeping her arms firm around the child on her lap.

Finally Willis expelled a breath. "Samuel, go to bed." He pointed down the darkened hallway.

Samuel pulled from her arms, sliding to the floor.

"And no more Navajo." Willis caught him by the shoulders as he passed. "Understand?"

Samuel stared at his toes.

After a moment, Willis released him, and Samuel fled down the hall toward the boys' dormitory, bare feet slapping the floorboards. A door in the distance opened, shut.

Silence stretched. A moment, two.

"You just don't get it, do you?" Willis's voice came quiet, tired. "But I've been easy on him long enough, on both of you."

Caroline bit her tongue against a retort.

"If that child is caught speaking Navajo again, he *will* be punished. I don't like paddling the children, but I'm not above a soap treatment."

"No, please!" She jerked to her feet. It would kill Tse if he learned his cousin suffered as he had. And what might it do to Samuel?

Willis folded his arms and stared at her.

"I won't play Navajo games with him anymore." She dropped her gaze, clenching her fingers together.

"I have your word?" Willis dropped his arms to his sides.

Caroline turned to the small table and gathered her papers with shaking hands. Like jumbled arithmetic figures, each time she thought she'd made progress, she only tangled things up further. "You have my word."

The fifth of October dawned chilly and windy, with heavy clouds to the north. Willis, stuffed-up and frog-voiced with a cold, kept to his room except for teaching classes, making Caroline's aim to avoid him somewhat more practical. The children were peevish and restless, perhaps reacting to the weather or the disruption in routine—she couldn't tell and felt too nerve-frayed herself to puzzle it out.

Willis appeared in the sitting room doorway just as Caroline headed to her room after dismissing class, craving a few moments alone before diving into supper preparations.

"Can you help Isaiah with the chores?" He blew his nose into his handkerchief. "My aunt says I shouldn't be out in the cold."

Caroline turned. He didn't look good—eyes and nose reddened, he leaned on the doorframe as if for support.

"I'd agree with her. But what would I do?"

"Milk, feed, whatever. Isaiah'll show you." He disappeared, sneezes echoing behind him.

Caroline sighed, trying to squelch the prickles of resentment. So much for a few moments of quiet. But Willis hadn't gotten sick on purpose. Milking, though? She wouldn't know where to start.

"You just crouch beside her—here." Isaiah grabbed a milking stool off the wall and set it on the milking stall floor beside Yázhí, who stamped her foot and stretched her neck toward the bucket of grain he held out of her reach.

Caroline lowered herself onto the stool, tucking her skirts as much out of the way as possible.

Isaiah squatted beside her, setting the bucket under Yázhí's nose. The goat ducked her head in and gobbled.

"Then pinch the top of her teat between the base of your thumb and forefinger—just so—and roll your other fingers down." A thick stream of milk hissed into the pail.

He made it look so easy. Caroline reached forward and gingerly took hold of the warm teat as Isaiah had demonstrated. She squeezed. Nothing.

"Be sure you close off the top first, or the milk goes back up." Isaiah leaned across her and squeezed another stream.

Biting the inside of her cheek, Caroline tried again. And again. At last, a few warm white drops dribbled out.

"Good." Flashing a rare smile, Isaiah stood and moved to the next doe.

Well. Hadn't she done scores of things she'd never attempted since arriving at Hebron? Caroline scooted the stool a bit closer. "Just the two of us, then, Yázhí."

She clamped and rolled and squeezed, the dribbles gradually becoming streams, albeit far weaker than Isaiah's. Caroline's hands ached. How had Tse handled this twice a day on his own, and for half a dozen goats?

Yázhí finished her grain and shifted her back foot, dangerously near the bucket.

"Almost finished, girl." Caroline scooted it away. How long could the milk keep coming out, after all?

At last the hissing streams began to slow. Caroline glanced into the pail. Nearly half full. Wouldn't Tse be proud? She leaned forward to massage Yázhí's udder as she'd seen him do to get the last drops.

Yázhí jerked her leg, banging against the pail. With a thud and a swish, it tipped over, milk gurgling out to soak into the straw littering the barn floor.

"Yázhí!" Caroline snatched up the pail, but only a spoonful remained, and that dirtied with manure. "Look what you did." She smacked the animal's rump. "Stupid goat."

Yázhí skittered away and out into the barnyard.

Her eyes hot, Caroline followed with the soiled pail.

Isaiah stood in the yard with the rest of the goats, holding a bucket of feed. He, of course, had finished milking all the rest while she'd done one. He gazed north, at the La Plata mountains of Colorado—or where they could usually see them, gilded with the last rays of sun at this time of day. Now only a dark bank of clouds lowered, covering the peaks. Must be raining hard up there.

"I've never seen the mountains hidden so long without break." Isaiah pointed with pursed lips.

"She kicked the pail over." Caroline set the bucket down and clamped her hands on her elbows. "I lost all the milk."

"It happens." Isaiah scanned the milling goats and rubbed his ear. "They are skittish tonight."

Indeed, they didn't seem able to stay still—now prancing with heads lifted and necks outstretched, then running together into a corner. Yázhí called for her kids, and her doeling trotted to her side while the buckling bleated madly from the males' pen. Ears flopping, Yázhí swung her head from one direction to the other as if reassuring herself her offspring were all right.

"You think the storm will reach down here?" Caroline stepped to Isaiah and touched his elbow.

"Don't know. But I better get them inside." With the same low whistle Tse used, he herded the goats into the barn, where the chickens already roosted, and shut the door.

Caroline glanced back over her shoulder as she followed Isaiah toward the mission. The air seemed oddly heavy, but the clouds stayed far away, the setting sun slanting amber rays against the gray. She halted and scanned the mission yard again. Gate latched, stock all safe in the barn.

She wished she hadn't slapped Yázhí. Lately she felt ready to snap at anyone and anything, but no doubt the little goat had only been tired of standing so long for a clumsy milker. "I'm sorry, girl," she whispered in the direction of the barn. "I'll bring you a treat tomorrow."

She turned and mounted the steps. Right now someone needed to fix supper.

During the meal, a knock came at the door. Willis had already taken to his bed, so with a look to Miss Spencer, Caroline rose to answer it.

Tse's father stood on the porch.

For a moment, Caroline couldn't think. "Mr. Tsosie—*Ya'at'eeh*."

He removed his hat, exposing his graying twist of hair. "*Ya'at'eeh*." He gestured to inside the mission, his eyes grave.

She stepped back for him to enter, then shut the door. What on earth?

Scanning the room, he said something in Navajo.

"Isaiah?" Caroline held up her hand.

The boy hurried to her side and listened, respectfully keeping his eyes from the elder man's face. "He wants to see Rev. Abernathy."

Caroline hesitated, then hurried to Willis's closed door and rapped.

After a moment, Willis appeared in shirtsleeves, bleary eyed.

"I'm sorry, but there's someone here to see you. It's—Tse's father."

Willis raised his eyebrows, then disappeared, coming back in a jacket and his spectacles. He strode into the dining room, amazingly brisk for his sickness. "Good evening, Mr. Tsosie. What can I do for you?"

Isaiah translated, then waited while Tse's father spoke, illustrating with gestures Caroline couldn't decipher.

"He says the river is rising." Isaiah shifted his gaze to Caroline, then back to Willis. "He thinks, with all the rain in Colorado, it could get very high. His father used to speak of a time like this long ago. He is moving his flocks and family to higher ground and says the children should be moved also."

Willis nodded in silence a moment, then locked his hands behind him and rose slightly on his toes. "Please thank Mr. Tsosie for his concern."

After the translation, Tse's father studied Willis's face and spoke again.

"He asks what you are going to do." Isaiah rubbed his ear.

"I do not believe the mission to be in any danger. But again, we appreciate his concern."

"Willis." Caroline gripped the back of a chair. "Perhaps we should consider what he has said."

"Good evening to you, Mr. Tsosie." Not looking at Caroline, Willis folded his arms and waited.

Tse's father looked the young preacher up and down and made a soft pffting sound under his breath. Then he turned and strode to the door.

"Mr. Tsosie." Caroline hurried after him.

He paused.

"Thank you." Her mind fumbled to remember what Tse had taught her. "*Ahe'hee'*."

He looked back at her then, and her breath caught. His eyes—so like Tse's.

His father reached out and placed his hand on hers. And then, he was gone.

Caroline shut the door and pressed her palms against it. The click of Willis's door within the sitting room turned her around. Pressing her lips together, she strode after him.

"Miss Haynes..." Miss Spencer softly remonstrated.

Caroline pretended not to hear, but she did shut the sitting room door before tapping on Willis's again.

He swung it open. "What now?"

"Don't you think we should do something?"

"About what? We haven't had so much as a raindrop. If there were any legitimate danger of flooding, they would send warning from Shiprock."

"How? We have no telephone."

"They would find a way."

"But this man knows the land. This country and its rhythms are in his blood."

"I'm not about to give some Navajo premonition credence over my own common sense. I'm going to bed."

The door shut, and Caroline stared at it a moment. *Go to bed.* How could he so dismiss a threat to the children's safety, no matter how unlikely? She paced the sitting room until the clatter of dishes signaled supper's end. Forcing herself calm, she smoothed her apron and went to wash up.

Perhaps Willis was right. She swished a soapy washrag across a plate, then dipped it in hot rinse water. But the way he'd looked down his spectacles at Mr. Tsosie... she scrubbed a tin cup, her middle heating again.

Caroline tossed in bed that night, recurring dreams flitting in and out like malevolent moths. At last she sat up, rubbing her eyes, then froze and listened.

Someone in the mission was sneezing, small explosions like repeat gunfire. And coughing.

Willis.

Caroline lay back down. Let him cough. He thought he could do so well without anyone else, let him try.

Something far-off clanged—the stove lids. Trying to make himself a cup of tea, no doubt. She stifled a sudden giggle. Had he ever even used the kitchen stove before? *Don't burn the mission down, now, Rev. Abernathy.*

More explosive sneezes, a fit of coughing. Silence for some time. And then a distant crash and clatter, as if he dropped the teakettle.

Land sakes. She swung her legs over the edge of her bed and stuffed her feet into her slippers. She might as well go and help. She certainly wasn't getting any sleep this way.

Caroline found Willis nursing a sore hand in a circle of lamp-light at the kitchen table.

"What did you do, try to lift it with your bare hands?" She found the cast-iron teakettle lid on the floor, replaced it, and used a tea towel to pour a cup of tea. "There."

"Sorry." He took the cup.

Her disastrous attempt at cooking in Dezbah's hogan flashed through her mind and stilled the sharp retort she had ready. What was the matter with her these days?

But she didn't trust herself to speak much. She stirred honey into his tea and had him scoot his chair near the boiling kettle to breathe the steam. Then she smoothed and turned down his bed, her stomach flinching at the intimacy of the act, though he did not enter his room until she had left.

Willis said little, just "good night" and thanked her before turning in.

She returned to the kitchen for a cup of tea herself. Sipping the calming brew, she glanced at the clock. Nearly five in the morning.

She headed through the sitting room on her way back to the dormitory. A sound caught her ear, and halting, she listened. Had the wind picked up? But it sounded different, steadier somehow.

She unlatched the front door and creaked it open. The noise filled her ears and struck cold trembling into her limbs.

Water. Rushing water.

CHAPTER THIRTY-NINE

"Willis!" Her hand shaking, Caroline rapped on his door for the third time that night, then barged in, heedless of propriety. "The river, it's coming ... it's flooding. I hear it."

"What in ... " He struggled up, threw on his dressing gown, and followed her to the front door, pausing to strike a match and light a lamp along the way.

Stepping out onto the porch, he lifted the lamp high. "Dear God."

Only a few hundred yards away, the road leading out from the mission had disappeared beneath a dark surge of water.

Willis stood frozen a moment, then spun and charged back inside, pushing Caroline ahead of him. "Wake the children. Hurry."

She stumbled from bed to bed, shaking sleepy-eyed and tousle-haired little girls awake, pushing uniforms into the hands of the older ones so they could help her dress the younger. *Please, Lord, keep the water down. Please, help us get out in time. Please ...*

Voices and thumps down the hall signaled the boys were up. Esther looked at Caroline with frightened eyes.

"It's all right." Caroline gave Anna a quick squeeze. "There's just—some water outside. We need to go to a safe place." But where?

"Bring them all on the porch." Willis spoke from the doorway. "The boys are already out there."

Fingers fumbling, Caroline tied a last pair of shoes and hurried the girls out into the dining room.

Miss Spencer piled food into a picnic basket on the table, her hands trembling like dry leaves in wind. A jar of apricot preserves crashed to the floor. "Lord, have mercy." She bent toward it, and Willis caught her before she fell.

"Leave it." He grabbed the basket in one hand and supported his aunt with the other. "Come on."

Caroline shepherded the girls toward the door. The water's roar filled their ears as soon as they stepped on the porch. Deborah and Anna started to cry. *Lord, help us.*

"I don't know what to do." Willis peered through the darkness. "We sure can't use the road."

"We should have left last night like Mr. Tsosie said!" Caroline clutched a whimpering Anna close, the little girl's arms tightening around her skirt. "Why wouldn't you listen to him?"

"There was no flood warning!"

"So you would have listened if it came from Farmington, but not from a Navajo man?" Caroline's voice was rising, but she couldn't help it. "Or do you only believe it when you see for yourself? Pride, isn't it? Foolish, stubborn, stupid pride!"

"We don't have time for this!" Willis grabbed her arm and hurried her down the steps, dragging Anna with them. The other children hurried behind. "We'll have to drive back up into the bluffs. Isaiah, help me hitch the teams."

Caroline blinked angry blur from her eyes. He was right, this was no time for a tirade. She gathered the children around her in the yard, trying to count heads in the gray pre-dawn.

A faint bleating caught her ear and skipped her heart. "Willis! What about the animals?"

"We'll let them out. Have to fend for themselves."

A moment later, pattering hooves filled the barnyard. A chicken squawked. A warm, solid shape brushed Caroline's knee. One of the goats. Yázhí?

The jingle of harness, snort and stomp of horses. Esther pressed against Caroline's shoulder, holding Deborah on her hip. Anna still hugged Caroline's skirts.

"All right, load 'em up!" Lantern light danced as Willis strode toward them. "Caroline, you go with Isaiah. I'll take my aunt. Children, get in. Hurry!"

They scrambled for the wagons. Caroline helped boost the smaller ones into the wagon beds. She scanned the shifting shapes—so difficult to see—and began counting off names.

From the other wagon, Miss Spencer did the same, her voice quavering. "Dorcas—Elijah—Asa—Esther."

"You got Samuel?" Willis hollered.

Wasn't he with his sister, in the other wagon? Caroline peered among the clumped shapes in the dimness. "Samuel?" Please, not again.

"Here, Miss Caro-line," he piped.

Thank You, Lord. "We have him."

"All right. Isaiah, keep a tight rein. I'll go first. Tell everyone to hold onto—"

A rush of cold drenched Caroline's boots, and she sucked her breath with a gasp. "Willis—the river!"

"Get in! Hurry!"

She scrambled, water sloshing, tugging her ankles, and heaved herself up on the seat.

A panicked bleating gripped her heart. "The goats!"

"Leave 'em—they're sure-footed, can find their way." Willis yelled at his team, and the wagon jolted forward.

Beside her, Isaiah slapped the reins, tension emanating from his lithe young body.

By the light of the lanterns swinging from each wagon, she could see the water spreading. A channel had somehow cut behind the school and now rushed to meet the surge in front. *Dear God, help us.*

Willis stayed ahead of it for a few moments, then the muddy river gushed around his wheels. The horses whinnied and shied, but he urged them on.

Beneath her, their horses' hooves sloshed through. The water still lapped low, but the current tugged already.

"Up this way!" Willis's call came through the darkness.

He was veering past the orchard up toward the bluffs where he had taken her that first day, the church site.

If only it were lighter, so they could see.

Isaiah half stood beside her, every muscle straining to control the team, murmuring under his breath in Navajo.

Was he praying? *Dear Lord, help us. Please.*

Then a thud, and the wagon jerked to a halt. The wheels spun, churning up fountains of muddy water. Isaiah slapped and slapped the reins, yelling, fully standing now. Several children in back began to cry.

"Willis—we're stuck." Caroline reached a comforting hand behind her.

"Tarnation. Wait, I'm coming."

A splash, a thud, then a scream.

"Miss Spencer!" Caroline gripped the wagon seat. *Dear God.*

"Some debris hit the wagon, the horse reared, Willis went down, and I don't know where he is!"

"I'm coming." Caroline swung her legs over the wagon side, fumbling for footing, her heart pounding in her throat.

"But Miss Caroline—"

For the first time, she heard fear in Isaiah's voice. "Stay right there." As if he would go anywhere else.

The cold rushed over her ankles again, and she clung to the wagon side to get her bearings. Still only mid-calf deep, but the current pulled slyly. She let go the wagon, holding her arms out for balance, and sloshed ahead. Once she nearly fell, but righted. At last she touched the corner of the other wagon.

"Willis?" She didn't want to marry him, but she didn't want him to die! She slid her hand along the wagon. On higher ground now, the water only lapped about her ankles here.

She stumbled over something and fell to her hands and knees. Reaching out, she felt a boot. "Willis? Can you hear me?"

A low groan.

She found his head, felt a lump. "We must get you back into the wagon."

The horses reared and plunged, shifting the near wheel dangerously close to Willis.

"Shh—easy there." Caroline jumped up and snatched at the reins. How did one calm horses? Oh, for Tse. *Please, Lord, calm them.* "Easy now." Miraculously, they stopped jerking at the harness like mad things, though they still snorted.

"Esther?" She peered up to the wagon.

A dark head popped up.

"Hold the reins for me. Hold tight and don't let go."

Esther scrambled onto the seat and snatched the leather straps.

"Good girl." Caroline dropped back beside Willis. "Work with me, now, Rev. Abernathy."

Another groan, but he shifted into a sitting position.

Caroline slung one of his arms over her shoulder and staggered to her feet. They stumbled a few steps, then Willis swayed and nearly took them both down.

A cry from Isaiah's wagon. "The water's getting deeper!"

Caroline began to shake under Willis's weight. With a final push, she rounded the corner of the wagon back and leaned him against it. The children helped pull him in, only his feet left hanging out. It would have to do.

"Miss Caroline!" The student's voices from the other wagon grew shrill above the horses' frenzied neighing.

She turned. In the graying toward dawn, she could see the water, surrounding the mired wagon. The horses lunged at their harness, foaming at the mouth. Isaiah sawed at the reins.

"Cut them!" Miss Spencer's voice, though quavering, sliced sharp. "Cut the horses loose, Isaiah."

He fumbled for his knife and whacked through the leather straps of the harness. After what seemed an eternity, the horses charged free through the water and galloped away toward the bluffs.

A child's wail sliced above the roar of the water.

Samuel. Caroline plunged into the muddy current, but the strength of its pull stopped her short. Past her knees now—it could tug any of them under. How in the world to get the children out?

"A chain." Again, Miss Spencer spoke from behind her. "Hold hands and form a chain."

Of course. Caroline crept as far out as she dared, then braced herself against the current and held out her hands. They were only a few yards away—surely this could work. "Isaiah, come down into the water and hold onto the wagon. We can pass the children between us."

He hesitated so long she wondered if he had heard, but finally he slid down the wagon's side, holding himself suspended a moment before finally dropping into the water. Hanging onto the corner, he spoke to the children. No one moved.

"What's wrong?" Caroline shifted her footing, trying to balance.

"They're afraid." Isaiah shifted, clinging tight. "Getting in muddy flood water is a bad omen."

"Tell them they must—the whole wagon could be swept away!"

Isaiah turned back and spoke again. A moment of silence—then Nathan's stocky legs appeared over the side. His knuckles straining against the corner boards, Isaiah reached one arm to steady the boy, helping him lower into the churning water. Then stretching as far as he could, he guided him toward Caroline.

She took a step closer, then another, pushing against the flooding tug, praying not to fall.

Someone gripped her hand from behind, and she turned to see Dorcas, holding the wagon side with her other.

Caroline nodded and squeezed the girl's hand, then stepped farther out. Almost—she could almost reach him—then Nathan's wet, pudgy fingers found hers, and she drew him safely to the other side. Air rushed into her lungs as she remembered to breathe.

Now again. *Continue to help us, O Lord.*

Anna came next, then another child, and another. At last only Samuel, Absalom, and Deborah huddled in the back of the wagon.

The water was deepening.

"Come!" Caroline waved her free arm wildly, beckoning, trying to stay upright.

But the children clung to each other and the back of the wagon, shaking, crying.

Isaiah hung onto the corner of the wagon, bracing himself against the water's flow, lacking the energy to shout any longer.

"Children! Come *now!*" Her voice rasped from shouting.

The wagon rocked. Deborah screamed.

Dear Lord, it was coming loose from the mud—any moment the entire wagonload could be carried away. A surge of panic choked her. *God help us, what do I do?*

Speak their language.

The answer came so swiftly, so suddenly, it startled her threatening tears away. Caroline took a deep breath and stretched out her hand once more. "Shashyáázh!" she called, using his Navajo name. "Shashyáázh!"

He stopped his panicked wailing and seemed to search for the voice, finally meeting her eyes.

She held his gaze and beckoned, just as he had that June day at the river when he wanted to show her the baby ducks. "*Hágo, Shashyáázh—hágo.*"

Shashyáázh stared at her. The air had lightened so she could see the jerky rise and fall of his chest. Then, his eyes never leaving hers, he inched forward on his bottom across the wagon bed, almost disappearing from her view as the front boards hid him. His head popped up, and he clung to the side, staring down at the churning water.

"That's it, Shashyáázh." Caroline hardly dared breathe. "*Hágo.*"

He hiked one foot over the side, turned on his stomach, and slid down toward Isaiah. The older boy caught his arm, but Shashyáázh slipped under the water. Isaiah yanked. The child came up sputtering, flailing bravely toward shore.

Caroline reached, her arms burning as she clung to Dorcas's hand and stretched toward Shashyáázh. And then her fingers closed around his, and he was pressed against her skirt, coughing, shuddering, safe.

"Good boy." She hugged him hard and gave him a push up the hill. "Go see Sháńdíín."

Caroline looked ahead once more to see Deborah clambering over the side. *Thank You, Lord—thank You.* Isaiah caught and passed her, then Absalom. Nathan came to stretch between Caroline and Dorcas, helping them reach far enough to pull Isaiah to safety.

The boy collapsed in the shallows, shaking, gasping for breath.

Caroline knelt beside him and hugged his soaked, quivering back. "You are a hero, Isaiah." If only she could tell him so in his own tongue.

But the water was still rising. Caroline touched Isaiah's shoulder. "Can you drive?"

He nodded and staggered to his feet.

Caroline surveyed the cluster of shivering children. "We can't all fit in one wagon."

Miss Spencer turned on the seat. "Let the smaller ones ride in the back with Rev. Abernathy. The rest will have to walk."

Isaiah took the reins from Esther, who scrambled down to stand by Caroline. Her brother clung to her.

Caroline hugged the girl's shoulders. "Where will we go?"

"We'll have to circle round and head for the trading post. The ground is higher there, and Willis needs a doctor." Miss Spencer's voice shook at the last.

It wasn't until they reached the dry tops of the bluffs that Caroline turned to look down. She pressed her knuckles to her lips to stifle a cry.

From hill to hill across the entire river valley rushed one brown, angry torrent, the mission buildings merely toy houses tossed in a mud puddle.

Father in heaven, I didn't mean for you to answer my prayer like this.

CHAPTER FORTY

"Move along!"

At the foreman's bark, Tse pushed harder, his muscles straining with Kee and another worker to wrestle a boulder off the track. At last it rolled aside with a crash, and he straightened and swiped at the sweat dripping off his nose.

"Now let's see you tackle one of these little rocks all yourself." Kee slapped him on the back.

Tse grinned and grabbed his pick again. "You first."

The foreman moved on down the track, shouting orders as the ring of picks and shovels clearing a rockslide from the steeply inclined track echoed through the canyon.

The sun climbed higher, blazing through his cotton shirt and sending streams of sweat down his back, beating upon the Navajo men around him and the Negro track gang working slightly farther down the pass.

Tse swung his pick against the rocks, falling into rhythm with the chanting of the darker-skinned workers down the line. Much like his people back home had songs for sheepherding and corn grinding, these men of African heritage seemed to have songs for everything. Once in a while he caught snippets of the words—sometimes they sang of Jesus, of heaven. But their songs were nothing like those of Willis and the Spencers at the mission. Instead, these melodies seemed wholly to belong to them, to be theirs. It awakened a throbbing in his heart, for his people too to have songs that were their own to sing to the Creator, not only ones borrowed and adapted from the *bilagáanas*. He wished he could talk to one of the black men about it.

"Watch out!"

Startled, Tse leapt from the path of a boulder crashing down the canyon. His heart pounded in his ears.

"That was close." Kee clambered up a pile of rocks for a better angle. "Gotta watch your toes, Tsosie."

After a moment's silence, the rhythm of picks and shovels picked up once more.

Tse blew out a breath and lifted his tool again, sending a half smile up to Kee. "You be careful too, my friend."

He aimed at a new rock pile, trying to push aside a niggling anxiety. If only he could be sure all the men had understood the safety briefing that morning. Rattled off in English at the break of day, he often sensed it served more to cover the railroad legally than to actually ensure the workers understood the conditions they would face that day. Even Kee, after a year or two in boarding school, still lacked proficiency in English. Some of the other Navajo men spoke barely a word and understood little more.

His muscles swung easily, the monotonous ping and scrape letting his mind roam. How was his father managing with the sheep, or did Dólii take them out these days? And Nezwood, had he stopped coming around? What of Willis, and the mission, and Caroline—no, he must not think of Caroline.

The rumble of sliding rocks, low and threatening, echoed through the canyon, pulling him back from the *Dinétah*.

Then a crash, a strangled cry, jerked Tse upright.

Men dropped their picks and ran to cluster near a settling cloud of dust, boulders tumbled loose where Kee had stood only a moment ago.

A head on the ground ... an outstretched arm.

Tse sprang, scrambling up the hillside. *No—please not Kee—please ...*

Two men struggled to shift the massive rock pinning his friend's body. Tse landed beside them, and with a final heave, it was off.

He fell to his knees on the rocky dirt. Dear God, the crushed arm ... the bloody, battered chest. He grasped the uninjured hand. "Kee?"

Kee coughed, bringing up blood. "Can't ... move."

"Don't try." *Diyin God, please.*

The foreman ran up, puffing. He stared down at Kee, shaking his head, and cursed under his breath. "Told you fellas to be careful." He pointed at one of the younger men. "You—go into Belen for a doctor."

The boy stared from the foreman to Tse.

Forcing his voice steady, Tse translated into Navajo, and the boy sprinted down the mountain.

"Tsosie—my wife—my baby—don't want to die!" Kee's fingers strangled Tse's.

"Your family will take care of them." Tse gripped his hand. It was true, it was the *Diné* way, they would be provided for. "And you're not ... "

But the words suffocated in Tse's throat.

"Don't want ... to die." Kee was shaking, turning cold, his eyes stark more with fear than pain.

"Jesus said, 'I am the resurrection, and the life.'" Tse swallowed down a choking in his throat. "'He that believeth in me, though he were dead, yet shall he live: and whosoever liveth and believeth in me shall never die.' He is the only *Doodatsaahii*—He alone has conquered death. If you repent of your sins, believe in Him—"

"Don't..." Kee was shaking his head. He coughed, more blood trickling from the side of his mouth. "Don't get it. Never... got it."

Tse's head pounded, his eyes blurring. *ShiDiyin God, help me! How do I make him understand?*

A heavy hand pressed his shoulder, and a man crouched beside him on one knee, placing his other hand on Kee's forehead. A hand darker than his or Kee's.

Tse looked up into the lined face of the white-haired black man he had heard the foreman call Martin. When he didn't just call him "boy."

"'The *Lord* is my shepherd—I shall not want.'" Martin lifted his face toward the sky. "'He maketh me to lie down in green pastures—He leadeth me beside the still waters. He *restoreth* my soul...'" His voice echoed from the canyon walls, his hand still firm on Tse's shoulder, gentle on Kee's head.

Tse's breath caught. *Shepherd.* He leaned closer to Kee.

"My friend, this man knows Jesus too." His heart thudding, Tse spoke into Kee's ear. "He reminded me how Jesus is called our shepherd. He cares for us just as we care for our sheep. He gave His life for us, just as we would risk our lives against wolf or bear for our sheep. All you have to do is tell Him you want Him to be your shepherd. He will take you home."

The fear in Kee's eyes focused, lightened. His eyelids dropped closed.

No. Tse clenched his jaw against the welling in his throat. *Oh, Lord, couldn't You have given him a little more time?*

"'Yea, though I walk through the valley of the shadow of death, I will fear no evil, for Thou art *with* me, Thy rod and Thy staff... they comfort me.'" Martin ran a gentle hand over Kee's still ribcage. "He's gone, ain't he?"

"Too late." A sob jerked from between Tse's clenched teeth. The man couldn't have understood Tse's Navajo words, so he tried to explain. "I tried to tell him—Jesus—"

"There, son." Martin patted his shoulder and eased himself onto the ground cross-legged beside Tse. "If it weren't too late for the thief on the cross, it weren't too late for him."

Perhaps. And there had been that peace that entered Kee's eyes at the last. But he could not know, could not be sure.

Tse pressed his fists to his forehead.

With the silent presence of one who knew sorrow, Martin wrapped a brawny arm about Tse's shoulders, and they cried together.

It was gone.

Caroline rose from kneeling on the muddy floorboards of her little room in the mission and stepped around the gaping hole by her bed, torn as the building slid from its foundation in the flood. If only she hadn't taken it off, that night before bed. But it was no use searching for Mama's locket anymore—nearly everything was gone, swept away in the surge of water that had torn through the building. Gone, or ruined.

She blinked back the stinging in her eyes as she made her way through the shambled dining room. Petty to grieve for a locket, with the devastation spanning the valley.

She retrieved the box of sodden books she had salvaged from the sitting room—the tightly closed door must have spared them the worst of the flooding—and paused in the open front doorway. The October sunshine comforted her cheeks, the fresh air cleansing after the stench of mold and mildew within.

In the yard, Willis and a few of the boys piled broken boards and muddied branches for burning. She'd never seen Willis so silent—he moved as if his mind were a score of miles away.

They had heard, though communication was slow with telephone lines, bridges, roads, and train tracks washed out, that Superintendent Shelton of Shiprock had sent a Navajo runner downriver in the middle of the night to warn of the flood. How Hebron had been missed was anybody's guess—perhaps Mr. Shelton had heard the rumor of them being shut down. Perhaps it had simply been an oversight. At any rate, it wasn't like they hadn't been warned.

Gripping the side of the doorframe, she let herself down into the empty space where the porch had been and headed toward Willis.

"A good two dozen are savable, I think." She nodded at the box in her arms.

"Put them in the wagon." He barely looked at her.

Biting the inside of her lip, she did so. She glanced at the barn, still in place, though with one wall caved in from the water's force. A single straggle-feathered chicken perched on a remaining fencepost, clucking discontentedly.

"Where are the other animals?" The anxiety that had niggled her all day pushed to the tip of her tongue.

"Who knows." Willis tossed another branch on the pile.

"Shouldn't we search for them?"

Willis began tearing the boards from a section of fence lying on the ground.

"Couldn't I at least take one of the boys and look?"

He tore off another board, yelped, and yanked off his work gloves to remove a splinter that had poked through. Flinging it aside, he looked up at her and blew out a breath. "Fine. Just don't be too long. I want to get back before dark."

Caroline nodded. Miss Spencer, back at the trading post with the few children whose families had yet to come for them, grew anxious with nightfall in recent days.

"Nathan." Willis turned.

The stocky child, youngest of the boys who had volunteered to help, looked up.

"Go with Miss Haynes to look for the goats."

Nathan dropped his branch and trotted toward Caroline.

They climbed the bluffs behind the mission, the crisp breeze teasing their hair and making Caroline glad of her shawl. At the top they paused for breath and gazed out over the valley. Cottonwoods flamed golden along the river, bright torches dotting the muddy sweep of destruction left by the deluge.

Caroline hugged herself. Where to even begin?

Nathan turned slowly round, scanning the high, junipered terrain behind them. Then with a tip of his head he was off, bounding over rocks and ducking under branches like a young goat himself, whistling that low call Tse always used.

Caroline struggled behind, her skirt catching on rabbit brush and snakeweed.

Lord, please… let us find them. At least some of them. At least Yázhí. But the goats would be together—they were herd animals, isn't that what Tse had always said? Assuming they had survived. Many ranchers had lost stock in the flood.

They seemed to hike for hours, finally circling back to the still-barren church site. Caroline paused to stare down at the rocky ledge where she had fallen that long-ago morning—a lifetime ago. The rattlesnake … and Tse …

"Miss Caroline!"

She whirled at Nathan's hiss, nearly losing her balance at the edge again. But she caught herself and hurried toward him, albeit with pounding veins.

"I heard something." He beckoned, his face alight.

Together they crept down the hillside, then rounded a clump of juniper brush. Nathan, ahead of her, froze and reached back his hand to her.

A glad cry escaped Caroline's lips.

There, lifting their heads to see about the strange noise, munching to hearts' content in sagebrush, grazed a small clutch of goats. Hebron goats—theirs.

Thank You, Father. Caroline hurried toward the animals, scanning each one. Yázhí—where was Yázhí?

"Some of the babies are missing." Nathan stepped to her side, his eyes darkened. "And two of the does."

No. Cold tightened Caroline's limbs and squeezed her throat. Yet somehow, she had known.

Sunset streaked the sky with orange by the time they pulled up back at the trading post. The boys piled out, but Willis stayed on the wagon seat, staring at the reins in his hands.

Caroline made no move to rise, either. Couldn't seem to summon the strength.

"I don't know if it's even worth it."

"What?" Caroline blinked and glanced at Willis, his profile dark in the falling dusk.

"The board is certain to close us down now. What's the use? We might as well sell the animals and be done with it, leave the wreckage for someone else to deal with." He swung down from the wagon and circled to assist her.

"You would just give up?" Caroline stood and let him help her down. She tried to withdraw her hand, but he closed his fingers tighter. A chill breeze rattled the cottonwood leaves in a near tree and sent a shiver through her.

"I have nothing to offer you now." His voice came husky.

"Willis … " She swallowed. She wasn't ready, hadn't expected to give her planned speech now, but it was time. "I can't marry you."

"I know, not now, I don't expect it. But perhaps, someday … "

"No." The word pricked her own heart with the stab she knew she was giving, but it would be crueler to hold out hope. "It can't be, Willis. Not even someday."

His fingers tightened on hers almost painfully. Then a long sigh with a catch in it. He released her, stepping to unhitch the horses. The clank and jingle of harness, a stomped hoof. He led the team off toward the barn, the falling darkness swallowing their shapes.

Caroline shivered again, a single cold tear seeping to tickle her cheek. No, she couldn't marry Willis, she was certain of that. But it still felt as though she had shut the door on her own last hope of marriage as well.

She stood there until her feet began to numb, then turned and entered the warmth and noise of the trading post.

Trader Hawkins joked with a few late customers clustered around the pot-bellied stove in the room's center. Tobacco smoke and coffee scented the air.

Caroline slipped past, averting her eyes from the men. Still shivering, whether from the warmth of the room or the heaviness in her heart, she reached the door to the back storeroom they had been granted and lifted her hand to the knob.

"Miss Haynes?"

She turned.

"Somethin' come for you today." Trader Hawkins rummaged behind the counter, then held forth a letter.

"Thank you." Caroline took the grimy envelope and turned it over for the return address. *Rev. Bernhard Jensen ... Pennsylvania.*

She softly pushed the door open and slipped into the room.

Amid boxes and barrels, the few children still under their care looked up from munching bread and cheese. Miss Spencer supervised from a straight-backed chair, set beside a crate supporting a kerosene lamp.

Caroline settled herself on a pallet next to Deborah, whose parents they still had not been able to contact since the flood. She ran her thumbs over the envelope, then bit her lip and slit the seal.

My dear Caroline,

With the salutation, she could suddenly hear Pastor Jensen's gentle, gravelly voice, see the little brick church, smell the peppermint scent of her Sunday school classroom.

I received your first letter with joy and took the liberty of sending copies of it to a number of other church mission boards with which I have connection, so moved I was by your descriptions of the children. After your second letter, though, I fear perhaps I was hasty, as it seems doubtful you will continue at the mission at all.

Little did he know how true that was now. Caroline shifted the letter closer to the flickering lamplight.

However, I have news that I hope will lift your spirit. I recently received an appeal from an old friend of my dear late wife's, who runs a school for impoverished boys and girls of the Philadelphia tenements. She is desperately in need of a teacher, one with a love for children and experience in handling them, and when I informed her of your inquiry, she was overjoyed. Should you wish to take the position, you could be instated as soon as you can arrive home ...

Caroline scanned the listing of pay and number of pupils, the headmistress's name and address. She lifted her head and gazed unseeing across the storeroom. So was this her answer, then?

With a yawn that squeaked like a kitten, Deborah cuddled against Caroline's side.

Leaning back against a huge sack of flour, Caroline pulled the little girl close and kissed her silky hair, grateful for the dim corner to hide her tears.

Yes, this must be her answer—she had nowhere else to go.

But that knowledge scarcely eased her aching heart.

CHAPTER FORTY-ONE

He missed him.

Tse stood in the line for the sweat lodge his tribesmen had constructed from earth and discarded railroad ties, mounding the earth in quiet defiance to the shabby bathhouse provided by the railroad. He shifted his feet, feeling oddly alone amid the line of men.

Kee's steady twinkle, his boyish laugh, his gentle teasing and quiet companionship had made the railroad bearable, had helped stem Tse's aching for home. Now the hammers and lining bars rang with a kind of hollowness, deepened whenever he thought of Kee's young wife and little daughter. He prayed for them each night, wondering if they had received the railroad letter with its coldly typewritten news, whether a trader would have to read it to them. Hoped he would be gentle.

Then the dream. Tse rubbed his nose. First come that night of Shashyáázh's illness, it had recurred twice since Kee's death. Soaring eagle-like over the beloved mesas and rivers of the *Dinétah*, he then would land in a field and hear that known voice.

Shiye', shepherd My sheep.

Always the same. But what did it mean? Tse stepped forward as a group of men began to emerge from the sweat lodge. He and the few ahead of him would be next.

His sheep—his people—were back home. And he couldn't be there, not now. Couldn't make enough to help support his own family. So what was he supposed to do?

"Hey, Tsosie." One of the foremen, reclining in a hammock strung between the supervisors' bunk cars, sat up holding a newspaper. "Ain't you from up Shiprock way?"

"Yes, sir." Tse waited while the man chewed his cigar. Those ahead of him were entering the sweat lodge.

"Huh." The foreman switched his cigar to the other side of his mouth. "Some flood they've had up there."

"Flood?" Tse stepped out of line, his pulse quickening.

"150 miles of land wiped out, three people killed." The man shook his head.

"May I have a look?" Tse held out his hand.

The man shot his eyebrows up, then glanced at his snoozing partners. "Sure, I guess, if you kin read."

Tse took the newspaper and scanned the article.

San Juan and Animas rivers higher than ever known in the memory of the oldest residents. Houses, lands, and bridges swept away. Only two bridges left in the county. Loss probably half a million dollars. The county of San Juan has just gone through the worst experience in its history since the coming of the white man.

"Where is the head foreman?" Tse handed the paper back, his head spinning.

His need for a sweat bath forgotten, he headed for the railcar used as an office. Sometimes a man just knew something, and Tse knew it now.

He needed to go home.

The foreman muttered and stalled, complaining that Navajos were "always up and leaving" for some ceremony or family need or other. Then days and nights passed, by boxcar, freighter, and on foot, before Tse sighted the first of the mountains guarding the four corners of his homeland. When he spied Shiprock's peaks spiring toward the sky, his heart seemed to take wings with the monolith's Navajo name.

But it crashed to earth at the destruction spanning the valley. Trees, houses, farms, bridges—all gone. Even much of the soil along the riverbanks washed away.

At last he hiked up toward the higher ground of Kai's winter family camp, recognizing each juniper, each cottonwood torched with gold. His pulse quickened as he sighted the hogans, the sturdy corral. Surely this was where his parents and Dólii would have come when the water rose, unless... please God, there wouldn't be an *unless*.

A lithe figure carrying a bundle of firewood halted, then turned and raised a hand against the lowering sun. The wood fell to the ground with a cry.

And Dólii was running toward him, calling his name. He met her and spun her around, her arms clinging about his neck, both of them laughing, crying, her deep-red skirt twirling around them.

He set her on the ground and touched her cheek. "I missed you, *Shideezhi.*"

"Come see *Shimá* and *Shizhé'é.*" Her eyes shone, bright with tears, as she tugged him toward the hogan.

He let her pull him along, drinking in the sweet scent of juniper needles, of autumn frost, of woodsmoke and—yes—his mother's coffee.

The door opened, and Sháńdíín and Shashyáázh tumbled out. Why weren't they in school? Behind came Kai with her baby on her back, her husband, Tse's parents, their smiles reaching him before their arms.

Home—thanks be to Creator, he was home.

"So the flood did not harm you, then?" he asked later, over roast mutton ribs and frybread. He felt like the Prodigal Son, save for the squandering and forgiving.

"Some of the horses who were roaming free—we haven't found them yet." His father's face shadowed. "And our winter hogan is gone. But the sheep, they are all fine." His smile lit his eyes again. "And so are we."

"Much better than some others." Kai stroked Shashyáázh's hair as he leaned against her shoulder.

"Did you hear about the mission?" Dólii reached for another piece of frybread.

Tse swallowed his bite. "What about it?"

"It's mostly destroyed." Dólii tore a corner of her bread with her fingers. "*Shizhé'é* tried to warn them to leave, but Rev. Abernathy wouldn't listen."

Tse's stomach clenched. *Diyin God, no.*

"When do *bilagáanas* ever listen?" His mother thinned her lips.

The memory of gray eyes filled with tears at hearing Nataani's story clamped Tse's heart. "Were they—did anyone . . . " Shashyáázh and Sháńdíín sat here safe and sound, that must mean something.

"Everyone escaped." His father shook his head. "No thanks to Rev. Abernathy. The wagon Shashyáázh was in got stuck in the mud, but Miss Haynes helped get the children out, somehow."

Tse rubbed his hands on his knees, trying to hide the trembling in his fingers at her name. "But the buildings destroyed?"

"No loss to anyone," his mother muttered.

"Only the schoolhouse still intact, I hear." Kai's husband leaned forward to throw a stick on the fire, then sat back with a contented sigh.

Tse sopped his frybread in the last of the mutton grease and stared into the fire, his mind shifting this way and that with the dancing flames.

"I will go down tomorrow. See if I can help." He popped the last bite in his mouth, savoring the taste of home, and brushed off his fingers.

His mother shot him a sharp look and opened her mouth as if to speak.

Tse glanced around at his family, all staring at him. "So. What other news?"

He had dreamed of sleeping in a hogan while on the railroad, had longed, while lying on his smelly bunk, for the comfort of a sheepskin on earth and stars through the smoke hole above. But Tse tossed long after the rest of his family had fallen into quiet breathing, his mind crowded with flood water and shepherds and falling rocks and Caroline's face.

At last he sat up, only to see his father crouched by the low-burning fire, sucking a cigarette.

"Can't sleep?" *Shizhé'é* glanced at him.

Tse shook his head, pushed back his blanket and scooted closer to the warmth of the coals. Felt to be a hard freeze tonight. They sat in silence some moments, only the sleepy snap of the charred wood, the far-off yip of coyotes, the flick of his father's ash.

Finally Tse tipped his head. "Are you all right?"

His father shifted, still staring across the flames. He took the shrinking cigarette from between his lips. "Why would you help at the mission?"

"Isn't that what you have taught me? That we help our family, our neighbors?"

"But they took your job." His father's hands trembled, crushing the twisted paper between his fingers. "They took your brother."

"They did." Tse drew a breath. "But Jesus told us to love our enemies. And you know I am a follower of Jesus, *Shizhé'é.*"

His father hesitated, then nodded. He stirred the coals with a stick.

Fire crackled. Coyote yipped. Ash flicked.

Tse's eyelids drooped.

"Why did you never tell me this God of yours spoke our language?"

"What?" Tse's ears tingled as from a thunderclap.

"Always, you say your God is for everyone, but you only talk to Him in the white man's tongue." His father tamped the smoldering paper butt into the earth floor, punctuating his words. "The *bilagáanas* say we must leave our ways, our people, our language to come to Him. That we must change who we are before He will accept us." He pierced Tse with his gaze. "But that is not what I heard, that night Shashyáázh was so ill. Nor what I saw, when he got well."

Tse's head pounded. So his father hadn't been asleep, when he prayed with Shándíín.

"You are right." Tse drew a breath. "For years I believed the God I knew accepted all peoples. But I knew in my head, not in my heart. I was afraid to pray to Him in our language. I had ... many wounds. But that night ... " His throat closed, and he worked his mouth a moment before he could speak. "I heard the Creator speak to me in our own language. And He began to heal me." He glanced at his father. "You have never wanted to speak of these things before."

"Before, I never saw why you wanted to exchange our *yei*, our chants to the Holy People, for a foreigner's ways." He rolled a fresh cigarette between his fingers and lit it. "I have always sought to walk in *hózhǫ́*, in harmony with the land, with others, with the spirits. But sometimes … " The twisted paper quivered between his strong fingers. "I am afraid. I have thought much, in this time you have been away. There is so much I do not understand. The flood—I see forces much stronger than I, and they do not care if I live or die." He drew a shuddering breath and passed his hand over his eyes.

Tse's chest ached. He sat silent, trying to pray, until his father continued.

"The *yei* do not care. I know that. We can only try to persuade them into showing us kindness. But that night … " He glanced at Tse with eyes that glistened. "You talked to Creator, that night, like He cared."

"That is why He sent Jesus." Tse pressed the ends of his fingers together and saw their trembling.

"Jesus." His father flicked ashes. "Always the *bilagáanas* say, 'Believe in the Lord Jesus and you shall be saved.' But they never really say who He is. Where did Jesus come from? What are His clans and who are His parents? You say God sent Him. How? And why did He?"

Tse rubbed his nose. Why had he never thought of it that way before? Always when a Navajo introduced himself, he gave first his mother's clan and then his father's. Tse was born into the *Tó'adheedlíinii*—Water Flows Together—clan and for the *Tódích'ii'nii*— Bitter Water—clan. What about Jesus?

The temptation pressed to dive into the brief Gospel presentation drilled into him at school, but something held him back. Kee had not understood "repent and believe" without context. Jesus came to the Jewish people within their culture, as a young Rabbi, as the Lamb of God, as the temple sacrifice and perfect high priest. How would He come to the *Diné*?

Help me, Lord. Willis always began with the New Testament. But what of all that came before? His father knew Creator had formed the world and placed First Man and First Woman in it. Why not begin with them?

Slowly, haltingly, Tse did. He spoke of how Creator had made the world good and beautiful, but First Man and First Woman rebelled against Him and broke the heavenly *hózhǫ́*, the peace and harmony and beauty between them and Creator. Yet He did not abandon them but planned a way to restore that *hózhǫ́* someday. But it could only happen through the shedding of blood.

He told of Abraham, a desert herder whom Creator promised a land for his own people, as the *Diné* had been given the *Dinétah*. He told how the descendants of this man became the twelve clans of Israel—a spark lit his father's eyes then, understanding clans. He told how finally, many hundreds of winters later, Jesus was born of the clan of Judah, but also of Creator Himself, for He had existed with Creator from the beginning, and through Him all things were created.

At last, while the coals lost their glow and the air chilled around them and his father's cigarettes turned to a pile of smoldering ends, Tse told how Jesus' own people despised and rejected Him, their Shepherd. How His shed blood finally healed the gap between Creator and mankind and made true *hózhǫ́* possible for all who would believe in Him. How He fought and conquered death.

His father stared into the fire a long moment after Tse finished. Then he dropped the last butt into the flames and rubbed his hands together. "Why has no one ever told it to us that way before?"

Tse sniffed back the burning in his nose. "I don't know."

CHAPTER FORTY-TWO

A pre-dawn breeze ruffled the pages of Tse's Bible as he sat outside the hogan, wrapped in a blanket against the chill. He ran his finger down the print of Isaiah 43, from which God had spoken to him that summer night Shashyáázh was ill. He wished he could read the whole thing in his language. Perhaps someday.

"'I, even I, am the LORD; and beside me there is no saviour … '" he murmured the words under his breath. "'Behold, I will do a new thing; now it shall spring forth; shall ye not know it? I will even make a way in the wilderness, and rivers in the desert. The beast of the field shall honour me, the dragons and the owls: because I give waters in the wilderness, and rivers in the desert, to give drink to my people, my chosen.'" Tse lifted his head and smiled. Even the owls.

His father stepped from the hogan and stretched his arms above his head, leaning from side to side. But he did not begin chanting his prayers as usual, instead scanning the horizon with a strange expression in his eyes.

"My son." He stepped closer to Tse. "How does one do morning prayers, when following the Jesus Way?"

Tse's hands froze on his Bible. He set it aside, unfolded himself and stood to meet his father's gaze. He saw the light, the wetness, in his father's eyes, and he knew.

"*Shizhé'é?*" he choked.

His father nodded. Then Tse was wrapped in his embrace, his father clasped in his, their arms tightening, gripping each other, their tears dampening each other's shoulders.

He didn't know how long they sat and talked and prayed together, their backs against the rough logs of the hogan, their shoulders pressed close. But as the sky pearled over the eastern horizon, stirring from inside signaled the women had wakened.

"I will tell your mother after breakfast." His father tipped his head. "She may take it better on a full belly, no?"

Tse smiled, but his thoughts suddenly ran ahead of him. *Caroline.* His heart quickened. She would want to know.

"I must get to the mission." He rocked to his feet.

"Breakfast first." His mother emerged from the hogan, her steps shuffling. Her knees always hurt worst in the morning. "*Ya'at'eeh abini.*"

"*Aoo'.*" Tse and his father affirmed the morning greeting.

She scanned them a moment, then bent to start the cooking fire, easing herself down with painful effort.

Tse's chest tightened. If only she would let them help more, but no. He glanced at his father, saw the flicker in his eyes. *Lord, please help her take his news well. Soften her heart.* He sensed it would be long before his mother could distance the death of her youngest from the message of the missionaries.

And Kee—Tse's throat tightened. He would not know about Kee, not until heaven.

But his father. His father!

As soon as his mother had heated the mush, Tse downed a bowl and headed for the corral.

He sang as he bridled his horse, praising Jesus in his language, letting the tune follow the natural pattern of the tones, as in the chants. It sounded genuinely Navajo, yet the truth of the words lent a wholeness to his tongue he'd never heard before.

"My son."

He looked up into his father's face and stilled at the gravity there, even with that new light in his eyes.

"Why do you want to go to the mission this quick?"

"I told you. To help." Tse shifted his feet.

"Yes. But I think there is more."

Tse met his father's eyes, saw the knowing there even as it dawned in his own heart. He focused on the knot in his horse's rope.

"It is her, then." His father sighed deeply. It wasn't a question.

Tse fumbled with the knot, then stilled. "Do I shame you, *Shizhé'é*?" He could hardly hear his own whisper.

Silence. At last Tse looked up.

His father leaned over the corral fence to scratch the head of a lame ewe nosing for attention. Lines etched between his eyes.

Tse stared at the sheep's back, at the wool growing thick for winter.

"Never would have wanted you to care for a white woman." His father straightened and spat off to the side.

Tse's heart sank like a stone dropped into the river. But what else could he have expected? He was a fool, simple as that.

"But." His father tapped the rail. "I saw her risk her position to come with you for Shashyáázh's mother and father. I saw her offer to stay with Dezbah in Kai's place so she could go to her child. I heard how her bravery helped save the children in the flood."

He reached over and laid his hand on Tse's shoulder. "I saw her eyes when she looked at you, my son. And the light in yours."

"Don't." Tse tried to pull away, shaking his head. "You are right, there is no way."

"So I meant to tell you." His father's grip tightened. "But Creator whispered to my heart this morning, that He makes a way where none seems possible. That I should not try to stand against what He wishes to do, with you and this Caroline of yours."

Tse stared at his father, his mind in a whirlwind. But unlike the whirlwinds his people feared as possessing evil spirits, this one brought hope, seeping light into the corners of his soul. And a strange clarity.

His father gave him a gentle shove. "Go, my son. And Creator and His Son be with you."

Tse pulled up his horse and scanned the wreckage of what had been Hebron Navajo Mission.

As his family had said, the schoolhouse seemed to have suffered only minor damage. And the barn could likely be repaired. But the main building, housing the dormitories, would have to be torn down. He could see that at a glance.

Tse swung off his mount and looped his bridle to the makeshift fence, glancing over the few goats milling inside. Had the others been lost, in the flood?

His chest tightened with an odd sense that he had lived this before, nearly a year ago when he came to ask for a job. Except it hardly seemed like the same place.

And now he was back, certain he was meant to come. But for what?

He found Willis in the orchard, stripping the branches from a fallen plum tree. Tse said nothing for a moment, just stood there watching the flex of his friend's muddied sleeves, his hands scraped and newly calloused as they wielded the ax.

Tse cast a glance around. So quiet, but for the thwack of the hatchet and an occasional bleat from the barn. Were the women in town?

The chopping stilled. Willis straightened and stared at him.

"*Ya'at'eeh*, Rev. Abernathy."

"Thought you were following the railroad somewhere." Willis narrowed his eyes.

"I heard about your trouble." Again, the sense this had happened before. "Thought you could use some help."

Willis puffed a half laugh and leaned to toss aside a chopped-off branch. "Still think you could do the job better than I, huh?"

Tse stood silent a moment, then walked away. He would look for Caroline, then be off. There was only so much a man could take.

"Tse."

He halted, then slowly turned.

Willis rubbed the back of his neck, weariness in his blue eyes, in the slump of his shoulders. "That was uncalled for. I'm sorry." He nudged the fallen sapling with his boot. "Give me a hand?"

His jaw still tight, Tse grabbed one end of the tree while Willis took the other. Together they hauled it down to a pile in the yard.

"Figure I can sell it for firewood, if nothing else." Willis leaned his hands on his thighs, catching his breath. He glanced up at Tse. "There are plenty more."

Not quite an invitation. But almost.

Together they worked, stripping off the dead-leaved branches, grubbing out stump remnants, hauling the lifeless trees. Sweat ran down Tse's neck, cooled and dried in the chill autumn wind.

At last they plopped down on one of the sturdier fallen trees to rest. Willis chugged from a thermos bottle, then offered it to Tse.

Tse nodded his thanks, took a swig, and coughed. Coffee, hot as if right from the stove. He turned the sturdy bottle in his hands. What would they think of next?

Silence stretched. Tse sensed the old wall there between them. When had it risen? When Willis came back from seminary and took over the mission? No, before that. With losing Nataani? Perhaps.

Willis sat hunched and unspeaking, staring at his broken fingernails.

Tse rubbed his thumb over the bottle cap. He should be helping his father cut logs for the new winter hogan today. Why had he come out here, anyway?

The answer beat in his heart. He should just ask Willis about her, straight out. His tongue stuck at the thought.

"Tse."

He turned his head.

"I believe I owe you an apology." Willis still stared at his hands.

"You already gave it."

"No, not that. I ... " The lump *bilagáanas* called Adam's apple worked in Willis's throat. "I shouldn't have fired you. You were right to go for Samuel's parents. I see that now. I ... apologize."

Tse's hands tightened on the thermos.

"I've treated you ... poorly. Don't blame you if you can't forgive me yet." Willis wiped his nose on his sleeve. "I keep thinking about that foolish man who built his house on the sand, 'and the floods came, and the winds blew, and beat upon that house; and it fell: and great was the fall of it.'" He leaned his elbows on his knees. "That's me right now."

"Willis." The old name slipped out, but Tse didn't take it back. He took a deep breath and laid his hand on his friend's shoulder. "I forgive you." The release in his chest brought burning to his eyes. So much, past and present, in those words—so much Willis didn't understand, hadn't meant. But they needed to be said. "I forgive you, my brother."

"I keep thinking of what you said, when I blew up that day you took the children to the river." Willis released a shuddering breath and let his head fall into his hands. "Dear God, have I really been teaching as doctrine the precepts of men? Is this His judgment upon me?"

Well, Willis had said it, not he. "There is no shame in needing to learn, in needing help. Only in thinking you do not."

"The board is sure to close us down now—our days were numbered as it was, unless something changed. Don't know why I even keep cleaning up this place." He sagged his hands between his knees. "Who knows if I was ever even doing God's work here."

"God is always working, I think." Tse rubbed his nose. "It is up to us whether we want to join Him."

Willis lifted his head and stared at him a moment, then one side of his mouth lifted. "Thanks."

They stood. Willis held out his hand.

Tse grasped it. Then suddenly, they pulled each other into an embrace. Tse blinked hard, gripping Willis's shoulders, his boyhood friend gripping his.

They pulled apart, not needing words.

"Thanks for the coffee." Tse held out the thermos.

"Caroline fixed it." Willis took the bottle absently.

A rush of heat warmed Tse's ears, followed by the singe of possessiveness. Since when had Willis gained the right to use her given name?

"She's leaving, you know."

Tse froze. The coarse cawing of a crow, the drying leaves on the trees, all seemed to still.

"Got an offer of a position back East. Couldn't expect her to stay on now, of course."

"Where—" His voice caught. Pain pierced behind his eyes. "Where is she?"

Willis looked at him oddly. "Down fixing up the schoolhouse. Trader Hawkins is getting cantankerous not having full use of his storeroom, and the children have all gone back to their families, so we figure we'll camp out there for now. You didn't see her?"

But Tse was already pounding down the hill.

CHAPTER FORTY-THREE

She hated good-byes.

Caroline leaned over the new barnyard fence, scrapped together from fragments left by the flood, to scratch the heads of the goats nosing near. She sneezed, her hands and clothes still dusty from the dried mud in the schoolhouse.

She and Miss Spencer would sleep in the younger children's classroom tonight, Willis in the older. Then tomorrow—she would be gone.

She stroked her fingers under the chin of one of this year's kids, now only half a head shorter than the grown does. Whiskery lips nibbled the cuff of her sleeve, and her throat tightened. "I will miss you, little ones."

"So you talk to them too."

Caroline caught her breath. That voice—could it be? She turned.

"Tse." The word came out a whisper, tinged with dreams, hopes, and heartache.

His broad shoulders, his strong hands, his hair hanging past chin-length again beneath his hat and silver earrings. His eyes— Caroline's stomach flipped, and she gripped the rough board of the fence behind her. "What are you doing here?"

"We help our family, our friends. It is our way." His mouth quirked with the hint of a smile, yet there was an anxiousness in it. He stepped nearer.

Her heart pattered till she was afraid he could hear it.

"Willis says you are leaving."

"What choice do I have?" She stepped away from the fence and gestured at the shambled grounds. Hugging herself, she felt her own trembling through her coat sleeves.

"We always have choices."

A moment's silence. He scanned the milling goats, lines between his brows.

"Yázhí and her babies... we lost them." Her eyes stung. "I'm so sorry."

"So am I." He laid his palms atop the fence.

Caroline stepped beside him, the lump in her throat pressing till she could hardly swallow. She clenched her fingers together, forcing back the tears, but her eyes blurred till the goats and Tse swam together.

"Caroline." He touched her shoulder. "What is it?"

"It might seem silly, but... I can't get it off my mind." She managed a shaky breath. "The night before the flood, Isaiah was teaching me to milk—Willis had a cold—and Yázhí kicked the bucket over, and I flew into a temper. It had been a hard day, and I scolded her and—and smacked her. She skittered away, and then that night, the flood... " She pressed her knuckles to her lips.

"It is not your fault." The warmth of his hand cupped her elbow.

"When Mama died, I was angry at her the night before." She hadn't meant to say this, but she couldn't seem to halt the words. "She was poorly, and I had stayed out later than I ought to have with a—young man friend. She scolded me—she almost never scolded me—but we had words, and I went to bed angry. Then in the wee hours, she went into labor, and I never told her—I was sorry." She covered her face with her hands. "Forgive me. You don't need to know all this … I don't even know what I'm trying to say."

He stroked her arm, saying nothing, the steady motion reminding her of how Father used to comfort her.

But today it didn't help. She lifted her face from her fingers. "How can you even come here, to help, with what this place has done to your family? Your brother died here!"

He flinched.

Guilt pinched, but she couldn't stop. "My people have done yours great wrong, and I have joined them. You don't need one more *bilagáana* here doing damage. We can't undo the wrongs of the past. It doesn't work." She moved from his touch, hugging her elbows, unable to stop her shaking. "I can't get anything right." The whisper choked, stopped.

"Caroline." He stepped behind her, took gentle hold of her upper arms. "You cannot carry the sins of the world, or even your own, on your shoulders. You were never meant to. Jesus has done that already."

She clamped her lips against the rising swell in her throat.

"No, you cannot undo the past." His grip tightened slightly on her shoulders. "But the wounds of the past and problems of the present are not going to just disappear. And if those who care about what is wrong leave, how will anything ever change?" His voice lowered to a whisper. "And you care. I know you do."

"I can't stay, Tse." Caroline shook her head, a tear squeezing between her eyelashes.

"Why?" He turned her to face him. "Why can you not?"

She traced his face with her eyes, his high cheekbones and strong nose, the earnest anguish in every line, the strength of his gaze.

"I want you to stay." His voice shook, and his grip tightened still more. "I—love you."

For a moment the world stood still around her, and she trembled in his arms, her heart winging skyward, then crashing to earth like a cut-winged bird. She bent her head, resting it against the rough woolen weave of Tse's poncho.

He lifted his hand, touched her hair, caressed it with a stroke light as a butterfly, his roughened fingertips catching on the strands. *Heavenly Father, help.* She lifted her head. "Don't—we mustn't."

"Why?" His hands froze, then dropped away, his voice hardening. "Because I am *Diné*?"

"No! Not like that." Though God forgive her, it might once have been. She clenched her fingers together, unable to bear the hurt in his eyes. "Tse—you are the finest man I have ever known. But I could never fit in your world. I realized that the night I stayed with Dezbah. The walls between our peoples are too high." Unable to meet his gaze any longer, she focused on his shirt buttons between the sides of the blanket. *Oh, Lord, why does this have to be so hard?*

"The Creator can make a way where none seems possible." Tse lifted her chin with a gentle finger. "My father told me that this morning."

"Your father?" She blinked to see him more clearly.

"He has decided to follow the Jesus Way." A sheen rose in Tse's eyes, and he glanced to the side. "He spoke to me also of you, or perhaps I might not have had the courage yet."

"But—how?"

"A number of things. Hearing me pray in our language when Shashyáázh was ill, then—"

"You prayed in Navajo then?" Her eyes stung. Why had he never told her? To be sure, they had hardly seen each other since.

He nodded, a softness touching his face. "And I do still. I'll tell you more later. But it was also you. Your staying to care for Dezbah touched him. He had never seen a *bilagáana* do such before."

Caroline dropped her gaze. Yes, she had stayed with Dezbah, because she was more afraid of Shashyáázh dying without his parents than she was of an angry elderly woman. Fear and desperation did not a heroine make. "You've been living your faith before your family for years. Certainly that had far more impact than anything I did."

"But it was that wall you spoke of, that still kept him from seeing. Until you helped break it down, just a little, with love." He took her hands in his. "Do you not see how God has used you? It is not for us to get it right—it is about His strength in our weakness. Think how He could use us, together, a bridge of healing between our peoples, if we were to ... " His throat worked. "Marry."

"Are you asking me to marry you?" Her voice sounded foreign. She could barely breathe.

"No." He gripped her hands, and she felt his trembling. "That would not be fair, not yet. I only ask you to be willing to think about it, to stay, to give our Lord a chance to show us what He has in mind."

She stood still a moment, staring into his eyes, no one in the world but they two. She had dreamed of a moment like this, once. He truly loved her—Tse loved her. And she him.

But she shook her head, pulling her hands from his, and turned away. "I can't."

"Why do you keep saying that?" His voice rose slightly, she heard the desperation in it.

"There's nothing for me here, nothing for me to do. Not that I was doing any good before, no matter what you say." She hugged her arms across her ribcage, lest she crack to pieces. "The school is destroyed. And you couldn't even find a way to support your family without traveling miles away. There's no place for either of us here. How could we do it? How could we possibly make anything work?"

"We could, I know we could. With God all things are possible."
He came behind her, touched her shoulder. "Why do you keep listening to fear?"

Caroline lifted her numbed hand to swipe the tears streaming down her cold cheeks, then brushed his warm fingers on her shoulder. "I'm sorry."

She ran, across the mission yard and up the makeshift steps back into the schoolhouse. She shut the door, then stepped to the window.

There he stood, gripping the fence, his head bowed. One of the goats stuck its head through to nibble the edge of the blanket hanging from his shoulder. He did not respond.

Caroline pressed her fingers to her lips and let the tears flow. *Tse ... my beloved ... I'm so sorry.*

She didn't know how she survived the evening without Willis or Miss Spencer asking what was wrong. But Willis stayed oddly silent himself, and Miss Spencer merely seemed glad to have returned to mission property, if only to a pallet in the corner, a salvaged woodstove, and a few straight-backed chairs to sit on while eating a one-pot supper from their laps.

At last, lamps blown out and Willis retired to his half of the schoolhouse, Caroline and Miss Spencer climbed under their quilts. The sounds of the night settled in—the low snap of fire burning low in the stove, the ever-present yipping of coyotes on the desert.

"You were very quiet tonight."

Caroline shifted under her quilt. She'd thought Miss Spencer already asleep.

"Does something trouble you?"

For a moment, she longed to pour it all out. But how could she? Miss Spencer would merely be shocked and counsel her as to why, indeed, she could never think of such a thing. And even if it were not so, what had happened between Tse and her was sacred, precious, not for laying open to other eyes, but to be saved in her heart alone.

"We've all been under a great deal of strain lately." Caroline tucked the quilt up to her chin. "I will be all right."

A moment of silence. Then a soft squeak, as if the elderly woman shifted on the pallet. "I am praying for you, my dear. We must not be afraid."

"Thank you." A tear leaked out and ran into Caroline's ear.

Quiet fell once more, soon punctuated by Miss Spencer's whiffling snore.

Caroline turned on her side. *Do not be afraid.* Could Tse be right, that she was listening to the voice of fear?

Ever since Mama died, it seemed she'd been afraid. Afraid that if she didn't do everything just right, something would happen to her family again—afraid of Lillian taking her place—afraid of not belonging anywhere, anymore—afraid she wouldn't get through to Samuel—afraid they would lose him—afraid of pushing Willis too far. Afraid of speaking up even when she knew something was wrong. Yes, she had spurts of courage, going for Shashyáázh's parents, speaking Navajo to calm him during the flood. But that came from the Lord, not from her.

But was that the point? Was that what Tse had been trying to tell her?

She drifted into a half-dreaming doze. And she was seventeen again, gripping the stairwell railing on the top floor at home, frozen in place as Mama's agonized groans from behind the nearby bedroom door tore at her heart. At last a nurse hurried out to fetch something for the doctor and banished Caroline to where Father paced downstairs. She looked to his distressed face for reassurance, but he only shook his head.

"She's in God's hands," he said, scrubbing his hand across his red-rimmed eyes.

At last, the cry of a newborn ... the doctor's frantic voice ... her father's sobs. Toby clinging to her as she rocked him, her ribcage aching with the tears she held in for his sake.

"*Mama!*"

Caroline sat upright on her pallet in the darkness, shaking, her eyes hot. Had she cried aloud? Yet Miss Spencer's snore still whiffled.

She lay back down and buried her face in the pillow. *O Lord, how am I supposed to trust my future and those I love into Thy hands ... Father put Mama there, and look what happened.*

What had happened?

The thought came so startling, she opened her eyes and turned to rest her cheek on the damp linen. Friends, family, neighbors gathering round them after Mama died, offering embraces, tears, and prayers, bits of motherly advice for her on caring for Benji. She and Father and Toby learning to laugh again at baby Benji's kicks and grins, to be a family again, even with Mama's place empty. Even Lillian's coming, bringing light to Father's eyes once more and a spring to his step. And Mama—she was safe and well in the presence of her Savior, never to suffer again, waiting for them until the day they would all be together, never to be parted.

Caroline's throat squeezed as hot tears pooled. The Lord hadn't promised they wouldn't have heartbreak. He had just promised He would never leave them or forsake them. And He hadn't. How had she never truly realized that until now?

"Forgive me, Lord." She used the corner of the quilt to wipe her cheeks. "I do trust You. I'm sorry for all the times I haven't. All the times I've held back because of fear. I trust you ... with me, with the children, with all this mess we've made. With ... Tse. Please bless him, Lord, and use him here, in this land, his land. And if in any of my plans, I am not within Thy will ... " She lay still a long moment.

"If you somehow want me to stay, please give me a sign." She let out a long, quivering sigh, a knot she didn't know she held loosening deep within her. "Thy will be done," she whispered.

She slept.

CHAPTER FORTY-FOUR

Caroline sat up with a start in the darkness. She listened hard, through the quietness of Miss Spencer's breathing and the rustle of drying leaves on the big cottonwood still standing undamaged beside the schoolhouse.

There—an odd snuffling sound, right beside the door. A prickle rushed down her arms.

She sat up and wiggled her legs from under the covers, stepping soundlessly to the floor. A coyote? But surely it would have gone for the barnyard. Should she scream for Willis?

She crept toward the door. A board squeaked beneath her foot, and she started.

Right beside the door now. More snuffling. She held her breath.

And then—a faint bleat.

Her heart skipped, then settled into a more normal rhythm. Of course, one of the goats had gotten out. That makeshift fence wasn't nearly as sturdy as the old one.

She slid the bolt on the door and eased it open, bending to block the opening with her hand.

In the frosty moonlight, a lop-eared head shook. A cold nose nuzzled Caroline's hand, *maa-ing* pitifully.

The goat was small, not fully grown. A bony back... rough coat stuck with burrs... one comical, crooked ear.

Caroline fell to her knees, laughing, crying, hugging the slender, fuzzy neck. "Willis! Come out here!"

Yázhí's doeling had found her way home.

"How in tarnation..." Willis set his lantern on the rocky ground outside the schoolhouse and knelt to feel the little goat's neck and legs for injuries. "Why would she come to the schoolhouse? You'd think she'd head for the barn and food."

"Maybe she remembers weaseling her way into the schoolroom last spring." Caroline stroked the dear little lop-eared head between her hands. "Could her family be nearby?"

"I'll go look." Willis took the lantern and stumped off through the darkness.

Caroline laid her cheek against the doeling's nose. *Thank You, Father—oh, thank You.*

"I can't see for beans without my spectacles." Miss Spencer peered from the doorway, her wrapper ghostly white in the moonlight. "But here's a bit of a treat for her."

A few carrot stubs landed at Caroline's knees. The little goat nipped them up as if starved, her soft lips nuzzling Caroline's dressing gown ribbons for more.

"Nothing." Lantern light came bobbing back across the yard with Willis. "Guess she's a sole survivor."

Caroline rubbed around the stubby horns, blinking at the burning in her eyes. So this baby had indeed lost her mama, her brother. But she was all right—she would be all right. They would all be all right.

"I'll put her in with the others, give her some feed." Willis looped a short rope around the doeling's neck and led her away toward the barn.

Caroline still knelt in the darkness. Miss Spencer had disappeared back inside the schoolhouse. From the barn came soft bleats of goats disturbed in sleep, the muffled thud of Willis tossing hay.

She gazed up into the blackness above, showered with stars, and hugged herself, the night's frosty chill seeping through the sleeves of her wrapper.

"Thank You, Father," she whispered once more. She bowed her head, tears of gratitude trembling on her lashes, something new and sweet and freeing stirring within her heart.

She had asked, and God had answered.

Caroline stood on the rocky ledge above the mission, watching the sunrise. How many times she had missed this miracle, amid the trees and houses of Pennsylvania.

First a deepening pink, a gilding of the clouds, hundreds of fluffy lamb's tails scattered across the pale blue of the sky—then a tiny sliver of white gold above the mesas, shooting its rays higher and higher before bursting in glory over the horizon, dazzling her eyes, sparkling on her lashes as she squinted against the brilliance.

At a low honk, she looked up to a wedge of Canadian geese cutting across the deepening blue overhead. She rubbed her arms, the frosty air biting through her coat sleeves. *O Lord, You guide the geese on their way… please guide me now. I'm trying not to be, but I'm still afraid.*

Willis had left for the trading post well before dawn, before she could tell him of her decision. He'd intended to haul one load of supplies, then take her to meet the freighter, the wagon meant to carry her away. But now…

She gazed across the autumn-cloaked valley, the cottonwoods a fading border of gold along the river, the muddy swathe of destruction somewhat gentled now.

Below, a figure rode silhouetted in the golden light, a horse and rider loping across the desert toward the mission.

Caroline's heart skipped. Could it be?

She strained to see, to be sure, then scrambled down the rocky side, half slipping. Across the desert she ran toward him, ran as she hadn't since she was a little girl, catching her skirt away from the sagebrush, frosted earth crunching beneath her boots. She had to do this, before her newfound courage seeped away like the floodwaters into the ground.

The rider loped nearer, reined to a stop, slid from his horse.

Caroline slowed, her breath coming in gasps. "*Ya'at'eeh*, Tse."

"What are you—are you all right?" His bewildered eyes searched her face.

"I forgot to tell you something, yesterday." Her heart pounded so she could scarcely think.

"Yes?" He stepped closer, tall and broad shouldered and smelling of sun and sweat and horse and autumn wind.

"I ... " Her stomach quailed at his nearness. She couldn't do this, couldn't remember the speech she had prepared, was foolish for even thinking she could. *Help me, Lord.* She groped for words. "I have been thinking."

He nodded, tipping his head for her to go on.

"You were right." She drew a breath. "I have been listening to the voice of fear, for so long now. And God has not given us a spirit of fear—has He?"

He shook his head. A quick rise and fall of his chest.

"I want to follow Him in faith, not fear. The whats and hows I don't know, but I do know—here He has placed me, at least for now. And here I will stay." She hugged herself and lowered her gaze to the dusty toes of her boots. Would he say—anything?

Soft leather moccasins stopped in front of her feet. Gentle hands took hold of her upper arms. "With me?"

Caroline lifted her head, looked into his coffee-colored eyes, and saw the sheen of tears. She nodded. "With you, Tse."

With a sound between a sob and a laugh, he caught her hands in his. "I can't . . . " He drew a shaky breath. "I was on my way to find you."

"Why?"

"At the trading post this morning—I had gone to ask about getting back on the railroad, but then Willis came in. Trader Hawkins gave him a letter, from the mission board. They have received so many unexpected donations toward Hebron, from various donors, that they've decided to fund the rebuilding of the mission. He said many of the donations came from some letter you had written, Caroline."

Pastor Jensen . . . the churches and mission boards he said he'd sent her letter to . . . the desert spun dizzily around her.

"They have decided to extend the mission's support another two years, maybe longer. Willis asked if I would come back on staff, as a teacher. And he thought it might be too late, but I said I would ask you also." His hands tightened on hers.

"But the mission—it's ruined."

"Listen." He ran his thumbs over the backs of her hands. "The schoolhouse is still in decent shape. Willis and I will tear the dormitories down this fall, build something smaller for staff living quarters. Then for the spring, Hebron can perhaps reopen as a day school."

"A day school?" His pulse thrummed against her palms, her own in her ears. Her mind was skipping, prancing every direction, she couldn't keep up with it.

"The children will come in the morning and go home at night. A few other places are trying it. It's still not best, I know, but it is better. And perhaps for those who live too far, you and I might sometimes take school to them." He paused for breath, clasping her hands close to his chest. "I have so many ideas since being on the railroad, ways of taking Jesus to my people, having gatherings at my family's hogan to talk about Him in our language, in a manner we are used to, singing in our own way... so much. But I couldn't think how it could happen, until this morning."

"He makes a way where none seems possible. Like you said." Caroline could barely breathe.

"He does." Tse brushed her cheek with a gentle knuckle. "But if you stay... it is no small thing I am asking, even if just to consider it... to join our lives into one. You must be sure."

She looked up into his face, tracing every beloved line. Then, her hand hesitant and trembling, she did as she had so often longed to and reached to smooth back a strand of his thick, dark hair, tucking it back within the headband.

"I love you, Tse Tsosie." She laid her hands on his chest, the fabric of his shirt nubbly beneath her fingers. "That's what I forgot to tell you yesterday."

He closed his eyes, then bent his head near hers until their foreheads touched, wrapping her hands close in his. They stood in silence sweet and hallowed, until the snort and stamp of Tse's horse lifted their heads.

Tse let go her hands and reached into the binding where his breeches and leggings met at the knee. "I did not know if I would even see you—I knew you were to leave today, but... I brought you this."

Silver and turquoise, glinting in the morning sun, caught Caroline's breath. She blinked against fresh tears as he held out to her a necklace even more delicate and lovely than Shándíín's.

"It's beautiful. My locket is gone—did Willis tell you?"

"No. But I guessed."

She turned, his fingers tickling at the nape of her neck as that long-ago Easter day when he fastened her locket. She touched the pendant nestled below her collar, the heavy blue stones in their settings of silver.

"Thank you." She twisted her head to look up at him. "Will you take me back to the mission?"

"Of course." He stepped back from her.

But she saw the flicker in his eyes. So many hurdles still to be crossed, so many walls, some that never would be broken, not in their lifetime. But this was not a day for fear.

So she smiled at him, even through the sparkle of tears. "Yázhí's doeling came back. I think she should be the first we tell, don't you? She brought us together in the first place."

Tse stared at her a moment, then threw back his head and laughed. He drew her to him and cupped her cheek with his hand. "Caroline… " He whispered something in Navajo.

"What does that mean?"

"My heart. You are my heart."

A tear slipped free onto her cheek.

He caught it with his thumb. "And I wish… your father did not live so very far away."

She laid her head on his chest, his arms wrapping her close, his heart thrumming beneath her ear. Around them spread the mesas, the arroyos and junipers and piñons of his land, of the *Dinétah*. Above them stretched the blue bowl of the sky, which the Creator had arced over all peoples, whom He would one day, somehow, heal into one through the blood of His cross. His Son had prayed it so.

Belonging isn't a place, Caroline. I hope you learn that. But it is something you can find.

Tse kissed the top of her head, then released her and led the way to his horse.

Caroline glanced up at the high back, the simple leather saddle. "How ... "

He swung astride in one easy motion, then reached for her hand, the smile she loved lighting his eyes. "Ride with me."

THE END

ISTORICAL NOTE

Between 1869 and the 1960s, thousands of Native American children were taken from their families and placed in both government and mission boarding schools across the United States. It is estimated that by 1926, over 80% of school-age Native children attended these residential schools, numbering over 60,000 students in 1925. "Kill the Indian, save the man," the motto of Carlisle Indian Industrial School in Pennsylvania, encapsulates the attitude of these schools and the time.

Many mission and government boarding schools existed on the Navajo Reservation in the early 1900s, from St. Michael's in Arizona to the government boarding school in Shiprock to Rehoboth in Gallup, which still functions as a Christian day school today. Rather than set my story at one of these schools, I chose to create Hebron Navajo Mission, a fictional school that nonetheless reflects reality as thousands of children lived it ... though I have shown only the milder side. Many children endured horrible physical and even sexual abuse at these schools, and many never returned home, often buried in unmarked graves and still unaccounted for by the U.S. government. However, I have tried to show how even well-intentioned teachers and missionaries did grave damage in taking children from their families—sometimes by force—and stripping them of their Native identity and culture, tragically equating the Gospel to Euro-American, "white" culture. Generations of children lacked parenting and endured punishment and trauma merely for speaking their own languages, trauma that still wracks Native communities today.

To learn more, visit The National Native American Boarding School Healing Coalition at https://boardingschoolhealing.org/

For a powerful true story of trauma and healing, look up the short film "The Cutting of the Tsiiyééł," by Susie Silversmith, a Navajo/*Diné* boarding school survivor and a dear friend of friends of mine.

$\mathcal{A}$CKNOWLEDGEMENTS

This story would not be what it is without so many, many people—first and foremost, Ted and Evie Charles. Ted and Evie, though this story was conceived in my mind before I met you, it has been through knowing you, being welcomed in your home, listening to your stories, exploring your beautiful *Dinétah* land with you that it truly found shape and heart and birth. Your own story of meeting and falling in love at a Navajo mission boarding school, Ted a young Navajo dorm supervisor and Evie a young Dutch American missionary nurse, mirrors the heart of this novel, though many details take different shape. Thank you for opening your hearts and home to me so many times, for all the authenticity you have lent to these pages, for reading my manuscript in multiple versions, correcting my Navajo words, names, spelling, and cultural portrayals, sharing your stories and pain and hope, even to Ted's grandfather's experience as a six-year-old on the horrific Long Walk. You have become family to me, and I will be forever grateful for your impact on my life. Any mistakes still held in these pages are my own.

Thanks also to so many other First Nations friends who have impacted this story: Mark Charles, who introduced me to his amazing parents above and whose prophetic voice for truth and reconciliation continues to challenge and impact me; Lora Church, who first told me about the Long Walk of the Navajo and prompted me to further research; Nicole Johnny, who told me of her grandmother's story; Annabelle Yazzie and John B. Dennison for sharing their memories as boarding school survivors; Casey Church, Richard Twiss, and Terry and Darlene Wildman for their trailblazing examples of following Jesus in life and ministry in uniquely beautiful Native ways. I'm also grateful to Paul Otoko for his model of indigenous leadership and leading a trip to Arizona where I met the godly Tsosie family, whose name I borrowed for Tse's. Thanks to Ben and Eunice Stoner, along with Tim and Joy Stoner and their family, for your example of how missionaries can represent Christ in humility and incarnational ministry, and how you seek to repair the wrongs that have been done.

Thanks to the San Juan College Library for allowing me access to newspaper microfilms covering the October 1911 San Juan River flood. I'm also grateful to the Farmington Library, Farmington Museum at Gateway Park, the Hubbel Trading Post, and Mr. Bill Foutz of Foutz Trading Company for other research resources, as well as the amazing collections and information at the Navajo Nation Museum in Window Rock, Arizona.

Thanks to Dr. David Esselstrom of Azusa Pacific University, in whose class this story was originally born as a screenplay. Thank you for telling me to "finish this puppy" and that you believed it was really meant to be a novel. Thanks to Dr. Adrien Lowery for your encouragement and for dragging me to my first writers conference at Mount Hermon—another turning point in my life! Thanks to my beloved critique partners whom I met there, Sarah, Sandra, and Marilyn—little did I know you'd become some of my dearest friends and prayer partners. Thank you for always believing in this story and loving these characters! Thanks to Randy Ingermanson and Natasha Kern for their valuable input on this story. Special thanks to Wendy Lawton, my amazing agent, for encouraging this newbie author even before I'd finished the manuscript and never giving up on me, or on this story.

Thanks to Lauraine Snelling, who first saw something in this story in your mentoring group at Mount Hermon, and for your endorsement of this book—what a joy and privilege it is to write with you! Thanks to Lori Benton and Laura Frantz for your generous friendship to "little me" over the years, your example of weaving Native history and characters so beautifully and sensitively into your own wonderful novels, and your willingness to take the time to read and endorse mine. Thanks to my newest writing friends, the Historical OWLs—what an inspiration you've been in my life! Thank you for your hearts for this story even before reading it.

Thanks to Sarah Elizabeth Sawyer (Choctaw) for your assistance to non-Native writers seeking to write faithfully and respectfully about Native history and characters—I'm so grateful for your excellent Fiction Writing American Indians course, and how you reached out to personally encourage me in my writing journey. Many thanks to my wonderful editor, Shelli Littleton, for the heart and skill you've poured into this story, Jill Kemerer of Story Architect for all your patience and expertise, and Roseanna M. White for designing the beautiful cover.

Special thanks to my beloved family—to Daddy, who led us to northwest New Mexico for five years in my teens and whose own interest in the Navajo people ultimately helped spark my own; to Mama, who first told me I had a gift for writing and unfailingly cheers me on; to my sister, Maren, who has always believed in this story and these characters; to my husband, Anthony, who continues to support me in this crazy life of writing books, and whose own Native heritage from the Tiwa people of New Mexico has deepened my commitment to telling these stories; and to my precious son,

Aeron, who is so patient when I spend time on the computer "writing books." I love you all with all my heart.

Finally, thanks to our Creator God and my Lord Jesus Christ for making all of this possible. He is the Son of Righteousness who rises with healing in His wings. (Malachi 4:2)

ABOUT THE AUTHOR

Kiersti Giron has been telling stories ever since she walked in circles around the living room as a little girl, telling them to herself. She loves digging into the lives and lessons of history and draws inspiration from her five years living in northwest New Mexico near the Navajo Nation, as well as her current setting in Southern California. After being published in several magazines and newspapers, Kiersti now has the privilege of collaborating on series of historical fiction with beloved author Lauraine Snelling. Kiersti loves writing about reconciliation, healing, and how God's story weaves into ours, and her novels have won two ACFW Genesis awards. When she's not writing, she keeps busy teaching 8th grade English online, homeschooling, and squeezing in precious time with her husband, lively little son, and two kitties. Learn more and sign up for her newsletter at kierstigiron.com.

MORE FROM KIERSTI GIRON:

Leah's Garden series,
by Lauraine Snelling with Kiersti Giron

The Seeds of Change
A Time to Bloom
Fields of Bounty
A Season of Harvest

Home to Green Creek series,
by Lauraine Snelling with Kiersti Giron

Land of Dreams
At Morning's Light (coming Dec. 2025)

www.ingramcontent.com/pod-product-compliance
Lightning Source LLC
Chambersburg PA
CBHW020515260626
47156CB00006B/2016